A matter of life, death, and revolution . . .

"Sit," Zuberi said, gesturing at the empty chair. "I won't have you looming over me."

Josan pulled out the chair and took his seat, using the time to study the two men. Zuberi's face was drawn with exhaustion, his lips compressed in anger. By contrast Brother Nikos appeared impassive, but one who knew him well could see the pleasure that he was trying to hide.

"What do you want from me, proconsul? Or is it Emperor Zuberi I by now?"

"Proconsul," Zuberi said.

"Then whom should I congratulate? Count Hector, perhaps?"

"Count Hector will be arrested for treason, once the new emperor takes his crown," Nikos said.

"So why have you brought me here?" Josan asked.

"I have been persuaded, against my own good judgment, to offer you a chance to stave off your execution," Zuberi said. "Count Hector must not be allowed to take the throne. And I cannot."

"So you are offering me the crown. Emperor Lucius," Josan said.

His words had been meant as a jest, but no one laughed. Zuberi's face tightened, as if he had bitten into a sour grape, while Brother Nikos smiled. . . .

Also by Patricia Bray
Published by Bantam Spectra Books

THE SWORD OF CHANGE TRILOGY

THE FIRST BETRAYAL

THE SEA CHANGE

Patricia Bray

BANTAM BOOKS

THE SEA CHANGE
A Bantam Spectra Book / August 2007

Published by
Bantam Dell
A Division of Random House, Inc.
New York, New York

Bantam Books, the rooster colophon, Spectra, and the portrayal of a boxed "s" are trademarks of Random House, Inc.

ISBN 0-553-58877-4

Printed in the United States of America
Published simultaneously in Canada

www.bantamdell.com

OPM 10 9 8 7 6 5 4 3 2 1

Acknowledgments

For the next generation—my nieces and nephew Marina Bray, Camila Bray, William Alers, and Mary Melander, and my godson George Benda.

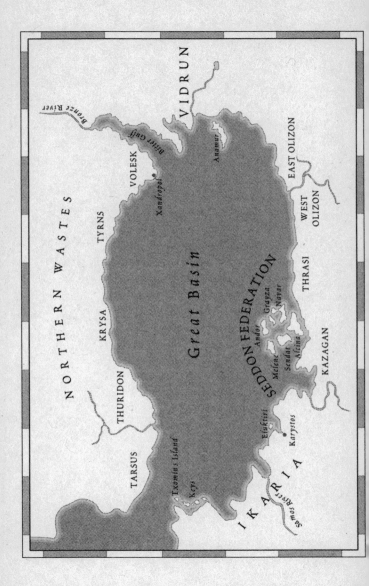

Chapter 1

Josan was hungry. And as his hunger grew, so too did his unease.

Missing a single breakfast would not harm him. It was an annoyance, but nothing compared to the true hunger he had experienced during those weeks in the northern wilderness when he had fled the twin perils of imperial justice and his growing madness. But those days were behind him. He had come to terms with the soul madness that had been inflicted upon him, and had yielded himself to the empress's justice. To his astonishment, in return for his obeisance she had spared his life—commuting a death sentence into mere imprisonment.

Not that he was called a prisoner. No, he was a most honored guest, given his own apartment within the imperial complex. And if the walls of that apartment were riddled with spy-holes, so that every moment of his life was observed, waking or sleeping, he knew better than to complain. There were far harsher alternatives.

His life was carefully scripted, as if unvarying routine was proof against treachery. Each morning he rose with the dawn, washed, dressed, and ate a solitary breakfast of hot porridge or cold soup, depending on the season. Then he would study his scrolls until it was time for lunch. After lunch he would take the two hours of exercise he was permitted, walking through the imperial gardens under the watchful eye of his escort. Returning to his rooms, he would read and meditate until it was time for dinner. When the sun set, he went to bed.

On the third day of each week, Ferenc came to play tiles. A minor clerk in Proconsul Zuberi's office, Ferenc had subtly tried to elicit information in his first visits. But Josan had deflected every question, and in time Ferenc had ceased his interrogations. He still came once a week, but now they played at tiles in silence, conversing only to discuss the game. Josan did not know why Ferenc continued to visit him, but he was grateful nonetheless.

On the last day of each week, a monk of the Learned Brethren delivered new scrolls for Josan to read and collected those that he had finished. Josan was never allowed to speak with the monks; instead they handed their precious burdens over to one of the slaves, who ensured that the scrolls were thoroughly inspected before they were passed on.

It had been three months before the empress had entrusted him with parchment and pen. The only communication he was allowed with outsiders was the weekly list of books that he sent to the brethren. Sometimes the books he requested were delivered promptly, and at other times his requests were ignored. There was never any explanation, which left him to wonder if another scholar was researching the tomes he had requested, or if they had somehow been deemed subversive.

His routine varied only slightly with the seasons. In the cooler months, he studied in the morning and took his exercise in the afternoon, but once spring came he reversed the pattern, taking his exercise in the morning, when there were fewer people around.

Occasionally the empress would summon him, breaking the monotony of his existence. Months had passed since the last execution she had required him to witness, but there were still formal occasions during which he was displayed as a symbol of her power. A proud man might have balked at being cast in such a role, but Josan knew better than to test the limits of the empress's patience.

He had played the role of Prince Lucius for ten months now. It had been even longer since anyone had called him by his true name. Now entire days passed when he forgot that he was playing a role, that Lucius was not who he was. He had allowed himself to sink deep into his role, knowing that any lapse might mean his death.

Yet none seemed to question his transformation from dissolute prince to studious scholar—perhaps because reading was the only occupation that he was permitted. It was fortunate that none of Prince Lucius's former friends came to see him—there were few left alive who could claim to have known him well, and they were far too intent on putting distance between themselves and the traitor. And as for the books he requested, he knew better than openly to request works on magic, instead reading histories of the early years of the empire and children's tales, gleaning what small nuggets of information he could from among their pages.

Yet for all that it had chafed, the unvaried routine of his existence also protected him. He was safe as long as he drew no attention to himself and gave the empress no reason to question his loyalties.

But now his routine had been broken, and he did not know what to make of this change. Could it be as simple as the servants having forgotten him? Though the servants were forbidden to gossip with him, yesterday he had overheard one of them tell his guard that Princess Jacinta had gone into labor. The birth of the long-awaited imperial heir might well have overwhelmed the palace staff, already burdened with the preparations for the public celebration of Empress Nerissa's birthday. At such a time, it would be easy to overlook the needs of a single man.

Or had the breakfast been tainted? It had been months since anyone had tried to poison him, but it would be foolish to believe that his enemies had forgotten him.

But neither would explain why no one had arrived to relieve the guard outside his door.

Not for the first time, he cursed his ignorance, which chafed far more than his confinement. A simple question to one of the palace functionaries would relieve his mind, but instead he was reduced to guessing blindly, constructing one improbable hypothesis after another.

Restlessly he paced his study, watching as a square of sunlight crept slowly across the floor. Time passed, and still no one came. Finally, nerves stretched taut, he broke the routine and opened the door to the corridor.

It swung inwards, revealing Balasi standing guard outside. By his calculations, Balasi had been on duty for nearly eight hours, rather than his normal four-hour shift. Yet neither Balasi's posture nor his carefully blank face revealed any hint of the unease that he must feel.

"Something is wrong. Did you send a servant for information?"

Balasi did not answer. He did not need to. The thin walls that made it so easy for others to spy upon Josan also made it easy for him to overhear his guards. Balasi could not leave his post, but it had been nearly two hours since he had asked a passing maid to take a message to his commander. It should have taken her no more than a quarter hour to deliver her message, and another quarter hour for an answer to return. The lack of response was damning.

"It is foolish to wait here. If Pirro is drunk, he will be in trouble, not you," Josan said, though by now he doubted that matters were so simple. "I will accompany you while you report to Farris."

"I have my orders. I am to watch, only. When Pirro comes, he will let you know if you are permitted to leave."

"And if Pirro never comes?"

"Someone will," Balasi said, his expression indicating that the conversation was over.

Josan was not satisfied. "Are you not curious? No one to bring breakfast, now your relief has gone missing? What if you are needed?"

"I have my orders. As do you." Balasi did not raise his voice, but he did not need to. He was as unyielding as one of the marble pillars in the great audience hall. Josan would have had better luck arguing with a statue.

He wondered what Balasi would do if Josan tried to push past him. Would he restrain him? Beat him as if he were a common prisoner instead of a royal hostage? Or would he simply follow disapprovingly, waiting for someone to tell him what to do with his recalcitrant charge? Josan was allowed to leave his rooms once a day, after all, and though Balasi was not his usual escort, that did not automatically mean that Josan was confined to his rooms.

He hesitated, weighing his need for information against the possible consequences. The empress would not look kindly upon an altercation between him and his guards. And it was foolish to risk her displeasure over something that might turn out to be nothing more than mere forgetfulness.

At last, he decided that he would wait until noon, when Pirro's replacement would normally arrive. If there was still no sign of either the guards or the servants who would normally have brought his meal, then Josan would take action. By then, he might even be able to convince Balasi of the rightness of this course of action.

No sooner had he made this resolve, however, than he heard the sounds of raised voices and rapidly approaching footsteps. Balasi turned in their direction, his left arm shoving Josan back inside his room, while his right hand grasped the hilt of his sword—a reminder that he was not only Josan's jailer but also his protector. No harm was allowed to come to him, except at the empress's command.

Proconsul Zuberi was the first to appear as he rounded the corner that led to Josan's apartment, accompanied by a half dozen guards.

"Stand aside," Zuberi ordered.

Balasi did not move. "My lord, I have my orders."

It was a bold act, since the proconsul was answerable only to the empress herself.

"Stand aside from the traitor, or I swear you will share his fate." The soft menace of Zuberi's voice was far more intimidating than a shouted threat. Behind him, the guards hefted their cudgels.

Josan was not surprised when Balasi merely nodded, then stepped to one side.

Now that Balasi no longer blocked his view, Josan could see that Zuberi's tunic had brown stains at the hem, as if he had knelt in filth.

Not filth, he realized. Blood. The stains were old enough to have dried, and yet the normally fastidious Zuberi had not bothered to change his tunic.

"What has happened?" Josan asked.

Zuberi came forward and slapped Josan hard, the unexpected blow rocking him back on his heels.

"Traitor," Zuberi hissed. "Murderer! I warned the empress not to trust you."

"I have kept my vows to the empress. I have done nothing—"

Zuberi struck him again. This time Josan braced himself for the blow, keeping his gaze fixed on Zuberi's face even as the pain blossomed.

Whatever was happening here, was happening with the empress's tacit or explicit consent. Zuberi was powerful, but he was no fool. He would not go against the empress's wishes. Some terrible deed had been committed, and the man they thought of as Prince Lucius was being held to blame.

"Nerissa should have killed you when she had the chance," Zuberi said, forgoing the empress's title in his rage. "I will not make the same mistake. You won't be allowed to live long enough to profit from your treachery."

"I demand to speak to Empress Nerissa. To hear from her own lips that she has found fault with my obedience."

And to give himself a chance to defend himself from whatever crimes Zuberi believed he had committed.

"Nerissa is dead, as you well know," Zuberi said.

Only Balasi's indrawn breath broke the silence that followed Zuberi's pronouncement.

The bloodstains on Zuberi's tunic suddenly took on ominous meaning.

Josan's heart raced, and he knew his face must have paled.

"If the empress has perished, then I regret her loss. But surely logic must tell you that I had no hand in this act. It was only her patronage that kept me alive."

Empress Nerissa had been secure enough in her rule that she had tolerated the presence of the former renegade prince, the last living link to those who had ruled Ikaria before her grandfather had taken the throne. Her eldest son, Prince Nestor, was unlikely to feel the same way.

Shock turned to rising dread as the depths of his

predicament became clear. Even his innocence would not be enough to save his life.

"Enough. I grow tired of your lies," Zuberi said. "Take him to the Rooms of Pain and do what you will as long as he is kept alive until he can be properly executed."

As Zuberi stepped aside, two guards came forward and seized Josan by the arms. He did not struggle, but that made no difference. A third clubbed the back of his head, and then they began to drag him away, not giving him the chance to find his feet.

It was a short journey from his apartments to the stairs that led down to the supposedly secret cells where the torturer Nizam and his minions held sway. Josan had been here before, and he did not relish his return.

He was halfway down the stairs when a push from behind propelled him forward. His arms flailed, but there was nothing on which to catch himself, so he fell forward, striking the stairs with his right shoulder, before tumbling over and over until he crumpled into a heap at the base of the stairs.

His vision blurred and he could not see the faces of those who stood over him. His right shoulder burned with agony, but the arm itself was strangely numb. His mind raced, but reason could not dispel the terror that welled up inside him. He knew what awaited him, and a broken arm was the merest taste of what was to come. Nausea roiled his stomach as a hand seized the front of his tunic and began dragging him down the corridor.

They threw him in a cell, and for one brief moment he wondered if it was the same cell he had occupied during his earlier visit. Then the first guard swung his cudgel, and there was no room for anything except pain. He tried to count the blows but lost count after the first dozen.

Pride abandoned, he began to scream.

• • •

As chief advisor to Empress Nerissa, Brother Nikos was seldom called upon to act in a spiritual role. Head of the collegium of the Learned Brethren, he had long ago delegated his religious duties to lesser monks, leaving them to offer prayers to the indifferent gods while Nikos reserved his energies for temporal matters. Some in the court had been known to mutter that Nikos wielded too much influence for one who called himself a monk, but these were the mere grumblings of those who had no power of their own. If the empress preferred to have him at her side dispensing advice rather than meditating in the collegium among musty scrolls and ancient tomes, who was he to question her judgment?

The last time he had served as priest was three years before, when he had officiated at Prince Nestor's wedding. Now he was called once again to take up his role as priest— this time to lead the public mourning for Prince Nestor's bride, who had died yesterday after giving birth to a stillborn son. The twin losses had shaken the imperial family, especially Prince Nestor, who had grown unaccountably fond of the bride that politics had chosen for him. Empress Nerissa, though normally free of the sentimental weaknesses that governed her sex, had chosen to delay the public announcement until today, to give the prince a chance to grieve in private. Once the announcement was made, the needs of the empire would take precedence over private mourning.

The death of the princess was a tragedy, to be certain, but Nikos was pragmatic enough to see it was also an opportunity. Ever since Prince Nestor had achieved his majority, there had been calls for Empress Nerissa to resign in favor of her son. She had only been intended as a placeholder, after all. There were many who had never been easy with a woman on the imperial throne, and they had found allies among those who had been unable to secure Nerissa's favor and thus turned to her sons.

Nikos had tutored the imperial princes, but they had never warmed to him. He knew that when Prince Nestor took the throne, his influence would be greatly diminished. Nestor would have his own advisors, and would undoubtedly overturn many of his mother's policies in his drive to set his own stamp upon the empire that she had ruled for so long.

Fortunately for Nikos, the empress had shown no signs of relinquishing her throne. Though the pressure on her would undoubtedly have grown even greater if Prince Nestor had an heir of his own. Now the prince's supporters had been dealt a mighty blow, while the position of Nikos and Nerissa's other allies had been strengthened.

A new wife would have to be found for Nestor, as soon as the official period of mourning was over. And perhaps it was time for his younger brother, Prince Anthor, to wed as well. Lost in calculating the favors that could be extracted from those who had suitable daughters, it took Nikos a moment to realize that they had arrived at the entrance to the imperial palace, where a large crowd blocked their way. With harsh words and sharp elbows, his acolytes cleared a path to the iron gates, which were unaccountably closed.

A man tugged on his sleeve, and as he turned he recognized Priam, a minor noble with an insignificant estate in the southern lands.

"Brother Nikos, do you know what is happening? The empress summoned us to her morning audience, but the gates are barred and the guards will not let us in," Priam complained.

Nikos had no answers for him. Even in the recent civil unrest, the palace gates had never been closed during daylight hours. But he would not betray his ignorance, not even before one as inconsequential as Priam.

"All will be explained when the empress wills," he said.

Brother Basil had managed to attract the attention of one of the half dozen guards who stood on the other side of the gate, apparently deaf to the strident pleas of those outside.

"This is Brother Nikos, summoned to counsel by the empress herself," Basil shouted.

It was undignified. Never before had he had to beg for admission.

But the guards did not seem impressed by Basil's words. Instead their eyes were hard, and their hands rested on their swords as if they feared attack.

It did not take a scholar to know that something was gravely wrong.

He pushed Basil aside and stood directly before the gate. "I am Brother Nikos, chief advisor to her imperial majesty Nerissa, and I demand to be taken to her presence," he said, in the booming voice best suited to leading the faithful in prayers.

He fixed his gaze on the sergeant, who nodded in apparent recognition. The sergeant gave orders to two of his men, who unbarred the gate. As it began to swing open, the crowd surged forward, but the remaining guards drew their swords.

"The priest only, no one else," the sergeant called out, and at the sight of naked steel, the crowd drew back.

Nikos slipped through the gate, not surprised to find that it swung shut before his acolytes could follow.

"Wait for me here," he instructed them.

The sergeant turned to one of the guards. "The proconsul asked to see this one. Bring him to the proconsul's office, and see that he stays there."

"The empress is expecting me—" Nikos began.

"The proconsul. Or I'll send you back through that gate."

Nikos nodded, accepting defeat for the moment, though he memorized every feature of the sergeant's face. When the time came, he would be punished for his disrespect. As the guard escorted him through the imperial compound, Nikos observed more signs of chaos—armed men were everywhere, but few servants were visible, and those that he did see rushed by with bent heads and ashen faces.

Was it possible that Princess Jacinta's death had not been a tragic accident? Had Empress Nerissa discovered evidence that the princess had been poisoned, and the baby's death was an act of deliberate malice? Surely the empress would want him by her side, but instead he was forced to cool his heels in Zuberi's outer office, under guard as if he were a common criminal. He waited with growing impatience until Zuberi finally returned to his office.

With a curt order, Nikos's escort was dismissed, and Zuberi led him into his private office.

"Sorry to leave you waiting, but Anthor just died," Zuberi said.

It took a moment for his words to penetrate.

"I must go to the empress," Nikos said. "She will be devastated."

Zuberi stared at him in disbelief.

"By the twisted fates, I forgot. You don't know."

"Know what? How did Anthor die?"

Zuberi sat down heavily, and after a moment, Nikos did as well.

"After you left yesterday, Nerissa, Nestor, and Anthor retired to the royal chapel to hold private vigil for the princess," Zuberi said. He took a deep breath, then continued. "Sometime during the night, an assassin entered. Nerissa and Nestor were slain. Against custom, Anthor was wearing a dagger, and he struggled with the assassin, killing him in turn, but he was gravely wounded. He must have bled for hours before they were found. The royal physicians did all they could, but he died just moments ago."

Zuberi's words made no sense. This was not possible. Nerissa, dead? And both her sons? How could such a thing have happened?

"How? Who?"

"The assassin bore the tattoos of a palace functionary, and thus was allowed to pass unquestioned. As for who, we both know Prince Lucius is behind this, and I have already dealt with him."

"No," Nikos said, the word escaping his lips before he could call it back.

"No?" Zuberi echoed, his eyebrows raised in astonishment.

Nikos thought furiously. He knew without a doubt that Prince Lucius was not behind this assassination, but he could not share the reason for his conviction with Zuberi. Not without exposing his own damning secrets.

"I do not think Lucius is behind this. His penitence seemed sincere."

Zuberi snorted. "You are too trusting."

"At the very least he must have had help," Nikos said. "He was too closely watched to hatch this plot on his own."

He waited, wondering if Lucius was alive, or if Zuberi had already killed him. In many ways, it would be better for Nikos if Lucius were indeed dead and his secrets buried with him.

"I will have Nizam drag from him the names of his accomplices," Zuberi said, confirming that Lucius was still alive. At least for now.

"How can I serve?" Nikos asked.

"I will draft the announcement, and you have a funeral to plan."

"Of course. And the next emperor . . ." Nikos let his

voice trail off delicately. "Shall I consult him as to his wishes?"

Zuberi smiled grimly. "You will know his name as soon as I do," he said. "For now, we have an empress to bury."

Interesting. He had half expected Zuberi to announce his own candidacy and try to secure Nikos's support. Perhaps Zuberi felt that it was too soon to make his move, with the empress's body not yet cold. Or perhaps Zuberi was merely being prudent—biding his time to see who else would try to claim the throne so he would know the faces of his enemies.

The difficulty was that there was no clear heir. Indeed, as a woman, Nerissa would never have been allowed to take the throne if there had been any legitimate male descendant of Aitor I. But Nerissa had been the only child of Aitor II, and had two sturdy sons of her own at the time of his death. The young princes had ensured the continuation of Aitor's line and their mother's seat on the imperial throne.

Now the field was wide open. With Nerissa's death, Nikos had lost a powerful patron, but if he maneuvered carefully, his own position might be strengthened. Whoever was chosen as emperor would need loyal advisors. And Nikos knew how to offer loyalty—in return for his own self-interest, of course.

What was good for the empire had proven to be good for Nikos as well, and he saw no reason why this should change. It was simply a matter of backing the right candidate for the throne—which made it all the more vital that those behind the assassinations be uncovered as soon as possible.

And if the emperor-to-be turned out to have blood on his hands, well then, there was always Prince Lucius. Nikos's first service to his new emperor would be to arrange evidence confirming Lucius's guilt ... for a suitable reward.

Prince Lucius was already doomed, from the moment the next emperor was named. At least this way his death would serve a dual purpose—to bring stability to the empire and ensure that Nikos remained in a position to guide the new emperor through the difficult days ahead.

Chapter 2

Nizam shook his head in disgust as he examined his newest charge. Prince Lucius lay sprawled on the floor of his cell, his naked flesh patterned in dark hues, clear evidence of the savage beating he had endured. Nizam motioned to his assistant to bring the lantern closer as he knelt down next to the prince.

They had not cut him, but from the swelling of his belly, he suspected the prince was bleeding inside his gut. His jaw was broken, and his face so swollen that he was incapable of opening his eyes. If the bleeding in his gut did not kill him, the broken jaw would.

There were lesser injuries as well—a broken arm, and knees swollen to twice their normal size. As Nizam turned the prince's body over, to check for injuries to his back, the prince moaned.

It was the sound of an animal in pain. There was no thought, no reason behind it. Lucius was beyond awareness, incapable of recognizing who was hurting him, or who had the power to end his suffering. It would be impossible to get any information from him in his current state.

Nizam understood that men could be driven by revenge, and many would say that Lucius had been treated as he deserved. But this was a pointless waste. It offended his sense of order, and he knew Empress Nerissa would never have permitted it.

The empress had understood his work as few others did. Even among his chosen assistants, most were merely competent rather than inspired. The empress had never personally wielded the lash nor the irons, but he had no doubt that she would have done so with skill. If she had been present in this cell, Lucius would have spilled all of his secrets before begging for death.

"Shall I send for the healer?" his assistant asked.

Nizam shook his head. "No. The proconsul's men said that he should be left untouched. I merely wanted to see him for myself before I made my report."

Rising to his feet, he gave the prince one last look before leaving the cell. He made his way swiftly through the passages and stairs that led from his secret domain up through the public spaces and finally into the palace itself. He knew the way, though he had seldom traveled it. Nerissa had preferred to meet with him in his domain, often insisting on being present for the interrogation of important prisoners, but her ministers lacked her spirit. Proconsul Zuberi had never set foot in the catacombs, preferring instead to summon Nizam to him on those rare occasions when he needed to speak with him.

Nizam smiled mirthlessly as servants blanched with fright, then quickly scurried out of his path. They did well to fear him. The assassin must have had help in gaining access to the palace, and until his accomplices were caught, all lived under suspicion.

Nizam had no fear for his position. Whether Proconsul Zuberi was crowned emperor or another, there would still be a need for a man with his talents. Especially now, with the assassin dead and Prince Lucius unable to speak, Nizam's services would be in high demand as they sought to ferret out the rest of the conspirators.

A dozen courtiers paced in the corridor outside the proconsul's offices, while more crowded inside the anteroom, along with an officer from the guard, and one of Petrelis's lackeys from the city watch. Each was badgering the clerks in turn, demanding immediate admittance.

Nizam said nothing, knowing his reputation would serve him far better than any words. True enough, the petitioners drew back as they recognized him and with a hasty swallow, the senior of the two clerks motioned him forward.

"Please, he is waiting for you," the clerk said.

The proconsul was still wearing the formal court attire he must have worn when he announced the deaths of the imperial family. The only concession made to the summer's heat had been to remove the black shawl of mourning, which was now draped carelessly over the back of his chair. The empress's death must have hit him hard. Though it had been only a few weeks since Nizam had last seen him, the proconsul seemed to have aged years in that time.

"You are authorized to use all lawful measures to enforce the peace—" Proconsul Zuberi's voice broke off as he saw Nizam.

The scribe, who had been taking notes, looked up, then rose swiftly to his feet even before Zuberi waved him away.

"Wait outside. I will summon you when I am ready to finish this," Zuberi said.

The scribe bowed as he gathered up his writing things, then swiftly backed away.

"There is a curfew in the city tonight, for all the good that will do," Zuberi said, by way of greeting. "I expect Commander Petrelis will have his hands full."

"Have him hang the first dozen violators that he finds and leave their bodies dangling as a warning to the rest."

It was what Empress Nerissa would have done. It would be impossible to arrest all of the violators, but the deaths would discourage honest citizens from trying to test the limits of the curfew. Then those still out on the streets could then safely be assumed to be lawbreakers and dealt with accordingly.

Zuberi shrugged. "And what of the hundreds of mourners out in the square? Now that sunset has fallen they are all in violation of the decree, but for each one that leaves, another two come to take their place."

Rumors had swept through the city far ahead of the official announcement, and the square had been packed for most of the day. Zuberi had ordered a curfew, to quell unrest, but privately Nizam doubted that there would be any riots tonight. The city of Karystos was in shock, the loss too enormous to comprehend. If trouble were to come, it would come tomorrow, once the shock had worn off and men began to reckon what they had gained and lost with Nerissa's death.

"Have the priests send them home. Or to the temples, where they may pray all night, and leave the streets free for patrols."

Zuberi nodded. He did not thank Nizam for his suggestion. It was not his way.

"What of Prince Lucius? My men said he told them nothing."

"Your men were ignorant brutes who smashed his jaw to stop his screams. Of course he told them nothing since he is no longer capable of speech."

He had thought to shock Zuberi with his bluntness, but Zuberi appeared unmoved. Perhaps he was no longer capable of being shocked after the tumultuous events of the past two days.

"He must have had accomplices, and I need you to discover who helped him."

"And how do you suggest I do that? The prince cannot speak and he is not fit to be questioned."

Zuberi shrugged and turned away slightly, his attention seemingly caught by the overflowing basket of scrolls on his desk. "Then we will question all those that Lucius has had contact with since he became the empress's guest. One of them must be guilty, and he will lead us to the others."

"And as for the prince?"

"He is to be burned alive at the foot of Nerissa's pyre, so the sound of his screams may ease her passage."

Zuberi had spent too long in the corridors of power, far removed from the realities of life and death. He could have benefited from a few hours spent observing Nizam's apprentices at their craft.

"The prince will not live that long," Nizam said. "Your guards were undisciplined and the damage they did too grave. The prince will die within days, either from the bleeding in his gut or from his broken jaw if he is unable to swallow water."

"They were under orders to leave him alive."

"He is alive. But he will not stay that way."

Zuberi growled in frustration. "I will not let him slip away this easily. The funeral is nine days from today. Do what you must to keep him alive until then."

"I will do what I can, but I do not think it will be enough," Nizam said.

Zuberi nodded, apparently satisfied. "If he dies, notify me at once, and we will display his body in the courtyard. I will send you a list of all those who have been in contact with him, and you may start questioning them immediately."

"As you command, proconsul," Nizam said, recognizing the dismissal.

Returning to the secret catacombs that were never shown on the official maps of the palace compound, Nizam sent a runner to fetch Galen the healer. He doubted that there was anything a healer could do to prolong Lucius's life, but he had promised Zuberi that he would try.

A former slave himself, Galen normally tended the servants of the imperial household, but he had worked with Nizam before when his special skills were required. As he entered Lucius's cell, followed by a slave carrying the tools of his trade, Galen took in the situation with a single glance.

"This was not your work," he said.

"No," Nizam agreed. "But now it falls upon me to keep him alive long enough that he may be properly executed."

Lucius had been moved to a low cot in preparation for Galen's visit, but other than that he was untouched. Unlike earlier, this time he did not make a sound as his abused body was turned one way, then another. Galen's face darkened as he manipulated the rigid abdomen, then carefully felt the shattered jaw.

"No matter what I do, he will be dead before morning," Galen announced.

This matched Nizam's own conclusions.

"Proconsul Zuberi will be most displeased." It was both a statement of fact and a warning. Nizam, by his position, was immune to Zuberi's displeasure but Galen was not.

"Why? Was this one of the assassin's helpers?"

"This is, or rather was, Prince Lucius."

Galen gave a low hiss of surprise, turning the prince's face toward the light. "So it is." Then he shrugged. "Prince or prisoner, it makes no difference. He will die nonetheless."

"Do what you would if you expected him to live," Nizam

advised. Galen had been of use to him in the past and there was no reason to sacrifice such a valuable tool to Zuberi's ire. "Bind his jaw and splint his arm. Let Zuberi see that we tried to save him."

"A waste of my time and supplies," Galen muttered, but he turned to his slave and gave the necessary orders.

Nizam watched as Lucius's broken arm was splinted, his swollen knees wrapped in compresses. His jaw was re-aligned and bound with linen strips, two reeds holding his lips parted to help him breathe. None of these efforts would save him but they were visible signs of the healer's arts.

Lastly Galen mixed powdered herbs into a bowl of well-watered wine. Soaking the corner of a rag in the bowl, he wet the prince's lips, then carefully allowed a few drops to fall into his mouth. They watched, as three drops became four, and then a dozen, but there was no sign of the reflex-ive swallowing that should have occurred.

Galen handed the rag and bowl to his slave. "Try again in half an hour, then every half hour after that. If his con-dition changes, send a guard to fetch me. I will be back to check on him myself later tonight."

The slave nodded, taking up his position crouched on the floor by Lucius's cot.

"I have done what I could, but it will not be enough," Galen said, as they exited the cell. "If I had been called at once, I might have been able to stop the bleeding in his belly."

"Or he would have died under your knife and you would have been held to blame," Nizam said. He did not believe in dwelling on what might have been. Facts were facts and the past could not be altered. A wise man accepted this and simply made the best of the present.

As Nizam intended to do. Whatever information Prince Lucius had held was lost to him, but there were others whose knowledge might prove equally valuable. He had preparations to make and suspects to question. One way or another, the next time he saw Proconsul Zuberi, he would have information that would distract the proconsul from the issue of where to lay the blame for Lucius's premature death.

Brother Nikos personally oversaw the transfer of the imperial family into the hands of the preservers, who would use their arts so that the bodies would still be seemly for viewing on the day of the funeral. The stillborn infant, having never breathed on his own, was handed over to the temple of the Daughters of the Moon, who would bury him in an unmarked grave in the cemetery set aside for such unfortunates. Such burials were normally done in secret, but the Daughters agreed to allow Lady Eugenia, the wife of Proconsul Zuberi, to serve as the imperial witness to the interment.

Then Nikos turned his attention to the details of the funeral itself. Ikaria had never before suffered such a loss— losing not just a ruler but also the entire ruling family. Many would want to pay tribute, and satisfying them would require all of his diplomacy and tact.

At first he had his own acolytes from the collegium to assist him, as the imperial functionaries were questioned. But they were soon cleared of suspicion—all fifty functionaries were accounted for, proving the assassin had indeed been an outsider. The senior of the household—who often filled the role of Greeter—had been swift to point out that the assassin's facial tattoos were a good copy, but his arm tattoos were wrong. Greeter and his fellow functionaries swore that they would have recognized the impostor at a glance, and there was no reason to disbelieve them. Pity that Nerissa's guards had not been as observant.

Once freed from suspicion, the functionaries were invaluable in helping Nikos make the arrangements for the funeral and ensuring that the palace was ready to accommodate the expected influx of mourners. Most of the nobles who would want to attend were already in Karystos, having arrived under the auspices of Nerissa's fiftieth birthday celebration; but many who had nearby estates now decided that they must stay in the city itself to ensure that they did not miss any moment of the ceremonies—or the political maneuvering. The birthday celebrations had perforce been canceled, but many of the arrangements could hastily be converted to serve this new need. There would still be a procession through the streets of Karystos; it was merely the date and the decorations that had changed. The plays honoring Nerissa's accomplishments could be staged, but now to the sound of funeral drums.

There was considerable commotion at the court when news came that Count Hector, Admiral of the Imperial Navy, had arrived unexpectedly, along with a half dozen ships of the fleet. He was visibly overcome with grief, insisting on seeing the bodies of his sister-in-law and his nephews with his own eyes before he would accept the fact of their deaths.

By now, the imperial apartments were overflowing with noble visitors, and the quarters that Count Hector normally used had been given over to Duke Seneca—who ordinarily outranked Hector; but, of course, there was Count Hector's connection to the murdered princes to consider. The count, professing to understand the functionary's dilemma, offered to stay in his nephew Anthor's now-vacant bachelor apartments. Or to remain aboard his flagship if no other quarters could be found.

Fortunately Zuberi intervened, and with some reshuffling and a few bruised egos, Hector's usual rooms were freed for his use.

Nikos heard of these maneuverings thirdhand, but he did not like what he heard. There had been little love lost between Nerissa and her brother-in-law. Nerissa's husband Prince Philip had been a pleasant enough fellow, with the proper breeding and a complete lack of ambition. He had fulfilled his role of stud admirably, and shortly after Nestor had passed his seventh name day, Philip had died of what the healers said was a summer fever. It might have been a fever, but most saw the empress's hand in his death. It was not that long ago, after all, that Empress Constanza had been usurped by her consort, and Nerissa had no wish to meet a similar fate.

Hector might have had his suspicions about his brother's death, but he never questioned Nerissa publicly, and for his silence he was rewarded with a post in the Imperial Navy, rising to the rank of admiral. Power, of a sort, but even here Nerissa was stingy. The army was where those with influence clamored to serve, and where noble fathers would offer favors to commanders who could advance their sons' careers. The navy held far less prestige, and far fewer opportunities to fatten the count's purse or increase his influence.

Still, it was possible that Hector, seeking to ingratiate himself into Nerissa's favor, had chosen to surprise her with a visit during the month set aside for her name day celebrations.

Or it was possible that he was here for some other reason. He must have been nearby, to have arrived so soon after the assassinations.

And perhaps Hector's grief was indeed genuine. If not for the loss of his nephews, then surely for the blow to his own political ambitions. Nerissa and her sons had reason to deal favorably with Hector, but when Zuberi became emperor, Hector would swiftly find himself without friends at the court.

Nikos's thoughts kept turning back to Count Hector, even as he busied himself with the funeral preparations. He glanced at the scroll in his hand, realizing that his assistant had handed him a list of musicians who would accompany the funeral procession.

"No, not this. The other list, of those who will be offering their blessings," Nikos said.

Brother Giuliano nodded and rummaged through the stacks on the table. "Here it is," he said, unrolling the scroll to reveal a list that had already been erased and reinked several times.

The official religion of the empire was the worship of the twin gods whom Nikos served, but Nerissa had been the mother of the empire, and thus spiritual leader of all its disparate religions. Each wished to honor her, and all were demanding a suitable role in the funeral. If he said yes to everyone, he estimated it would take three days for the rites. Possibly four, judging by the latest request from Fadil, high priest of the triune godhead.

"How many priests is Fadil bringing?"

Brother Giuliano ran his finger down the scroll till he found that entry. "Four, it looks like. They are to recite the blessings for the martyred dead and anoint the bodies with perfume made from hyssop flowers."

"Tell him he can have three priests, no more. There should be no objection, since he professes to believe in the power of three. And the only ritual anointing will be done by the Daughters of the Moon, before the bodies leave the palace."

Giuliano made a notation on the parchment.

It helped to understand that the true gods did not care about funeral offerings nor the order of prayers. These things were done for the benefit of men; the gods had far weightier matters to attend to. Even the passing of an empress was insignificant to beings who had seen a thousand emperors reign and die. As long as the ceremony was dignified, and no lesser religion was favored over another, it would be acceptable.

The funeral orations were a more complicated matter. Proconsul Zuberi would deliver the main oration, of course, and Nikos, as head of the Learned Brethren, would deliver his own as he led the funeral services. Others had demanded to speak as well, to serve as a public reminder of how close they had been to Empress Nerissa. To these requests Nikos said neither yes nor no, explaining that he was considering them all and must consult with Proconsul Zuberi before making any final decisions.

Count Hector proved harder to dissuade. First he sent a messenger with his request, then, dissatisfied, sought out Nikos himself.

The count had not been in Karystos for the past two years, having been occupied with his duties in the Imperial Navy. But he looked much as he had then—tall and slender, with enough muscle to prove he was a warrior and not a courtier. Time had been kind to him, for his dark hair held not a streak of gray. Only his weathered face showed that he was not much younger than Nerissa had been.

"Brother Nikos, I must start by thanking you for your services in such a difficult time. I know how hard this must be for you. We have all lost a great empress—but you have lost a patron, and I . . . Well, I have lost a friend, along with my beloved nephews," Count Hector said.

Nikos felt his eyebrows raise. By reminding Nikos of his family ties to the empress, the count had neatly implied that Nikos was laboring on his behalf, turning his own presumed grief into a subtle assertion of power.

"The burden of sorrow is heavy on us all, but it is our duty to serve the empress in her death just as we served her in life," Nikos said. It was a platitude fit for a child, but Hector seemed to accept it at face value.

"I have come to speak to you about the funeral orations. I have prepared a draft, and would welcome your suggestions."

Clever. He had not asked Nikos if he could offer an oration, but rather implied that his participation should be taken for granted, and he merely needed advice on his turn of phrase.

"There are many who wish to honor Empress Nerissa in this way—" Nikos began.

"Of course," Count Hector interrupted. "And I would not take that honor away from them. But someone needs to speak for the murdered princes, Nestor and Anthor. And who better than their own father's brother?"

Nikos had not expected this. He had assumed that Hector was like the rest, intending to praise Nerissa and her sons in a single speech. But Hector was more clever than he had supposed, reminding him that Prince Nestor had been a royal prince, heir to the imperial throne. By custom and law he, at least, deserved his own oration, and Nikos was a fool for not having seen this before.

Hector was Nestor's closest living relative. Nikos could not deny him, not without provoking a public scandal.

"Who better indeed?" he echoed. "And I would be happy to look over your speech and offer my humble advice."

The count smiled, content with his victory. After exchanging mutual insincere pleasantries, he took his leave.

Nikos waited until the count's footsteps had died away before turning to his aide. "Put those scrolls aside and run to Zuberi's office. Tell his clerk that I need to meet with the proconsul. Today."

"Yes, Brother, at once."

Count Hector was up to something. Nikos could taste it.

• • •

Officially Prince Lucius had been an honored guest of the empress, but in fact he had spent these last ten months as a prisoner, albeit a noble one. Each day had been carefully scripted—his every action, every conversation, dutifully recorded. Nothing in those records had indicated that he was conspiring against the empress, but now Nizam delegated an assistant to read through them again, looking for clues they might have missed. As well as to compile a list of all those who had come in contact with the prince, which he would then compare against the list that Proconsul Zuberi's clerks had provided.

Nizam went over the list, selecting those he wanted to question first and delegating others to his assistants. The initial interviews would take place in his offices, on the level above the Rooms of Pain. Those who could not provide satisfactory information would be sent below, for the stricter forms.

Slaves, of course, received no such consideration, and all would be lashed first, then interrogated. Most of these interviews could be safely left to his assistants, who knew how to inflict pain without permanently damaging a valuable asset. If anything of interest was discovered, Nizam would be summoned to complete the interrogation.

He began with the guard Balasi, who had been with the prince at the time of his arrest. The prince had been sleeping when Balasi began his shift, but after the prince had awoken he appeared restless. At the time Balasi had ascribed this to the disruption of routine, and indeed when Balasi's replacement had failed to arrive on schedule, he had been disturbed enough to send a message to his watch commander.

Balasi was a veteran of the guard—steady, reliable, with a reputation above reproach, which was why he had been chosen for such a delicate assignment. He answered each of Nizam's questions fully, but unlike most who were summoned to the room, Balasi showed no signs of nervousness. Balasi held himself blameless, and after an hour of questioning, Nizam privately agreed.

Not that he told Balasi this, merely dismissing the guard and instructing him to hold himself ready to be questioned further.

As the night wore on, a messenger brought word that Lucius had recovered sufficiently to swallow some of the medicine that Galen had prepared. It would not be enough to save his life, but Nizam cautiously hoped that Galen's efforts would appease Proconsul Zuberi.

Day was much the same as night here in the catacombs, and it was only by the turning of the clock that Nizam knew dawn had arrived. He had finished questioning Lucius's guards, discovering only the usual petty crimes. Pirro had twice been too drunk for duty in the last six months, but both times his fellow guards had chosen to enforce discipline themselves rather than reporting the matter. Sifu and Oles were in the habit of swapping shifts without notifying the watch commander, but even this was a minor infraction. There had been no unauthorized visits, no messages or packages secretly slipped to Prince Lucius. If there was a conspiracy, the guards had no part in it.

After a hasty breakfast of hot tea and sweet rolls, Nizam descended to the interrogation rooms below to assess the progress of his assistants. The maid who cleaned the prince's quarters was currently being questioned, and he watched with satisfaction as Akil coaxed the sobbing woman into confessing that she had once thought the prince well-favored and offered to lie with him, but he had brusquely declined.

Foolish girl. The prince had saved her life by refusing her offer, for Nerissa would not have allowed even the slightest possibility that Lucius might breed an heir. The maid's infatuation and subsequent pique were duly noted, but she had little of value to reveal.

After conferring with his other assistants, Nizam decided to check on the prince. To his surprise he found both Galen and his slave in the cell with their patient.

"How much longer does he have?" he asked.

"I honestly don't know," Galen said. "See for yourself."

As Galen moved aside, Nizam could see that the prince was sweating heavily. His breathing was torturously slow, but his bruises seemed to be fading, and while his belly was still swollen, a touch confirmed that it was no longer rigid.

"Remarkable."

"Unexpected, I would say," Galen said dryly. "But none of my doing."

"Will he live long enough to satisfy Zuberi?" The funeral was still eight days away.

"It is too soon to say. If he is still alive tomorrow, perhaps."

As the day wore on, Nizam continued his interrogations, interspersed with messages from Galen charting the prince's progress. The healer's natural caution shone through in his choice of wording, but as the prince's condition improved from deadly to grave, then to merely serious, it was hard not to see his improvement as miraculous.

Magical, even, and Nizam recalled the statements taken last year from the prince's followers. He had intended to read those statements again, to see what could be gleaned from them, but now he had a dual purpose. At the time, he had dismissed those statements as signs of the conspirators' gullibility, but what if there was something to their tales? If Prince Lucius did indeed possess an inner magic that was healing him, then it opened up a new range of possibilities for Nizam to explore. Should he recover sufficiently to be questioned, the prince would come to regret his gifts and wish that Zuberi's men had indeed killed him.

The human body had limits. Nizam knew just how much damage he could inflict before the effect was fatal. The secret of his craft was to vary the types of pain and injuries inflicted until the subject had passed the limit of what he could endure. That limit varied from one man to another, but Nizam was always able to find it and push his subjects over the edge into mindless, abject cooperation.

Sometimes he was surprised, when one of his subjects exhibited a weak heart, or uncontrolled bleeding, and on these occasions Galen was summoned. But he had never before been surprised by a man's ability to heal.

For three days he left Lucius in the care of Galen and his assistant, letting him build his strength as the interrogations of his compatriots continued. They found evidence of thievery, drunkenness, and two illicit love affairs, but nothing that spoke of treason or murder.

Still, Nizam was not discouraged. His effectiveness at his job came not just from his skill at inflicting and withholding pain but also from his meticulous checking and rechecking of each fact. Though it would hardly do for him to make this known, when his reputation ensured that most spilled their secrets long before they were strapped to the punishment frames.

Nizam did not care whether the prince was guilty or innocent; these were questions for another to decide. His interest was in sifting truths from lies. Let others interpret the facts that he found as they would.

He waited until all the other interrogations had been completed, and he had carefully memorized everything that they had learned about the prince. Then, and only then, did he order that Lucius be brought to the Rooms of Pain.

His assistants knew the routine by heart and had stripped the prince and bound him to the upright punishment frame, where the bright torches cast the prince's features into harsh relief. Nizam waited in the outer room a full half hour after the summoning, giving the prince's fears time to build.

The frame had been positioned so the prisoner could not see anyone entering, but as the door creaked open, Lucius stiffened and futilely tried to move his head so he could see. Nizam came up behind him, admiring the smooth flesh that showed only faint marks where days before there had been livid bruises.

Magic indeed. The lizard had been the symbol of Prince Lucius's forebears, and Nizam wondered what traits the lizard and the prince had in common. He had already survived injuries that would have killed an ordinary man. If Nizam cut off his hand, would he grow a new one, as a lizard would grow a new limb? If he were blinded, would he grow new eyes?

It was said that a lizard could survive anything, except having its head chopped off. He wondered if the prince could say the same.

His assistants were masked, but in this room Nizam wanted the prisoners to see his face. They must learn to read his expressions, to know when he was displeased.

He moved to the front of the frame, watching Lucius's eyes widen as he recognized Nerissa's chief torturer.

"I did not kill them. I knew nothing of this," Lucius said. His voice was steady, though his pallor indicated his fear.

"So you say now. We will see what you say when we are better acquainted."

Nizam gave a hand signal, so subtle that most prisoners never knew to look for it, and his assistant drew back his arm and lashed the prince across his back.

The prince hissed, as much from the shock as from the pain. At Nizam's nod his assistant continued, the whip leaving dark marks on the prince's newly healed skin. He did not expect the prince to reveal anything under the lash, but such a whipping was customary. The prince would expect it.

He would not expect what Nizam had planned for him next.

Chapter 3

Josan jerked as the whip cut into his flesh again, but his bindings held him securely in place. Pain flared for a moment, as sharp as a knife cut, then faded into the dull agony that consumed him.

He could feel blood running down his legs—see it puddling on the floor beneath his feet. He was sickened by its stench and the sharper tang of his own fear.

It unnerved him that he could not see his tormentors, but the punishment frame prevented him from turning his head. He did not even know if Nizam was still present, though surely he must be.

"I am innocent," he began, then hissed as the whip struck again. "Please, there is no need for this. I will tell you whatever you want to know."

No one answered him. He had begun by trying to reason with Nizam and swiftly been reduced to begging. But neither Nizam nor his assistants acknowledged Josan with so much as a single word. There was only the whip, and a pain that was beyond anything he had imagined.

He had tried to count each blow but lost track after

three dozen. The total might have been fifty. It might have been more.

Did they mean to kill him? Simply to whip him until he bled to death? He trembled as he wondered how much he could endure before he fell insensate.

There was no point in pride. There was no point in pretending to be anything other than the coward he knew himself to be.

He screamed as the whip cut into him again. Then, sobbing, he found enough voice left to beg. "Please, have mercy."

There was no answer.

"Please," he cried again, reduced to a single word, as the measured cadence continued. Four more blows struck, patterning him from his shoulders down to his thighs.

He braced himself for the next blow, but it did not land.

He waited as a minute passed. And then another. Josan did not move, did not say a word, unwilling to do anything that might jeopardize this reprieve. The only sounds to be heard were his harsh pants as he struggled to regain his breath.

He flinched as he felt something stroke the back of his neck. A gloved hand, or perhaps the handle of a whip.

Josan shivered as Nizam came into view. He strained to read his expression, but Nizam's face was blank. He was as calm as if he were regarding a statue, rather than a man.

Josan tensed himself for a blow as Nizam raised his right hand, but Nizam simply stroked Josan's face, which was damp with sweat and tears.

"I had nothing to do with Nerissa's death," Josan said. "She was my protector—I had no reason to wish her ill. You must see this."

"I see that you are still keeping secrets from me," Nizam said, fixing him with a pitiless stare.

Josan felt naked, exposed under that gaze, and his eyes

dropped, without conscious decision. Hastily he wrenched his gaze back up, but it was too late.

"Your body betrays you," Nizam said.

"Ask me anything. Whatever you wish, I will answer."

Nizam had yet to ask any questions of his own. He had let Josan babble, proclaiming his innocence, recalling to mind each deed or conversation that would prove he had not violated Nerissa's trust. Josan had told him everything he could think of.

But he had not mentioned his true name. Nor had he mentioned the spell that had placed the soul of a dying monk into the body of a prince. Did Nizam somehow sense these secrets? Or was Nizam simply a brute who received his pleasure from the torments of others? Did he care about the answers he received or was he more interested in seeing Josan bleed, savoring the sound of his screams?

If he offered up his secrets, would they be believed? Or would Nizam punish him for a truth that was so strange it seemed a lie?

The agony of his flesh made it impossible to think clearly. Reveal himself as the victim of sorcery and he would be condemned to death as an abomination. Keep silent, and risk the same fate.

The question was not if he would die, but rather which choice would earn him a swifter death.

"You held out longer than I thought," Nizam said. "Two dozen lashes before you began begging."

He supposed it was a compliment, of sorts. He had screamed almost from the first.

"But even a prince would have been whipped as a boy," Nizam said.

Josan shook his head. Perhaps Lucius had endured canings from his tutors, but the monks did not beat the boys in their care. Discipline was enforced through fasts or time spent alone in contemplation of one's mistakes. While he had worn his own flesh, no one had ever raised a hand against him. It was only after he was joined to Prince Lucius's body that he had learned what violence was.

"Pride is the obstacle that must be overcome. Only when a man is stripped of his pride will he reveal the full truth." Nizam's tone was as even as if they were two acquaintances in polite debate. He had yet to show any signs of emotion.

"I have no pride," Josan said.

"We will see."

Josan could hear Nizam's assistants moving behind him, and he trembled, wondering if they were about to resume the lash.

"Akil has never fucked a prince before," Nizam said.

Josan drew in a sharp breath.

"I'll bet you were pretty when you were a boy," said a voice from behind him.

"There is no need for this," he said. He searched Nizam's face, but there was no trace of sympathy—no recognition that Prince Lucius was anything more than an object to be broken. "Just tell me what you want me to say."

He would confess to murdering Nerissa with his own two hands, if that was what they wanted.

"Of course a prince is bound to be tight," Akil said. "But we'll loosen you up."

He felt something press at his most private entrance, and his mind rebelled. Desperately he tried to flee, to banish himself into oblivion, but he could not do it. Only Prince Lucius's spirit had the power to dispossess him, and Prince Lucius had vanished months before.

Josan closed his eyes, unable to bear Nizam's gaze. He held his breath as a blunt object was brutally shoved inside him, tearing the delicate flesh. Tears rolled down his face— tears of shame mixed with those of pain. Akil rocked the object back and forth, opening him up for what was to come.

His eyes flew open as he felt Nizam's hand cup his balls, a thumb stroking his prick. It was a parody of intimacy that revolted rather than aroused.

He could not have been more humiliated if he were indeed the sheltered Prince Lucius, who had never known the touch of another man.

The hand around his balls tightened suddenly.

"What would you do to keep these?" Nizam asked. "What if I were to cut them off?"

Josan could not reply. His gorge rose. This, this was not happening. At any moment he would awaken, and discover this was a nightmare.

But the pain was all too real.

The object was removed. Two hands held his hips, and he felt something nudge against his backside.

He looked directly at Nizam. "I killed her. It is my fault, all of it. Tell Zuberi that I confessed."

Nizam shook his head. "You are still lying to me," he said. With a final pat he released Josan's prick.

At the same time, Akil begin to force himself inside Josan. It felt as if he were being fucked by a horse. The wounds on his back burned as Akil pressed against him.

Josan whimpered, his breath coming in short pants. His head swam, and for a moment he hoped that he was about to faint. But there was no such respite, as Akil began to pound into him, over and over again, long past the endurance of an ordinary man.

Josan must have had lovers in the past, though they were lost in the fog that hung over his years with the Learned Brethren. He supposed it was because they had not been important enough to be remembered, not the way that his studies had been. The monks understood that men needed the physical release of sex, and thus relations between them were allowed. As long as such relations were transitory, and the monk's primary focus remained his duty to the order.

But it was forbidden for a monk to lie with one not of the order. The penalty for taking an outside lover was castration, and banishment from the order, which was seen as the far harsher of the two. In the years of his exile, there had been opportunities for Josan to stray, but not once had he been tempted.

He did not know whether his inexperience made this easier or harder to endure. Perhaps if he had pleasant memories to contrast this with, it would not have felt so much like a violation.

Or perhaps it would have felt even worse.

Nizam's eyes glittered darkly, missing no detail of Josan's humiliation. This rape was more than a rape of his body. It was a rape of his soul. Nizam would not be content until he had utterly degraded Josan. In this moment he hated Nizam, more than he had ever hated any other. If it had been within his power, he would have held his tongue, to deny Nizam his victory.

Yet it was not within his power. As much as he hated Nizam, he feared the pain even more.

"Pretty, pretty princeling," Akil said. "You take my prick as well as any low city whore."

Josan ignored the taunting words, his attention focused on Nizam. He knew where the true power lay in this room. And as he watched, he saw Nizam's focus move to those who stood behind Josan. Nizam nodded slightly, apparently giving permission for what was to come next.

"He'll take more than that before we're done with him," an unseen man said. "You've stretched him long enough. Now let him feel a real man."

Akil thrust a few more times before pulling out. Josan

felt liquid running down his thighs, a mixture of blood, se-
men, and filth.

His gorge rose. Nizam stepped back, just as Josan spit
bile in his direction.

"Be done with this," Josan said. "Whatever you want, I
will do. I will say anything."

"I want the truth," Nizam said.

"I have told you the truth."

"I do not believe you."

Josan despaired as he realized that it did not matter
what he said. He could not reason with his captor. Truth,
lies, it was all the same to Nizam. He was as impervious to
logic as he was to Josan's suffering.

This was not about truth. It was about breaking him,
until there was nothing left of the man he had once been.

Akil's companion took his place, and the rape began
again. Josan endured, his mind narrowing its focus until
the room faded from his consciousness. There was room
for nothing but the sensation of pain, and the small, stubborn part of himself that refused to die.

The shock of cold water roused him to wakefulness.
His body ached from head to toe, and he stared at the
blood-soaked floor with a distant fascination. That was his
blood, he realized, his life's essence that spread in an ever-
widening pool toward Nizam's boots.

It was impossible for a man to lose that much blood and
live. His light-headedness was the precursor of the death
that he longed for.

"What do you know of Empress Nerissa's murder?"
Nizam asked. He stood so close that his breath wafted
across Josan's cheeks.

"Nothing," Josan whispered. "I know nothing."

"And what are you hiding from me?"

"How much I hate you."

He tensed, expecting a blow, but at this Nizam smiled.

"I knew you would be my favorite," he said. "And you know why?"

Josan refused to respond.

"Because you can heal yourself," he said. "So we can do this again, and again, until I am satisfied."

"No!" It was not possible. No man could survive this. Josan's terror rose, even as the darkness of unconsciousness beckoned. He prayed that he might never awake—even as he feared that Nizam was telling the truth.

"I am confident that Lucius had no knowledge of the plan to murder the empress. Nor was he in contact with others who might have plotted this on his behalf," Nizam concluded.

Proconsul Zuberi scowled, the fingers of his left hand tapping impatiently against his desk. His expression had grown increasingly grim as Nizam related the results of his investigations and his repeated interrogations of his royal prisoner.

Brother Nikos was surprised to be included in this meeting. In the past he and the proconsul had often been at odds, and Nerissa had relied upon their differing perspectives to inform her own opinion. But since Nerissa's death, Zuberi no longer held himself aloof, and indeed seemed to welcome Nikos's counsel.

Of course, Nikos already knew that Lucius was innocent, but that did not mean that there weren't other damning secrets that Lucius might have revealed during his agonies. But so far, at least, Nizam was convinced that the prince was innocent, much to Zuberi's apparent frustration. It was clear that the proconsul would prefer an easy answer, and an obvious villain.

"He may not have planned the murders, but if his followers committed the crimes, then he is still guilty," Zuberi argued.

Nizam inclined his head in agreement. "That is for you to judge. I can only tell you the facts. Make of them what you will."

"And he has told you everything?" Zuberi asked.

"About this matter, yes. But he has other secrets, which I have not yet explored."

"What are you waiting for?" Zuberi demanded.

"I need your permission before I destroy him. Once I am done, the prince will be a witless shell, fit for nothing except killing."

"Do it."

"No," Nikos interrupted.

"No?" Zuberi's voice rose in anger, and Nikos knew that he trod on dangerous ground. One did not lightly cross a future emperor.

"I would speak with you privately," Nikos said.

As Zuberi's gaze locked with his, Nikos could feel his palms sweat and his heart begin to race. But he kept his face calm, reflecting none of his inner turmoil. After a long moment, Zuberi gestured, and with a half bow Nizam left the room.

"Why do you care what happens to the prince? Nerissa's funeral is tomorrow morning. We do not need him sane, nor whole, in order to play his part. A madman screams just as loud as any other."

This was not about whether Lucius died on the morrow. As far as Brother Nikos was concerned, it would be better if Lucius were killed and took his secrets to the grave. Lucius knew too many of Nikos's own secrets for his comfort. In fact, Nikos had spent the past few days preparing his own explanations for anything that Lucius might reveal. Though so far it seemed that his former pupil had kept his silence long after an ordinary man would have confessed all in the hopes of earning an easy death.

But there was more at stake than Nikos's own misdeeds. The stability of the empire demanded that they find and punish those who had conspired in Nerissa's death. And if the search for the conspirators took attention away from whatever secrets Prince Lucius still held, well, then, it was for the good of the empire, after all. And no one would suspect him of protecting the prince.

"You heard Nizam. And Farris, who commanded the guards assigned to watch the prince, also concluded that Lucius could not have planned this," he pointed out.

In fact, Farris had called Lucius a half monk, scornfully dismissing a man who spent hours each day absorbed in his studies.

"Even your own clerk, Ferenc, saw no sign of treachery," Nikos continued.

"Why do you defend him?"

"I care not what happens to the prince. But I do care about finding those who murdered Nerissa and her family. Allowing Lucius to shoulder the blame gains us nothing."

More than once it had crossed his mind that Zuberi, as the emperor presumptive, had the most to gain from Nerissa's death. But Zuberi was not acting as a man pleased to be thrust into prominence, nor was he seizing the reins of imperial authority. He was either innocent or a master at dissembling.

And if not Zuberi, then who? The treacherous Lady Ysobel had fled home to the Seddonian Federation once her role in the aborted insurrection had been revealed, but was it possible that the bitch's schemes were still being carried out in her absence? Or was there a new adversary, one who had yet to reveal himself?

Zuberi frowned. "Even if Lucius did not conspire with the assassins, he is far from innocent. He rebelled against the empress not once but twice, and his example may have inspired others. For this alone he deserves to die."

"The next emperor will have to work hard to secure the peace and support of his people," Nikos pointed out, continuing the pretense that the identity of the next emperor was still to be determined. "If Prince Lucius is executed, and later we arrest another for Nerissa's murder, it will breed resentment among the old Ikarians."

"So what do you advise?"

"Do nothing in haste. Let Nizam keep Lucius, but tell him not to damage Lucius irrevocably. For our part, we will be wary, and watch who seeks to profit from Nerissa's death. The traitor will reveal himself; it is just a matter of time."

Nikos waited patiently as Zuberi mulled over his words, his right hand absently rubbing his belly. Nikos's own belly ached with hunger as well. The proconsul might be accustomed to working long hours without considering the needs of his body, but Nikos was used to a more civilized existence.

"I will do as you suggest," Zuberi said. "The prince will live, for at least another day. You will see that a suitable sacrifice is found to take his place?"

"Of course."

Fittingly, the moon was high over Karystos as the Daughters of the Moon arrived to prepare the empress and her family for their final journey. The preservers had done marvels, and what could not be concealed by their arts was hidden by the carefully draped garments of imperial purple silk. But not even the preservers' art could stave off decay forever, and a faint smell of rot hung in the air, until it was banished by the perfumes and ointments that the priestesses applied.

Brother Nikos inspected the priestesses' work, then retired to an antechamber to don his vestments. Underneath he wore an alb of unbleached linen as a sign of humility, and over this an open cloak of red, brocaded silk. Red was traditionally worn by the brethren for both naming ceremonies and funerals since it signified both birth and death. Here it was doubly fitting since both birth and death had visited the imperial family within a few short hours.

As the first rays of dawn broke over the city, Brother Nikos stood by as the bodies were loaded onto biers, and then placed on carriages draped with black silk. Nearly five hundred official mourners filled the courtyard, and he could hear raised shouts as the functionaries cajoled them into the proper order.

Brother Nikos's impatience grew, until finally Brother Giuliano reported that all was in readiness. As he took his place, Brother Nikos gave the signal to start.

The procession began with slaves of the imperial household waving palm branches, which occasionally dipped as they paused to remove spectators who crowded the way. Flute players followed, and behind them were young officers bearing standards that proclaimed Nerissa's military triumphs. The two tallest of his acolytes had been chosen to play the parts of Nerissa's father and grandfather, and they wore masks of beaten gold as they stood in a chariot, pulled by three matched horses.

Behind them, Brother Nikos walked alone, followed by the heads of the lesser religious orders. The streets were lined with people, some wearing black shawls of mourning, while others had only been able to find dark-colored ribbons to tie on their arms. Flowers crunched under his feet, as mourners cast blossoms in their path, the mingled scents rising in a sickening miasma. The excited murmuring of the crowds gave way to cries of grief as the bodies came into view, interspersed with chants of Nerissa's name.

The official mourners followed the funeral carriages, led by Proconsul Zuberi and Count Hector. Those nobles who could walk did so, even those who ordinarily would summon a chair to bring them from one end of the imperial complex to the other.

It took over two hours for the slow-moving procession to reach the outer walls, and the sacred grove outside the city where imperial funerals were held. The commoners who tried to follow were held back by the honor guard—only the select would be allowed to witness the funeral ceremonies.

Nikos wondered if there would be violence, as there had been when Aitor I had been buried. It was said that a thousand citizens had forced their way into the grove, crying out their grief. But today's followers, after some objections, allowed themselves to be turned aside.

The depth of their grief was surprising. Nerissa had not been a beloved figure. Indeed, twice in her reign she had been on the verge of being overthrown. But it seemed the manner of her death had bound together in outrage those who ordinarily would have rejoiced over her passing.

From the highest to the lowest, all felt the void left by Nerissa's death. There would be no security until the next emperor was named and Nerissa's killer caught and executed. As the mourners slowly filed into the grove, he could see the uncertainty in their faces and watched the careful maneuverings as old friends sought each other out and others purposefully distanced themselves from their former allies.

In the center of the grove were three funeral pyres, constructed of carefully arranged stacks of oil-soaked timbers capped with level planks of cedar. Under Brother Giuliano's direction, the imperial functionaries placed the bodies of

Prince Nestor and Princess Jacinta side by side on the first pyre. Prince Anthor's body was placed on his own pyre, and finally, Empress Nerissa's body was placed on the tallest pyre, flanked to either side by the bodies of her sons.

The dignitaries formed a loose circle around the pyres as the religious lined up to offer their final blessings.

The Daughters of the Moon were the first to pass by the pyres, bowing their heads in respect as their leader sang in prayer. The priest Fadil followed, chanting the praises of the three gods so beloved of the old Ikarians. Other religious orders followed, in increasing order of importance, until at last it was Brother Nikos's turn.

The acolytes wearing the masks of Aitor the Great and his son Aitor II flanked him as he approached the pyre where Anthor's body lay. Bowing deeply, Nikos commended the young prince's soul to the care of his noble ancestors. Next he moved to Nestor's pyre. Here, too, he offered prayers that Nestor be allowed to join his noble ancestors. Princess Jacinta, being merely his wife, was not mentioned. As one of his possessions, it was understood that she would share whatever afterlife he had earned.

Finally, Nikos stood in front of the pyre that bore the body of Empress Nerissa. Brother Giuliano held the scroll as Nikos read out the blessings for the dead. While he proclaimed Nerissa's accomplishments, the acolytes playing the role of her ancestors stood on either side, their arms outstretched, signaling their willingness to carry her spirit up into the next realm.

As Brother Nikos and the acolytes stepped back, Proconsul Zuberi stepped forward to give the first oration. The crowd grew silent, ready to hear the words of the man that most assumed would be their next emperor.

Zuberi's speech revealed his mastery of politics. All the anger and frustration that he had expressed over these past nine days were put aside, as he spoke of Nerissa's life and triumphs. Zuberi reminded his listeners that Nerissa had brought peace to her realm through her victory over the empire of Vidrun. *Victory* was perhaps too strong a word for what had been merely a negotiated truce, but none of his listeners were ready to challenge him. The empress was praised for her fairness, and for her mercilessness toward the enemies of Ikaria. Here Zuberi paused, and the crowd shifted uneasily at the reminder that there was at least one enemy who had yet to be uncovered.

Zuberi concluded his speech by promising that Nerissa's noble legacy would be carried on and that the Ikarian Empire would emerge strengthened from this tragedy. He promised that Nerissa would join her noble ancestors in watching over her empire and guiding the next emperor along the paths of wisdom and justice.

In a show of humility, Zuberi did not name himself that next emperor. Today was a day for mourning, and the shadow of Nerissa still loomed large. Once her funeral was over, it would be time to name her successor. Nikos knew it would not be long before the imperial councilors demanded that Zuberi take the throne and put an end to this dangerous interregnum.

Minister Atreides was next to speak, and the elderly councilor's voice shook as he recalled the woman he had known since her birth. In recent years, Atreides had been the leader of the conservative courtiers who had been encouraging Nerissa to resign in favor of her eldest son. Now such differences were forgotten, and the old man wept at her passing. His rehearsed speech forgotten, Atreides rambled incoherently. When he could no longer speak through his tears, Nikos signaled to Brother Giuliano, who moved forward to escort the old man back to a place among the mourners.

Seven others spoke, carefully selected from among the ranks of the nobility to ensure that no faction was slighted.

They, at least, managed to stick to their prepared speeches, though their careful words of praise for the late empress were not always enough to disguise their own worries over what the future would bring. Anything that Nerissa had accomplished could be undone by the next emperor, and those who were in power now could swiftly find themselves cast out.

Finally, it was Count Hector's turn. His booming voice, suited to barking out commands at sea, now served him well; his words carried to every corner of the grove. As he lauded the two princes, he shed tears of grief—though, unlike Atreides, Hector's tears did not interfere with his speech. Hector finished by reminding his listeners that Prince Anthor had survived long enough to kill his assassin, and only later succumbed to his mortal wounds.

It was a masterful performance, especially considering that Hector had never before shown any inclination for public oration. No doubt he was hoping to trade on the grief for his murdered nephews to secure his own position. And, indeed, Zuberi might well decide to leave Hector in his post as admiral of the navy. Replacing him would cause upheaval at a time when continuity was needed, and it was hardly a plum post. Zuberi's clients would be maneuvering for far more important positions in the new government.

When Hector stepped back, two bullocks were led forward—one of deep black and the other the purest white. Their handlers forced the bullocks to kneel in front of Nerissa's pyre, then Brother Giuliano slit their throats. Despite his care, blood sprayed, soaking Giuliano's red vestments, and Nikos knew he had been wise to delegate this task to another.

More than two hours had passed since they had first entered the grove, but now, at last, an imperial functionary handed Nikos a lit torch. As he touched the torch to the base of Anthor's pyre, the oil-soaked wood caught in an instant, and Nikos stepped back hastily to avoid setting his robes on fire.

Prince Nestor's pyre was lit next, then finally Nerissa's. The flames swiftly leapt up, obscuring her body. The fragrance of the cedar boughs that were laced into the pyres could not disguise the stench of burning flesh, and Nikos was relieved when he was able to step back.

One by one, the funeral guests lined up in strict order of precedence to pay their respects. From highest to lowest, they bowed before each of the pyres and cast their offerings upon the flames.

Once the ritual death offerings would have included slaves of the imperial household, as well as priceless objects such as favorite weapons and jeweled crowns. Now most of the offerings were miniature versions meant to show the giver's regard, but even these tokens were of the finest quality. There were caskets of rare spices, porcelain dolls to take the place of servitors in the next life, and enameled jewelry in the shape of mythical beasts.

When Count Hector's turn came, he was followed by an aide bearing a large chest. Ignoring protocol, Hector went first to Nerissa's pyre, where his aide placed the chest on the ground and opened it. Reaching into the chest, he handed Hector a silk-wrapped object, which the count opened to reveal a splendid jeweled torc of rank, which he placed on Nerissa's pyre.

Next Hector moved to Prince Nestor's pyre, where he placed a necklace of moonstones—the traditional gift for a new mother—on the side occupied by Princess Jacinta. For Prince Nestor he offered a glass sculpture of the imperial city, so large it had to be held in two hands as he leaned forward to place it on the pyre. Swirling sparks fell on his arms, but Hector showed no sign of the pain he must be feeling. Within seconds, the priceless sculpture had begun to sag and melt.

It would have taken a master craftsman weeks to create such a work, and Nikos wondered where Hector had found it. It was, by far, the most expensive offering that had been made and would ensure that Hector's largesse would be talked about for days.

Hector waited until the sculpture was devoured by the flames before moving to Prince Anthor's pyre. There he bowed far more deeply than he had to the empress. His aide handed him a second glass sculpture, this one of a noble stallion since horses had been Anthor's passion. Imploring the ancestors to take charge of the spirit of his beloved and most worthy nephew, Hector placed the sculpture on the pyre. Then he unbuckled the belt of his dress sword. Stabbing the sword into the heart of the pyre, he asked the War God to look after one of his own.

Nikos shivered, despite the blazing heat of the pyres. He knew that Hector's every move had been calculated, first to remind his watchers of his family ties to the murdered princes, and then to remind them that Hector himself was a warrior, proven in battle.

Nikos looked to his left, where Proconsul Zuberi stood, and as their gazes met, he saw his own concerns reflected in Zuberi's grim expression.

Hector's offerings were not spur-of-the-moment gifts, gathered in the days since Hector had arrived in Karystos and learned of the imperial family's tragic deaths. These had been planned well ahead of time. Were they merely the signs of a man who had prepared for all contingencies? Perhaps remnants from the time of the rebellion, when Nerissa's hold on the throne had been in doubt?

Or had they been specifically made for this occasion? Had Hector somehow learned of the plot to assassinate the imperial family?

Whether willing conspirator or merely someone who had come into possession of another's secrets, one thing was clear. Hector had come here prepared to stake his claim as the true heir of his nephews—and the next emperor of Ikaria.

Chapter 4

Alcina was the largest of the islands that made up the Federation of Seddon, but it was the smaller island of Sendat that served as the federation's capital, the center of both government and commerce. There was a lesson to be learned from this: that size did not equal power.

Or so Lady Ysobel had been told, when she had been a bored child, impatient to exchange her lesson slates for a berth on a trading ship. But her tutors had been wrong. Sometimes size did equal power. Having earned the wrath of not one but two nations, she had swiftly found herself outmatched, and spent much of the past year fighting for the survival of both herself and her ambitions.

A fight that she was slowly losing. Each day her capital dwindled, and her efforts to repair her reputation had yet to bear fruit. Reluctantly, she had decided to ask her father for help, but such a request could not be confided in a mere letter. Instead she had had to wait until her father made one of his rare visits to Sendat.

Lord Delmar Flordelis of Flordelis of Alcina had become head of the house of Flordelis six years ago, when his cousin, Lord Etienne, had chosen to step aside. Though most of his time was spent in the countinghouses and dockyards at their home on Alcina, all of the major trading houses maintained a presence on Sendat, and the house of Flordelis was no exception. Her father journeyed here two or three times each year, as duty required, and to consult personally with his representatives.

Ysobel had seen her father only once since her return, a visit that had coincided with the annual merchants' council held each fall, before the winter seas made travel too risky. It had been a tense reunion, his love for his daughter balanced against his concern for the rest of his children and the extended family that depended upon the house of Flordelis for their livelihood. In public they had kept their distance, lest Flordelis be tainted by her tarnished reputation.

Both Ysobel and her father had seats on the merchants' council, but they did not sit together, nor did they acknowledge each other in any way. When the representative from Charlot proposed that Ysobel be stripped of her seat, it had been left to others to speak in her defense. And those who defended her did so only out of self-interest. Their words had saved her, but the margin in her favor had been a mere twelve votes.

To this day, she did not know if her father had been one of the twelve.

When her father had arrived on Sendat two days ago, Ysobel had sent one of her clerks to request a meeting. She had known better than to arrive unannounced and risk public rejection. The response to her request had been in a clerk's hand, inviting her to call at her father's residence today at the third hour. There had been no personal message, but she took heart from the fact that her father asked to see her at the Flordelis family residence rather than at the countinghouse.

As the appointed hour drew near, she dressed with care,

selecting a tunic and trousers of light wool, suitable for one master trader calling upon another. A simple leather clasp held back her hair, and sandals of the same leather adorned her feet. Only a keen eye would notice that the rare, wine-dark woven leather was imported from Kazagan. The only obvious sign of wealth was the signet ring on her left hand, with the seal of her personal trading company.

She hesitated, wondering if she should wear the family ring as well but reluctantly set it aside. She had worn it for years, ever since her father had gifted it to her on her sixteenth name day, but of late the ring had remained in her jewel case. It seemed presumptuous to wear it, when her family's support could no longer be taken for granted.

Any success she achieved would bring reflected glory upon the house of Flordelis, while the burden of failure was hers to bear alone. She had known this from the moment she had accepted her aunt's gift of a trading vessel and chosen to make a path for herself separate from that of her siblings. Even now, despite all that had happened, she did not regret her choice. Let her brothers and sisters toil under their father's direction, patiently biding their time. She was made of sterner stuff, unwilling to stay in shallow waters when there were riches to be gained by venturing into the deeps.

By the standards of Sendat, the mansion owned by the house of Flordelis was large, having been acquired when Flordelis was at the height of its power. Their influence had diminished in the hundred years since, but Flordelis was still a name to be reckoned with. The mansion was both a symbol of past glories and the so-far-unfulfilled pledge that those glories would return again.

But if Flordelis was ever going to regain its prominence, she knew it would not happen under the leadership of her father. Lord Delmar was too cautious, intent on preserving the assets under his care, unwilling to risk falling further into decline. Great rewards came only with great risk, and he was unlikely to see either.

Ysobel squared her shoulders as the mansion came into view. The white stones gleamed in the morning sun, and a flapping pennant flew over the door, proclaiming that Flordelis himself was in residence. The central door was open, with a boy of about nine or ten standing guard.

"Good morning, master trader," he said, as his gaze dropped to her left hand and the ring that she wore. "How may Flordelis serve you?"

She spent a moment trying to place his features. He was not one of her nephews, but he could easily be the child of one of her many cousins. Then she shrugged, dismissing it as unimportant. She had spent much of the past seven years away from Alcina, either on trading missions or in service of the federation. It was no wonder that she did not recognize him, nor he her.

"I am Lady Ysobel Flordelis of Alcina, here to see my father."

His features showed neither surprise nor curiosity and she felt a stir of pride. Flordelis's power might be diminished, but they still bred true, and their training could not be faulted.

"Of course. Do you need a guide?"

She shook her head. "I know the way."

With a nod, the boy stepped aside, and she passed through the gate into the large foyer.

No trading family could afford to keep a mansion merely for the occasional visit by the head of house, and Flordelis was no exception. The mansion was divided into apartments. Those on the ground floor were set aside for use by the senior captains when they were in port. The second floor was given over to the use of the trading representatives who lived year-round with their families in Sendat. The third floor held a suite of rooms for her father, and other suites that could be used by members of the family when their affairs called them here. Ysobel had once had use of a small bedroom, until she had earned her master trader's ring and set up her own establishment.

At this hour of the day the mansion was mostly empty, its residents at the countinghouse or down at the docks. As she climbed the stairs to the second floor, she passed a servant carrying a basket of soiled linens, and a pair of young girls who dashed by, giggling, as they played a game of tag. She spared a moment to wonder if her father had chosen this time deliberately, so that there would be few witnesses to her visit. Her breath quickened as she raised her hand to tap on the door that led to her father's private rooms.

A distant voice called "Enter," and she opened the door.

Her father rose from his seat behind a desk covered high with books and advanced to meet her.

"Greetings and welcome, beloved daughter," he said. Taking both her hands in his own, he kissed her first on the right cheek, then on the left.

"Greetings of the day to you, honored father," she replied. The analytical part of her mind noted that he had welcomed her as a daughter rather than a fellow trader, and wondered what this might mean for her errand.

"Let me offer you some tea." He led her to his private balcony, where a pair of chairs flanked a table set for a late breakfast. She declined a pastry but allowed her father to pour her a cup of dark red tea, which she tasted for politeness' sake, then set aside.

From the balcony they had a fine view of the ships in harbor and the warehouses that lined the wharves. Flordelis could literally look down upon their property—and their competition.

"I know why you are here," Lord Delmar said. "My

agents have kept me informed. They tell me that the course you have chosen brings you neither honor nor profit."

Ysobel bristled at the criticism. She would not have tolerated this from another; but he was her father, and so she chose her words carefully. "It is true that my difficulties have persisted longer than I would have wished, but the situation is not so dire as that."

"Is it not? Honest captains refuse to sail for you, and merchants do business with you only when they can find no other. When is the last time that one of your ships brought in a profit?"

"Captain Zorion and the *Swift Gull* turned a profit on their last voyage, and he has high hopes for the new route," she said.

Though it was true that the profit from the *Swift Gull* had been measured in mere pennies. Even her most experienced captain could not overcome the taint that her name now bore. As for her other three ships, two of their captains had left. The oldest of the three, Captain Mercer, had chosen to retire. He had been replaced by an even older man, a friend of Zorion's called out of his own retirement to serve. Captain Jeanette, the youngest of those who sailed for her, had also left. Ambition had brought her to Ysobel's service, in hopes of rising as quickly as her mistress. When Ysobel's fortunes declined, Jeanette left for richer shores. Ysobel had promoted Jeanette's first mate Elpheme to take her place—though not without reservations. Elpheme was inexperienced for her position, but in these difficult times her loyalty outweighed this disadvantage.

With Ikarian-controlled ports closed to her ships, she was forced to look elsewhere for cargoes. The contracts that she was offered were on terms she would once have scorned, but now she gritted her teeth and accepted. Even if the voyages ran at a loss, it was better to keep her ships on the seas and their crews together. She had hoped that time and the continued proof of honest dealings would serve to restore her reputation, but she had not expected it would take this long. As each month passed without making a profit, she was forced to dip deeper and deeper into her capital reserves.

If the situation did not change soon, she would be forced to consider leasing her ships to another house, or even selling them outright.

And a trader without ships was a pitiful creature indeed.

"It was a mistake for you to try to curry favor at the court. A trader's attention should be reserved for her ships, not caught up in politics and scheming."

"At the time, you said that Lord Quesnel's favor would be a valuable thing to have," she reminded him.

"And it would have been if it had been honestly earned. As it is, he shares your disgrace and is in no position to help anyone."

Lord Quesnel had been the minister of trade, one of the most important positions in the government. It had been his idea to send Lady Ysobel to Ikaria. Officially her position had been to promote trade; unofficially her mission had been to promote revolution and destabilize the Ikarian Empire.

Accepting the assignment had been a calculated gamble, one that Ysobel could afford to take, while an established house like Flordelis house could not. At the time, her father had approved of her boldness, but it seemed her subsequent disgrace had merely confirmed his views that prudence was the only sure path to fortune.

Still, she had not failed in her mission, though it seemed that many, including her father, had forgotten this truth. "I did not fail," she reminded him. "I did as the council asked. Empress Nerissa's court is in chaos. Over two dozen nobles have been executed, and the imperial fleet was re-called home."

"You failed when you were implicated in the scheme, bringing disgrace to yourself and the federation," her father amended. His words were cruel, but his tone was as calm as if they were discussing the weather.

"There is no proof of my involvement, merely suspicions. And the council has refused all requests from Ikaria to return me for questioning."

"Instead they confined you to this island, which shows their support is lackluster at best."

This was the punishment that rankled most. She was convinced that if she could take personal command of one of her ships, she could turn a profit. She trusted Zorion and Telfor, who had been with her from the start, but her other two captains were either too old or too young for their posts.

Of course, Ysobel was not the only one who had paid the price for their role in the ill-fated scheme. Lord Quesnel had been too powerful to be dismissed entirely, but he had been given a new post as minister of war. Only one intimately familiar with federation politics would recognize the change as the insult that it was. In the federation trade ruled all, and any other ministry paled beside it.

But she had not come to her father for a history lesson. She could not undo what had been done. She had learned the hard way that politics and business did not mix. Now it was up to her to chart a new course for the future.

"I have come with a proposition," she said, changing the subject.

Her father nodded for her to continue and refilled their cups, giving her a chance to organize her thoughts.

"It is true that the contracts I have been offered have been less than favorable. Though no merchant has ever lodged a successful complaint against me or one of my ships, the rumors of cheating still persist. I need time to recover, but I cannot let my ships stand idle. Instead I propose to lease three of my ships to the house of Flordelis, leaving the *Swift Gull* to bear my standard. You gain three well-run ships, at terms that will be favorable to your house. I gain the time that I need to rebuild my reputation, without the burden of supporting all four vessels."

With effort she kept her face impassive, revealing no trace of how hard it had been to make this offer. In some ways, this would be as if she was starting anew. But eleven years ago she had been given a single ship and used it to build a successful trading house. She could do so again.

Still, offering to lease the ships to Flordelis rankled. It smacked of failure—a child whose ambitions had outstripped her grasp and had to come running back to her family to rescue her. The only thing that would rankle more was if she was forced to lease her ships to strangers.

"No," Lord Delmar said.

"No?"

"No."

Anger rose, but she kept her voice calm. "Why not?"

"Leasing the ships only prolongs the inevitable, and I will not use the resources of our house to fund further folly."

She drew in her breath to protest, but he continued. "I have a counteroffer. Flordelis will buy the ships from you, at a price to be set by an arbiter, with payment over seven years. You will resign your house and return to us. You may keep your status as master trader and work here in our countinghouses, negotiating agreements on behalf of Flordelis. When the council lifts your restrictions, you will be allowed to petition to sail as captain if you so choose."

She gulped her tea to cover her confusion. The fruit brew was bitter on her tongue, or perhaps that was merely the taste of humiliation.

"Is this my father speaking? Or Flordelis of Flordelis?" she asked.

"Both," he said. He leaned forward and took her hands in his own. "You know I've worried about you ever since Tilda encouraged your madness by giving you your own ship. I knew that I wouldn't be able to protect you, and I was right. But if you come back to us, I can shield you from the consequences of your folly. Lean on the strength of the family and we will protect you."

She knew that many would call his offer generous. Bold even, in that he was risking tainting his own house's reputation by taking in his wayward daughter.

All she had to do was to give up her dreams of building her own trading empire. To admit that her ambitions had been mistaken, and yield to the wisdom of her elders. To follow a carefully circumscribed course for the rest of her days, knowing that her judgment might never be fully trusted again. There was little chance that she would ever achieve the rank of head of house, able to implement her own vision for the future.

But would it really be so bad? She would be a master trader, still—a feat that none of her brothers or sisters had yet achieved. She would have more power than most, and she knew the move would go a long way toward restoring her reputation. Those who had disparaged her previous accomplishments would take pleasure in her reduced status, and ironically this would make it easier for her to deal with them.

Gently she withdrew her hands from her father's. "It is a generous offer, but I must decline. I am committed to my course, and there is no turning back. If Flordelis will not oblige me, I will find another house to lease my ships."

"And if no one comes to your aid? What then?"

"Then I will do what I must," she said. "But better

bankrupt and laboring on the docks than returning to Flordelis and denying my ambition."

He winced and she knew her words had hurt him.

"I love you and I will always honor our family," she said, "but I need to make my own way in this world, for good or for ill."

"I do not understand you," he said.

"I know." He had never understood his wayward middle daughter, no more than he had understood his sister Tilda, who had left one day on a routine trading voyage and returned a pirate hunter. There had been no place for Tilda in the house of Flordelis, and there would be no place for Ysobel, either. She was too independent ever to be happy steering another's course.

In a way, his generosity hurt more than a flat-out rejection would have. It gave her nothing to rage against. She had hoped that he would see her as an equal and deal with her accordingly, but now she realized that he would always see her as a child. An unruly child, but beloved all the same and in need of protection.

She wondered if things would have been different if Lord Etienne had remained head of the house. Was it only her father's love for her that blinded him to her worth? Or would Lord Etienne, too, have seen her as too headstrong, too much of a gambler to be a worthy business partner?

"I thank you for the gift of your time and counsel, Flordelis of Flordelis," she said, using the ritual phrase to signal that they were finished speaking of the business of her house. "Now tell me what other news you bring from Alcina. Mother is well? And my nieces and nephews?"

Her father frowned, but allowed the conversation to be steered toward matters on which there could be no disagreement.

•   •   •

Having failed to convince her father to back her, Ysobel began cautiously approaching representatives of other trading houses, looking for one that would partner with her. The reputable houses would not consider leasing one of her ships—or, if they did, the terms they offered were insulting. And as for the less reputable houses, well, she was not quite that desperate. Yet.

She reckoned the sums several times and came to the conclusion that even if her ships brought in no profits, she could continue to sail for the rest of the season. But there would be little capital left to buy new cargoes come spring. If matters had not changed by that time, she would have to sell one of her ships. The *Swift Gull* was the newest and fastest, and would bring the most profit. But it was also her best chance for rebuilding her fortunes. Likewise, the *River Sprite* had been built to her specifications. Smaller than the *Gull,* it was more versatile, with a shallow draft that meant it could sail up rivers as easily as it could cross the great sea. Both of these ships were too valuable to lose.

Her two other ships—the *Leaping Dolphin* and the *Eastern Star*—were less impressive, being older and more conventionally designed. Alone, neither would bring the money that she needed, so she would have to sell them both. But as yet, the situation was not that dire. There was still time for the tide of her fortunes to change.

With all four of her ships at sea, there was little to occupy her restless mind. Instead she took to prowling the dockyards, carefully observing the newly arrived ships and their cargoes. She frequented the traders' guildhall, inspecting the registry of contracts, as was her right. The intelligence gained on business partnerships was valuable, but that was only part of the reason why she visited. The other part was to remind the traders that she was still one of them, with all the privileges that this entailed.

Not long after her meeting with her father, she returned

from the market to find a marine lieutenant standing inside her rented room. His polished brass shoulder cords shone brightly in contrast to his dingy surroundings. Hardly a fitting place for a master trader to live, but she had better things to spend her coins on than mere lodging.

She did not bother asking him how he had managed to gain entry. The manager of the apartment block seldom inquired as to the comings and goings of those within, and the cheap lock on the door would not have stopped a determined child. That was why Ysobel kept nothing of value in these rooms, using them merely as a place to sleep.

"What brings you here?" she asked.

"We've been combing the city for you," he said. A brief grin crossed his face, taking several years off his apparent age. "Luckily I thought to wait for you."

"Who is looking for me?"

"Lord Quesnel. Come, he said to make haste."

She did not protest, merely setting down the bag that contained the ingredients for her dinner. If it had been a simple matter, Lord Quesnel would have sent a servant. Even the minister of war did not use marines for his personal errands. Whatever the reason for this summons, it was bound to be of the gravest importance.

Her belly churned. She wondered if the council had changed its mind about her fate. Were they even now preparing to hand her over to the Ikarians? If so, surely the summons would have come from the council rather than Lord Quesnel.

Her curiosity grew as she followed the marine, who led her not to the War Ministry, but rather to Lord Quesnel's private residence.

Lord Quesnel dismissed the marine with a swift thanks and assurances that he had earned the promised reward, which explained the marine's pleasure at being the one to find her.

She had expected the tidings to be grave, but to her surprise Lord Quesnel appeared gleeful, almost manic. As soon as the marine left, he embraced her and kissed both of her cheeks, a greeting reserved for trusted friends and allies.

"I had hoped they would find you earlier, but now our time together must be brief. No matter; there will be other opportunities to celebrate."

"Celebrate?"

Rather than answering immediately, Lord Quesnel turned away. He poured pale star-wine into two crystal glasses and handed one to her.

"To success beyond all measure," he proclaimed, lifting his glass in a toast.

"Success," she echoed, raising her glass, then taking a small sip. "Now tell me, how have we succeeded?"

"A ship brought news from Ikaria. The captain is an old friend, so he came to me first. But it won't be long before others bear the news to the council." Lord Quesnel took another sip of his star-wine, clearly enjoying drawing out the suspense.

Ysobel refused to be drawn. She waited in silence, knowing that in time he would not be able to resist sharing whatever news he had received.

"Empress Nerissa has been assassinated," he said.

Now it was her turn to sip her wine as a cover for her confusion. This was what she had worked for, the event that would destabilize Ikaria and ensure that their empire would no longer be a threat to the federation. Still, hearing the news was a shock. She had never truly expected they would succeed. Their schemes had been meant to turn Nerissa's attentions within her own borders and keep the empress far too busy to cast covetous eyes upon the federation's valuable ports and colonies.

The empress had been a threat, but she had also been a

strong ruler and worthy opponent. Lady Ysobel felt a stir of regret, though it was swiftly smothered by more immediate concerns.

"How did she die? And is there any sign that Prince Nestor suspects the federation of involvement in his mother's death?"

Not that they could have carried out such a crime. Those who had schemed with Ysobel to bring down the empress had since been executed, or had fled Ikaria in disgrace. Still, she had no doubt that Lord Quesnel would take credit, if he could.

And as Lord Quesnel's fortunes rose, so, too, would hers. It seems her gamble might have paid off after all.

"Nestor is dead as well. And his wife, and his brother Prince Anthor. The house of Aitor is no more."

It was too much to take in. It was as if she had cast her line for a salmon and hooked a whale instead. The empress and her two sons both gone? All of Ikaria must be reeling from the shock.

"There will be civil war."

"Indeed." Lord Quesnel chortled with glee. Draining his glass, he refilled it, but she waved aside his offer to refill her own. She needed a clear head to chart her course.

"What of Prince Lucius?" The prince, sole heir to the former rulers of Ikaria, had been the figurehead for the two previous rebellions. It was logical to conclude that he would be blamed for this one as well.

He shrugged. "My source tells me he was handed over to Nerissa's torturers. No doubt he has already been executed."

"No doubt." She repressed a twinge as she contemplated the death of yet another acquaintance. Circumstances had forced her to work with Prince Lucius, but she had not liked him. Reportedly he had surrendered himself to Empress Nerissa in order to bring an end to the last rebellion, but such courage and self-sacrifice did not seem in character with the man she had come to know. Perhaps she had never known him at all.

And now she never would. Lucius had joined a long list of those who had once trusted her, and gone to their deaths. No stranger to death at sea, she had discovered that she had little stomach for the senseless killings that their convoluted plots inspired. Politics was a far uglier business than she had imagined, and she was well clear of it.

She had been naïve to think that she could emerge unscathed from such foulness.

Lord Quesnel glanced at the mechanical clock on his desk, then set down his glass. "I must go, but I am glad that we were able to speak. You should hold yourself in readiness. The council will want to speak with you, to hear your opinions on who is most likely to win the throne and who among the contenders will be open to a discreet partnership with the federation."

In other words, he wanted to start the games again. He would take oblique credit for the demise of the imperial family and persuade the council to permit him to launch a new scheme, one that could very well be even bloodier than the last.

But he would have to do it without her help. She had already decided to swear off politics, and news of the slaughter in Ikaria only strengthened her resolve.

"I will be happy to give the council the benefit of my observations," she said, hoping her face showed none of her inner revulsion. "And naturally, if the council should feel fit to recognize me for my service, I would be most grateful. I can think of no better reward than being allowed to sail once more upon one of my ships."

"Of course," Lord Quesnel said.

From the sobering of his expression she knew that he had understood her message. She would testify before the council and say nothing that would contradict whatever claims he might make. And, indeed, it was not as if she would be lying. It was possible that some of their allies who had fled Ikaria had later returned to seek their vengeance. Or even that a small group of rebels had survived undetected, biding their time until they could strike.

But the price of her cooperation was the restoration of her reputation—and an end to his attempts to use her in his schemes. "It is good when friends understand one another," he said.

"And it is important to know who your friends are," she replied.

Chapter 5

Lady Ysobel's testimony before the council was brief. She answered their questions truthfully, reminding the councilors that it had been a year since she had hastily left Ikaria. Much could have changed in that time, as new political alliances would have formed in the wake of the mass arrests and executions. Former friends would have distanced themselves from each other, and old enemies might have found common ground.

The supporters of Prince Lucius were widely assumed to have been behind the assassinations, though there was no word as yet if he had been tried and executed for the crime. The council issued a carefully worded statement of sympathy to the people of Ikaria, lamenting the death of their great ruler. Buried within the formal letter was a reminder that Nerissa had spent much of her reign focused on imagined conspiracies from outside her own shores, ignoring the danger from within that had finally claimed her life.

Copies of the letter were sent to federation emissaries around the great basin. The official federation position was clear—Nerissa had tried to blame earlier unrest upon agents from the federation to draw attention away from the growing disloyalty of her own subjects. But such deceptions could not last forever, and now all could see the truth. Thus neatly absolving the federation of any blame.

In public the federation offered its sympathies, while in private there was cautious rejoicing. It was clear that Nerissa's death and the inevitable struggle for succession would weaken the Ikarian Empire, but King Bayard and his councilors had not yet decided how best to take advantage of the situation.

Not that Ysobel was privy to their debates. After her testimony, she had been dismissed so they could deliberate in private. The next day she received confirmation that all official restrictions upon her had been lifted. The council offered its regret that she had been inconvenienced because of baseless, vile rumors from Ikaria and thanked her for her patience and loyalty in the face of such calumnies. A copy of that letter was filed with the traders' guild.

A second letter, enclosed with the first, asked her to make herself available for further consultations with the council during this difficult period. The letter was for her eyes only, but the meaning was clear. Officially she was free to go wherever she wished. In reality, though, she would not be allowed to leave Sendat. Not while each day brought ships carrying new rumors of what was happening in Ikaria. Her expertise might still be needed.

But the long-sought public approval from the council did little to change the opinion of the other traders. They were wise enough to recognize her restored status as a political favor—payment for services rendered rather than a judgment on her trustworthiness. Her mission to Ikaria had been a secret one after all. Even now, only the most senior councilors knew that she had been sent there specifically to offer federation aid to those who sought to overthrow Empress Nerissa.

Surely the next ship from Ikaria would bring news of the new emperor. Privately she expected that Proconsul Zuberi would take the throne, though she had been careful to downplay her certainty when she testified before the council. She did not want to make herself appear too valuable, after all.

With a new emperor on the throne in Ikaria, the council would have no further use for her. And once she was set free, she would leave on the first of her ships that came into harbor.

A successful voyage under her command would do far more to restore her reputation than a dozen letters of praise from the council. Sailing was in her blood, and she desperately longed to exchange the stench of politics for the clean scent of a favorable wind. The salt sea was calling her, and she anxiously awaited the day that she could once more answer that call.

The threat posed by the Seddonian Federation was not forgotten, but Brother Nikos had far more immediate matters to occupy his attention. In the days following the funeral of Empress Nerissa and her sons, he had been a near-constant presence at the imperial compound. Proconsul Zuberi, who had once held himself aloof, now frequently sought Nikos's counsel. Others sought him out as well, perhaps seeing him as impartial, while the rest of the court maneuvered to back their favorite candidates for emperor.

Many assumed that Proconsul Zuberi would take the crown, and indeed there were those who asked Nikos to urge Zuberi to make his announcement now, rather than decorously waiting until a full month had passed. To these Nikos offered his reassurances, though as the days passed he began to suspect that Zuberi had no intention of claiming the throne for himself. And with each day that passed, the other claimants to the throne grew bolder, interpreting Zuberi's silence as weakness.

Darius, one of the few native Ikarians left in Nerissa's court, suggested that an election be held to name the new emperor, following the barbaric customs of the Seddonian Federation. Both Darius and his suggestion were widely mocked, his detractors finding common ground in their disdain—though they could not agree on anything else.

Finally, with only two days left before the official period of mourning was to end, Zuberi summoned Nikos to an informal dinner. The location, Zuberi's private residence rather than his official apartments in the imperial compound, was perhaps meant to disguise the meaning of the invitation, but anyone watching would know that this was not a mere dinner but rather a council of war.

In addition to Nikos, Zuberi had invited Petrelis, head of the city watch, Simon the Bald, who served as Chancellor of the Exchequer, and Demetrios, the leader of the senate. With the imperial bureaucracies firmly under Zuberi's control, these were four of the most powerful men in the empire. Five, counting Nikos himself, who wielded power not by official position but rather through the reliance of others on his counsel.

As Nikos took his place on the last empty couch in the dining room, an unwelcome thought occurred to him. Anyone wishing to complete the destruction of Nerissa's legacy need only assassinate the men in this room, and there would be none left to oppose him.

He hoped fervently that Zuberi's servants were loyal and that Petrelis's guards on watch outside could be trusted.

Dinner itself was a modest affair, a mere six courses, accompanied by wine so heavily watered that it was impossible to guess its provenance. The dishes were mild, almost peasant fare, when contrasted with the heavily seasoned meals that were offered at the palace. Nikos and the others ate enough to seem polite, though he noticed that Zuberi himself ate only enough to assure the others that the dishes were not poisoned.

They spoke of trivial topics until the servants had cleared the last plate away and shut the doors firmly closed behind them.

"My men intercepted one of Commander Markos's lieutenants trying to enter the city today," Petrelis began. A man of modest stature, his unprepossessing appearance caused many to underestimate his ruthlessness. Though little known outside of Karystos, within the city walls he was a man to be feared. "He took poison before we could question him, but it is obvious that Markos is in contact with his supporters in the city."

"He must be closer than we suspected," Demetrios said.

"But did he bring his troops? Or are they still in the north?" Simon asked.

"He would be a fool if he moved without them," Petrelis said.

Commander Markos was one of the five regional commanders of the imperial army, and married to Atlanta, the great-granddaughter of Aitor the Great. There were a handful that championed Atlanta's claim to the throne as the only living descendant of the imperial line. But most had lost their taste for an empress, even if it was understood that Markos would rule in his wife's name.

"Who knows what the armies will do? If Nerissa had replaced General Kolya, then we would not have this uncertainty," Simon grumbled. As the oldest of those present, and one who had known Nerissa from her childhood, he was often freer in his criticisms of the late empress than the rest.

"And then we would be dealing with one man, rather

than five. One man might be tempted to seize the throne, but if Markos tries to bring his troops into the city, the other commanders will oppose him," Demetrios said.

Perhaps they would. Or perhaps Markos had already found common cause with one or more of his fellow commanders, offering a promotion in return for supporting Markos's wife's claim to the imperial throne. It was what Nikos would do, in his place.

"Zuberi, we've had enough of your modesty," Simon said. Second in power to Zuberi, he could speak bluntly where another might have tried a more delicate approach. "Propriety is good enough in its place, but the longer you delay, the more time your foes have to gather strength and form alliances. Have Demetrios call the senate into session tomorrow, and when they offer you the throne, you will accept for the good of the empire. Then we can put the schemers in their place."

"No," Zuberi said.

Simon sat upright. "No? What madness is this? With us to support you, who will gainsay your right to the throne? Why else have you gathered us here?"

"Would that matters were so simple, but the gods have other plans for me," Zuberi said. With his right hand he rubbed his stomach, a gesture that had become habitual with him in the last weeks. "I have a cancer in my stomach that will kill me before the year is done."

Nikos drew in a sharp breath. It was scant comfort that the others seemed to be equally stunned.

"Are you certain?" Simon asked.

Zuberi nodded.

Nikos thought frantically, his careful calculations in disarray. If Zuberi was not to take the throne, then who?

"You could still rule," he said, after a moment's thought. "Ikaria needs your guidance for however long you have left with us. And your son Bakari will make a fine emperor himself one day."

Bakari was only ten or eleven, as Nikos recalled. After his father's passing, he would need regents and advisors to help him govern. Zuberi had many trusted friends, himself among them, who would gladly offer such service.

Zuberi shook his head. "I will not do that to my wife, nor to my sons. Has anyone forgotten what happened to Lady Zenia's children? Not to mention the two princes? Once I am gone, my family will be easy prey."

"The people will not rally behind a boy emperor, no matter whose hand guides him," Demetrios added.

"Then it will have to be Count Hector," Simon said. "Prince Anthor did survive after his mother's death, as Hector's supporters constantly remind us. With Nestor dead, Anthor would have inherited his mother's titles. And under the law, without children of his own, Anthor's possessions pass to his father's nearest relative."

"And if Hector merely wanted Anthor's stud farm, I would see it given to him. But Nerissa sat on the imperial throne, not her husband. If Nerissa's consort Philip could not call himself emperor, neither can his brother," Demetrios argued.

Nikos realized that Zuberi had not told the others of Hector's guilt. He, alone, had been privileged with this information, since he had been the first to cast suspicions upon Hector.

"Hector must not rule," Zuberi said quietly. Zuberi's calmness was in stark contrast to his frantic guests. Then, again, Zuberi had known of his death sentence for months, while Nikos and the rest were still trying to fathom the consequences of his illness.

"I know Nerissa never liked him, but he's served the empire faithfully," Simon said. "We could do worse."

"I have proof that Hector arranged for Nerissa's assassination," Zuberi said.

Petrelis slammed his fist down on the table. "Proof? What proof do you have? And why have you kept it from me?"

Ordinarily Petrelis deferred to the others, conscious of his common birth. But he guarded the privileges of his office fiercely and would be slow to forgive any slight. He leaned forward, ready to demand answers, and Nikos wondered how Zuberi would respond. If Zuberi had indeed discovered proof of Hector's treachery, it was news to him as well.

"Hector's ships anchored off the coast three days before the empress's murder. The duke has said that he was waiting to make a grand entrance on the day of her birthday celebrations, but when he sailed into Karystos harbor, he saw the black ribbons of mourning and learned of the tragedy," Zuberi said.

This much was public knowledge.

"He played the role of grief-stricken uncle so well that no one questioned him, no one except the learned Brother Nikos and myself. We could not question Hector, so we questioned his lieutenant."

"Lieutenant Azizi? He was reported missing—my men found signs of a struggle in his quarters but no trace of him," Petrelis said. "This was your doing?"

Petrelis was angry over the slight to his authority.

"On my orders," Zuberi said. "As for the lieutenant, well, after two days in Nizam's care, he told the tale of a heavily cloaked stranger who boarded Hector's vessel when they stopped in Kazagan. The stranger stayed in his cabin for the entire voyage, until Hector's ships anchored off the coast. A skiff rowed from shore to meet the flagship, apparently by prearrangement. As the passenger descended from the ship to the waiting skiff, the wind disturbed his cloak, and the lieutenant is prepared to swear that the stranger's face was covered in tattoos."

Nikos stared at Zuberi, trying to read the truth from his face, but the proconsul was inscrutable. It was hard to believe that Hector could have been so careless as to transport the assassin on his own ship, knowing that the assassin bore the damning tattoos of a functionary. Then, again, who else could Hector have entrusted this errand to?

"Why haven't you given the order to arrest him?" Petrelis asked.

"Only the next emperor will be able to order him jailed," Zuberi replied.

"If Zuberi will not take the crown—" Simon began.

"I will not."

"Then the empire is doomed," Simon continued. "Only you or Count Hector had a chance at uniting the various factions. Anyone else will launch Ikaria into civil war."

"What of yourself?" asked Petrelis.

"I am too old and have made too many enemies," Simon said calmly, as if he was discussing the weather. "Demetrios, you have the power of the senate behind you, but you also have an older brother. We cannot elevate your blood by slighting his."

Demetrios nodded, no doubt having already reached this conclusion days before. Ambitious and charismatic, he had friends among commoners and nobles alike. Next to Zuberi he was the best-known official outside the walls of Karystos and would have made a suitable emperor were it not for his older brother. Though if the struggle for succession stretched on, his older brother would do well to fear for his life.

"Petrelis is baseborn, and the city watch is as high as he will be allowed to rise. And as for Nikos, only a fool would name a celibate monk as emperor," Simon concluded.

The insult stung, but Nikos recognized the truth of

Simon's words. The next emperor must have a son of his own to follow him.

Zuberi picked up the pitcher and refilled their wine cups, but no one drank. The five men sat in silence, their heads bowed as if they felt the weight of the empire pressing down upon them.

Strange to think that five men, lingering over the remains of an indifferent dinner party, held the fate of Ikaria in their hands. And yet, who else was there to guide the empire in these crucial days?

"We are agreed that Hector will not be allowed to rule?" Nikos asked.

"I will kill him myself before I see Nerissa's murderer crowned in her stead," Petrelis swore. It was not an idle threat.

"Then we must choose the next emperor ourselves. We cannot wait to let the factions fight among themselves and plunge Ikaria into civil war. I had come here tonight to pledge my loyalty to Zuberi, but if the proconsul will not rule, then there is another we should consider. A man who will owe no loyalty to the factions, but instead allow himself to be guided by us. And one whose claim to the throne cannot be disputed."

"There is no such man," Zuberi declared. "But would to the gods that he existed."

"He does. And he is in Karystos at this very moment," Nikos said.

Josan tensed as he heard booted footsteps approach his cell. After weeks spent in the dark confines of the dungeon, he was intimately familiar with its routines, and he knew that this sound boded ill.

Two sets of booted footsteps meant that the guards were coming with his daily allowance of food and a bucket of water. One man to bring them into the cell and a second who stood watch lest the prisoner try to escape.

The sound of sandals meant that the healer Galen or his slave was approaching, though it had been days since Josan had required the service of a healer.

This was the sound of several guards approaching, and he trembled, knowing what was to come.

It had been over a week since Nizam had last questioned him, but he knew better than to think that the chief torturer had forgotten him. The long intermission merely meant that Nizam had run out of questions to ask, and Josan had run out of answers to give him.

He wondered what new questions Nizam would put to him and whether this would be the day that Nizam finally learned the truth about his royal prisoner.

Not that Josan had been able to conceal anything that Nizam wished to know. Nizam had shown himself a master at his craft, capable of inflicting unimaginable pain— and stripping a man's soul bare in the process. In the end, Josan had found himself begging to be allowed to answer Nizam's questions.

After his first torture session he had been convinced that he was dying, a fate he welcomed. But instead he had awoken to find himself being tended by a healer. And to his utter disbelief, in a mere two days he had healed well enough for Nizam to begin his work again.

Over and over again he had recounted his activities during the months of his confinement in the palace, knowing himself blameless and desperate to convince Nizam of his innocence. Nizam had given no sign whether or not he believed his prisoner, merely moving on to questions about his role in the aborted rebellion.

Josan had told him everything he could remember. The names of everyone he had met with, every conversation he could recall, every detail that he had known or guessed about the conspiracy. All information that he had given the empress before, though this time his statements were punctuated with screams, his veracity guaranteed by the torments of his flesh.

Nizam had seemed equally interested in his magical abilities, though a talent for fire-starting seemed a paltry enough trick. It had taken a careless comment from the healer's servant for Josan to realize that there was other magic at work—his body was healing itself. Injuries that would have killed another man were instead mere inconveniences. Broken bones mended within days, open wounds closed themselves overnight.

And as for the other—each rape hurt as if it were the first.

At times Josan cursed his body's ability to heal—death would have been preferable to the repeated agonies that he had been forced to endure. Nizam had taken Josan's healing as a personal challenge and tested the very limits of this new power.

Strange to think that he had learned more about the Old Magic under Nizam's care than he had in all his months of surreptitious studying. But it was knowledge that he could have lived without.

Josan had answered every question that Nizam put to him, usually more than once. But for all his thoroughness, Nizam had yet to touch upon the biggest secret that his prisoner concealed.

The magic that sustained him was not his. It belonged to Prince Lucius, the heir to the former rulers of Ikaria and the rightful owner of the body that Josan now wore.

Both Josan and the prince were victims of a plot by Brother Nikos, who had sought to mold the prince into an obedient servant. Forbidden magics had been used to place the soul of a dying monk in the body of the rebellious prince. But rather than a compliant pawn, the spell had produced a damaged man who was neither prince nor monk. After years spent in exile, last summer Josan had learned the truth of what had been done to him as the prince's spirit finally roused from its long slumber.

After struggling to cast the invader from his body, Prince Lucius had finally reached a truce with Josan, and the two had united to bring an end to the bloody rebellion. Then, as they surrendered to the empress and certain death, the prince's spirit had fled. There had been no trace of his presence since. Josan had striven to awaken him but could not afford to rouse Brother Nikos's suspicions by requesting works that dealt directly with the forbidden magics.

In the weeks before the empress's murder, Josan had begun to fear that the prince's spirit had indeed passed, leaving Josan alone to pay the price for the prince's misdeeds. But his miraculous healing indicated otherwise. Some part of the prince still lingered.

And if any part of the prince survived, it was up to Josan to keep that secret for as long as he could. At first he had kept silence out of respect for the members of his order. Brother Nikos deserved punishment for his crimes, but the rest of the Learned Brethren were innocent. Once it was discovered that the collegium was studying forbidden magics, all members of the brethren would be seen as equally guilty.

Now he kept silent for the prince's sake. And for his own. He had been very careful not to imagine what Nizam would do once he realized that he had two souls to toy with, but he suspected it would make his prior torments pale in comparison.

He could not withstand Nizam's questions, so he must give him no reason to suspect that there was anything left to discover.

Josan rose to his feet as the door to his cell swung open,

refusing to let his captors see his fear. A foolish gesture, perhaps, since Nizam and his assistants had already witnessed his degradation, still, such gestures were all he had left.

He was not a particularly brave man, and these weeks had taught him far more than any man should know about the depths of his own cowardice. But bravery wasn't all there was to a man. Sometimes stubbornness would serve just as well, and a blind refusal to accept that he was defeated. It was not bravery that drew him to his feet and kept him calm as the hated guards approached. It was a refusal to grant them any more power over him than they already had. He feared them, yes, but he was still Josan. Still the man he had always been, even as he wore this borrowed body. And perhaps there was a bit of Prince Lucius's arrogance still lurking, enough to help him stand without trembling, his face a mask of calmness.

"It has been too long," he said. "I was beginning to think that Nizam had found a new favorite."

There was no reaction from the guards, but he knew his words would be reported to Nizam. It was a subtle challenge, one he knew Nizam would understand. Josan had not broken. Not yet. Nizam might be able to make him bleed, but he had to work for his triumph, every time.

No doubt used to prisoners who were too damaged to walk on their own, two of the guards seized his arms, prepared to drag him if necessary. Their bruising grips discouraged any thoughts of resistance. Indeed, if he escaped them, where could he go? These underground catacombs were Nizam's domain. Even if he had the strength to flee, Josan would not get ten yards without being recognized and recaptured.

Two more guards stood outside his cell, and as Josan was led out they formed up behind him. It was a curious sign of respect, that he was considered so dangerous that four armed men needed to watch over him. Then again, he supposed there was no established protocol for dealing with a man who was both royal prince and suspected regicide.

When they reached the end of the corridor, he automatically began turning left, toward the Rooms of Pain. His escort had other ideas though, and he stumbled as the guards jerked him to the right.

"Where are we going?" he asked.

They did not answer. Neither did they strike him, the usual reminder that he must keep silent in the corridors.

Interesting.

He was brought to a small room, with a proper wooden door instead of an iron grate. Bright lanterns illuminated the room, and he blinked furiously as he tried to take in his new surroundings. It was not one of the torture rooms, that much was clear. Instead there was a plain wooden table holding a basin of water, with a pile of folded cloth next to it.

"Clean yourself up," a voice said, and Josan turned to find that one of his escort had followed him inside. Strangely enough, the others remained outside, with the door shut.

"If you won't do it, I'll have my men do it for you," the guard said.

Josan nodded. Swiftly, he stripped off his filthy rags, dropping them carelessly on the floor. The water was tepid, but even this was bliss to a man who had gone without bathing for weeks.

A cake of soap rested on top of the folded towels and with the help of a small towel he scrubbed himself as clean as he could. The water was black when he was finished. He dried himself with the second towel, for the first time able to see the faint scars that were all that remained from his injuries. His skin felt better, but he was all too conscious of his rank hair and the itching of his unkempt beard. He stood there for a moment, holding the towel, unwilling to put on his filthy rags.

"Put these on," the guard said, handing him a small bundle.

Josan opened it to find a cotton tunic and leather sandals. Plain enough garb, but luxury for a prisoner. He wondered at the meaning of this. He knew that Nizam had no interest in his comfort, but perhaps he was trying a new tactic—offering his prisoner courtesies that could then be withheld.

Though even that rang false. Perhaps the answer was simpler.

In the dark of the catacombs it was difficult to distinguish night from day. By his reckoning he had spent thirty-seven days here. But what if his count was wrong? What if today was the thirty-ninth day?

The empress would have been buried on the ninth day after her death, and then there would have been thirty days of mourning. By custom, on the thirty-ninth day the new emperor would take up his crown.

And what more fitting time could there be for the execution of the man who had killed his predecessor?

Josan was being prepared for his death, his ablutions meant to ensure that none could mistake the man being led to his doom. He searched inside himself for outrage or fear, but instead he found only calmness. He had known from the beginning that he could not expect his freedom. Regardless of whether or not he was found guilty of Empress Nerissa's murder, the new emperor could not afford to let Prince Lucius live. Death was inevitable, and a swift death was preferable to remaining Nizam's personal plaything.

"I didn't kill the empress," he said, needing to make this

much clear. He would face his death calmly but not out of any sense of guilt.

"I know," Nizam said.

Josan started. He had not heard the door open.

With fingers that shook only slightly, he finished tying the straps of his sandals, then straightened up and turned around.

The guard had left the cell, and Nizam stood in his place. Josan felt his closeness as if it were a blow, cold sweat breaking out along his spine, and his stomach clenched in anticipation. He was grateful that he had not eaten anything since yesterday.

If Nizam came closer, he knew his limbs would tremble. He could not control how his body reacted to his torturer, but he was more than mindless flesh.

"If you know I am innocent, then why wasn't I freed?"

Nizam shrugged. "It is my job to uncover the facts. Others decide what to do with what I find," he said.

Nizam stepped closer, and Josan locked his knees to keep himself from sagging as Nizam tugged at the folds of his tunic until it was arranged to his satisfaction.

"I will miss our conversations," he said, giving one of his rare smiles. Josan had learned to dread those smiles. Then Nizam stepped back. "Come, they are waiting for you."

The waiting guards had been dismissed. Apparently Nizam himself was considered sufficient escort. They climbed the stairs that led up from the catacombs in silence, emerging from an unmarked door into a small courtyard that accessed the buildings set aside for the ministers of state. It was a different route than the guards had taken when they took him to the dungeons, and Josan wondered just how many entrances and exits there were to the secret realms.

With each step, he grew more puzzled. He'd expected to be met by a contingent of soldiers, ready to lead him off in chains, and to hear the distant roar from the great square as the crowds prepared to witness his execution. Instead he was greeted only by the soft rays of dawn and the sounds of birds twittering as they splashed in the ornamental fountain.

But he was given no time to savor the peaceful scene, for Nizam urged him across the courtyard and into the nearest building. Prince Lucius might have once known what offices this building held, but Josan the monk could only speculate on where he was being taken.

And why.

At this early hour the ministry was empty. They encountered no one until they reached their destination—an unmarked door. Nizam rapped on the door once, then opened it.

"As you ordered," Nizam said, pushing Josan into the room.

Caught off guard, Josan stumbled for a few steps until he was able to regain his balance. Looking up, his gaze met that of Proconsul Zuberi, whose frown of displeasure boded ill. Seated next to the proconsul was Brother Nikos.

There was no one else. He had expected Petrelis, the head of the city watch, or his deputy at the very least, but there were no guards. No irons. Merely two of the most powerful men in Ikaria, seated at a table that held the remains of their breakfast.

"Should I wait for him?" Nizam asked.

"Yes," Zuberi said, just as Nikos said, "No."

It seemed the two men were not in accord. They glared briefly at each other, then Zuberi said, "Wait outside."

"Sit," Zuberi added, gesturing at the empty chair at the opposite side of the table. "I won't have you looming over me."

Josan pulled out the chair and took his seat, using the time to study the two men. Zuberi's face was drawn with exhaustion, his lips compressed in anger. By contrast Brother Nikos appeared impassive, but one who knew him well could see the pleasure that he was trying to hide.

Brother Nikos picked up the teapot and poured tea into an empty cup, sliding it across the table to him.

Tea? They were offering him *tea*? The last time he had seen Zuberi, the proconsul's men had beaten him nearly to death. And now he was expected to drink tea with him?

"What do you want from me, proconsul? Or is it Emperor Zuberi I by now?"

He was proud of the steadiness of his voice, despite his parched throat and cracked lips. The rising scent of cinnamon tea made his mouth water, but he carefully ignored the cup, assuming that it was either drugged or poisoned.

With a small smile, Brother Nikos filled his own cup and took a hearty sip. And then another.

Only then did Josan drink from his own cup.

"Proconsul," Zuberi said.

"Then whom should I congratulate? Count Hector, perhaps?"

With little to occupy his mind besides the pains of his own flesh, Josan had spent many hours carefully tracing the imperial genealogies in his head, wondering who would be named emperor. It had been purely an intellectual exercise, for he knew better than to hope that whomever they chose would pardon him.

"Count Hector will be arrested for treason, once the new emperor takes his crown," Nikos said.

From the glare that Zuberi gave the monk, it was clear that this was a tidbit that Zuberi would have preferred to keep secret.

"Treason?" Josan repeated, too stunned to say anything else.

"For the murders of Empress Nerissa and her sons," Nikos clarified.

It was fortunate that Josan was sitting, for his muscles sagged in sudden relief.

During these past weeks he had proclaimed his innocence, even through the taste of his own blood and the agonies of his flesh.

But a small part of him had wondered if he did bear some responsibility for her death. Some of his followers had escaped Nerissa's justice, among them Josan's former friend Myles, who possessed both the skills and fanaticism necessary to carry out the deed.

Instead, if Brother Nikos could be believed, it was Count Hector who had let his ambitions overrule his conscience.

"So why have you brought me here?" Josan asked. He kept his gaze locked on Zuberi's face, knowing where the true power lay.

"I have been persuaded, against my own good judgment, to offer you a chance to stave off your execution," Zuberi said.

"What do you want from me?"

"Count Hector must not be allowed to take the throne. And I cannot," Zuberi said.

"So you are offering me the crown. Emperor Lucius," he said.

His words had been meant as a jest, but no one laughed. Zuberi's face tightened, as if he had bitten into a sour grape, while Brother Nikos smiled.

"Yes," Brother Nikos said.

"What?"

"We want you to take the crown and ensure that Nerissa's murderer is punished."

This had to be a trick of some sort. A bizarre test, intended to reveal that he had been scheming for the throne all along. But he would not play their games. "Why not you?" he asked Zuberi.

"The proconsul——" Nikos began.

"I have my reasons," Zuberi interrupted, "and this is not a jest. Already Ikaria trembles on the brink of civil war. The ministries and nobles would follow me, but I cannot rule. Count Hector has the next strongest claim, which he must have known when he put his foul scheme in action. No other candidate can hope to unite Ikaria and keep our enemies from taking advantage of our disarray."

"So you want me? As what, a decoy for the next assassin?"

He could not believe what he was hearing. He had been prepared to beg for a merciful death. He was not prepared for this.

He longed with all his heart to accept—even an assassin's blade was preferable to the prospect of returning to the dungeons and Nizam's care. But to be named emperor . . . he could hardly comprehend it.

"If you will not deal with me, Nizam is waiting for you," Zuberi said, proving that at least some of what Josan felt must have shown on his face.

"Why me? The newcomers will not follow one of the old blood, and you cannot truly intend me to reign over you."

"Your blood gives you a legitimate claim to the throne, but you owe allegiance to none of the factions. Given a choice between you or one of their enemies, the nobles will prefer you," Brother Nikos explained. "Proconsul Zuberi controls the ministries, and our allies control the treasury and the city watch. Our backing will be enough to see you seated on the throne."

"You will be emperor in name only," Zuberi said. "I will name your circle of advisors, and you will heed our advice or meet with a swift death at the hands of your personal guards."

They *had* thought of everything.

"I know Prince Lucius will be pleased to serve his people, and to do whatever is necessary to protect his empire," Nikos said, taking care to stress Lucius's name.

Josan knew this was intentional, just as he knew the reason for Brother Nikos's barely contained triumph. This was the moment that Brother Nikos had striven for when he had performed the forbidden magics linking the soul of a monk to the body of a prince. Nikos had long dreamed of having the next emperor under his control, and his dream was about to come true.

"You have given me no choice," Josan said. "I will do as you ask."

In the end it did not matter. Emperor or prisoner, he was still damned.

Chapter 6

The Ikarian Empire had seen its share of violence and bloody conquest, and the scrolls of history contained the accounts of at least one emperor who had been crowned while still bloody from battle. But never before had a man gone from condemned prisoner to emperor-to-be in the space of a few short hours.

A part of Josan was convinced that this was a dream—a fevered fantasy created by a mind intent on escaping the horrors inflicted upon his flesh. But as each hour passed without his awaking, he was forced to concede that this was no dream.

After accepting Proconsul Zuberi's bizarre proposition, Josan was handed over to the care of one of the imperial functionaries, who led him to the suite of rooms that had once belonged to Prince Nestor. There, body servants helped strip off the garb he had only recently donned, and Josan gave himself over to their ministrations. He had a proper bath for the first time since the assassinations. His beard was shaved off, his hair trimmed, and the servants brought him new clothes to wear—a knee-length tunic of white silk, banded in the shade of purple reserved for the imperial family. From the size of it, the tunic had once belonged to Prince Anthor, and it hung loosely on Josan's emaciated body, as if he were a child wearing his father's robes.

Which, he supposed, was a fair analogy. The functionary, who refused to give his personal name, treated Josan as if he were a child, even as he helped him don the garb of an emperor-to-be. Each carefully phrased request was in truth a command.

Lest he forget his new status, he had only to glance at the entrance to his suite, where Farris stood at attention. Farris, who had once been assigned by Empress Nerissa to watch over Prince Lucius, with orders to kill him at the first sign of treachery. He wondered if Zuberi had given Farris similar orders, to ensure that the new emperor remain firmly under his control.

All that Josan knew was that his coronation would occur tomorrow, and that only a handful of court members had been informed of the identity of the next emperor. Nikos had suggested this, stating that it was better to present the nobles with a *fait accompli* than give them a chance to unite behind another candidate. To Josan, this seemed a spectacularly poor idea. Surprising the courtiers with such unpalatable news was inviting trouble.

But Josan's words were not heeded. Instead he was sent off to his rooms like a child, so Zuberi and Nikos could plan out his life. Though to be fair, his new cell was an improvement over the last.

The functionary waited until he had finished his breakfast before suggesting that he adjourn to the dressing chamber, where a waiting tailor took his measurements, muttering under his breath all the while. A purple robe was draped over Josan's tunic, but it was obvious at a glance that it had been made for a man both shorter and broader than he.

"Too tall," the tailor muttered as he knelt next to Josan, measuring the distance between the hem of the robe and the floor. "Too tall, and there's no time."

"Too tall?" Josan repeated.

The tailor ignored him, his eyes still focused on his work. "I don't know what Zuberi is thinking," he muttered. "He should have consulted with me weeks ago. Creating ordinary court robes in this short time would be a miracle, but an emperor's robes . . ."

Laughter welled up inside Josan at the absurdity of it all. The tailor's dilemma was real enough, but he was merely the first of those whose plans were to be thrown into disarray by the realization that Zuberi was not the man who would be crowned tomorrow. A few yards of silk tacked to the hem of the robe would serve to lengthen it, but the other challenges Josan faced would be far harder to solve.

Grasping the fabric of the robe in his hands, Josan tugged the garment until the tailor looked upwards.

"You are done here. Unless you intend to sew the robe while I am wearing it—"

"No, no, you are right, I am finished," the tailor stammered, scrambling hastily to his feet, as he suddenly realized that he was complaining to the future emperor himself. "There's no one your size among my assistants, but I have the measurements I need, and I'm sure I can find someone to stand in for the future."

"Yes. Fine. Go," Josan said, as he pulled the robe up over his head and handed it to the startled man.

The tailor, clutching the robe to his chest, backed out of the dressing room, with promises that he would work all day and night.

Josan's next visitor was the healer Galen.

"Prince Lucius, I have come to offer my services," Galen said.

It was the first time Galen had called him by name.

"I do not need a healer."

"Because of your recent ordeal, Proconsul Zuberi thought—"

"Proconsul Zuberi should concern himself with the empire," Josan snapped. "If Prince Lucius needs a healer, he will send for one."

He held his breath, wondering if the hovering functionary would choose this moment to override his wishes. But instead the man merely nodded, then escorted Galen outside.

His *ordeal*. A polite way of saying that Josan had been repeatedly tortured in the bowels of this very palace, brought to the brink of death again and again, but never permitted to cross over. Galen had seen him at his worst, treating his injuries with competence but without compassion, as if Josan were a broken object that needed mending rather than a man of flesh and blood.

Even if he were still suffering from the effects of his imprisonment, he would not turn to Galen for help.

He wondered what Galen had been told. Had he merely been told that the prince had been declared innocent and set free? Surely he must have wondered why the former prisoner was now to be found in the rooms once occupied by Nerissa's eldest son and heir.

First the tailor, and now Galen. Along with the servants who had attended his bath and fetched his meal. The functionaries and the guard Farris could be trusted to hold their tongues, at least for the span of a day, but surely it was too much to expect that the others would stay silent. Brother Nikos was a fool to think that such an explosive secret could be kept for long.

Then, again, even if they did talk, who would believe them? Perhaps it was the very absurdity of the news that Nikos was counting on.

After the tailor left, the functionary politely suggested

that the prince should rest. It was a sensible suggestion. Lucius's magic might have healed their shared body, but Josan was still weakened from his long imprisonment. Catching a glimpse of his reflection in one of the many mirrors that adorned Prince Nestor's chambers, Josan saw the face of a man stretched to his limits—exhausted and confused by the abrupt change in his circumstances.

The bed he had glimpsed earlier called out to him, with the promised luxury of a soft mattress and clean linens, but Josan resisted its temptations. The proconsul had said that he would speak with him later, but if Zuberi came and found Josan asleep, the proconsul might well decide not to awaken him, leaving Josan in ignorance.

He ignored the functionary's increasingly firm suggestions, pleased to win a minor victory when the official finally relented. As dusk fell, another meal was brought. The first functionary was replaced by another—an older man who also refused to give his name. Their identical tattoos gave them a similar appearance, but after careful observation Josan noticed that the second functionary had darker eyes than the first, and his ears protruded slightly from his head, as if to catch the faintest sound. In his head he decided to call this man Two, to differentiate him from the first.

Farris was replaced by Balasi, who had last seen Josan as he was dragged away by Zuberi's men. Balasi showed no sign of surprise at the change in his charge's circumstances and resolutely refused Josan's attempts to draw him into conversation.

The oil lamps had burned low when a grim-faced Zuberi finally sought him out. Zuberi scowled at Josan's attendants, who quickly removed themselves to the outer chamber, leaving Josan and Zuberi alone.

Josan braced himself for the news that Zuberi had

changed his mind—that he would once again be condemned to death. Or worse.

"Hector's dead," Zuberi said. "Poisoned, we think."

This was not the news he had been expecting, and it took a moment for Zuberi's words to sink in.

"Count Hector?"

"He was already dead when Nizam's men found him, or so I am told," Zuberi elaborated.

"But I thought he was to be arrested after the coronation—" Josan's voice trailed off as Zuberi gave him a contemptuous glance.

"And have him disrupt the ceremony? The plan was for him to be taken into custody today, quietly. Then once you were crowned, we would announce his arrest and set a date for his judgment and execution."

These plans had obviously been made after Josan had been dismissed from Zuberi's presence, but he would not remind Zuberi of that fact. He wanted to see what other information Zuberi would let slip in his distraction.

"Did he take the poison himself? Or was there another hand in his death?"

Zuberi shrugged. "It seems unlikely he would kill himself—"

"If he knew you had evidence of his role in Nerissa's murder . . ."

"Perhaps," Zuberi said, though from his tone it was clear that he was skeptical. "Or perhaps there is a second conspirator. If Hector had lived, he would have told us what we needed to know to prove his guilt. Now there will be those who see him as a martyr."

"And they will place the blame for his death on my shoulders," Josan said.

Would Hector's supporters unite to bring down the new emperor? Or would they obey him, at least publicly, out of fear for their own lives?

Josan drummed his fingers on the side of the couch, impatient with his own ignorance of court politics. His studies had done little to prepare him for the role he must play, and there was no time to remedy his deficiencies. Only experience would aid him—if he survived long enough to be schooled.

"We will worry about them when the time comes," Zuberi said.

"The list of our worries grows longer by each hour," Josan pointed out.

"You need only concern yourself with doing as you are told. Leave the empire in my hands."

"And what orders do you have for me?" Josan asked, frustration lending a sarcastic edge to his words.

"You will be crowned tomorrow at noon, in the great chamber. Brother Nikos will place the lizard crown on your head, and accept your pledge to serve Ikaria faithfully. I will be first to swear my allegiance, followed by Demetrios and Simon the Bald. The rest will fall in line."

"I admire your confidence."

Zuberi snorted. "Petrelis will have his men inside the chamber to quell the dissenters."

"Then what happens?"

"Demetrios will retire to the senate, where the senators will unanimously vote to confirm you."

"Surely there will be some who object. Hector's supporters will want to avenge his death, and there are others who will wish to support their own claimants to the throne."

"Demetrios assures me that the majority will follow his lead. As for the rest, regardless of their personal opinions, no one will want to be seen taking the losing side. Not publicly."

It seemed Zuberi had matters well in hand. Which only made Josan wonder, once again, why Zuberi wasn't taking the crown for himself. Surely it would be far easier for him to rule directly rather than through a proxy.

Unless, of course, Josan was not a proxy but a target. A distraction, meant to draw the eyes of whatever conspirators still lurked. If Count Hector had indeed been murdered, then Zuberi's caution was well-founded. He knew that Zuberi would cheerfully sacrifice the puppet emperor if it meant drawing his enemies out into the open where they could be dealt with.

"My clerk is drafting a series of orders for your signature. Once you are crowned you will sign all of them, without question," Zuberi added.

"Understood." This, after all, was the bargain he had made in exchange for his life.

"Among them is an order for compensation for the men who were executed today."

"Which men?"

"The guards who arrested you," Zuberi said.

"But those were your men, obeying your orders—"

"They laid hands upon you, and then boasted of what they had done." Zuberi shrugged, then spread his hands wide in a gesture of helplessness. "Letting them live would make you appear weak."

"So you had them killed. Your own men." After the tumultuous events of this day, Josan had thought that there was nothing left that could shock him, but Zuberi had just proven him wrong.

He had underestimated Zuberi's ruthlessness and the depths to which he would sink to gain his own ends. If the proconsul could so casually speak of killing his own men, then what else he was capable of?

A new thought occurred to Josan. "So I may expect to see an order for Nizam's death?"

He objected to murder, but that was one decree that he

would sign with a clear conscience. Surely if anyone deserved to die for his crimes, it was Nizam.

"Nizam is too useful. And he knows how to keep his mouth shut, as do his men," Zuberi said.

Pity. Josan would have enjoyed watching Nizam die.

"Your freakish powers protect him," Zuberi said, with a malicious grin. "If he had left you visibly scarred or maimed..."

In that moment Josan knew that Zuberi didn't merely despise him. Zuberi hated him, as evidenced by the pleasure he took in reminding Josan of his torments, and that he was powerless to take revenge upon those who had injured him.

He did not understand why Zuberi would scheme to put a man whom he hated on the throne of Ikaria; but it did not matter, for Zuberi had unwittingly given Josan a new goal. He wanted to do more than survive. Instead he would strive to gather enough power that he was able to act on his own, free of Zuberi's restraint.

And when that day came, Nizam would do well to fear him. And to fear what Josan had learned in these past weeks.

His feet were numb. Josan tried to wriggle his toes within their too-small boots, but he could not tell if his efforts had been successful. The boots, which had belonged to one of the late princes, were made of dark purple leather that had been elaborately decorated, and were intended for occasions of state. They were also intended for a man with smaller feet.

"I don't see why I couldn't have worn sandals," he complained. "I will make a poor impression if I stumble in front of the court because I cannot feel my feet."

Proconsul Zuberi turned to glare at him. "You will look

the part of an emperor. Any discomfort you feel is a small price to pay."

Indeed, his cramped feet were a mere trifle compared to what he had endured in the past weeks. But it gave Josan's mind something to focus on as he and Zuberi waited in the antechamber behind the main audience hall.

A heavy brocaded curtain separated the chamber from the hall, muffling the sounds of the crowd gathered on the other side. From time to time, Zuberi drew back a corner of the curtain to peer through, but he had firmly rebuked Josan when he tried to do the same. Josan had time for no more than a quick glance before the curtain was pulled from his grasp.

At last the functionary whom Josan had named One entered the room. Bowing low, he said, "All is in readiness, your graciousness."

His words were addressed to Josan, as the emperor-to-be, but the functionary waited for Zuberi's dismissal before bowing a second time and backing out of the room.

Josan's stomach clenched in anticipation of what was to come.

"Wait twelve heartbeats, then follow," Zuberi reminded him, his hand poised to pull the curtain back.

"I know what I have to do," Josan snapped.

Zuberi turned to scowl at Josan. "Remember that neither purple robes nor that ancient crown gives you any power. You live or die as I command, Lucius."

Apparently satisfied that he had put the upstart prince in his place, Zuberi drew back the curtain and stepped through onto the dais at the head of the audience chamber.

Josan could hear the rising hum of voices as the crowd realized that Zuberi was dressed in the white silk of a minister of state rather than the robes of an emperor. Squaring his shoulders, he counted off twelve heartbeats, then stepped through the curtains.

The murmuring voices fell silent as Josan advanced across the dais and took his place in front of the throne. To his left stood Proconsul Zuberi, in his role as the chief minister of state, while to his right stood Brother Nikos, accompanied by an acolyte who held an open case containing the lizard crown.

His eyes swept the assembled gathering, noting that armed guards with naked swords lined the three walls of the audience chamber. An ordinary ceremony would have arrayed the witnesses by rank, but today the front row contained only those whom Zuberi had enlisted in support of this farce—Simon the Bald, Chancellor of the Exchequer; Demetrios, the leader of the senate; Duke Seneca, a cousin by marriage of the late empress; Aristid, arguably the richest merchant in Ikaria; and several others whose rank would not have ordinarily entitled them to a place in the front row, including Petrelis, whose guards ensured that there would be no disruption.

Josan waited, expecting angry shouts and demands for his death, but there was only a low murmur.

Zuberi turned to address the assembled crowd. "An evil plot took from us our beloved empress, and struck down her sons before they had time to fulfill their promise. We will never forget their loss, but today we look to the future. Our next emperor is a man who has given ample evidence of his devotion to Ikaria and his personal loyalty to Empress Nerissa."

Josan marveled as Zuberi continued to praise him, showing none of the contempt that he displayed in private. Surely the courtiers knew that these words were exaggerations at best, if not outright lies? At any moment he expected someone to call out a challenge; instead he saw only the nodding of Zuberi's allies.

He forced his wandering mind to pay attention as Zuberi continued, "This was not an honor that he sought, but in all humility Prince Lucius has accepted our plea to devote himself to the service of the empire. I can think of no worthier candidate, and thus we are honored to bear witness as he accepts the crown of Ikaria and the stewardship of the empire."

Zuberi turned back to face him once more, and at his signal Josan knelt, presumably for the last time in his life.

Brother Nikos came to stand beside his shoulder, ensuring that all present had a clear view of their future emperor. As Brother Nikos prayed to the twin gods, Josan's attention was caught by the acolyte who stood at his side. He looked familiar, though from his age he would have been a boy when Josan was last in the temple. Minsah was his name, or perhaps Mensah. The acolyte's shifting gaze and the faint tremors that ran through his outstretched arms indicated that he was overwhelmed by the occasion, and Josan felt a twinge of sympathy.

Then his gaze drifted upwards to the burnished crown, wondering where they had found it. Called the lizard crown because of the lizards that lurked among the twined olive leaves, it was the traditional crown of Lucius's forebears. Scurrilous legend had it that the crown had bitten the usurper, Aitor the Great, at his coronation, though it was likely that the ancient crown had merely scratched him. Whatever the reason, Aitor had had a new crown made—a wide band of gold heavily encrusted with costly gems—that had been worn by his son and his granddaughter.

That crown was presumably held in safekeeping, meant for the next true emperor. Prince Lucius was deemed only worthy of the lesser crown, a sign that he had not truly taken Nerissa's place.

"Do you swear to carry out the legacy of Empress Nerissa, to safeguard and protect her people, and to give your life in service of the empire?" Brother Nikos asked.

Giving his life in service of the empire—or in service of Nikos and Zuberi's schemes—was exactly what he had promised, so his voice was steady as he gave the reply that they had drilled into him. "I swear to honor the memory of Empress Nerissa, to rule as she would have done, with mercy and compassion, guided by the wisdom of those around me." Thus he proclaimed himself a mere puppet for those who had not the wit to see this on their own. "I swear to devote my life to the service of the empire, and to safeguarding her people."

Brother Nikos reached into the case and lifted the crown high, so that all could see.

"Accept the crown of Ikaria and the devotion of your people."

Josan had a brief moment of panic. What if the crown did not fit? What if it was like the boots, so small that it appeared a jest?

But Brother Nikos did not appear concerned as he raised the crown one final time, then lowered it onto Josan's head. The delicate filigree fooled him, for it was heavier than he had expected, and he braced himself at the unaccustomed weight.

As Brother Nikos removed his hands and stepped back, Josan felt a flash of warmth where the metal touched his skin. The acolyte gasped, and Brother Nikos's eyes widened. A few in the crowd cried out in amazement, though he didn't know why.

Proconsul Zuberi, his face now pale with anger, gestured for him to rise.

Surprise welled up inside him, then triumphant glee. *At last.* In his mind he heard a voice that had been silent for nearly a year. The scene before him blurred, as if he were seeing it through another's eyes. For an instant he lost all sensation in his limbs, as he heard Prince Lucius's voice ask, *What dream is this?*

Josan stumbled as he tried to rise to his feet, and only Nikos's quick grasp of his arm kept him from falling.

He knew he should be pleased that Prince Lucius's soul had survived, but the prince could not have chosen a worse time to make his presence known. *Please,* Josan thought furiously, *I will explain everything. But we must do nothing to rouse their suspicions.*

As sensation returned, he slowly seated himself on the backless ivory throne, wishing for an ordinary chair with a back that he could lean against. He took his time arranging his robes around him as he fought for composure. He could feel Lucius trying to take control of his body but he could not let that happen. Not when one false word could result in their deaths.

This is no dream? They have crowned me emperor?

Yes, but in name only. Zuberi holds the chain around our neck, and we must do nothing to rouse his suspicions.

Josan tasted fear, but it was quelled beneath Prince Lucius's pleasure.

Lucius, who had been spared the past twelve months and knew nothing of what Josan had endured to preserve their lives.

Lucius, who had always wanted to be emperor, and only in the final days of his existence had learned to reckon the cost of his ambitions.

I can wait, Lucius said. *For now, let us enjoy the sight of Zuberi on his knees.*

Josan shivered. Lucius had only reluctantly come to terms with the invader who had taken possession of his body—a truce forced upon them by circumstances that had demanded their cooperation. He had no reason to welcome Josan's presence, and indeed many reasons why he would seek to banish him. And while Zuberi had the power to confine Josan's body, Lucius had a far more insidious power. He could banish Josan's soul, locking his intellect away in a kind of endless sleep, denied even the relief of dreams—a prison from which there would be no escape.

Josan had as much to fear from Lucius as he did from his enemies—and Lucius was the one person from whom he could never escape.

Chapter 7

Lady Ysobel watched from the foredeck as the hoist swung the last load of crates into the *Swift Gull*'s main hold. From where she stood, she could not see what was happening below, but mere moments later the empty cargo net was raised again, indicating that her sailors had unloaded and stowed the cargo with the practiced speed of a well-trained crew.

"That was the last of them," Captain Zorion said.

"I know."

"There's a favorable tide tonight, and good weather . . ." His voice trailed off as she turned to face him.

"I know that, too."

Zorion was not merely one of the captains in her employ, he was a friend—in fact, her oldest friend. He had entered her service more than ten years ago, when her aunt Tilda had seen fit to chart one course to serve two ends— gifting her favorite niece with a captured pirate vessel and sending along her favorite captain to serve her niece, so that Tilda would be free to take him as a lover.

A fever had taken Tilda from them, but the bonds she had forged had outlasted her death. Zorion's wisdom helped guide Ysobel from novice ship owner to master trader, with all the privileges and responsibilities that entailed.

Zorion knew Ysobel better than anyone. Better than the young men who sometimes graced her bed, better even than her own father. In the past he had never hesitated to offer his advice, nor to point out when she was behaving foolishly. She knew the only reason he held his tongue now was that he did not need to speak. There was nothing that he could say that she had not already told herself a dozen times over.

It was just over a month since she had testified before the council. As each day dawned, she was confident that this would be the day that she was finally released by the council, free to leave Sendat and resume the life she was meant to lead. The arrival of the *Swift Gull* in harbor had seemed an omen that her fortunes were about to change, and she had spent long hours in conference with Captain Zorion, plotting her next voyage and negotiating their cargo.

Time spent in harbor was coin wasted, and the federation rightly boasted that no harbor in the world made quicker work of supplying ships, or of loading and unloading cargo. The repairs to the *Swift Gull*'s rigging had been completed yesterday, and with the last of the cargo on board, she was ready to sail tonight, a mere four days after she had arrived.

Her ship was ready, but Ysobel was not.

A freshening breeze brought the clean scents of the open sea, banishing the familiar stench of the dockside. Ysobel closed her eyes and took a deep breath.

"Take the *Gull* out into the harbor and anchor there tonight," she said. Space at the wharves was at a premium, and each hour they spent tied to the wharves drained more coins from her dwindling reserves.

"A trader listens to her head, not her heart," Zorion said, his lips tight with disapproval.

She placed her hand on his forearm, in silent entreaty. "It has been a long time since I lived as a trader. Nearly two years since I last stood on the deck of one of my ships as she sailed from harbor. Give me one more night. If the council does not release me on the morn, you may sail without me, on the noon tide."

"One more night," he said. "You know nothing would make me happier than having you on board but—"

"But your duty is to my house. As is mine."

"I'll pray to the Sea Witch that the land-bound officials see wisdom," he said, with familiar scorn for those who chose to make their living on dry land. "And I'll ask your aunt Tilda to put in a good word with her as well, seeing as she was so devoted to her."

Ysobel laughed, as he had meant her to do. The contrary Sea Witch brought fortune both good and ill to sailors, who swore by her fickle charms. There were many stories about her, most of which contradicted each other. One thing all agreed upon was that the Sea Witch had a wicked temper and a tongue to match. Much the same could have been said about Tilda when she was alive.

Zorion surprised her with a quick embrace. Ordinarily such gestures were reserved for when they were in private. In public he was careful to treat her with the deference due his employer. From the strength of his arms around her, she knew that he expected that this was good-bye, and that tomorrow he would set sail alone.

"I hope to see you in the morning," she said. "And if I do not, I wish you fair winds, calm seas, and a profitable voyage."

After leaving the *Swift Gull,* Ysobel made her way to the western end of the fish market, where street vendors set up stalls to feed dock laborers and those who had no kitchens of their own. By now, most of the vendors knew her—or knew *of* her at least, since it was seldom that a master trader chose to eat such humble fare. But with every coin she could lay claim to earmarked to support her ships, there was little left over for self-indulgence.

She knew that tonight Zorion would dine better than she, but that was as it should be. Zorion and the sailors aboard the *Swift Gull* were an asset, their labors bringing valuable coin to her house. They deserved every consideration, while she was merely a drain on her resources. Until the council released her, she could do little. And despite her brave words, she had little hope that the next day would bring a change in her circumstances.

Such grim thoughts did nothing to whet her appetite, and so rather than examining today's offerings, she simply wandered through the stalls till she found one that was less crowded than the others. She recognized the proprietor, Brice—a white-haired former sailor who had lost both legs below the knees some years ago. His forced retirement seemed to sit easily, as he could often be found chatting cheerfully with his customers, and when no customers were to be found he gossiped with those who minded the adjacent stalls. She'd heard the tale of how he lost his legs at least a dozen times, and each time it was different.

Today it was a pair of apprentices that held his attention, listening with wide-eyed fascination as he spun a tale of his encounter with a beautiful mermaid. Ysobel caught his eye and pointed to the grill. Brice nodded, not missing a single beat in his story as he grabbed a chipped bowl from the stack at his elbow, then filled it with fried fish balls and two stuffed cabbage leaves.

The bowl and metal fork were worth more than the price of her meal, so like the rest of the customers she ate standing up, careful to keep within his sight lest she be accused of theft. The spicy batter disguised the plainness of the fish, while the red cabbage leaves were stuffed with a mixture of goat cheese, beans, and herbs. Cheap fare, but filling. She ate swiftly, finishing her bowl just as Brice reached the climax of this story—this time the mermaid's jealous lover transformed himself into a shark. She'd heard this variation before, so she handed her bowl back to Brice and left.

Making her way to the seawall that formed one end of the fish market, she climbed the stairs and looked out into the harbor, where she saw that the *Gull* was already anchored among the others waiting for their sailing orders. With all of her heart she longed to be there, and for a moment she contemplated simply hiring a lighter to take her to her ship, and leaving in the morning with the *Gull*, whether the council approved or no.

But she knew better than to indulge in such folly. The council jealously guarded its privileges, and they would take swift retaliation against one who flouted their will. And, indeed, from their perspective they were not punishing her. Most traders spent their lives ashore, managing their trading houses and fleets of ships. Her own father set foot on ship only when he needed to travel between the islands.

Sea captains had the freedom to explore. Master traders led lives that were more circumscribed, maneuvering for power.

She had known when she entered diplomatic service that she was giving up the sea, but it had seemed a fair trade at the time. She had imagined spending a year or two in service, then returning to the federation, where her experiences would elevate her to the first rank of traders. But as time passed, she had come to regret her ambitions. Though she wondered whether it was truly her love for the sea that drove her, or merely her contrary nature that made her long for the one thing that was denied her.

Her mood now grim, she descended the stairs and left

the market, but not before purchasing a skin of cheap wine. Returning to her apartment just after sunset, she was not surprised to find that there were no messages for her. Throwing back the shutters of her window to catch the night breeze, she placed the oil lamp on a nearby table, then dragged her chair over. She could not see the harbor from here, but she knew where it was. Lifting the skin in the direction where the *Swift Gull* lay anchored, she offered a silent toast to her crew. Then she opened the skin and drank.

The wine was bitter, tasting of vinegar with an undertone of mud. The second swallow was worse than the first, but she persisted, and after consuming half the skin, the wine seemed merely bad rather than wretched.

Her thoughts turned back to Brice, wondering how he endured his fate. He had once been a sailor, but now he was land-bound, spending his days serving others who lived the life he had once possessed. Such a fate would drive her mad. Indeed, it *was* driving her mad. But Brice seemed happy enough.

Or maybe his happiness was a deception—an illusion meant to charm his customers, as false as the stories he told. Perhaps Brice pretended to be happy because he could not bear the sympathy of others.

She frowned at the wineskin, feeling restless, as if waiting for something—though she knew not what. She sat by the window in silent contemplation until midnight came, and she knew the tide had begun to ebb.

Only then did she move to her bed. The wine had been a poor choice, for it seemed she had barely fallen asleep when she suddenly awoke, heart pounding as she recalled being pursued by a merman who had transformed himself into a shark. Her limbs shook as if she had indeed been frantically swimming for her life.

She took a deep breath to calm herself, then she heard

the sound of someone banging on the door to her apartment.

"Ysobel, awake," she heard Zorion call out.

"G'way," a man's voice yelled, while another called out "I'll wake the lazy bitch."

"Enough," she called, as she scrambled out of her bed. Both Zorion and her disgruntled neighbors quieted.

The oil lamp was still burning, so she raised the wick, the soft light dispelling the shadows. The terrors of her dream were banished by the very real fear of the present. She wondered what tragedy had brought Zorion at this hour.

"The *Gull,* she is safe? And you?" she asked as she threw open the door.

"We're safe," he said, brushing by her and shutting the door behind him before he added, "There's news from Ikaria."

"And it could not wait until morning?" Her frantic heartbeats slowed as she realized that there was no immediate danger, but whatever news had brought him here must be grave indeed.

"I wanted you to hear it from me, before the council summons you."

Ysobel perched on the edge of her cot as Zorion dragged the chair away from the window.

"They've crowned him. Emperor Lucius, of the house of Constantin."

"That's impossible. Absurd." Briefly she wondered if this was another wine-fueled dream. Or an elaborate hoax.

But Zorion seemed convinced, and far too solid to be a mere dream. "I heard it myself, from Amitee, the captain of the *Liealia,* who slipped into harbor after sunset. She's just back from Kazagan, so I rowed over to ask about conditions there and learned more than I had bargained for."

"The captain must be mistaken. This is mere rumor put

out by Lucius's supporters, meant to create confusion. Proconsul Zuberi would never stand for it."

"Captain Amitee swears it is true. She heard it from the harbormaster herself, and saw the official decree, signed by the proconsul and the head of their senate. Lucius has made himself emperor with the help of Nerissa's ministers."

"Emperor Lucius," she said, tasting the strangeness of the words on her tongue.

She had dismissed the prince as a weakling, unable to command his followers, too troubled by his newly discovered conscience to do what must be done. Even Empress Nerissa seemed to agree with this judgment, for she had permitted the rebellious prince to live as a symbol of her mercy.

But it seemed Ysobel had misjudged him. And so had Empress Nerissa. He must have been secretly scheming for months, if not years, all the while playing the role of a naïve and helpless pawn.

"Ikaria must be in chaos," she said. Even if he had done the impossible and secured the support of Proconsul Zuberi, surely others would be displeased to see one of the old blood elevated to the rank of emperor. They guarded their privileges jealously.

It would be chaos. This was precisely what the federation council had schemed to bring about, when it sent her to destabilize the Ikarian Empire. Belated, but a triumph nonetheless.

"It's what the council hoped for," Zorion said, echoing her thoughts. "But it's a gift of the Sea Witch for certain. No telling if this is good fortune for you, or ill."

She did not need his words to know that it was too soon to rejoice. Chaos brought danger as well as opportunity. She must steer a careful course in the coming days.

"I thank you for this news," she said. "And now you should return. You will set sail in less than six hours."

She sighed as she realized that he would sail on his own. As one of the few who had met Prince Lucius, the councilors would surely wish to hear her impressions of the man. But then, hopefully, they would reward her service by releasing her.

"I'll return as soon as I can," Zorion said. "Look for our sails within the month."

"Safe passage," she said.

"Safe passage to you as well," he replied.

Morning brought not one but two summonses—one from Lord Quesnel and one from the council itself. With wits that cleared as the sun rose, she realized that she should have sent her own messenger to Lord Quesnel last night, on the off chance that his own spies at the docks had failed to give him early warning. He did not like surprises. He would want to know everything she did, so he could appear all-knowing before the council.

But the summons of the council took precedence over Quesnel's desire for a private meeting, and thus she followed their messenger to the residence of Lady Felicia. The location of the meeting indicated that this was an informal gathering rather than an official meeting of the council. There would be no scribes to record the debates nor duly mandated observers from the plebeian class.

What was said today would be said in secret, but the decisions made would have the full force of law to back them up.

Ysobel was shown to a small receiving room where two men were already waiting. She did not recognize them, and they did not offer their names. Following their lead, she did not offer her own name, merely sipping the offered tea and watched the play of light over the small garden that she could see just outside the window.

She wondered at the circumstances that had led to Prince Lucius's rise to power. What had led Zuberi to support the prince's claim rather than taking the throne himself? How long had the two been scheming together? Was Zuberi's disaffection with Nerissa a recent occurrence? Or had this plot been simmering before the federation offered its assistance to the rebellious prince? Would Lucius be grateful to the federation for past favors? Or would he see them as betrayers who had abandoned him to Empress Nerissa's clutches, forcing him to find new allies?

The answer to these questions would shape the federation's own response. She suspected that the councilors would want her opinion, but she had no guidance to offer them. Since she had not been able to anticipate Lucius's elevation, she could hardly claim to be able to predict his next move. Only time would reveal his intentions, but she knew this answer would not please the council.

Though, in this situation, ignorance might serve her best. If she were intimately acquainted with Prince Lucius, the council might well find a use for her. But as it was, she had nothing to offer them, so there was no reason for them to insist on her continued presence.

She sat for hours, her well-trained nerves showing no signs of impatience as the sun climbed in the sky. The two men, dressed in the smocks and leggings worn by travelers and master sailors, sat side by side without speaking. In time, a servant arrived to summon the younger of the two men, who left without a word to the man she had assumed was his companion. A short time later the second man was summoned.

Finally, it was her turn. Inwardly she composed herself, stilling her emotions, as if she were about to enter negotiations with an unknown adversary. There must be no sign of weakness or doubt. She had done them a service, one they had only recently acknowledged, but the councilors were not her friends. Not even Lord Quesnel, who was an ally at best, and thus she must be on her guard.

Ostensibly this was a private gathering, but the room she was led to was even grander than the official council chamber. Lady Felicia sat at the head of a long table of polished mahogany, while Lord Quesnel sat at the opposite end. Arrayed between them on the far side were a half dozen councilors, while on the side of the table closest to the door there was a single empty chair.

At Lady Felicia's gesture, Ysobel took her seat. She nodded respectfully to the other councilors, trying to judge their mood. Lord Quesnel's face was blank, but his stiff posture hinted at inner tension. Lady Solange, who had taken Quesnel's place as minister of trade, appeared troubled, as well she might be. Quesnel had been campaigning to resume his former post, and anything that strengthened his hand would weaken hers. Ysobel did not know the others well enough to be certain, but to her eye they also appeared anxious, as might be expected, given the gravity of the news.

Of course most of the councilors were master traders themselves. They might well be choosing to show the appearance of anxiety to hide their true feelings and intentions.

"You do not seem surprised by your summons to this meeting," Lady Felicia began. "May we assume that you have heard the recent news from Ikaria?"

Ysobel turned her head toward Lady Felicia, as was polite. But this meant that she could no longer see Lord Quesnel's expression, and she realized that the council seats had been deliberately chosen so he could not offer her any guidance.

She wondered who it was that they were testing. Was it her or Lord Quesnel they sought to keep in check?

"One of my captains brought the news to me late last night. I intended to report to you this morning, but your summons arrived before I could send word." Her words were addressed to Lady Felicia, but they were meant to appease Lord Quesnel.

Telfor, who had held nearly all the ministerial offices at one time or another in his long life, eyed her with disapproval. He was no longer a minister, but still served as both councilor and private advisor to King Bayard.

"A month ago, you stood before this council and assured us that Prince Lucius would be executed and Proconsul Zuberi would assume the throne. What have you to say for yourself?" Telfor demanded.

"I believe I merely said that Proconsul Zuberi was the most likely of the candidates, based on my knowledge of Ikarian politics. But that knowledge was several months stale, as I informed you at the time."

"Not good enough," Telfor said.

"Lady Felicia, may I ask if you are certain of this news? There is no possibility of deceit or confusion?" Ysobel asked.

Lady Felicia nodded. "Two different sources have brought us word of Emperor Lucius's ascendance, strange as the turn of events may seem to at least some of us."

"I beg your pardon?" Ysobel did not have to feign confusion.

"You were sent to Ikaria to foster rebellion. You used federation gold and contacts to help Prince Lucius and his followers in their rebellion. Since your return, you have argued that your diligence in carrying out your duties was worthy of reward."

Ysobel was shocked by Lady Felicia's frankness. In the

past the councilors had been careful to couch Ysobel's acts in the most general of terms, using the language of diplomacy to mask treacherous deeds.

"While I was in Ikaria, I did my best to carry out the wishes of the council," Ysobel replied, choosing each word with deliberate care. "And I have never asked for a reward, merely acknowledgment that my service was complete and that I was free to return to my duties to my trading house and my ships."

She wondered if this was the reason for her summons—they wanted to make it clear that she should expect no reward from them.

"So you knew nothing of Prince Lucius's schemes, correct?" Lady Solange asked.

Ysobel knew this was the moment of danger. She risked a quick glance toward Lord Quesnel, but his face was impassive, giving no hint of how he had responded when this question had been put to him. She cursed herself and the wine that had fuddled her wits the night before. As soon as Zorion had given her the news, Ysobel should have sought out Quesnel, regardless of the impropriety of the hour.

But it was too late. It was too risky to try to guess what he might have said. She could only answer honestly and hope that he had done the same.

"I reported everything I knew to the council when I returned last year," Ysobel said. Such knowledge had been deemed too dangerous for written reports, so they had only their own memories to guide them. "As I said at the time, I believed Prince Lucius to be completely without friends or supporters, with the possible exception of his former tutor, Brother Nikos. I was as surprised as any when Empress Nerissa chose to let him live, and I am even more startled by this latest turn of events."

Some might have been tempted to claim credit for

Lucius's unlikely success, but Ysobel was wise enough to avoid this trap. Claiming knowledge of his schemes now would leave her open to charges that her previous reports to the council had been deliberately misleading, perhaps even treasonous.

"Prince Lucius played you for a fool. And us as well," Telfor said.

Ysobel kept silent. She could not defend herself from the truth.

Lady Solange smiled. It was not a pretty smile, but rather the grimace of a predator—one whose appetites were about to be satisfied. Lord Quesnel's face, by contrast, was flushed with anger or humiliation.

In that instant, Ysobel knew she had chosen wrongly. Lord Quesnel must have responded quite differently when asked that same question. He might even have tried to claim credit for Lucius's ascendance and the civil war that would almost certainly erupt. He must have counted on her being greedy enough to back him.

He had misjudged her. She was ambitious, yes, but not deceitful. She had shaded her answers to the council as carefully as she could, but she would not lie. Not for him, and not even for herself.

"Your comments have been most enlightening," Lady Felicia said. "I thank you for your time, and must ask that you remain on Sendat lest we need the benefit of your views in the future."

"I am, as always, at your service," Ysobel said, rising to her feet and giving a short bow.

She left, knowing that she was leaving behind at least one enemy. Lord Quesnel had been displeased with her before, but they had achieved a fragile truce, one that she had just unwittingly broken.

Lord Quesnel had no reason to love her, and while the

other councilors might enjoy his discomfiture, this did not mean that they would willingly take up Ysobel's cause as their own. She had left behind no allies in that room, only enemies.

She would have to watch her back.

Chapter 8

The monk who shared his flesh had promised to explain all, but the story he told was so fantastic that a part of Lucius was convinced that he must be dreaming.

Nerissa dead, and her sons as well. It hardly seemed possible. She had sat on the throne since before he was born, a commanding figure whose decrees had ruled every moment of his existence. He had hated and resented her in life, and even in death he felt no pity for her. But it seemed somehow wrong that she had been struck down while he was unaware. A great ruler—for such she had been, usurper though she was—a great ruler should meet defeat on the field of battle—not at the hands of a cowardly assassin.

He was still shocked to find himself among the living. The last time he had been conscious, he had fully expected that the empress would have him killed. He did not understand why she had chosen to spare his life. There was no one left who could be trusted to tell him her thoughts, just as there was no trace of her left in the place that had once been her inner sanctum. The rooms were spotless, but there were neither tapestries nor paintings to brighten the walls nor carpets to soften the floors. As he wandered through the smaller of the two sitting rooms, his fingers ran idly along the back of one of the half dozen bamboo chairs grouped around a low table. As a boy, he had been summoned to this room from time to time, his mother's warnings reminding him to display his best manners in front of the empress and her sons. In those days, the room had been filled with couches decorated with ivory and piled with silken cushions, and he wondered when Nerissa had decided they no longer suited her.

Perhaps the servants had been ordered to remove her things, replacing them with the furnishings he saw. A subtle insult, implying that Lucius was not worthy to touch the late empress's possessions.

Or perhaps the rooms had simply been changed to ready them for the presence of an emperor, for all must have assumed that Nerissa's successor would be a man. The furnishings he saw did not seem to be in Zuberi's taste, which he would have guessed ran to the classic styles. Instead the disparate styles hinted at furnishings hastily assembled, or a widely traveled man with eclectic tastes.

Belatedly, it occurred to him that the servants might have readied this room for Count Hector. They would not be the only ones shocked by the sudden reversal in Hector's fortunes.

Hector's guilt is certain? Lucius formed the question in his thoughts, but dared not speak aloud. He had dismissed the hovering servants, and the functionary whom the monk, for some reason, referred to as One. But the servants had not gone far, merely to an outer room. An emperor was never truly alone.

Brother Nikos and Zuberi told me of Hector's guilt. He heard the monk's voice in his mind, as clearly as if he were speaking aloud. *But merely because they say it does not mean that it is true.*

Then why did Zuberi put me on the throne? Why not take it for himself?

Lucius felt his body shrug. The monk had no answer. For all that the monk had spent the past year living in the palace, it seemed he had learned nothing.

Lucius's anger grew. This was his body, by right. His name. His lineage that had earned him the crown. Yet he had spent the last year exiled to dreamland while the monk had played his part. It was unseemly that he had to rely upon whatever scraps of information the monk deigned to share with him. Who knew what the monk had done in his name? What promises had he made, what alliances had he forged?

How could he trust that the monk was telling the truth? Josan's words might be nothing more than lies meant to deceive so that Lucius would allow the monk to remain in control. The monk had already shown that he could tap in to Lucius's knowledge, but Lucius could not return the favor. He could feel the monk's emotions but knew only what the monk chose to tell him.

It was time to remind the monk how it felt to be powerless. Lucius gathered his thoughts, preparing to cast the invader into unknowingness, but before he could do so, Proconsul Zuberi strode into his chambers as if he owned them, followed by the attendants Lucius had previously dismissed.

"I suppose you think yourself clever, with that little display," Zuberi growled. His face was flushed with anger, and his hand was raised.

For a moment, Lucius feared that the proconsul would strike him, heedless of the servants who would bear witness. But at the last moment Zuberi relented, lowering his hand.

"*We*—that is *I*—did as you instructed," Lucius replied. "Nothing more."

Zuberi's lips twisted in derision. "We? Giving ourselves airs already?"

He did not need the monk's whispers to know that he had made a dangerous mistake. It was time to soothe Zuberi's ire and ensure that he did not dwell upon that slip of the tongue. "Whatever I have done to offend, tell me so that I may make it right."

"Do not pretend to innocence. A few fools may have been impressed when you made that bauble glow, but your trickery will gain you no friends."

"Glow?"

Zuberi spoke slowly, as if to an idiot. "The crown glowed when it touched your brow. As you well know."

Lucius shook his head firmly. "How could I? There were no mirrors for me to see myself." Then, prompted by the monk, he added, "The choice of the lizard crown was yours, not mine. I could hardly have anticipated this."

Though it was satisfying to know that the crown of his ancestors had recognized him. It had acknowledged him, at the very moment when his consciousness had returned to his body. Or perhaps it was the crown that had summoned him, like calling unto like.

The crown had been given to One for safekeeping, but now he wished to hold it for himself, see what other secrets it might hold.

"You will perform no more such trickery," Zuberi said. "You will keep your magic to yourself. You will remember that your every moment is watched. The next time you disobey me, it will be your last."

Zuberi glared at him until Lucius dipped his head in acknowledgment. "I understand," he said.

The reckless prince he had once been would have argued, but Lucius had changed. He would obey, for the moment.

Zuberi spun on his heel and left, in violation of protocol. So great was his scorn that he could not be bothered to keep up the pretense in front of the servants.

It seemed the monk had told the truth when he said that Zuberi hated Lucius. Which made it all the more strange that he had put Lucius on the throne. Was this a bizarre form of punishment, to give Lucius the title he had longed for but not the power that went with it? Or was it merely the first move in some complex scheme that would ultimately destroy him?

He stilled his thoughts, ready to listen to whatever advice the monk could share, but the monk's voice was silent. For all that he had lived in the palace for the past year, the monk knew nothing of Zuberi's motivations or the political climate.

I could not afford to ask those questions, Josan's voice sounded in his head. *Any hint that I was gathering information would have been seen as a threat, and the empress would have acted accordingly.*

So what did you do with yourself for the year that I slept?

I did everything that Nerissa requested of me. When I was allowed to, I read. Books of the early years of the empire, and children's tales mostly.

A waste of time.

He felt Josan's impatience. *I could hardly ask for books on magic,* the monk thought. *Not with Brother Nikos inspecting each request I made, and Nerissa's men reading every scroll looking for hidden messages.*

And did you learn anything?

I learned that your forebears had powers similar to yours—the ability to call fire, and to heal. Some scrolls implied that they could control the weather, others that they were merely able to predict the weather to come. But nothing that would help undo what Nikos has done to us.

He felt disappointment echoing across both halves of his soul.

There are more scrolls in the collegium, ones I did not have access to. Brother Nikos will not want to share them, but in time we can force his hand.

Why not now?

Brother Nikos is the one who urged the council to put you on the throne. Do you think you can survive if he turns against you?

It seemed the monk had some political instincts after all. Patience was not one of Lucius's strengths, but he recognized that he needed to gather power to himself before he could challenge Brother Nikos.

Sunset brought a change of servants. The new functionary referred to himself as keeper of the emperor's chambers, as had his predecessor, but the monk called him Five. Giving a functionary an individual name was against all custom, but the monk's conceit appealed to Lucius's sense of humor.

Not to mention that knowing the functionaries as individuals might well have saved Nerissa's life—a lesson not lost on either Lucius or the monk.

A short time later, Five informed him that supper had been laid out in his private dining room. He dined lightly on grilled fish and summer vegetables dressed with vinegar, musing that this was a very odd way for an emperor to celebrate his coronation. A public celebration would have been fitting, or at the very least a private dinner surrounded by friends and trusted allies.

But he had no friends. Only those who had agreed not to harm him out of political expediency. He could not think of a single person that he would want to share bread and oil with.

What little appetite he'd had fled with this realization. Pushing the dishes away, he rose from the table. He could feel that the monk wanted to say something to the hovering server—an apology for the wasted food, perhaps—but

Lucius easily overrode him. He would never win the respect of the servants by stooping to their level.

The monk's presence remained a subtle pressure in his mind, but his mental voice fell silent, granting Lucius the illusion of control. But he knew it for just that, an illusion. He did not command the monk any more than he commanded these servants. The servants took their orders from Zuberi, and as for the monk . . . Well, as much as the monk claimed to regret this spell, for him this shared existence was better than the finality of the grave.

Five followed him from the dining room, reciting a list of the appointments for the next day. The imperial tailor had sent word that the first garments in Lucius's new wardrobe were ready to be fitted. In the afternoon, Proconsul Zuberi and Demetrios would accompany him to the senate for his first public appearance. Lucius let the words wash over him, knowing that it was not up to him to approve the arrangements that had been made on his behalf.

Not yet. The time would come when he had true power. But until that day he would play Zuberi's games, lulling his enemies into a false sense of security.

The functionary broke off his recitation as Lucius yawned once, then twice. It was still early, but Lucius could feel the bone-deep tiredness within him. He dismissed the functionary and retired to his bedchamber.

There the servants had lit oil lamps, which provided a soft glow as he stripped off his tunic, leaving it crumpled on the floor by his wardrobe. Crossing to his bed, where nightclothes had been laid out, he glanced down at his own body, needing reassurance that nothing had changed. He was far thinner than he remembered, his sunken belly flanked by jutting hipbones. He was not yet thirty, but hardship had given him the body of a man a decade older. As he cupped his belly with his right hand, he felt a sharp ridge on his skin. Questing fingers revealed three long parallel lines.

What is this?

There was no answer. The soft light hid more than it revealed, so he picked up the lamp from his bedside, and brought it close. The flickering light revealed three white scars, which appeared to be several months old.

He stared, seeing a faint shadow that might have been another scar, this one leading down toward his groin.

What happened?

Still the monk remained silent. Replacing the lamp, Lucius made his way to the adjacent bathing chamber. A surge of anger and the lamps within the bathing chamber blazed to life, filling the room with their radiance.

Here he studied his body with the dispassionate gaze of a stranger. The three raised ridges on his belly were the most prominent, but the mirrors revealed that his body was covered in faint scars, from his neck down to his thighs.

Were these the marks of a lash? A knife? What had happened? And why?

He was outraged. Here was the evidence that his body had been violated, not once, but repeatedly.

Who did this to us? Whoever it was, he deserved death.

He could taste the monk's anger as if it were his own.

After Nerissa was assassinated, we were Nizam's special guest for thirty-eight days, the monk said. *We were only released from his charge two days ago.*

The monk was lying. *Nizam did not do this. These scars are too old.*

You healed this body. Each time Nizam brought it near death, your magic brought it back.

Lucius shivered, wishing suddenly for a robe to cover himself.

What did he do to us? I have a right to know.

You have no rights, the monk lashed out, in a rare display of temper. *You abandoned us to Nerissa, left me to die for your sins while you chose the peace of oblivion. Now you must live with the choices you made, as must I.*

With that the monk's presence disappeared, leaving Lucius alone to endure his guilt.

And his shame. Shame not just for abandoning Josan last year, but for that moment of relief he had felt when he realized that he had been spared torture.

Caught up in the heady pleasure of his coronation, it had been easy to forget just how much he owed the monk. Easier to dwell on the lost months than to admit that the monk had not chosen his fate.

Surrendering to Empress Nerissa had been Lucius's decision, not Josan's, though in the end they had both agreed that it was the only way to end the senseless slaughter being committed in his name. That final night, as they faced the prospect of torture and an agonizing death, Lucius had sworn that he would not leave the monk alone to face what was to come. But he had broken that promise.

It had been his decision to leave. The monk had not forced him into oblivion. Instead, Lucius had fled headlong, so terrified by what was to come that he had broken his word.

It was no wonder the monk was angry. Lucius had shown himself a coward, while this monk, the bastard son of a nameless peasant, had proved the stronger man.

The irony was that his fears had been for naught. Nerissa had not tortured him, after all. Whatever the monk had said to her had convinced her to spare his life. Lucius's cowardice had served only to rob him of nearly a year of his life.

Though from the evidence of his body, the last month had been every bit as horrific as he could have imagined.

Thirty-eight days. Dry-mouthed, he turned his back on

the mirrors. His hands shook as he extinguished the lamps one by one, concentrating on the task so that he would not have to think about what Nizam had done to him. To them.

When he woke the next morning, he could feel the monk's presence again, though Josan was silent. In the quiet darkness of the night before Lucius had rehearsed his apologies, but now the words seemed inadequate or self-serving. And the growing discomfort he felt from the monk made him suspect that the monk was not interested in his apologies, nor indeed in anything that would force him to recall his trials.

Lucius let the moment for explanations pass in silence, not knowing whether he had chosen this path out of wisdom or cowardice.

The tailor arrived soon thereafter—an unprepossessing man trailed by three lackeys carrying garments in various stages of completion. Conscious of his scarred body, Lucius insisted on wearing his undertunic throughout the fittings. The tailor appeared ready to object, but a raised eyebrow was all it took to quell his mutterings.

It had been far too long since he had worn decent garb, but though the tailor was anxious to hear his preferences, Lucius could find no pleasure in discussing fabrics or styles. Instead, after confirming that the completed garments fit well enough, Lucius dismissed the tailor with instructions to make whatever he saw fit.

The half dozen outfits delivered included a set of court robes, nearly as fine as those he had worn to his coronation. After lunch a servant helped Lucius dress, and the functionary One brought Lucius the lizard crown. He'd half hoped it would glow or show some other sign of magic, but to his disappointment it did not react to him, instead resting quietly on his brow, the heavy weight an unsubtle reminder of the weight of his responsibilities.

Proconsul Zuberi and a dozen of the household guard escorted him from the palace to the senate. A stranger glancing at their grim expressions might have assumed that they were escorting a prisoner rather than acting as an honor guard. Demetrios met them at the steps of the senate hall, offering his official welcome as he led the procession into the hall. The hall consisted of a semicircle of thirteen courses, which descended to a speaker's platform, where orators would stand in debate when the senate was meeting. At the rear of the dais was the emperor's chair, a marble throne used only for occasions of state. Today a purple drape softened the cold stone, but as Lucius took his seat he realized that it was a damn uncomfortable piece of furniture. Perhaps deliberately so, as a means of encouraging the emperor not to spend too much time interfering with the workings of the senate.

Proconsul Zuberi, who was not a member of the senate, took a seat at the left end of the bottom course while four of the honor guard arranged themselves at the corners of the dais. The assembled senators had risen to their feet when Lucius entered, and remained standing as Demetrios repeated his oath of fealty.

The senators turned and formed into a line that snaked along the courses. One by one they approached the throne to pledge their allegiance to their new emperor, with varying degrees of enthusiasm. As Lucius accepted their oaths, he was surprised by how few faces he recognized. Some of their names were familiar, likely cadet members of powerful families, or sons who had taken their fathers' places. Others were newly come to power, as Nerissa cleansed her government of those suspected of being sympathetic to the rebellion. These men, brought to power because of their personal loyalty to Nerissa, would have no reason to look favorably on their new emperor. Lucius would need to look elsewhere for allies, if he was to challenge Zuberi.

Demetrios is an unknown, the monk thought. *Zuberi could not have done this without his support, but I do not know how he convinced him to set aside his own ambitions. If Zuberi did not want to pursue his own claim, it seems likely that Demetrios would have been the next strongest candidate.*

Demetrios has an older brother, Lucius replied, absurdly pleased to have knowledge that the monk did not. *Though I would not want to wager on Prokopios's continued good health.*

The monk made no reply, but Lucius could feel his shock at the implication. It amused him to realize that, despite everything he had witnessed, the monk could still be shocked. His expression must have revealed something of his thoughts, for the councilor in front of him blanched and lost his place, stammering as he began reciting his oath anew.

He schooled his face to a neutral expression, knowing that he could not afford to indulge his boredom. He would never earn the respect of the councilors if he did not at least appear to respect them in return. Still, patience had never come easily to him, and thus when he felt his grasp upon consciousness slipping, he did not fight it. He would save his strength for another day, confident that the monk would do nothing that might imperil them.

As he let control of his body slip from his grasp, a brief flare of panic engulfed him as he remembered how long he had slept the last time. What if he did not awaken for days? Or months, or even years? He strained toward the light, but he was too weak, and his thoughts dissolved until all that remained was an echo of his fear.

Josan felt the moment when the prince's consciousness drifted away. He shifted uneasily on the marble seat as he again grew accustomed to the sensations of this body. He tasted the copper taste of fear, and in his mind he called out: *Lucius? Prince?*

But there was no answer. Nothing to tell him what or whom the prince had feared.

At last the final senator had sworn his allegiance and returned to his place, his name and features carefully memorized. Josan had spent the ceremony observing the senators, noting who had kept their eyes fixed on the dais, refusing to acknowledge their neighbors, and which ones had gossiped among themselves when they thought his attention elsewhere.

Josan rose and thanked the senators for their confidence, and pledged to work with them to fulfill Nerissa's legacy. Zuberi, who had spent much of the ceremony hunched forward, his arms crossed on his chest, unbent enough to nod with grudging approval. It seemed his master was pleased with the performance of his lackey.

Returning to the palace, Josan handed the crown and the court robes over to the functionaries, who carried them away for safekeeping. For a moment, he fancied that they would carry him off as well, relegating him to a musty storeroom until the next time Zuberi needed to display his pet emperor.

But even Zuberi did not dare go that far, however much he might have wanted to. Instead the new emperor was treated with seeming respect, though his new life was as circumscribed as it had been when he was Nerissa's honored prisoner.

His chambers might be larger, but there were guards at every door, and he could not leave his rooms without an escort. His guards had orders from Zuberi that the new emperor was not to leave the palace grounds—for his own safety, of course. In the days that followed his coronation, his only visitors were the tailor and Zuberi's former clerk

Ferenc, who had been assigned as the emperor's personal secretary. Ferenc kept him busy signing official decrees that had been drafted by Zuberi and his cronies, as well as responding to the formal messages of congratulations that had started to arrive.

Council meetings were held, but the emperor's presence was requested only after the council had reached agreement among themselves. The emperor was kept informed of the policies of his new government, but powerless to effect them. It was enough to frustrate even the calmest of men, which was perhaps the reason why Lucius remained a faint presence at the edges of his mind rather than coming to the forefront.

He was surprised that no one sought him out to request favors, or to try to discover for themselves what strange alliance had brought Lucius to the throne. But as the days passed, he realized that the functionaries, with Ferenc's help, must be discouraging all such requests.

A month after his coronation, he emerged from the bathing chamber to find his court robes laid out, and in this manner he discovered that today he was expected to hold his first court session. His skin crawled as he remembered Nerissa's twice-monthly gatherings, when he had been ordered to present himself. He had been the only member of her court required to perform a formal obeisance, demonstrating his complete subjugation. A petty humiliation that had saved his life even as it chafed his pride.

The audience hall was crowded, as those who had come to the capital for Nerissa's funeral had stayed, lest they and their interests be overlooked as new alliances were formed. There were only two petitioners, both minor nobles requesting that the emperor confirm their inheritance. In both cases, Josan asked the ritual question: "Is there any here who would deny this man's claim?" giving Zuberi a chance to object. But there were no objections, and so he confirmed them in their new status.

The two men were both newcomers, giving credence to his suspicions that Zuberi had deliberately chosen them so that Lucius could play the part of emperor while reassuring the courtiers that the newcomers had nothing to fear.

At least from him. Wild rumors came even to his ears—some claimed gangs roamed the streets of Karystos, murdering any who dared cross their paths. Others said the legions were in open revolt, their commanders battling each other to determine who would rule as emperor. Even if he believed only a fraction of what he heard, these were perilous times indeed.

And he was powerless to act—he could no more protect his people than he could himself.

Demetrios had invited Zuberi to join him at the senatorial baths, but Zuberi had insisted on meeting Demetrios at his offices in the senate instead. A meeting at the baths would have provided the illusion that theirs was a casual encounter between friends, but it would have also required Zuberi to disrobe, something that he was loath to do. Artfully draped tunics and the heavy silk robes of state concealed his illness, but stripped of these and all would see his swollen belly and know his deadly secret.

If his enemies even suspected his weakness, they would not hesitate to strike. It was only their fear of him—and of his influence over the new emperor—that kept them in check.

When he reached Demetrios's offices, he found Demetrios deep in conversation with several senators, all wearing the banded tunics of office indicating that they were performing their official duties.

Interesting. Demetrios had not mentioned that the senate would be in session today.

"I understand your concerns," he heard Demetrios say. "But now is not the time to debate such matters."

"If not now, then when?" The speaker's back was to Zuberi, but the accent was unmistakable. Senator Columba, who represented the far western provinces.

"Allowing the regional governors more control—" chimed in another senator.

Demetrios nodded as he caught sight of Zuberi. "And the senate will consider your suggestions, at the proper time," he said. "Now, if you will forgive me, I believe the proconsul and I have matters to discuss."

"Honored senators," Zuberi said, as he reached them.

Senator Columba nodded curtly, then stalked off. His supporters mumbled what might have been greetings before scurrying after their leader.

Demetrios led him into his office, where open shutters offered a fresh breeze as well as a clear view of the imperial palace. Zuberi settled himself into a straight-backed chair, disdaining the couches, and Demetrios settled himself in another chair.

"Columba must be watched," Zuberi said. "He will not be content until he elevates the governors at the expense of the empire."

Demetrios shrugged. "Columba has little support for his views. As you see, only four senators joined with him— not enough to call for a debate, let alone have any chance of passing their legislation."

"In Nerissa's day he would not have dared even mention such a proposal. Today he has four other senators who are willing to lend him their support publicly, and who knows how many privately agree with him? Left unchecked, he could win others to his cause."

"Of course," Demetrios said. "I did not mean to make

light of your concerns. I merely meant that Columba's ambitions are not our most pressing problem."

It was as much of an apology as he could expect, but it did little to assuage him.

"Your brother, he continues to recover?" Zuberi asked.

"So he tells me," Demetrios said. "I have not seen him since he left for the family estate, but naturally I receive reports each day."

"It is the gods' own luck that he was spared," Zuberi said.

That, or incompetence. Prokopios's litter had been attacked as he was returning from a banquet—his bearers killed, and Prokopios himself stabbed in the abdomen. A passing patrol had chased off the attackers before they could finish the deed.

Such attacks against the wealthy were increasingly frequent in Karystos, straining Petrelis's city watch to the breaking point. It was possible that Prokopios was just another victim of thieves, or of rebels taking advantage of the increasing lawlessness to settle old grudges against the newcomers.

But it was equally likely that the attack had been a clumsy attempt at assassination. With Prokopios dead, there would be nothing to prevent his younger brother from becoming the next emperor—once the upstart Lucius was disposed of.

It was a move that Zuberi had been prepared to support. In the weeks since Lucius's coronation he had been unable to find a better candidate. But the bungled assassination, if that was what it was, troubled him. Nerissa would never have allowed such incompetents to serve her.

Then, too, Demetrios seemed oblivious to the danger that Columba represented. Either his political skills were far less than Zuberi had previously believed—or he was forming his own alliance with the provincial governors and did not want Zuberi to know.

Zuberi frowned. He wished it were possible to question Demetrios openly about his brother's attack but knew such was folly. Demetrios would never admit to planning fratricide, even if Zuberi offered his tacit approval.

"Markos and his legions are far more of a threat to our control of the provinces than any schemes of Senator Columba," Demetrios said, returning to their earlier topic.

"Commander Kiril should arrive within the week, and the other commanders will follow," Zuberi said. If they obeyed their orders. And if they were willing to fight for Emperor Lucius.

Lucius. Emperor. The very thought enraged him, for all that he had agreed to this farce. Nizam might have declared Lucius innocent in the deaths of Empress Nerissa and her sons, but Zuberi knew better. Lucius's rebellion had been crushed, but not before exposing the empress's weaknesses and inspiring others to try where he had failed.

Belying the frailties of her sex, Nerissa had been a cunning politician who had led her people wisely. A true empress, and worthy successor to her illustrious ancestors. She had elevated Zuberi from obscurity to a position of power second only to her own, and thus commanded his absolute loyalty. Even after her death, he continued to serve her.

Compared to her, Lucius was nothing. A worm who did not deserve to live. He had cheated death again and again—first spared by the empress's mercy, then spared by the perverted magic that flowed through his veins. For a man facing the prospect of his own impending death, this was an insult that could not be borne.

Lucius would remain emperor only as long as he was of use to Zuberi. Then he would be killed—his death as agonizing as Zuberi could contrive. He currently favored poison—it gave him satisfaction to think of Lucius writhing and twisting in pain as the poison destroyed his organs. And if Lucius's powers spared him from poison—well, not even a sorcerer could survive decapitation.

"Kiril will want something in return for his support," Demetrios said. "And as for the senate, our alliance is fragile as well. We need a list of favors that the emperor can dispense to his loyal supporters to keep the factions in line."

"Agreed," Zuberi said.

And they needed a new emperor. Once Markos was dealt with, and order restored, it would be time for Lucius to name his heir—before his tragic death.

He listened as Demetrios outlined which imperial ministries had vacancies, and which officials could be persuaded to retire so that their lucrative posts could be offered to others. But even as he nodded his agreement, his mind returned back to the problem of who would succeed Emperor Lucius. Demetrios had disappointed him, but he would give the senator a chance to prove himself worthy of the honor. If he could keep the senate under control, and if he managed to dispose of his brother without being implicated in scandal, Zuberi would throw his considerable influence behind Demetrios and convince others to do the same.

And then Zuberi would have the dual satisfaction of knowing that he had secured the future of the empire, and seen the last of Nerissa's enemies destroyed.

Josan's days continued to pass quietly, with no official engagements that required his presence. But he was well aware that it was the quiet before a storm. Despite Proconsul Zuberi's best efforts, it was doubtful that the new emperor's reign stretched any farther than the city walls. Josan could feel Prince Lucius's presence in his own growing frustration, though for now the prince remained in the background. He suspected that the prince's reticence was his way of avoiding the tedium, using Josan as a servant to endure what the prince chose not to.

It would not be the first time.

He shook his head, knowing that such thoughts were dangerous. No good could come of recriminations, nor of fighting among his selves.

Rising swiftly to his feet, he left his inner chamber. He did not pause as he swept by his startled clerk, merely calling over his shoulder, "We will visit the gardens."

His steps were swift, fueled by an anger that he dared not acknowledge. Two of the guards fell in behind him, hurrying to keep up. Servants scurried to open doors before him so the emperor did not have to sully his hands.

Even the brutal heat of the late-afternoon sun was not enough to slow his progress. He was sweating freely by the time he had crossed the courtyard and passed through the ornamental pillars that marked the edge of the imperial gardens. Behind him, the guards were red-faced with exertion.

There was no one else to be seen on the tree-lined paths. The rest of the palace's residents were either busy with their duties or too sensible to take their exercise in the heat of the day. Everyone had an assigned task—everyone except the emperor, that is. He was of no more use than the statues surrounded by their carefully tended greenery.

But his anger could not be sustained. Gradually as he walked, his thoughts calmed. If the past year had taught him anything, it was that his circumstances could change in an instant. Already he had gone from reluctant guest to condemned prisoner to emperor in name, if not in fact. Time was his ally. Time and the patience to build a base of power for himself, free from those who sought to control him.

Josan had no wish to rule, but neither was he content to let others rule in his name. Here, his and Lucius's goals were the same.

Leaving the pathways, he entered the first of the inner gardens, where late-season roses bloomed alongside beds of violets, acanthus, and fragrant jasmine. A gardener knelt by a topiary dragon, apparently pruning it, though the bush seemed flawless to Josan's eyes.

Hearing footsteps behind him, the gardener turned his head, then scrambled to his feet and hastily bowed, gaze fixed on the ground so he did not commit the impertinence of staring at his emperor.

On his own, Josan would have turned to leave the garden rather than disturb the servant at his work, but he knew Lucius would never have done so. Such petty matters were of no concern to one who would style himself prince. Or emperor.

Josan kept walking, choosing a curved path that would take him into the next garden. As he passed the servant, he was surprised to see the man raise his head.

"Emperor Lucius, if you please," he called out.

Josan stopped.

The gardener, seemingly emboldened by such notice, took a few steps closer so he would not have to shout.

Josan's gaze fell on the garden shears that he carried. It was less than a year ago that another man had tried to kill him in this very garden.

"Hold. Approach no farther," one of the guards ordered.

For the first time since his coronation Josan was grateful for their presence.

The servant flushed, and as he realized the direction of Josan's gaze, he hastily dropped the shears on the ground.

"Most Gracious Emperor, I beg your pardon for disturbing you, but we—that is, those of us who tend your gardens—would know your will."

"My will?"

The man nodded. "Yes. Ordinarily I would have asked for instruction from the Master of the Gardens, but since you are here . . ."

Josan felt his eyebrows rise, and the gardener's voice trailed into silence as he realized the enormity of his error. A mere servant did not stop the emperor to ask a question. Ever.

Nerissa would have had this man flogged.

Then again, this was the first time anyone had sought out the new emperor for advice. Only moments before he had been bitter because he was ignored. It seemed the fates had a malicious sense of humor.

"What is it that you want?"

"Lizards," the gardener said. "There's a new nest in the east garden, where the flowering cacti are. Empress Nerissa would have had us destroy them, but I thought that you, well, you might wish differently."

Josan gave a grim laugh. "Lizards," he repeated.

"Yes," the gardener said, frantically bobbing his head in agreement. "The small spotted ones, not the royal lizards, but still . . ."

The symbol of his house. By Emperor Aitor's decree, lizards had been banished from the imperial gardens for a century, and the nobles in Ikaria had followed suit. He knew that there would be some who took this as a sign— that Emperor Lucius had somehow drawn them here by his very presence.

But Josan would not play such games. Instead he shrugged.

"The lizards mean nothing to me," he said, gaining

petty pleasure from the puzzled look on the servant's face. "Do what you will, for the good of the garden."

He turned and left, the gardener's stammered thanks trailing after him like the perfumes of the gardens.

He chuckled softly as he realized that Emperor Lucius had just made his first independent decree, free from those who controlled him.

His first, but not his last, he vowed, and he heard Prince Lucius's voice echo in agreement.

Chapter 9

It was strange to surface and feel an emotion from the monk other than that of worry or fear. Lucius savored the humor of their encounter with the presumptuous gardener—it was a petty victory but a victory all the same.

His spirits remained high as they left the garden behind. As they crossed the great courtyard, preparing to return to the imperial apartments, Lucius was surprised to see a military commander entering on the far side, followed by an aide. The monk's gaze would have passed him by, for to the monk one soldier looked much like another, but Lucius took control of their eyes, squinting as he saw the red cloak, fastened at the shoulder with a gold brooch. This was no mere officer, but rather one of the regional commanders, and at Lucius's urging, the monk turned their steps to intercept him.

I know this man, Lucius thought, mindful of their uneasy truce. He would not seize his body without warning, not unless there was no other choice. *Let me speak with him.*

He felt rather than heard Josan's agreement, and the monk's consciousness retreated. Cooperation eased the transition, and Lucius assumed control of their shared body without a single misstep.

For a moment, he regretted that he was dressed simply in a plain tunic with only the merest banding of purple at the hem to indicate his royal lineage, and not even a circlet on his brow. But he need not have worried, for as Lucius drew near, Commander Kiril's eyes widened and he came to an abrupt halt.

"Emperor Lucius," he said, raising his right fist in salute and bowing.

"Commander Kiril," Lucius replied, acknowledging the salute with the barest nod. Kiril commanded the legions of the south, whose main responsibility was the pacification of the border with Kazagan. Kiril was far from his post, and where the commander led, his troops would not be far behind.

"I was not expecting you so soon," Lucius added, wondering what, or whom, had brought Kiril so far from his post.

Kiril flushed slightly as he replied, "I could not let Karystos stand alone in her time of need. I was already on the march when your orders reached me."

Lucius recalled no such order, and the monk, who took the time to read each piece of parchment that Ferenc thrust before them, agreed.

Lacking an overall leader, the five regional commanders had reported directly to Empress Nerissa, which meant in practice that their orders had come through Proconsul Zuberi's office. It must have been Zuberi who summoned Kiril here, in the name of the new emperor.

Their encounter was a stroke of luck, for Zuberi would never allow Lucius to speak with Kiril alone—or at least not until he had privately informed Kiril of the emperor's impotence.

"Your arrival is well-timed, for I was on my way to consult with my councilors," Lucius said. "You will walk with me."

"I am honored," Kiril replied, inclining his head.

As Lucius turned, Kiril fell into step at his right, a quarter pace behind him, close enough to hear what Lucius had to say without presuming himself his equal. It was a sign of respect, and perhaps a sign that Commander Kiril, at least, was unaware that the new emperor was a mere figurehead.

Their escorts trailed several paces behind, out of earshot.

Here was the opportunity he had been searching for if Lucius only knew how to use it. He thought frantically, dredging up what bits he could remember about Kiril. Among the more conservative of the newcomers, his family had a long tradition of military service. He had briefly served in the empress's personal guard before being posted to the far-flung sections of the empire. Lucius risked a sidelong glance, trying to reconcile the gallant officer of a dozen years before with the impassive man who walked at his side.

The last time he had seen Kiril, it had been at the wedding of Kiril's sister. All of the members of Nerissa's court and her dependents had been invited to attend, including himself. He had forgotten the name of Kiril's sister, a plain thing who already looked the part of a matron though she was barely sixteen. Still, the groom had seemed happy enough, for with the sponsorship of his new father-in-law, Anatoli had begun a rapid rise through the military ranks.

Anatoli, who at last report was a senior aide to Commander Markos, whose armies marched toward Karystos.

The vague outlines of a plan began to form in his mind. Zuberi would never agree; he would order Kiril to help fortify Karystos, but that would be a mistake. If the fighting reached the walls of the city, then win or lose the battle, they would have already lost the war.

"Your sister's husband, Anatoli, he is well?"

Kiril's face gave away nothing, but his feet betrayed him, as he froze for a moment, then hastened to catch up.

"It has been some time since I heard from him—"

"Nonsense. If my messengers found you, so have Markos's. And even one as stupid as he would know enough to bait the trap with a letter from Anatoli."

Kiril's complexion turned gray, perhaps recalling the Rooms of Pain that lay under this very complex. "My emperor, I would never betray you—"

"Of course not," Lucius said. At least not without sufficient incentive. Which was why Kiril was here. Markos must have made him an offer, and Kiril had come to see if the new emperor would better it.

A dangerous gamble, but it showed he had courage. And he would need that in full if he was to agree to Lucius's scheme.

"I do not fear the pretender Markos," Lucius said.

"Of course," Kiril murmured.

Lucius stopped so swiftly that their escort nearly collided with him. Turning to Kiril, he held out his right hand, palm upwards. Ignoring the monk's protests, he searched deep within himself, rejoicing as the power of his ancestors sprang forth at his command. Yellow flames danced on the palm of his hand, and Kiril gasped.

Lucius waited several heartbeats, then closed his fist, quenching the flames within.

"Markos's destiny is already writ in the stars. He will be destroyed, utterly. I fear not him, but for those he may lead astray in his quest for power."

Lucius resumed walking, and after a moment Kiril once more fell in at his side.

"I knew Markos," Lucius said. "He was a bully and a

liar then, and he has not changed since. Whatever promises he has made you, I assure you they are worthless."

As a boy, Lucius had joined Nerissa's sons as they were tutored in the military arts. Markos, an ensign at the time, had been in charge of their physical training. Their lessons had been supposed to instill discipline, but Lucius had learned something else. Markos had repeatedly praised him to his face, then later blamed him publicly for being unruly and the source of all mishaps in the training hall. Markos had been swift to curry favor with those who could be useful to him, only to discard them once their use was over. Well regarded by his superiors, he was despised by his underlings—a fact that Kiril must know.

"Emperor Lucius, I seek only to serve," Kiril said, still visibly shaken by Lucius's earlier display.

He was hardly likely to confess to considering treason, though it would have saved time if they could have spoken plainly to each other.

"You will take your armies north, where, on your signal Anatoli will arrest Markos and turn him over to you, along with those who conspired with him. Restore order to his legions, and bring Markos here to me to face judgment, and I will name you general of the armies."

It was probably the same offer that Markos had made him—generalship of the armies in return for supporting Markos's claim to the throne.

"As your first act, you may promote Anatoli to your place as commander of the southern legion. Though if Kazagan has used your absence to rebel, your first task will be the reconquest of those lands." Lucius kept his tone casual, implying that disagreement was inconceivable.

They walked in silence for several paces, and Lucius fought the urge to hold his breath. He must not show any sign of weakness.

"What of the other commanders?"

"I would have made the same offer to any of them," he said. "You arrived first, but if you do not feel up to the task, I will raise another in your place."

Lucius gave a cold smile. If he failed today, it was unlikely that he would have a chance to make this offer again, but Kiril did not know that. Kiril believed he was speaking with an emperor, a man favored by his gods. Once he met with the councilors, he would gain a far different impression.

Lucius said no more, striving to give the impression of a man negotiating from a position of strength. He fought to appear confident, but his heart sank as Kiril remained silent. As the doors to the council chamber came in sight, Lucius realized that time had run out.

Bitter disappointment welled up within him. If he could not convince this man to follow him—a man who believed that he was emperor in truth—then what hope did he have of ever being more than Zuberi's slave?

As their escort opened the doors to the council chamber, Kiril finally spoke. "I will be honored to carry out your orders. My emperor."

Lucius did not bother to conceal his pleasure, which grew at the anger he saw on Zuberi's face as he realized just who it was who had intruded on the council session.

"Lucius," Zuberi began, the informal address a marked departure from the imperial protocol they observed in public. Then Zuberi paused as Commander Kiril followed Lucius into the chamber.

Lucius's eyes swept over the small gathering. Zuberi, Brother Nikos, who was never far from his side these days, Demetrios, and Simon. Four men who ruled the empire in his name and ruled him as well.

"My trusted servants," he said, ignoring Zuberi's obvious displeasure. "Commander Kiril begs your attention as he explains how he will bring the traitor Markos to justice."

Demetrios frowned thoughtfully as Zuberi swallowed whatever remark he had been about to make. He had surprised them, and men of power did not like surprises. Despite his announcement, Lucius was the focus of all eyes, not Commander Kiril.

Lucius took the vacant seat opposite Zuberi, nodding to each of the councilors as the monk cataloged each of their expressions. Then he turned toward their guest.

"Commander, if you would?" Lucius prompted.

Kiril saluted, then began to speak. If he wondered why his emperor wanted him to claim ownership of their plan, he gave no sign, instead speaking as if he had been considering this strategy for weeks rather than mere moments.

He had chosen his first ally well. Lucius leaned back in his seat, savoring this moment of triumph. He knew that the councilors were suspicious, but what could they accuse him of? Conspiring with Kiril to achieve a victory that would benefit them all?

A part of him wanted to claim credit for winning Kiril over to their cause, but the monk's voice urged him to caution. *Zuberi will let us live only as long as he thinks he holds the whip,* Josan reminded him. *And we cannot stand against him.*

Not yet, Lucius replied. *But that day will come.*

After a short debate, the council approved Commander Kiril's plans and dismissed him. At the monk's urging, Lucius also departed, so as not to give Zuberi a chance to vent his anger. His glee was tempered by the monk's dry reminder that he had won a minor skirmish, not the war, and that the cost of victory was still to be reckoned.

The monk's presence in his skull was a constant

irritation—an itch he could not scratch. The monk yielded when Lucius asked, but he never quite disappeared. He could force the monk into silence, but such an effort of will would drain him, ensuring that his solitary control would not last long.

The monk had no such difficulties. Once in command of his stolen body he could remain so indefinitely, until the next time Lucius was strong enough to regain awareness. It was fundamentally unfair—this body was Lucius's by right, but the monk's ties to it were the stronger, perhaps because his presence was more recent, or perhaps it was merely the result of the long years when Lucius's spirit had lived in the dreamworld.

It was as if Lucius had returned from years spent in a foreign country to find a stranger living in his villa. The villa was his by law, but the stranger had the advantage of long occupancy and servants accustomed to obeying their new master. Even after asserting his rights, he was still no more than a mere guest in a place that had once been his personal domain.

It was no wonder that he felt angry, yet that anger was mixed with shame, knowing that Josan had not chosen this fate. There were far worthier targets for his anger. For both of them.

And such targets were close to hand as Zuberi swept into Lucius's private quarters.

"How dare you?" he demanded.

Lucius carefully set down his glass of chilled fruit juice, and with a wave of his hand he dismissed the boy who had brought it.

"What is it that you believe I have done?"

"You broke our agreement when you conspired with Kiril."

Zuberi's complexion was dangerously red, his face beaded with sweat from the heat of the day. He appeared close to losing control, and this shocked Lucius more than anything else. Zuberi was famous for his self-possession. If Zuberi had indeed changed so greatly, then it was difficult to predict what he might do next.

"I did not conspire," Lucius said. "Kiril encountered me as I returned from the gardens, and I could hardly deny him, not when he had been summoned in my name."

"And it was mere chance that you happened to be there to greet him?" Zuberi's voice dripped with scorn.

"How could it be anything except chance? I knew nothing of his summoning."

Lucius remained seated even as Zuberi paced furiously around him. Strangely, the angrier Zuberi became, the easier it was for him to remain calm. Here, at least, was an enemy he could fight, even if the only weapons in this battle were his wits and his temperament.

"I will not tolerate your disobedience," Zuberi said. "You swore to take no action on your own. If you cannot be trusted, then you will be replaced."

He did not doubt that Zuberi had the power to have him imprisoned, even executed. But he wondered why Zuberi had come alone to confront him. Could it be that the rest of the councilors did not share Zuberi's sentiments? They had much to gain from peace and little to gain from strife. If Commander Kiril succeeded in his task, Lucius might well find he had allies among Zuberi's former cronies.

But first he must survive.

"The army serves the emperor. If the commander judged me a weakling, what reason had he to support me? He would have rushed to offer his sword to Markos and returned to Karystos at the head of a conquering army."

"You do not give the orders."

"And I did not. I merely listened to Kiril as I escorted him to the council, so you and the others could judge the worthiness of his proposal."

Zuberi turned away abruptly. "We had other plans for his legions."

"Then you could have overruled him. Couched your orders as advice to me, and I would have endorsed them. The worthy commander would have left the council room believing the orders were mine even as he hastened to do your bidding."

Zuberi growled, apparently unable to find fault with Lucius's logic. As he resumed pacing, Lucius allowed himself to believe that the danger was passed.

Then Zuberi halted. He turned, and his anger was gone, replaced by a cruel smile.

"Your cleverness will be your undoing," he declared. "If Kiril succeeds in uniting the legions, we may find we no longer have a use for a mock-emperor."

The thought had occurred to him as well, but he would not show fear. He would not give Zuberi that satisfaction.

"If you are so eager for the throne, why not take it today? There are none who would deny you."

He felt the monk's anger at his challenge. But Lucius was counting on Zuberi's intelligence overriding his anger. Zuberi had put Lucius on the throne, and for whatever reason he still needed him. Zuberi would not move against him.

Not yet.

"The scales of balance remain in your favor. For the moment. Challenge me again, and I will accept your offer."

"Understood," Lucius said, inclining his head as if Zuberi had just complimented him.

And, indeed, he understood his position well. He must keep Zuberi satisfied while at the same time gathering enough supporters to himself so that, when the time came, Zuberi would not be able to act against him. It would be a close race, but one he must win, or die trying.

• • •

Prince Lucius had declared his goals, but it was left to Josan to strategize how they could achieve his objectives. He agreed that they needed to gather power to themselves if they were to survive, but despite the lofty title of emperor, he had very little with which to work. Lucius had no former friends in positions of power, nor could he dispense favors—the traditional means by which emperors built their followings. Even his purse was constrained—the senate had confirmed him as emperor but, for the moment, at least, Nerissa's private fortune was out of his grasp. The functionaries saw that he was fed and clothed royally, but he had not a single coin to his name.

His clerk Ferenc routinely refused all invitations on his behalf, for reasons of security. Those few who attempted to wait upon him in person were turned back by the functionaries long before they reached the imperial apartments. The court must think him an arrogant recluse, which was hardly likely to gain him any allies.

Days passed with no change to the tedium of his existence. Josan could feel Lucius growing impatient, and tried to reassure the prince that any change to their situation would take time.

Josan very carefully did not think about what had happened the last time the prince had decided to take decisive action, abandoning calm calculation for bold action. He had survived two internments in the Rooms of Pain. He had no wish to endure a third.

There had been no word yet from Commander Kiril, and privately Josan wondered if Kiril would keep his oaths or if he would throw in his lot with Markos. It was what Josan would have done, if he were in Kiril's place.

It seemed as if each day brought more bad news. The mood of the council grew grim, and Zuberi's distemper gave him a haggard appearance. On those rare occasions when the emperor was called into the council's presence, he noticed that the other councilors couched their words carefully, lest they draw Zuberi's wrath. Weeks passed, and Josan was no closer to making allies than he was to discovering why Zuberi had placed him on the throne.

Then came the news that Simon the Bald had been killed—murdered while he slept. As a prominent supporter of the new emperor, it was hard not to see this as a prelude to an attack on Lucius himself.

Simon's funeral was a private affair, supposedly at the request of his family. Though Josan suspected the real reason was that Petrelis and his guards were not certain they could guarantee the safety of the emperor and his supporters if they chose to attend.

When the emperor's bimonthly court reception was abruptly canceled, supposedly for reasons of ill health, Lucius would have protested, but Josan held him silent. He no longer trusted Zuberi's grasp on the shreds of his temper. It seemed increasingly likely that Zuberi would forget himself, or, worse yet, forget his need for his pet emperor and take irrevocable action against him.

Everyone's tempers were frayed as the heat of the summer wore on and fevers swept through the poorer districts. A few nobles left for their country estates, but most remained in the city to ensure that their rivals did not take advantage of their absence. Karystos had the feeling of a city under siege, as all waited to see if the emperor could hold on to his throne or if the legions would rise up against him.

Finally, a messenger from Commander Kiril arrived bearing a tersely worded note stating that the legions had been restored to order after Commander Markos's suicide. He might have skimped on his words, but the messenger also brought gruesome proof in the form of Markos's severed head and hands.

The grim trophies were displayed in the central court-yard of the palace, an unsubtle warning to those who might have contemplated treason. The city enjoyed a general celebration, even as the politicians rushed to proclaim that there had never been any real reason for concern.

With relative calm assured, at least for the present, Proconsul Zuberi declared that he would take a fortnight's holiday on his nearby estate.

Senator Demetrios waited until Zuberi had been gone for two days before requesting a private audience with the emperor. Ferenc was obviously troubled when he handed the invitation over to Josan, but with Zuberi gone he had no one to consult.

Josan's preference would have been to meet with Demetrios at once, but on the advice of Lucius he agreed to a private dinner the next day, so as not to appear too eager.

It was Lucius who made the arrangements for the dinner. Breaking with tradition, it was to be held in the emperor's private garden, where they could enjoy the cool night air—and an open venue that assured no spies could overhear their conversation. Lucius bathed, perfumed himself, and selected their attire for the evening, his elaborate preparations still puzzling to the former monk. But it was Josan who kept them both calm as the appointed hour drew near.

Protocol dictated that the emperor be last to arrive, so Demetrios was already in the garden, apparently admiring the night-blooming moonflowers. They played their parts for the hovering servants. Demetrios bowed low in respect, and Josan assured him that this was an informal occasion and they need not stand upon ceremony. Servants handed them glasses of chilled wine, and they drank a toast to the continued prosperity of the empire before taking their places on the adjacent couches.

They began with a simple course of olives to whet their

appetites, and as the servants brought each succeeding course, they conversed on general topics ranging from the unseemly weather to the anticipated date when Kiril would arrive back in Karystos. Safe topics—nothing that would arose suspicion if reported back to Zuberi.

Josan drank sparingly, heavily watering his wine, and he noticed that Demetrios did as well. He ate lightly but the food still sat heavily in his stomach as he tried to project an air of confidence. Finally, after three hours had passed, the last of the courses was cleared away and the servants were dismissed.

Demetrios rose, pouring a goblet of unwatered brandy for himself, and, at Josan's nod, another for his emperor.

"So what is it you have to say to me that you cannot say in Zuberi's presence?" Josan asked.

Demetrios smiled, taking a sip of his brandy.

"Perhaps I merely wished to get to know my new emperor and for him to know me."

"You could have done so anytime in these past weeks, but you have never sought out my company. Until now."

"You are not what I expected, nor as I remembered you. When Brother Nikos proposed you as emperor, I had my doubts."

"Then why did you agree?"

"Because no other had a better claim to the throne. It is what Empress Nerissa would have wanted," Demetrios said, parroting the official statements.

Josan gave a bitter laugh, and after a moment Demetrios unbent enough to smile.

"I find myself in agreement with the results, but I'll admit I'm curious as to why Brother Nikos proposed you."

"And if I could enlighten you, what would you do for me?"

Demetrios's eyes sharpened as he sat upright, no longer pretending that this was mere casual conversation. "I will give you something of equal value in return."

Josan hesitated. He had picked Demetrios as the one of the four most likely to be open to alliance, but he was loath to give away what advantage he held without any guarantee of return.

Then again, this very meeting was a gamble. He had not come this far only to hesitate at the brink.

"Brother Nikos is not the innocent that he portrays himself to be. He may have been Nerissa's man, but during the years of my exile, it was Nikos and his order who sheltered me."

"I do not believe you."

"Believe what you like," Josan said, shrugging to indicate his indifference. "But be cautious in your dealings with him. He has no morals save his own advantage in all things."

Demetrios appeared to ponder his words. "Why would he do such a thing?"

"One day, if I count you friend, I may tell you that tale."

But privately he knew that day would never come. He could never trust any man enough to call him friend, not while he must still conceal the twin souls inside him.

"I will give you coin of my own in return," Demetrios said. "The proconsul is dying."

Josan blinked.

"He has a cancer in his bowels that will kill him before the end of the year."

He should have seen it for himself. Zuberi's increasingly haggard appearance should have roused his curiosity.

"How many know?" he asked.

"Nikos, Simon, Petrelis, and myself for certain, and I assume Zuberi's wife knows as well. As for the rest— Zuberi's physicians have done what they can, but soon enough there will be no disguising the matter."

Which explained why Demetrios had been willing to share this with him—the secret had value today but soon it would be public knowledge. And once it was known that Zuberi was dying, his influence would be drastically diminished. Many would scheme to take the proconsul's place—perhaps Demetrios among them.

He now understood why Zuberi had not taken the crown for himself. But Zuberi's illness did not make the proconsul any less of a threat. For as long as Zuberi lived, he would remain a danger to Josan.

Chapter 10

Lady Ysobel stood at the stern rail, feet braced against the pitching deck, as Sendat's harbor slowly faded behind them. With one hand she shielded her eyes from the wind-driven rain, straining to see if they had been followed. But so far, it seemed, they were alone.

For months she had longed for this day—schemed, cajoled, even lowering herself to beg the council for permission to return to sea. Finally, her wish had been granted, but it was a bitter triumph.

She turned as she heard the sailing master's shouts and saw the hands scrambling to obey. They worked swiftly, despite the rain that lashed both ship and sailors. She knew from long experience that wet ropes made each task more difficult, and even the most surefooted of sailors could slip on a rain-slicked deck. It was a foul night to have set sail, which hopefully meant any potential pursuers had been caught off guard.

She watched as Captain Elpheme conferred with the sailing master. A part of her wanted to overhear their conversation, but Ysobel forced herself to remain where she was. Elpheme was captain of the *Leaping Dolphin,* while

Ysobel was merely an honored guest, and it would not do publicly to undermine Elpheme's command.

The *Dolphin* was the second largest of her ships, having originally been built as a raider for the federation navy. After two decades of service, she had been replaced by a faster, more agile ship and sold off to a merchant house. Her new owner had removed the heavy ram and replaced the lateen sail with a third mast. Belowdecks, the former marines' quarters had been converted into storage holds. When Ysobel had purchased the ship a half dozen years ago, she'd noted the signs of a martial past—the reinforced bow meant for ramming, and the double-thick deck intended to support the weight of weapons. Her construction made the *Dolphin* heavier than other ships of her size and thus slower, but this meant the merchant was willing to part with her on favorable terms.

She had served Ysobel well as a hauler of bulk cargoes, but now the *Dolphin* was being called upon to remember her days of glory. The *Dolphin* was being sent to war, and Ysobel with her.

At least she had a ship of her own under her feet rather than the weed-draped hulk that Lord Quesnel had offered. After explaining that the demands on the navy meant he had no better ship to serve her, he could hardly refuse when she offered up a ship of her own. She would have preferred the *Gull,* naturally, and the steadiness of Captain Zorion at her back rather than the aged *Dolphin* with its relatively inexperienced captain. Still with this ship, at least, she had no fear that she would drown before her mission had begun.

Though whether she would survive the war to come was another question. For war it was, though anyone with sense could see that it was an ill-advised folly.

True, Ikaria was in disarray if the news was to be believed. Admiral Hector was dead, some said murdered by the new emperor, his fleet kept in harbor, not trusted to set sail. Buoyed by fresh rumors from Ikaria that indicated the empire was on the verge of civil war, the royal council urged King Bayard to destroy the Ikarian navy, which had long harassed honest federation ships. With their navy crippled, and Ikaria consumed by internal conflict, the federation could once more claim its place as the preeminent power on the sea. Trading colonies that had been seized by the Ikarians would be retaken, and shipping routes reopened.

If the federation moved swiftly, they could seize the ports before the end of autumn and use the long winter to fortify them. Even if the civil war was over in months rather than years, Ikaria's lost ports would prove too costly a prize for them to reclaim. It would take time to rebuild their navy, and all the while the federation would grow stronger.

Or so the councilors had argued, and King Bayard had agreed.

What others saw as bold action, Ysobel saw as reckless folly. There were too many assumptions, and their intelligence on Ikaria had failed them before. An empire weakened by civil war would indeed be reluctant to go to war with the federation. But if Emperor Lucius was able to unite his people and bring the full force of Ikarian military power to bear, then the struggle between the two countries could well prove long and bloody, and there was no certainty that the federation would emerge triumphant.

It was a fool's gamble. A chance no sane trader would take, where the risks far outweighed the rewards. And it worried her that the council had been so quick to follow Lord Quesnel's lead. As minister of war, he had the most to gain should his efforts be successful, but surely the others should not be blind to the risks.

Perhaps the councilors saw the risks as well as she did. Perhaps they endorsed Lord Quesnel's scheme not because they thought it would succeed, but rather because they thought it would fail. They sought to destroy Quesnel, not reckoning the cost to the federation.

She shook her head to clear it of such grim imaginings. Surely the council members would not imperil the federation merely to settle scores among themselves. There was no profit to gain from burning down a house that all must share.

With one last glance at the empty seas behind them, she made her way below.

Captain Elpheme had offered her own cabin, but Ysobel had refused. She was the owner, yes, but she was not sailing as captain, and instead made do with the adjacent sailing master's cabin, as she had on her prior voyages. It was a show of respect for Elpheme's authority as captain, meant for the crew as much as for Elpheme herself.

Between the two cabins was a small office that was shared by both, and it was there that Captain Elpheme found her, as Ysobel pored over the charts showing the entrance to Gallifrey harbor. The charts provided by the War Ministry were good, but her own—copied from the charts maintained by generations of the house of Flordelis—were better.

"Wind's backed off two points and the storm is easing. It will blow itself out before morning," Elpheme reported.

"Good. And the marines, are they settled?"

"Bedded down for the night, those who aren't heaving their guts up."

The two women shared a grin. Like most sailors, they despised the marines, who took up valuable space and refused to earn their keep aboard ship. For ordinary journeys, the *Dolphin*'s crew was capable of protecting itself, but for their current mission four dozen marines had been crammed into the *Dolphin*'s hastily converted cargo holds.

"Keep an eye on them and watch those that appear too

comfortable. Their lieutenant knows more than he is saying, and I'll wager at least some of his marines were sailors
not all that long ago," she said.

Quesnel would have his spies among the marines, but
she hoped their orders stopped short of mutiny. Still, it was
best not to take any chances. The marines outnumbered
her sailors, and that was assuming that all of her sailors
were loyal.

Elpheme leaned over the table, looking at the charts.
Her eyebrows raised. "Gallifrey harbor in Thuridon? Do I
need to set a new course?" A more senior captain might
have questioned why Ysobel had directed her to spend the
last two hours sailing south if their intended destination
was north and west, but Elpheme's voice was even, giving
no hint of her feelings.

"If you would be so kind," Ysobel said.

"And once we arrive at Gallifrey harbor?" Elpheme's
voice trailed off delicately.

"We are to take the harbor and hold it until reinforcements arrive."

"You jest." Elpheme's face flushed, anger overriding
her usual deference.

"I wish I did."

Ysobel had been ordered not to inform anyone of the
details of her orders until after she had sailed. She was not
certain if the ministry was trying to preserve the advantage
of surprise by protecting the secrecy of her mission or
merely ensuring that no one would interfere.

"One ship? It's not possible."

It was meant to be impossible. Ysobel was a trader, not
a warrior, but she had been to Gallifrey harbor many times
before. A half dozen warships with a full complement of
marines might have been able to seize the port, but it was
folly to ask a smaller force to make the attempt.

It was more than folly. It was murder. Or so Lord

Quesnel intended. This was how he repaid Ysobel for challenging him. If she disobeyed his orders, she would be branded a traitor, forced to flee into exile. But following his orders would result in her death as well as destruction of her ship and her crew. And that was a price she was not prepared to pay.

"We will have the element of surprise, at least," Ysobel said.

Elpheme gave her a long look. "I assume you have a plan?"

"I will," Ysobel said. "My personal luggage was stored in the aft hold as I instructed, correct?"

"Yes," Elpheme said. "I did as you asked, and made certain to complain loudly about master traders who had grown soft with city living and could not travel without the comforts of home."

Elpheme had been very careful not to inquire as to what exactly was in those crates, which had been marked as personal food stores and chests of clothes sufficient to outfit half a dozen noblewomen.

"You'll need to put together a working party tomorrow. There are six ballistae in there, along with ammunition stored in the wardrobe chests. I want them installed on the deck and the crew practiced in loading and firing. Our crew only, mind. The marines are not to touch them."

Elpheme straightened and saluted, as if Ysobel were indeed a war captain. "If it comes to a fight, the *Dolphin* will give a good account of herself."

"I know we will," Ysobel replied, careful to keep her doubts to herself. The armaments would give them an edge in a ship-to-ship battle, particularly if the enemy was expecting an unarmed merchant ship. But ballistae would be of little use against a fortified harbor. She had the next weeks of sailing to come up with a plan that would keep her ship and her crew intact, and still carry out the war minister's orders.

Landers, the sailing master, had spent the last forty years at sea. He boasted of having sailed aboard every type of ship in the Ikarian fleet, from the smallest skiffs that plied the island trade to a stint in the great crewed warships of the navy. When Ysobel had promoted Elpheme to captain of the *Dolphin,* she had sent along Landers as second-in-command, so that his experience could offset Elpheme's lack. Landers had helped train up a generation of captains and was skilled at making orders sound like mere suggestions. He listened carefully as Ysobel described how she wanted the ballistae spaced evenly along the sides of the ship. By the time the conversation was finished, she'd agreed to placing two flanking the prow, with four amidships.

He wasted no time in setting the sailors to work. Ysobel could not resist following him up on deck, bringing with her the cup of citrus tea that had taken the place of breakfast. She leaned casually against the deckhouse, where she could watch as the first crates were brought on deck and opened. There were a few knowing looks and low-voiced comments, but with so many eyes upon them, the sailors knew better than to voice their questions aloud. Rumors would be saved for belowdecks and the privacy of their quarters.

After all, with a cargo of marines instead of trade goods, it was already plain that this was no ordinary voyage. The armaments were merely reinforcing what everyone knew—and was forbidden to discuss.

They had barely finished unpacking the first crate when Lieutenant Burrell appeared by her side.

"Lady Ysobel, a word if you please."

Ysobel took a sip of her tea, watching him out of the corner of her eye. There had been no marines on deck when the first crate was unboxed, so one of the sailors must have brought him word.

Too late, it occurred to her that she should have been watching the hatch that led below to see who had borne tales. It was a precaution she would have taken on any other ship, but the habit of trusting her own crew was one that died hard.

She continued to sip her tea, testing the limits of Burrell's patience, but he refused to be drawn. He bore up steadily under her regard, even as her gaze surveyed him from head to toe.

A frown marred features that would otherwise be handsome. Pity, for the rest of him was well put together. His nearness reminded her that it had been far too long since a man shared her bed. Under other circumstances she would have been tempted, but she knew better than to lie with one who might betray her.

Tired of baiting him, she drained her mug, then placed it in the deckhouse rack for retrieval later. Burrell turned toward the hatch, but instead Ysobel led the way to the prow, stepping carefully around the work crews.

The seas were still rough after yesterday's storms, but Ysobel's sea legs had never deserted her, and she made her way without resorting to the handrails. Burrell proved equally adept, reinforcing her belief that he was more sailor than soldier.

As she reached the prow, she looped her right arm around the deck rail, bracing her feet as she turned her back to the spray that swept over the deck each time the prow sliced through the waves.

Burrell stood beside her, holding the rail with both hands. "This isn't the place for this," he said, his voice raised to carry above the sound of the spray.

"I like it." She felt more comfortable above deck than below, where who knows what reception awaited her. A half dozen of his marines already in her cabin waiting to take her in chains? It was not beyond the realm of possibility.

"What was so urgent that it could not wait?" she prompted.

"Those weapons were not in your orders," he said.

"Neither was there anything forbidding them," she countered. She watched his face, trying to get a sense of his character. Old for the rank he claimed, it was possible that he was as much a victim of Quesnel's schemes as she was—another enemy to be disposed of. But it was equally likely that he was Quesnel's man, ready to carry out his own secret orders to ensure her failure.

How he reacted to the ballistae was a test—unless, of course, he was clever enough to see this for what it was.

"You've stolen armaments that the ministry needs for its own ships—"

"There was no theft," Ysobel said, drawing herself to her full height.

"Then where did they come from?"

"Unlike the navy, merchants rely upon themselves. My warehouses hold more than you would imagine, and can supply whatever my ships need," she said. Though technically the ballistae had belonged to the house of Flordelis until she had traded her remaining favors for their loan. Her orders from Quesnel allowed her to equip her own ship at her own expense, though he might have phrased those orders differently if he suspected she had access to weaponry.

"These ballistae will not help you take Gallifrey harbor," he said. It was not quite an accusation.

"They do no harm," she replied. "They give my crew something to occupy their attention on the voyage."

"But you still intend to carry out your orders?"

"Of course. And you?"

He merely nodded, tight-lipped.

"That's not enough," she said. "On my ship, you and your marines are under my command. So I ask your solemn word, will you support me as I take Gallifrey harbor?"

"Yes, ma'am," he said. "As long as this ship keeps course for Gallifrey, I will not interfere."

So he thought her likely to make a run for it, perhaps to turn pirate aided by her new toys. A reasonable assumption, given what he must have been told about her. Still, it seemed that he was prepared to play his role, at least for the present, and that was all that she needed.

It was telling that he had not asked how she planned to take Gallifrey harbor, nor how his marines would be used in the assault.

"I think we understand each other," she said. "I suggest you return to your marines and make sure that they are settling in. Given the activity on deck, I ask that you send no more than six at a time on deck to take the air."

And if she saw more than six, she would know that mutiny was afoot.

He simply nodded once more, then turned and left without any acknowledgment. She knew she had not won that encounter, but merely bought herself time to craft her scheme.

As the dawn rose, the *Dolphin* dropped anchor outside the entrance to Gallifrey harbor—close enough to be seen, but far enough away to make it clear that they did not intend to enter. The yellow plague flag fluttered from the mainmast, while a dozen of her sailors lay on the deck under canvas screens, their skin dyed green with boiled weed.

The sails were furled sloppily, canvas drooping and lines

seemingly tangled. It was as she had ordered, yet such disorder disturbed her soul. Ysobel clenched her hands into fists, her nails digging into her palms as she fought the urge to admonish her sailors for the careless work.

There was one final touch. Ysobel watched as two sailors lowered their grisly burden onto a canvas sheet. Orva had been a plain woman in life, and the week her body had spent pickling in brine had done nothing to improve her appearance. The sharp tang of the brine did not cover the stench of rot, and the sailors were white-faced as they backed away from the corpse.

Orva's death had been a stupid waste, a moment's carelessness that led to a lethal fall to the deck below. But even in her death she could be made to serve.

"And what will you do if they do not come?" Lieutenant Burrell asked. Ysobel had grown accustomed to his constant presence in the days since she had first revealed her plans. He questioned her at every turn, but nonetheless followed her lead.

She still knew no more of his loyalties than she had at the start of the voyage, but now was the time that both of them would be put to the test.

"Only a fool would let a plague ship anchor outside their harbor. They'll send a party to warn us off. Or if they don't, I'll send a rowboat in to parley."

The narrow entrance to Gallifrey harbor was guarded by two small forts on each side, with deadly catapults that could rain stones or lead shot upon enemy ships. A massive iron cable closed the harbor entrance at night, or in case of attack. As per their treaty with Thuridon, Ikarian marines controlled the forts, and they could call for reinforcements from the Ikarian merchant ships that filled the harbor.

A single federation ship could do little damage. Even a full-scale attack by the navy might not succeed.

Which was why Ysobel had chosen stealth and deception instead. She had kept her doubts to herself, knowing that the crew needed to believe in her if they were to play their parts. Still, she could not resist a sigh of relief as her eyes caught sight of a small gig leaving the harbor, heading toward them.

As she waited for the gig to draw near, she took a final stroll around the deck, occasionally bending down as if to reassure the stricken sailors, but in truth reminding each of their part.

Burrell, wearing the tunic of a sailor, joined her amidships as the gig approached within hailing distance. While Ysobel posed as captain, Elpheme stood in the deckhouse, within calling distance of the hatch where the rest of the sailors crouched belowdecks, awaiting her orders. If their deception was discovered, Elpheme would rouse the crew for a speedy escape.

The gig stopped a cable's length away, close enough that they could hear each other and see each other's faces.

As the rowers shipped their oars, the man sitting in the front of the gig stood up. "I am Antonius, the harbormaster. Your ship is denied entrance to our harbor, and we order you to set sail within the next day."

Ysobel gave an exaggerated shrug. "If I have enough crew alive tomorrow, I will gladly set sail."

The gig was close enough so that she could see the sailors blanch, but the harbormaster was made of sterner stuff.

Ysobel mopped her brow with a linen handkerchief. At this signal, Elias, the youngest of the crew, rose from his pallet and staggered to the rail, where he vomited barley soaked in red wine. To an onlooker it would appear as if he had vomited blood.

The ability to vomit at will was not something she had previously considered an important qualification in one of her sailors, but rather served as proof that even the most unlikely of talents could be turned to serve the ship.

"I need fresh water and to pass along a warning," Ysobel said, raising her voice to be heard over the sounds of Elias's choking heaves.

"A warning?"

"Last night I anchored offshore, not wanting to try my luck with the reefs. This morning I discovered one of my longboats missing along with several of my crew." Ysobel gestured to the empty davit. "I fear they may have snuck into the harbor, and brought their contagion with them..."

"The harbor is chained and watched—" the harbormaster said.

"Of course you know best," she said. But both knew that the chain was meant to keep out ships, not small boats that drew only a shallow draft. And according to her intelligence, the marines had grown lazy, relying upon the chain rather than making regular patrols by rowboat as was the custom in other ports.

"I will see that water is sent, but be warned that your ship will be watched. Your crew must remain on board, and you must depart in two days," Antonius said. He sat down heavily and gestured to his crew.

Ysobel placed her right hand behind her back, and at this signal the sailing master called out "We've lost another one."

The harbormaster flinched.

"By the gods," Ysobel swore. "She's the second this morning."

"The third," Burrell corrected her. "It's getting worse."

She watched as Landers tied lead ballast weights to each of Orva's legs, then bound the canvas sheet around her body with rope. At his signal a sailor lifted the body by the shoulders, while Landers picked up her feet. They carried the body to the rail and heaved it unceremoniously over the side. As planned, the loosely knotted ropes gave way in the air, revealing Orva's bloated corpse. With a small splash, her body sank beneath the waves.

Shocked exclamations arose from the crew of the gig, who bent their backs to their oars as if they were being pursued by monsters. Only those who had grown hardened to death would have treated a corpse so shamefully, and Ysobel knew that this would do more than anything else to convince Antonius that she had been telling the truth. There could be no doubt that the *Dolphin* was cursed by vile contagion.

So far all had gone according to plan. Ysobel made a circuit of the deck, ostensibly checking on her dying sailors, but in reality reminding them that the ship would be watched from shore, so they had to keep up the pretense of illness.

Barely an hour had lapsed since the harbormaster's visit, when the first trading ship left the harbor for the open sea, carefully skirting a wide berth around the *Dolphin*. Such a departure could have been routine, but she was swiftly followed by a second, then a third. By noon, more than a dozen ships had left the harbor, their captains abandoning cargo and profits rather than risk being caught in a port overrun by plague. As the day wore on, the tangle of masts in the inner harbor thinned, as one ship, then another, chose prudence over danger.

Ysobel's spirits rose with each departure, though she was careful to keep her face grim while on deck. The canvas screens, which covered both ballistae and supposedly dying sailors alike, could only conceal so much.

There was no sign of the promised provisions from shore. If there truly had been contagion aboard the *Dolphin,* fresh water might have meant the difference between life and death. Such callous disregard was against all customs of the sea, where even the most deadly of rivals were required to set aside their differences in the face of a common enemy. Then, again, Antonius was Ikarian, with all their inbred arrogance and disdain for the ways of others.

She wondered if Antonius had forgotten to send the water lighter, or if he had been unable to find any willing to approach the plague ship, when so many ships already in harbor were no doubt clamoring for fresh water and willing to pay generously for service so they could set sail.

Or maybe the delay was more ominous in nature. Perhaps they were preparing to send not water, but rather soldiers with flaming arrows, ready to set fire to the *Dolphin* and execute her dying crew before they could spread their illness. Though such a course held its own peril. They had anchored near the western edge of the harbor mouth, close enough that they could be seen through spyglasses from the watchtower. Which meant that they were also close enough that a strong swimmer could make it to the breakwater. Presumably those who were already infected and dying would drown before reaching shore, but would the harbormaster want to take that chance?

Such fretting accomplished nothing, so after a quiet word with Captain Elpheme, Ysobel stretched out on the deck for a nap, taking her turn playing the role of a stricken sailor. A short rest would aid her for later, and had the advantage of scandalizing Lieutenant Burrell, who viewed her idleness with deep disdain.

As she closed her eyes, she wondered why he had left the planning of this mission to her since it was clear that he did not trust her. Either he was grossly incompetent, or he was trying to ensure that the responsibility for failure would be hers alone.

She dozed lightly, until the late-afternoon sun slipped below the canvas awning. Rising to her feet, she made her way below to her borrowed cabin, where Elias, the vomiting sailor, was waiting. She congratulated him on his earlier performance as she inserted wax plugs into her nose, then stripped off her clothes. A sponge soaked in a mixture of tea and boiled weed painted her skin a sickly yellow-green. Then she put on a blouse and leggings that had been soaked in some foul concoction thought up by the cook. Even through the nose plugs she could smell their stench, and wondered how Elias stood there without gagging.

Once dressed, she entered the chart room, where Lieutenant Burrell and Captain Elpheme were waiting. Burrell, who proclaimed himself a skilled swimmer, wore similar attire to her own. Elpheme's face was green, but from honest nausea at the stench, not paint. She would remain with the ship.

"The volunteers are ready," Elpheme said. "They're assembled by the stern, waiting for you."

Ysobel looked at Burrell. "If your marines fail us—"

"My marines will be in position, as I commanded," he said. "They know their duty."

"Good," she said. "I would hate to be executed alone."

If the harbormaster had boarded the *Dolphin,* he would have seen that the empty space on the davit was meant to hold not one but rather two rowboats. Yesterday, two dozen of Burrell's marines had been crammed into the boats, and set ashore down the coast, with instructions to hike along the rocky coastline until they were in sight of the fort that guarded the eastern edge of the harbor.

The western edge was joined to land by a narrow breakwater, which meant that it could only be approached from the water. While Burrell's marines secured the eastern fort, Ysobel and her sailors would take the western fort. Timing was everything, and there was no room for hesitation or second-guessing. Either the plan worked, or it didn't.

If they failed, it was likely that Burrell would execute her before the Ikarians had a chance to capture her. He had only agreed to her plan after insisting that he be allowed to accompany her—and he assigned only half of his marines to the raiding party, ensuring that enough remained behind that she could not act against him.

"The *Dolphin* is ready, and I will be waiting for your signal," Captain Elpheme said. "May fortune be with you."

After so much anxiety, the actual battle itself was over nearly before it had begun. Confronted by diseased-ravaged, cutlass-wielding madmen, many of the garrison threw down their weapons and fled. Those who chose to stand and fight were quickly disarmed.

There were a few anxious moments before signal lamps from the eastern fort indicated that Burrell's marines had seized it as well.

Ysobel ordered the Ikarian flag struck down, as the agreed-upon signal, and a short time later boats arrived from the *Dolphin* bearing the rest of Burrell's marines. Under his direction they took control of the watchtower and its catapults.

Ysobel had taken charge of interrogating the senior of the surviving soldiers, who proved remarkably cooperative as long as she did not approach him too closely. The long swim had done little to lessen her stench, and the soldiers seemed convinced that this assault was the last act of a crew desperate to escape their dying ship. She did not bother to inform them otherwise.

His tally of ships left in harbor matched her own observations—a mere ten seagoing vessels, with a like number of smaller river craft. What she hadn't known was that there were two federation flagged vessels in harbor, along with four Ikarian-owned ships.

It spoke poorly of her fellow traders' instincts that they had not chosen to flee, but since they had remained behind, she would have a use for them.

Elpheme had proven her worth by sending along fresh clothes for Ysobel and the rest of the swimmers. A hasty wash took care of the lingering stench, though her skin would stay green until the dye wore off. Leaving a marine sergeant in charge, she joined Lieutenant Burrell in a skiff that rowed them across to inspect the eastern fort. At the entrance to the fort, drying bloodstains told the tale of fierce fighting. Two of the marines had been killed, and three others wounded, but the fort was secure.

The skiff ferried the wounded marines to the *Dolphin*, and brought back sailors to help secure the fort. Ysobel had stripped the crew of the *Dolphin* as much as she dared—leaving barely enough hands aboard to make sail if trouble came.

When dawn came, both forts flew the flag of the Federated Islands of Seddon, as did the nearby *Dolphin*, which had moved to guard the harbor entrance from approach by sea. She had lowered her yellow plague flag, as well as the canvas screens that concealed her ballistae.

At Ysobel's orders, the harbor chain remained drawn, ensuring that no ship could enter or leave the harbor without permission.

It was midmorning when two men approached the fort, bearing the palm leaves that indicated their wish to parley. They were brought into the fort, through the central courtyard, where her marines were massed to give the impression of overwhelming numbers.

Ysobel met them on the far side of the courtyard, Lieutenant Burrell at her side. The resplendence of his dress uniform nearly made up for his sickly complexion.

The harbormaster Antonius glared at her, while his companion, an older gentleman with the pale complexion of the native Thuridons, merely looked around the courtyard with interest. "I am Calvino, mayor of Gallifrey," he said. "I come to you under the truce of parley."

"I welcome you in peace," she said. By custom, no harm would come to the emissaries while under truce, though such truces had been known to be broken. It spoke much of their trust in her honor that they would send the mayor on such an errand, or perhaps it showed how poorly he was regarded.

Calvino nudged Antonius.

"I come in truce," Antonius muttered. She had spoken, but it was Burrell to whom he addressed his words and gaze. It appeared that Antonius shared the disdain of his countrymen toward women in positions of authority. It would gall him to have to treat with her.

"I am Lady Ysobel, in command of the Federation forces, and this is Lieutenant Burrell."

"Your presence is an act of war. Surrender these forts at once, and we will spare your lives," Antonius blustered. "And if you cannot see reason, surely your lieutenant will."

Burrell kept his silence, playing the role of a dutiful subordinate.

"We should not judge. Perhaps their illness has impaired their thinking—" Calvino began.

"There was no illness," Ysobel declared.

Calvino merely nodded, as she confirmed what must have been evident. It was to him that she addressed her next words.

"These forts are the lawful property of the Federated Islands of Seddon, by treaty between our people and your government. We do not blame you for allowing Ikaria to seize them, but neither may you accuse us of doing anything other than reclaiming our property."

It was a subtle distinction. True, the treaty between their two peoples had never been dissolved, but Ikaria had held the port for nearly twenty years and made their own agreements with Thuridon.

"You are one woman with but a single ship. You cannot hope to hold on to this harbor," Antonius said.

"Why not? I have sailors in plenty to hold the forts, and my marines are far too skillful to fall for a child's ruse."

"And he who controls the forts, controls the harbor. Or have you forgotten that the catapults may be aimed at the docks as easily as at the sea?" Burrell added.

Antonius cursed under his breath.

"That sounds like a threat," Calvino said. He remained calm, even as his companion grew visibly enraged. From his control, she concluded that he was mayor in truth, not a mere figurehead.

Now it was time to sweeten the deal. "The federation is prepared to honor the old treaty and all of its terms," she said. "As you may recall, the years of our partnership were a profitable time for both our peoples."

"You can't make a deal with these people! Just look at how they deceived us," Antonius said.

"They deceived *you*," Calvino replied.

Ysobel bit back a grin.

"May I invite you to dine with me this evening, so we may discuss the details of the new treaty?" Calvino said.

"I would be honored," she replied.

Antonius grumbled and blustered, but the mayor paid him little heed as the two were escorted out of the fort.

"We've won," she told Burrell. "Antonius hasn't the men to retake the forts, and he'll get no support from Thuridon. I'll dine with the mayor tonight and let him win a few concessions in return for his immediate expulsion of Antonius and his lackeys."

Burrell blinked, and his frame momentarily sagged as the exertions of the past two days caught up with him.

"You'll need to recruit sailors from the ships in harbor

to replace those we've borrowed from the *Dolphin*. How long until your reinforcements arrive?"

"I don't know."

"You don't know?"

He shook his head, then unaccountably he grinned. "I don't know. We'd planned for everything—except the possibility of victory."

It was a confirmation of what she had long suspected. "Then it is time you made new plans," she said. "Lord Quesnel will not be rid of me this easily."

Burrell's face grew sober. "Don't underestimate his anger."

"And he should learn not to underestimate me," Ysobel replied.

Chapter 11

It did not take long for Lieutenant Burrell to adapt to success. No longer constrained by his secret orders from Lord Quesnel, Burrell threw himself into planning the long-term occupation of Gallifrey harbor. He drafted sailors from federation vessels in port to man the forts, freely promising Lord Quesnel's gold in return for their service. With no sign of the transport ships that were to have supported Ysobel's mission, Burrell convinced a reluctant captain to divert his ship, bearing a message to the nearest naval base.

While Burrell did not speak of it aloud, both knew that their reinforcements were neither tardy nor the victims of ill fortune. Quesnel had deliberately withheld them before the attack, hoping that she would fail. But having succeeded against the odds, not even Quesnel would throw away victory for his personal vendetta, and she was confident that reinforcements would soon be on their way.

While Burrell secured their military position, Ysobel took control as acting harbormaster. She met first with the mayor, then the leading merchants, assuring them that the federation had no intention of disrupting trade. As a sign of that good faith, she reopened the harbor. The first ship to leave was an Ikarian merchant, with the former harbor-master aboard. He would report what had transpired, but the federation was gambling that the Ikarian Empire would be too consumed by its internal conflicts to worry about retaking a small foreign port. Gallifrey was a vital trade link for goods coming down from the Northern Wastes, but it had little military significance.

After two days, trading vessels began arriving, their captains far more concerned about rumors of plague than they were about the change in control of the harbor. The *Dolphin* remained on guard outside the harbor entrance, sending work parties to board and inspect each vessel before it was allowed to enter the harbor. A few captains objected to such treatment, but Elpheme's crew made it clear that they were searching for weapons and soldiers only. They had no interest in whatever cargo the vessel carried.

Though naturally they reported all cargo to Ysobel, legitimate goods and contraband alike. Knowing which captains and houses were honest, and which were not above a bit of smuggling, was invaluable intelligence for a master trader.

Ysobel's second decree abolished the schemes that had given preferential dock space and reduced cargo fees to Ikarian vessels. Antonius had fled his office in such haste that he had left behind ledgers recording the bribes that each captain had paid. It was a complicated scheme based on the nationality of the captain, the type of cargo carried, and the frequency of one's visits to Gallifrey. Half of the bribes were remitted to Ikaria as special docking fees, while the rest went directly into Antonius's purse.

Instead Ysobel began assigning dock space as was done in the federation—according to a published schedule of fees based on the length of the ship and time spent in port. The docking fees were higher than they had been, but the elimination of bribes meant that even an Ikarian captain would pay less than he had before.

With more coin flowing into the official coffers, this meant more tax dollars for Gallifrey's mayor, who was quick to signal his approval of her plans. He even offered Ysobel the service of one of his own clerks to help run the harbormaster's office. The clerk's skill at keeping records quickly brought order out of chaos, and Ysobel's scrupulous honesty in dealing with the traders meant that he would have nothing but favorable words to report to his master.

She would make sure her replacement understood the importance of keeping the mayor content. Gallifrey was the largest port in Thuridon, but it was not the only one. Goodwill built here would extend along the coastline. And the federation could have need of that goodwill someday—if it kept on the path to war with the empire.

Ysobel had never realized the full scope of a harbormaster's responsibilities. Previously she had been on the other side of the counter—now she was the one negotiating with merchants over duties and trying to smooth tempers among captains, all of whom insisted that their needs took precedence. A captain herself, she sympathized with their plight, even as she pointed out that no amount of shouting or threats could create an empty berth out of thin air.

It was a valuable opportunity. Each lading list that she reviewed, every argument with a captain, each request for supplies, provided her with insights into the local trade and the conditions of her competitors. Consider the house of Laurent, which was generally believed to be prosperous: The ship they sent to Gallifrey was undermanned and carried a cargo of fleece and leathers, which would bring only a meager profit. On the other hand, the local trading vessels from Vidrun were ancient single-masted relics, but their derelict appearance disguised their valuable cargoes of perfumes and exotic spices.

As the days passed, incoming ships brought news of other skirmishes between the Ikarian and Seddonian navies, though reports of how the conflict was progressing depended on the nationality of the captain telling the tale. So far all agreed that no pitched battles had been fought between the fleets, but there had been a handful of encounters between vessels. One reported that the federation had claimed the island harbor of Eykstra, another that the incursion had been beaten back.

She could glean no clear picture of the federation strategy. At times, it seemed as if the strategy was merely to nibble away at the edges of Ikaria's foreign possessions, reckoning that no single piece would be seen as worth reclaiming. At other times, she thought grimly that there was no overall strategy, merely individual commanders making a grab for whatever they could in the confusion.

Her darkest imaginings gained strength when a battered ship sailed into harbor, bearing a federation prize crew on a vessel that she had last seen flying an Ikarian pennant. The acting captain claimed to have seized the vessel from pirates, and such was legal under federation law. But she was troubled that there were no survivors aboard who could prove the truth of the tale.

With nothing to back up her suspicions, she could take no official action against the captain. Indeed, it seemed hypocritical to suspect him—after all, her aunt Tilda had started as a pirate hunter herself and, without that legacy, Ysobel would never have achieved her own success. Yet Tilda had always been careful to turn over the surviving pirates to the authorities on dry land, even when keeping them alive meant short rations for all else on board.

She worried about her own ships, and whether they had been swept up in the madness. Since her flight from Ikaria, her ships no longer ventured into Ikarian waters, but that did not mean they were safe. She wrote to her factor, sending new orders to her captains, instructing them to only accept cargoes bound for the east.

Elpheme was busy aboard the *Dolphin,* and Ysobel saw little of her. By contrast, Burrell was a near-constant presence, as he divided his time between the two forts. Having been assured of his worth, she found herself turning to Burrell as a sounding board. She would not call him a friend, but there was no one else that she could speak to frankly.

Working closely together gave her a new appreciation for Burrell—he had demonstrated both courage and wit, two qualities she greatly admired. She could feel the attraction simmering between them—saw proof of it in his gaze when he thought himself unobserved.

But this was neither the time nor the place to indulge herself. While the people of Thuridon were not quite as rigid in their views on women as the Ikarians, it was still unusual for them to place a woman in a position of power. News that she was involved in a liaison with one of her subordinates would be seen as a sign that she was untrustworthy, and she needed the support of Mayor Calvino and his people if she was to keep control of this harbor.

Weeks passed, and finally, just when she had convinced herself that she would have to hold the port through the winter, two navy ships arrived. Using the message semaphore atop the customs house, she sent orders that they be allowed to anchor in harbor and an invitation for their captains to meet her in her office at their earliest convenience.

After a moment's consideration, she sent a runner to fetch Lieutenant Burrell. It was a courtesy, though his own watch would surely have informed him of the ships' arrival.

She wondered what orders the ships brought. Would she be allowed to return home? Or did Lord Quesnel have a different fate in mind for her?

Nerves taut, she forced herself to continue reviewing the day's accounts until the two ships had dropped anchor in the harbor. Only then did she send her clerk to fetch hot apple wine and fresh nut rolls from the bakery stall that catered to the docks. Plain fare, but bound to be appreciated by those who had been on sea rations. Burrell arrived as she was giving the orders to her clerk, having taken the time to change into his dress uniform and don the brass shoulder cord that proclaimed him the ranking officer at this post.

"At last," he said. "The sailors we impressed will no doubt rejoice tonight."

Though Burrell did not have the look of a man who was pleased. His expression was guarded, as it had been during the earliest days of their acquaintance.

She offered him apple wine, which he declined, choosing instead to pace restlessly, peering around her office as if he had never seen it before. He circled the large meeting table twice, then came over to her desk. Picking up a scroll from the basket on the far left side of her desk, he juggled it idly in his hands before replacing it with another.

"My clerk will have both our hides if we disturb his filing system," she said, carefully lifting the scroll and returning it to its place.

He flushed. "My apologies," he said, before clasping his arms behind his back and retreating a few paces.

Strangely enough, seeing his nerves calmed her own. She was able to wait with seeming diffidence until the sharp knock on her door announced the arrival of her guests.

The first to enter wore the dress uniform of the navy, showing he had taken time to change before presenting himself, his graying hair tied back neatly in a plait. "Lady

Ysobel," he said, inclining his head in respect. "I am Captain Justin, born into the house of Bendat, and this is Major Armand."

Major Armand was the younger of the two, with a ruddy complexion and light brown hair that curled close to his scalp. He, too, wore a dress uniform, fit for a court presentation and not the deck of a ship.

Their immaculate attire did not impress her—it gave them the air of courtiers, not sailors.

"Captain; Major," she said, nodding to each in turn. "And this is Lieutenant Burrell."

Burrell saluted. The major stared at him for a long moment, his gaze dismissive, before finally returning his salute.

"I was surprised to receive your message," Major Armand said. He was speaking to Ysobel, but his gaze flickered back over to Burrell, and this time she could see the animosity. It appeared that the two knew each other and had not parted on friendly terms.

"Surprised, but pleased by your success," Captain Justin hastened to clarify.

"Please, have a seat, gentlemen," Ysobel said. "We have much to discuss."

Her guests accepted goblets of the warmed apple wine, in deference to the damp chill of autumn, but declined the nut rolls, giving a look that said they had far more important considerations than their stomachs. Seized by an imp of contrariness she took a roll for herself and made sure to offer them to Burrell before taking a seat at the table.

The visitors had chosen to sit side by side, with Burrell to their left. She sat to their right, so she could watch them with ease, while they would be forced to divide their attention between herself and Burrell.

"Tell me, how did you take Gallifrey with so few men?" Captain Justin asked. "I would have sworn it couldn't be done."

"A trader knows how to improvise," she said. It took only a few moments to recount the taking of the harbor—a reckless, heart-stopping gamble recounted as if it were a children's tale. Burrell then took up the thread of the narrative, discussing the improvements to the defenses that he had made since he had taken over.

Major Armand grunted in apparent approval though he did not speak his praise aloud. His attitude irritated her, for what harm could there be in acknowledging Burrell's efforts? A few words of honest praise would cost him nothing, yet his refusal to utter them spoke volumes about his character.

She had expected her own efforts to be dismissed. She was a master trader with no military experience—failure would have been her responsibility, but any success would be credited to luck or the skill of her advisors. She had come to this meeting ready to fight for her role to be acknowledged. She hadn't expected to have to defend Burrell. The lieutenant had shown himself courageous and deserving of respect.

But despite his posturing, Armand was not in charge—as a mere marine, he would take his orders from the navy. Captain Justin was in charge of this mission, and it was his words that would be heeded.

Justin, who'd introduced himself as born into the house of Bendat, but not of that house. Some saw the navy as honorable service, but for one born into a trading house, such service was seen as the lesser path. The favored sons and daughters of the house would have followed the merchant's path. Ysobel outranked him twice—as a master trader who had earned the title of Lady, and as the head of her own house. She might be constrained to follow Lord Quesnel's orders, but these men were her inferiors. A fact that they seemed to have forgotten.

"Justin, how many marines have you brought, and how

quickly can you take control of the harbor?" she asked, deliberately omitting his title.

He blinked in surprise. "Major Armand has a full contingent of one hundred marines——"

"Good," she interrupted. "Lieutenant Burrell, after their shift, send the impressed sailors to me and I will see that they are paid for their service. If any choose to remain, have them see Major Armand. Otherwise, I will find them temporary work at the docks until they can find a berth on a ship."

"As you command," Burrell said.

"You overstep yourself. My marines will need time——" Armand began.

"Time? To learn garrison duty? Lieutenant Burrell was able to seize these forts and hold them for over two months with half as many marines, but if your troops are incapable, I suppose I could ask the sailors to remain...at double their pay."

Burrell's face was studiously blank, while the major's naturally ruddy complexion darkened. "I will take command of the fortifications as soon as my marines can be set ashore."

"Good." She had won that point. It was time to find out if Quesnel had sent instructions for her, as well. If not, she would seize this opportunity to implement her own plans—they could not hold her here on their own authority. "Justin, you will need to appoint a harbormaster to take my place."

"My quartermaster can take charge until a replacement arrives. And we will need to review any agreements you have entered into on the federation's behalf," Justin said.

Here was the trap they hoped to catch her in. If they could prove corruption, or that she had exceeded her authority by entering into new treaties, then Quesnel would have the justification he needed to destroy her.

But they had misjudged their prey. She was far too cunning to be caught in such obvious misdeeds. "Never steal anything worth less than the sum of your house," Tilda had once advised her, and as of yet she had never come across anything that tempted her to break that rule.

"Of course. I made no new agreements, but merely reaffirmed the old treaties under which the port was governed. If you feel you can negotiate better terms, I am certain the mayor is willing to hear you."

Captain Justin's smile faltered in the face of her self-confidence.

"Unless you have new orders for me, I believe this concludes our business. I will, of course, make myself available to meet with your quartermaster and to answer any questions you might have about the running of the port."

"There is one more thing," Captain Justin added, withdrawing a scroll from a pocket in his tunic. "Upon satisfactory completion of your duties here, you are instructed to join the fleet to assist in the campaign against Kazagan."

"Kazagan?" she asked. It had been too much to hope that Quesnel had forgotten about her, but this was beyond anything she had expected. "Have they gone mad? Kazagan was the pride of Nerissa's house—the new emperor cannot let it go, not without alienating his supporters. The Ikarian navy will attack us at sea, and their armies will crush us should we attempt to land."

Justin bristled. "It is not your place to question the minister's orders."

"The Ikarians have other concerns—the legions from the north march to the capital in support of their own claimant to the throne, while their navy is still confined to harbor by order of the emperor. By the time they learn of our attack, we will already be victorious," Major Armand said.

It was a risky gamble. Even if the rumors were true, and Ikaria was consumed in a civil war, circumstances could change. An external threat could unite the rival factions behind the emperor, and in that case, federation victory was far less certain.

She had no doubt that their ships would prevail in their initial attack, thanks to the superior skills of their sailors. But should the federation try to invade Kazagan...

It was madness. She shook her head in disbelief even as she accepted the scroll from Captain Justin. Her orders were simple—return at once to the naval base on Melene and place herself and her ship at the disposal of the commodore there. There was no mention of when the orders had been written or the target for their attack.

Perhaps the talk of Kazagan was a diversion. Or perhaps the plans were not firm—there was still time for the council to come to their senses.

Or perhaps the war had already started.

"And what of Lieutenant Burrell?" she asked.

"I can find something to keep him occupied," Major Armand said.

So Burrell's success had not redeemed him. And the look on the major's face did not bode well for the lieutenant's future.

"You may enjoy garrison duty, but the lieutenant is far too valuable to be allowed to rot away here," Ysobel said. She knew her hasty words were making an enemy, but she did not care. If these men were so blind that they could not see the looming disaster, then their respect was not worth having. "My instructions from Lord Quesnel allow me to retain my own crew, so if the lieutenant will agree to continue under my command?"

"The lieutenant is an officer of the marines—" Major Armand began.

"And I am *Lady Ysobel,* acting under the direct authority of Lord Quesnel, the minister of war," she countered. "I answer to the minister, not to you."

"Your point is noted," Captain Justin said. He turned to face Burrell. "I am certain the lieutenant would prefer to remain in the service of the marines, and to assist Major Armand as he takes command of the harbor. Is that not so?"

Burrell took a deep breath, his gaze wandering over the two officers then fixing itself on Ysobel's face. "I have no doubt Major Armand will serve ably in his new role," he said. "As for myself, I would be honored to serve under Lady Ysobel's command as she goes into battle."

"So be it," Justin said.

He stood, and Major Armand hastily rose to his feet as well.

"I will see that the necessary arrangements are made for the transfer of command," Captain Justin said. "You may instruct your ship to prepare to sail the day after tomorrow."

"Excellent," she said.

With insincere bows, the visitors left. Ysobel waited until the door had shut behind them, then said, "I did you no favors."

"You did me no harm. The major and I have long disliked each other. Any service with him would have been unpleasant."

She wondered if he would ever trust her enough to tell her the reason for such animosity, and whether his tale would explain why a man of his age was still a mere lieutenant.

"Any service with me is likely to be brief," she said.

Burrell shrugged. "If it is to be war, then eventually all of us will be called upon to fight. I'd rather do so with someone I trusted."

"And I as well. Come now, there is much to be done.

Most of your marines will have to stay behind, but you can pick a dozen of them to come with us. I'd suggest volunteers, but I'll leave that up to you."

Justin would not challenge her over a dozen marines, not when she could insist on the full complement that she had brought with her on the *Dolphin*. Indeed, she was tempted to ask for them all, but doing so might leave Gallifrey shorthanded should an attack come. And since the major seemed remarkably lacking in cunning, he would need to rely upon superior forces instead.

She would have to rely upon her wits, and on those she trusted. She could only hope they would be enough.

Chapter 12

The servingwoman looked up at Lucius through lowered lashes, smiling demurely as she handed him a cup of chilled tipia. "The bath, it is to your liking, your graciousness?"

He returned the smile. "I find much to like," he said, letting his gaze wander down from her face to her lithe form.

She blushed, as if she were a modest maiden. Then she leaned forward, reaching in with one hand to stir the rose petals that floated on the surface of the water. The pose gave him a clear view of the tops of her firm young breasts.

She was very much to his taste—a change from the matronly servants who had been his previous attendants, and he wondered whom he had to thank for her presence. Were the functionaries finally ready to treat him as an emperor should be treated? Or was this woman's presence here mere happenstance?

He took a sip of his drink, the chilled mixture of fruit juices mixed with soft wine providing a perfect counterpoint to the heat of the baths. Lucius felt a stirring in his groin, as she once more leaned in—this time close enough that her breasts brushed his arm as if by accident.

Yet it was no mere accident, but rather the dance of seduction—a game that he had played in his youth, though never as often as he had wished. The imperial princes had been the subject of most women's ambitions; he had had neither wealth nor influence to tempt them.

"You are far more beautiful than my last attendant," he said, taking up his part in the game. "Tell me your name so that I may ask for you again."

"Tiphene, your majesty," she said. "It is my honor to serve you."

She boldly met his gaze, then dropped her eyes, this time not in modesty but in frank appraisal of his form. The scars from his torture had faded, and he knew that what she saw would please her—as it would please any woman. He was young, handsome, and well endowed—a far cry from the withered old men who were his advisors.

Well, perhaps Demetrios was not old, though he was far from handsome. But as for the rest—only a mercenary would sleep with them by choice.

Lucius stood, letting the water drip from his body. His male bath attendant held out his arm to help Lucius descend from the bathing pool, while Tiphene picked up a large towel. She dried him slowly, her touch lingering as she reached his waist, and he felt his flesh respond.

He cast his mind back, but he could not remember the last time he had lain with a woman.

He could feel the monk's presence in his mind, and so he asked, *How long has it been?*

Since what?

Since my body felt the touch of a woman?

Not since I was joined to you.

Lucius shuddered. Was the monk only half a man? Could he really have spent the past years in a celibate existence?

"Quickly, fetch his robe," Tiphene ordered her fellow

servant, mistaking his shuddering for a sign that he was chilled.

He allowed her to slip his arms into the robe, then held still as she belted it around his waist. She stood there for a moment, her hands lingering on the ties.

"I can think of another way to warm up," he said. He took her hand in his, then turned to his other attendant, saying, "You are dismissed."

He did not miss the flash of triumph that crossed Tiphene's features, though it was swiftly hidden beneath another maidenly blush. Still, for all her feigned demureness, it was she who tugged gently at his hand, leading him toward his bedroom.

He was content to be led. The monk might have wasted these past years, but he would not allow such an opportunity to pass him by.

A thought crossed his mind. Perhaps those years had not been wasted—the monks of the Learned Brethren were known to lie with other men. Not solely by preference, though no doubt there were those who preferred the rugged embrace of a man to the softer joys of a woman. But the monks—who drew their ranks from the bastard outcasts of noble families—lay with their fellows in order to ensure that they would breed no challengers to the rightful heirs.

Lucius had never felt an attraction toward another man, and the thought that Josan might have used his body in that manner was distressing. *Tell me, did you lie with male lovers?*

Josan was silent, for so long that Lucius feared he would not speak. Then, finally he said, *Since the time I was joined with your body, I have taken no lover, neither man nor woman.*

Lucius was relieved. Even if he had no memory of such an act, it was still distasteful to contemplate. Perhaps Josan found the idea of sex with a woman equally distasteful, for he could feel the monk's presence retreating, allowing Lucius to take full control of his body.

He climbed upon the bed, reclining back against the pillows, then unbelted his robe, letting it fall open.

"Let me see you," he said.

Tiphene slipped her right shoulder free of her chiton, exposing one breast. She held the pose with the skill of a practiced courtesan, then slowly slipped her left shoulder free, and let the chiton puddle on the floor at her feet.

She was not classically beautiful, but her skin was unblemished, her breasts generous and firm. White teeth flashed in a smile as she climbed onto the foot of the enormous bed and began to crawl toward him.

He waited, enjoying the sight of a beautiful woman anxious to please him. As she approached he held out his hands, drawing her to him so that she knelt astride his thighs, the tip of his sex brushing the softness of her belly.

She bent her head to him and he brushed her lips with a kiss as he reached forward and caressed her breasts. Their soft weight filled his hands, but it was not as pleasant as he remembered.

He withdrew his hands, and Tiphene took this as a signal, for she brushed a kiss against his chin, then his neck, then continued down his chest, exploring him with lips and hands.

He smelled the perfume of her hair and gazed upon her soft curves. But his attraction was waning—what should have been a delight instead felt wrong.

She was too fragile, too yielding. Plump and curved where he wanted hardness and strength. He grasped her waist, but it was as if he were clenching a bolster rather than a lover.

Tiphene's lips reached his sex, which now lay flaccid

against his leg. He heard her soft gasp of surprise, then she began to stroke him with her tongue.

You, this is your fault! Leave, before you unman me.

I would if I knew how. I am sorry.

But the monk's apologies were useless, and Lucius could not summon the concentration necessary to force him into oblivion.

Lucius imagined sinking his hardness into Tiphene's soft curves, remembering the pleasures to be found in joining with a woman, but it was no use. He could not recapture his earlier arousal. Despite his efforts, and Tiphene's increasingly frantic ministrations, his body remained unmoved.

He was a eunuch. Crippled by the cursed spell that had stolen so much else from him.

He shoved Tiphene so that she toppled to her side. She looked up at him, pouting lips topped with dark accusing eyes.

"I am bored of this," he said. "Leave me."

"But—" she began.

"Leave," he said, in a voice that would not countenance disagreement.

Tiphene scrambled to her feet, picking up her garment but not bothering to don it as she raced from the room. She must have feared that he was about to order her whipped for her presumption.

I should have her whipped, he thought. *By tomorrow the whole of the palace will know that I am not a man. In a few days the news will spread throughout the city.*

They will think her words a sign of pique—the spite of a serving girl angry that the emperor refused her advances, the monk observed.

But he was not in the mood to be reasonable. *And what if this happens again? What if I can no longer lie with a woman? An emperor must have an heir.*

Lucius was furious, but the monk's mind voice was calm. *It is likely that we will fall victim to Zuberi's machinations long before the question of an heir arises. And, if by chance it comes to that, I am certain Zuberi would be happy to father our heir. He has already assumed the rest of your powers.*

And how is Zuberi any different from you? Lucius asked. *He, at least, is honest in his intentions. You are just as much of a usurper, but you cover your deeds with apologies and feigned regret.*

He felt a flash of rage from the monk, then silence. He could still feel the monk's lingering presence, an unclean shadow lurking in his mind. He vowed that he would not endure this partnership forever. Someday he would find the means necessary to rid himself of the monk's spirit—whatever it took.

There could be only one emperor, and Lucius was determined to be that man.

The mood of the palace had lightened, perhaps owing as much to Zuberi's absence as it did to the news that the rebellion in the north had been put down. Other news was less encouraging—Ikarian merchant ships were returning to port with tales of harassment by coastal raiders, and several had gone missing entirely. Their absence could be the result of storms or pirates, or there could be more sinister forces at work. There were many countries that might seek to take advantage of Ikaria's internal distractions—chief among them the Federation of Seddon.

At least Josan no longer languished in ignorance. His tentative accord with Demetrios had already borne fruit—each morning at breakfast a clerk would arrive to brief him on the news of the previous day. As troubling as the rumors had been, the bare facts were even worse.

The mood of the populace was grim. Violence remained a daily fact of life in Karystos, and Petrelis's guards were hard-pressed to maintain even a semblance of order. Two of the provincial governors reported that they had suppressed rebellions, though Josan wondered if they were merely using this as an excuse to seize the assets of their rivals.

Some nobles who had remained in the capital throughout the summer now chose to return to their estates. Perhaps they were fleeing the violence, or perhaps they sought to return to their bases of power, in preparation for the civil war that most feared loomed on the horizon.

Today's briefing brought the disquieting news that the federation had recalled their ambassador for consultations—a diplomatic phrase that meant he was suspected of wrongdoing, or considered too valuable to leave as a potential hostage in case war broke out. Ambassador Blaise had only served a short time, replacing Ambassador Hardouin, who'd been expelled for not noticing that his assistant, Lady Ysobel, was conspiring with the Ikarian rebels—Prince Lucius among them.

Josan wondered what had happened to Lady Ysobel after her escape. Had she returned to the life of a sea trader? Or was she weaving new schemes, once again risking her life to fuel her ambitions? She must have been astounded by his rise to the throne though he had no doubt that she had somehow found a way to claim credit.

What would he do if the federation sent her back as part of their delegation? Would he be expected to greet her as an ally? But surely she, at least, knew better. After all, he had betrayed his supporters to Empress Nerissa, Lady Ysobel among them. Having once fled Karystos to save her life, she could not be anxious to return.

This morning's report brought more troubling news, a rumor that the federation was massing its naval forces, converting merchant vessels to troop transports. It was a single report, but if true, it boded ill. Especially with the Ikarian navy still captive in port and no likely successor for Admiral Hector found.

The navy is unimportant. The strength of the empire has always been in her armies, Lucius thought. It was he who took control of their shared body and dismissed the clerk with a wave of one hand, ordering the hovering servants to bring him a pot of fresh citrus tea.

Josan despised citrus tea, and Lucius knew this. He had taken a perverse pleasure in requesting it as often as possible, savoring each sip, while Josan inwardly winced. At times like this he almost wished for the days when Lucius could temporarily banish him, but Lucius could no longer force Josan into unknowingness. Josan could not rest—he could try to silence his own thoughts in meditation, providing the illusion of solitariness, but he was always present.

He could not bring himself to apologize for something that was not in his control. Nor could Lucius accept the situation gracefully. They had begun to rub each other raw, as would any two men who had been chained together against their will.

We need the navy to protect our coast. And our ships. Unless you plan to give up the teas of Olizon, along with at least one quarter of the gold that flows into the imperial coffers.

Lucius grimaced, but accepted this point. *Then what do you suggest?*

Josan had the beginnings of a plan, but he was not ready to share. If he mentioned it, Lucius would insist on implementing it at once rather than waiting until the right moment. Josan resented having been forced into the role of parent, constantly reining in Lucius's intemperance, urging caution over folly. But each time he was tempted to let Lucius simply have his way, he reminded himself that the consequences to both of them might well prove fatal.

We must ponder our strategy, Josan replied. *Zuberi will return tomorrow, and I know the council will have their own ideas.*

Think as much as you like. The voice in his mind was scornful. *I am in the mood for fencing, unless you plan to interfere with this pleasure as well?*

Josan thought a wordless agreement and wondered if the embarrassment that he felt was reflected on their shared visage. When Lucius's mind slumbered, Josan was content to read his scrolls, consult with the clerks, or stroll in the gardens. He had learned to accept these limitations, but Lucius was used to a more energetic life. Forbidden to leave the city to engage in his favorite pastime of riding, he had taken to visiting the training hall, practicing with a sword as if he were expecting to lead his armies in the field. An unobjectionable pastime for an emperor, and far more to Josan's taste than Lucius's other attempts at diversion.

Lucius had still not forgiven Josan for his role in their failed attempt at seduction, though it was not clear what Josan could have done differently. Neither Josan's apologies, nor his reminder of how such a liaison would be seen by Zuberi, was enough to deflect his wrath.

Since then he had been careful to defer to Lucius in small matters whenever Lucius was present. It would not take much to break their tentative truce.

He could feel Lucius attempting to take control of their body, and Josan let his focus diminish, ignoring the physical sensations in favor of contemplation of the mysteries of the sacred numbers that had once formed the central portion of his studies.

• • •

Lucius felt the monk's presence diminish as he resumed full control of his body. He knew the retreat was meant as an apology, but he could not bring himself to feel grateful. The monk had done him no favors, merely ceding back to Lucius what was his by birthright—control of his own body. Though he knew from bitter experience that this control was but a temporary interlude.

It chafed that he had no way to strike back at the monk. Any action that hurt Josan ultimately hurt Lucius as well. He could not harm him, nor could he banish the monk to silence. Instead he was reduced to petty tricks—eating foods that he knew the monk disliked, insisting on vigorous exercise when the monk would have preferred to study.

He wondered if it would have been easier if they were friends. There was no common ground between them other than their mutual desire to survive. Left to his own desires, he would never have spoken two words to the monk, yet circumstances had bound them together more intimately than any friendship.

Though it was a decidedly unequal partnership. He knew that Josan considered him reckless, constantly chiding him as if the monk were his elder brother. The monk seemed to have forgotten that it had been Lucius, not Josan, who had won over Commander Kiril to their cause. Lucius had engineered their first victory against those who would see him cast off the throne, yet instead of being inspired to even bolder actions, the monk continued to counsel patience.

If the monk had his way, Lucius would turn into a mere statue, surrounded by dusty tomes.

It was not as if the monk's studies had any value. He still refused to send for books on magic, or anything that might help them discover how to undo the original spell. At times Lucius wondered if the monk truly wished to be free of this curse. For him, this stolen half-life was better than no life at all.

But it was not enough for Lucius, whose restless spirit craved action. In the days before his exile, Lucius had engaged in mock duels with other young nobles of Nerissa's court—younger sons who showed their daring by befriending the object of the empress's charity. He had considered them true friends at the time, and indeed some had died in his name in that first aborted rebellion. Those that had survived had done so by denouncing him. Now fortune had turned in his favor, but so far none had shown signs of being willing to trade upon their old friendship. And for his part, he made no overtures to them.

He did not need friends. He needed allies, and the company of those who had once gambled, drunk, and wenched with him would only serve to remind others of the wastrel he had been.

And that Josan still considered him to be.

As he reached the training hall he saw that Ermanno, his usual partner, was already there.

He doffed his robe, revealing a thin tunic underneath, belted with a linen cord. Ermanno was dressed in similar fashion, though his tunic was undyed cotton rather than silk. Lucius began by stretching to limber his muscles. Ermanno mirrored him, performing his own stretches with a fluid grace that Lucius envied. The muscles needed for fighting and swordplay were far different from those required by the menial existence of a lighthouse keeper or fugitive, and his body was only slowly regaining its former suppleness.

At last Lucius straightened up. "The heavy swords today," he said.

"As you wish, emperor," Ermanno said. Crossing to the wall he selected two wooden broadswords. Bowing low he extended the first to Lucius, hilt first, before taking his own.

Lucius swung his arm in a serpentine pattern, accustoming himself to the weight of the sword. Usually they practiced with the lighter dueling swords, but he was in the mood to test himself today. The polished ironwood was nearly as heavy as an actual sword would be, though the dull edge would draw no blood.

No man would risk dueling an emperor with sharpened steel—not even if he commanded him to do so.

They took their places in the center of the hall, a dueling circle outlined by dark red stones set in the marble floor. It had been years, perhaps decades, since an actual duel had been fought here, but the circle still remained, testament to a bloodier past. These days the circle was used as a training device—as long as both players stayed within the circle, points were awarded by judges based on the difficulty of the attacks and speed of execution. A swordsman forfeited the match if he stepped outside the circle, or was so careless as to draw blood from his opponent.

Today there were no judges. Lucius raised his sword in salute, and Ermanno followed. As he lowered his sword, Lucius lunged forward in attack.

Ermanno blocked his strike with a blow that made Lucius's arm ache, and the contest was joined. A part of Lucius's mind was wholly engaged by the swordplay, though it was merely an extension of the training exercises, as Ermanno essayed one choreographed drill after another, testing his pupil's skill and stamina. Lucius recognized the attacks, and was nearly always able to block them, though he struck few blows of his own.

But even as he sparred, a part of Lucius's mind was still focused on his anger with the monk. The revelation of Zuberi's fatal illness should have spurred them to take decisive action, but the monk insisted on moving slowly.

If only there was someone he could trust to give him

counsel. But even if he found a political ally, he could not trust him with the secret of his twin existence. Neither friendship nor political expediency would be enough to counter the horror of realizing that the emperor was a monster.

His lungs burned, and sweat covered his body, while his opponent was as fresh as if he were merely describing the moves rather than sparring. Lucius's anger rose. Putting his left hand over his right, he lifted the sword high, then whirled, the sword cutting a clean arc through the air, right where Ermanno's neck would be.

In his anger he had forgotten that a blow above the shoulders was considered in poor form. But it did not matter, because, before he could complete his turn, Ermanno hooked one leg around his own, and Lucius crashed to the floor.

He lay there, winded, his aching body protesting the bruises he had already received, and the new ones that he had just earned. He would regret this folly later.

"My apologies, emperor," Ermanno said. He said the same thing every time he bested Lucius, as if superior skill was something to apologize for.

"I will not make that mistake again," Lucius said.

Ermanno extended his left arm, and after a moment Lucius took it, allowing the man to pull him up.

Lucius swayed for a moment, still breathing heavily. "Enough for today," he said.

"It was well fought, until the end," Ermanno said.

Lucius shrugged. He wanted to believe Ermanno's words, but suspected that they were mere flattery. Still, he could take pride in having lasted longer than he had in his last bout with the heavy swords. Next time he would last longer still.

The monk was wrong about him. Lucius had learned how to be patient when it mattered. But he had also learned when to take risks, and that was a skill the monk needed to learn. And if the monk was unwilling to learn, then it would be up to Lucius to take decisive action, regardless of the monk's objections.

Josan raised his right arm to tug at the fold of his tunic, grimacing as his muscles reminded him of yesterday's exertions. Almost as soon as the training session was over, Lucius's presence had begun to fade. Rather than fighting his retreat, Lucius had cheerfully accepted his banishment, pleased to leave the burden of their aching body to Josan.

It was a child's trick, letting another be punished for his sins. Shameful in a youth, it was contemptible in a man who claimed to be ready to rule as emperor. Any sympathy that Josan had felt for Lucius had been slowly worn away by such tricks until now he felt only anger at Lucius's shortsightedness.

Zuberi had returned to the city last night and set a council meeting for this very afternoon. The emperor had been informed of the meeting as if he were the one who had called it and the functionary was merely confirming the time. A subtle play, meant to give the appearance that the emperor was in control. Though if matters followed true to form, any decisions would be made before the emperor arrived, so his presence was a mere formality.

Josan had been waiting for an opportunity to test his newfound alliance with Demetrios and see just how much goodwill the victory over Markos had won him. He had considered his proposal long and hard over many hours and believed he could sway the majority of the councilors to his side.

But it meant acting without Lucius's agreement, something he had sworn not to do. Each had promised to take no action without the agreement of the other. Yet this opportunity might not come again. If he acted without Lucius, he would incur his anger. If he waited until Lucius was once more present, the moment to act might well have passed.

No matter what he did, he could not win. He had spent most of the morning desperately trying to rouse Lucius's consciousness, to no avail. As the council chamber came in sight, he gave one last mental shout but heard only silence.

So be it. He was on his own.

Josan did not break stride as he approached the council chamber, trusting that the guards would open the door at the correct moment. It was a trick he had learned from Lucius—an emperor expected others to serve him. The more he behaved like an emperor, the more others were likely to perceive him as such.

Entering the chamber, he was not surprised to see that the councilors were already seated, apparently having been here for some time. Mindful of the watching guards, they rose to their feet and remained standing, until he took his seat, then resumed their own as the doors swung shut behind him.

He used the opportunity to study Zuberi carefully. He looked better than he had—not quite as worn, his complexion warmed by the sun rather than the pale gray of exhaustion. But he was not a well man, and Josan wondered how he could have missed seeing the signs of illness.

Perhaps it was because he had seen Zuberi only as his enemy, not as a man. It was a blindness he could ill afford.

"Proconsul Zuberi, Senator Demetrios, Brother Nikos," he began, acknowledging each man in turn. "It has been too long since I heard your words of wisdom."

"Fortunately there has been little to discuss," Nikos said.

"Oh? Then the news that our colonies are under attack were mere rumors, not fact?" Josan pressed.

"A single colony," Zuberi said. "And the attackers were repelled."

"One colony that you know of," Josan pressed. "And how many ships lost at sea?"

Zuberi frowned.

"It is difficult to determine if the ships are lost, or merely delayed," Demetrios said.

"Delayed." Josan let the word hang in the silence. "And how many ships must be *delayed* before you will believe that there is a threat?"

"We did not summon you here today to talk about ships," Zuberi said.

"Then you are overlooking a grave danger. Or do you truly think that the Federation of Seddon has forsaken its ambitions?"

"And what makes you think the federation is behind our losses? Perhaps you are still in communication with the treacherous Lady Ysobel?" Brother Nikos asked.

Josan shrugged. "Lady Ysobel's plans are her own. But those who sent her here to stir up trouble are still in power in the federation, and it is not likely that they will miss any opportunity to take advantage of our weakness."

"What would you have us do?" Demetrios asked, drawing a sharp glare from Zuberi.

"The fleet needs a new admiral. The captains blame me for Hector's death, seeing him as a martyr to my ambitions. They will not follow me unless they are led by someone they trust."

"We have discussed this before. The senior captains are all Hector's men, chosen by him and personally loyal to him," Nikos said, with the air of a teacher correcting a difficult student.

"And most are of the old blood," Josan said. "We need one of the old blood who can hold their loyalties yet who would be faithful to us."

"Every candidate we've proposed either has no experience at sea or enough experience that he will decline this honor. We waste our time discussing this," Demetrios added.

"But we all agree that the need is urgent?" Josan asked. There were reluctant nods from all present. "Then I suggest we publish a decree recalling Septimus the Younger."

"No," Zuberi said, slamming his fist against the table. "I will not see a traitor go unpunished."

The others startled at his vehemence though Josan had expected no less. Simon the Bald had been the only one who could reach him in his anger, and since Simon had been murdered the council had lost an important voice of reason.

"Septimus the Elder was a traitor. I myself gave evidence against him," Josan said. "As for his son, not even Nizam could find a whisper linking him to the conspiracy. Septimus's flight from Ikaria was a sign of prudence, not guilt."

"The guilt of the father is shared by his sons," Demetrios pointed out. Such was true by law, though the law was rarely enforced.

"I will not stand for this," Zuberi said. "You think to grasp power—"

Demetrios laid a hand on Zuberi's forearm. "Hear him out," he said.

Josan took a deep breath, forcing himself to display a calmness he did not feel. These men held his life in his hands, and the moment they thought him beyond their control, they would dispose of him. The trick was to guide them while letting them make the final decision.

"Septimus was an experienced captain before he became master of Karystos harbor. He is of the old blood, and well known to the navy. Moreover, if we are seen to deal with him fairly, it will set an example for all those captains who might feel threatened by our rule. Give them a reason to serve faithfully, and they will fall in line."

"And if not?" Brother Nikos asked.

"If not, are we any worse off than we are now? Our fleet and sailors are rotting in harbor, while our enemies' aggression goes unchecked," Josan said.

"I do not believe the situation is as dire as you say. Still, it would do no harm to recall Septimus the Younger and put our own questions to him," Demetrios said. He turned slightly away from Josan so that he was facing the other councilors. "If we then see fit to offer him a post, that will be our choice."

Demetrios was a master politician. By reminding Zuberi of where the power lay, he had both supported the emperor while simultaneously undercutting his position.

But it was enough for Zuberi. "So be it. Draft up a decree recalling Septimus, guaranteeing his safety. But do not think yourself clever, princeling. You have not gotten your way. Not yet."

"The final decision will be yours, of course," Josan said. "I merely offered my advice."

"And have you any other words of wisdom for us today?" Zuberi asked, his voice dripping with scorn.

Josan shook his head.

"Then be still as we tell you what we have decided. Emperor."

Josan resisted the urge to mop his brow. He had won this skirmish, but Zuberi's resistance had been greater than he expected. He would have to tread lightly in the coming days if he wanted to avoid further suspicion.

Chapter 13

"I am flattered that you think I may serve, but I do not know what it is you think I can accomplish," Septimus said.

Josan ground his teeth. If Septimus continued to refuse, Josan would be made to look a fool. And they would still face the same problems.

The situation had deteriorated in the weeks since the council had issued a decree assuring Septimus the Younger of his safety should he choose to return to Ikaria. Perhaps inspired by patriotism—or perhaps by memories of the property he had left behind—Septimus had gambled on these promises and returned. He had shown courage by returning and a fine sense of diplomacy before the council.

Mindful of his precarious standing, Josan had held his tongue and let Demetrios be the one to suggest that Septimus could prove his loyalty by taking charge of the Imperial Navy. The honor of being named admiral should have been a dazzling incentive for a man who had been living in exile, but Septimus, so far, was proving resistant to the idea.

"The navy needs an admiral, so we can carry the fight to the Seddonians," Josan said.

Navies were not like armies—they were often out of contact for weeks if not months at a time. The navy needed to be led by someone they could trust—someone who could set tactics in response to the ever-changing situation. Someone who knew how to use ships to their best advantage. There were easily a dozen men who had the experience to be general of the armies, but finding a man who could lead the navy and be counted on not to commit treason was a much harder task.

"And you are certain the federation is behind our recent losses?" Septimus asked.

"We know they seized Gallifrey harbor," Zuberi said.

"They've long disputed our claim upon that port," Demetrios countered. "It is not surprising that they took advantage of our distractions to reclaim their former possession."

"So we should let them keep it? I suppose next you will propose handing Kazagan back to the barbarians." Zuberi's voice was sharp—his temper flared more often these days, as the signs of his illness grew obvious to all. There had been no announcement yet, but all knew that the proconsul had mere months to live.

He's too stubborn to die, Lucius thought. Despite his firmly held belief that the navy was irrelevant, Lucius had been furious when he discovered that Josan had proposed the recall of Septimus without first consulting him. It had taken hours of silently waged arguments before he had agreed that Josan should remain in control for this meeting, but even now Josan could feel his lingering disapproval.

"We yield nothing," Demetrios said. "But practically, Gallifrey is a minor port. We have more pressing concerns."

"What do you want the navy to do?" Septimus asked. "To protect our merchant ships as they ply the coastal trade routes? To defend our ports against incursion? To carry the fight to our attackers? We do not have enough ships or men to do them all."

"All know our navy is currently in harbor," Demetrios said. "Learning that it is once again patrolling our shores will give these so-called pirates pause."

Septimus shook his head. "And what if it is the federation behind these attacks, and they choose not to be discouraged? It is not clear to me that Ikaria would prevail if it came to open warfare between our two countries. In the past, the federation has hesitated to attack, but if they decide the time is right . . ."

"The federation is a motley collection of islands. They could never defeat our empire," Zuberi said.

"On land, no. But on the sea? Their navy is no match for ours, but their merchant fleet is vast. If they begin arming their merchant ships . . ."

"So you take the coward's path, believing us already defeated?" Demetrios asked.

If he was hoping to draw a spark he was disappointed, for Septimus remained unperturbed.

"I think the challenges are grave," Septimus said. "I do not want to start by misleading you. If you still want me to serve, I will do so to the utmost of my abilities. But if you want ready promises of easy victory, then you must find another."

Josan looked at his councilors, waiting until he saw Zuberi's nod. "Your candor does you credit," he said. Inwardly he celebrated his triumph, but he was careful to appear grave, not wishing to give the councilors any reason to doubt him. "The empire accepts your service, Admiral Septimus."

"It is my honor to serve you, my emperor."

At least there was someone who was honored to serve the emperor. A few meetings with Zuberi would swiftly teach Septimus where the true power lay in Ikaria, but no matter. By agreeing to name Septimus as admiral, the council had handed Josan a victory—recognizing the new emperor as someone to be reckoned with. Not their superior, nor even their equal. Not yet. But the next time he spoke, they would pay heed to his words.

To our words, Lucius reminded him. For all Lucius's anger over the scheme, it seemed he was ready to claim whatever advantage Josan had won for them.

"If I may, I would like to summon my senior captains for consultation and review any reports the ministries have received on naval activity," Septimus said. "Winter is fast approaching, but there is still time for a few sorties and to arrange regular patrols along those coasts where the weather is not too severe."

"At least the season hinders all equally. The federation sorcerers know no tricks to steer a path around the storms of winter," Zuberi said.

His words resonated oddly in Josan's mind. "They are not sorcerers—" he began.

"It matters not whether their captains are sorcerers or if they merely employ the tools crafted for them by magic," Brother Nikos interrupted, glaring at Josan as if he were a novice caught in some mischief. "I am certain that Admiral Septimus is well aware of the advantage that their ships have and will plan his strategy accordingly."

"Of course," Septimus said, seeming oblivious to the tension between his emperor and the head of the Learned Brethren.

There was something wrong. Something Josan had said angered Nikos—was it his denial that the Seddonians employed sorcerers as navigators? Did Nikos think the emperor so arrogant that he would claim himself as the only true magic user?

Or had Nikos realized what the others had apparently

missed—that now both the Admiral of the Navy and the General of the Armies owed their appointments to the emperor's influence? Should he ever wish to cast off the council's yoke, these men could form the basis of his challenge.

Yet neither of these explanations felt right. For the first time in months, Josan felt that odd sense of dislocation—that there was something he had once known but could no longer recall. Much of his past had been lost when the spell had placed his soul in the body of Prince Lucius. He had gradually grown used to the gaps in his knowledge, but each time he found a new one, it hurt, as if another piece of his soul had gone missing.

He did his best to cover his confusion, listening with seeming attention as the council concluded its business, then withdrew to his chambers. But the problem would not leave him alone. It was a relief when Lucius demanded control of his body, leaving Josan to sift through the fragmented memories that he claimed as his own.

Only the most credulous believed that dreams brought enlightenment, but when morning came, Josan knew why Nikos had moved so swiftly to discourage yesterday's discussion of sorcery. It was not the discussion of magic that Nikos feared, though as one who had dabbled in forbidden spells, Nikos would do well to be wary.

Instead Nikos feared that Josan was about to expose his discovery that the federation navigators relied on skill, not sorcery, to ply their craft. Josan's studies had enabled him to unravel a mystery that had baffled the Learned Brethren for decades. It was mere ill luck that he had been struck down with a fatal fever even as he returned to the collegium to share his knowledge with them.

Nikos would have guarded that knowledge as closely as

he guarded the memory of Brother Josan, waiting until the time was right to reveal it.

That is, if he even understood the contents of Josan's notebooks. Josan felt a pang as he realized that his discovery might have been lost—the knowledge rotting away in the shelves of the great library, waiting for another scholar to stumble upon it.

Lucius seemed to be slumbering, but still Josan clutched this revelation to himself. Lucius claimed not to be able to read Josan's thoughts, but Josan did not trust his assertions, and this new knowledge was too precious to be shared. Not until he had decided what he wished to do about it.

A general audience had been scheduled for that day, and when Lucius's consciousness returned, Josan allowed him to take charge of the preparations, as was their custom. Lucius enjoyed the process of grooming himself and selecting which robe to wear from a selection of seemingly identical garments. Josan generally roused enough of his awareness to peruse the list of petitioners and Proconsul Zuberi's instructions on how to deal with each, but today he left even that to Lucius, trusting that the prince would not be foolish enough to go against the council's wishes.

Instead he stayed silent, meditating to keep himself calm. When it came time for Septimus to present himself and be acknowledged as admiral in front of the court, Josan could not repress a bitter surge of anger, as the sight of Septimus reminded him of the dilemma he faced. He felt Lucius's curiosity, but quickly buried himself in recollections of dusty scrolls until Lucius's attention turned outwards again.

Such tactics could not protect him forever, but he needed time to think. To weigh his options. He knew that Lucius would see his actions as betrayal, but he had no alternative. All of his choices were equally fraught with risk.

Whatever he chose to do with his newfound knowledge, it would be a betrayal of some part of himself.

He had only to choose which bits of himself he wished to sacrifice. He was not a whole man; he had come to terms with that knowledge months ago. But each decision since then had led to a further diminishment of self, until he no longer recognized the man he had been. He had fought hard to preserve this strange life he led, as much for his own sake as for the sake of the man whose body he wore. But there were times he no longer remembered why he had tried so hard to survive.

For a long moment he wished that he were more akin to Lucius, able to rail against the unfairness of his situation, to whine like a petulant child denied a promised treat. But he was no child. It was neither the gods nor the cruel forces of a fickle fate that had forced him into his situation, but the actions of men. He and he alone must decide how he would face this latest challenge.

In the next days, Lucius's presence remained strong. Josan used every trick he had learned in his years of study at the collegium to avoid thinking on his dilemma, but he could not prevent his anxiety from leaking through. He was short-tempered, and Lucius grew short-tempered as well, believing that Josan's fears came from his lack of confidence in Lucius's ability to rule.

It did not help that he could not deny the accusation. He did not trust Lucius to deal with the perils that faced them. Aitor himself might have quailed before the challenge of a restive populace and a council of advisors that had chosen him solely because they knew they could control him. Anytime he felt himself safe, he had only to trace the faint scars on his body to remember that this safety was but a momentary respite. Should Proconsul Zuberi order the guards to arrest the emperor, he had no doubt that they would comply.

Josan told himself that there was no urgency in deciding what to do about his discovery, but he knew that he was playing the coward's part. Still he waited, paralyzed by indecision, until Admiral Septimus came before the council to deliver his recommendations.

Josan had not seen Septimus since his court presentation, though he knew that he had met privately with Zuberi on more than one occasion. Thus he was not surprised that Septimus directed his attention toward Zuberi rather than to his emperor.

"So we are agreed," Septimus said. "I will send a small fleet under Flavio to patrol the northern coastline, with instructions to winter over in the Keys," Septimus said. "A second detachment will sail for Kazagan, to combat the so-called pirate raiders. I will sail with the remainder of the fleet to accompany Flavio as far as the Samos River, then return along the trade routes, to discourage attacks and escort any vessels we encounter."

It was a sensible plan, one that would give Septimus time to learn the intricacies of his command. Once the storms of winter began, only a few coastal ships would ply their trade, careful not to stray far from safe harbors. The rest would remain lying safely at anchor, where they could be guarded by the navy. Even the federation was not so foolish as to launch an attack in winter.

"There is no hope of retaking Gallifrey?" Demetrios asked.

Septimus shook his head. "It is too late in the season to sail for Gallifrey. A federation captain might make it, but not one of ours."

Ikarian captains sailed coastal routes, as their fathers and grandfathers had done before. An Ikarian vessel would take months to reach Gallifrey, while a federation vessel could journey there in less than half the time.

"Perhaps it is time to seize one of their captains and let

Nizam convince him to share with us the secret of their magics," Zuberi said.

Josan felt his head nodding, as if Lucius were prepared to consider the idea. For the first time in days he took control of their body, letting Lucius feel his revulsion at the thought of anyone in Nizam's hands. *You are quick to condemn another to a fate that you could not endure.*

Lucius's mental voice fell silent.

"We've tried it before, with no success," Septimus said. "There are no federation-crewed vessels in Karystos, and if we seize one of their captains at sea, it will be as good as a declaration of war."

He wondered why Nizam had failed. Had his victim been one who lacked the true knowledge? Had Nizam simply lacked the ability to understand what his prisoner told him? Or was the captain a victim of his country's deception? Having convinced the world that their skill at navigation was based on magic, any other explanation would be seen as a lie.

What do you know of this? Lucius's mental voice was sharp, and Josan realized his mistake. *Later,* he promised.

"We are not ready for war with the federation," Josan said. From the corner of his eye he could see Brother Nikos staring at him, but was careful not to return his regard. Nikos had no means of knowing which memories of Josan's had survived, and he must give Nikos no reason for suspicion. "But we must be ready come spring, for the decision may be taken out of our hands."

"So we are agreed to Septimus's plans," Zuberi said.

"And the senate will authorize the funds you requested for improving the fleet," Demetrios added.

The monk was hiding something. Lucius had been right to distrust him. He had known that no man could be as noble and selfless as the monk held himself to be—and yet now that he had proof of his suspicions, he could not repress a feeling of disappointment. He had wanted to be wrong.

The monk had been pitiless in his judgment, but his own flaws were equally as great.

I never judged you, the monk thought.

But you did. Every time you condemned my ignorance, my so-called cowardice, my failure to do what you wished.

That was not my judgment, that was the voice of your own conscience, the monk replied.

And what does your conscience tell you now?

There was no response.

Despite the monk's lowly opinion of him, Lucius could be patient. He did not want any trace of his internal debate to be visible to the council. He let the monk hide in silence while the council finished its deliberations, then made his way back to his chambers. Dismissing the waiting functionaries, he poured himself a glass of harvest wine, savoring its earthy flavor. Less than a fortnight before, this wine had been grapes on the vine, and he fancied he could taste the sunshine.

He felt Josan's impatience with such a comparison, but the monk had no head for the finer things. He knew only the appeal of musty books. And treachery.

It was not treachery, Josan thought.

But you are hiding something from me. Something to do with Septimus. Perhaps he was not innocent of the rebellion after all.

It is not that, Josan thought, but he volunteered no further information.

If it was not Septimus himself, then it was something else. The monk had been angered at the idea of interrogating a federation captain—understandably so, given his own history.

Lucius knew the monk thought him ignorant, but merely

because he had not memorized hundreds of scrolls did not make him any less clever. The monk had been disturbed by the mention of magic, yet all knew that federation captains traveled secret paths on the sea by using magics passed down from one captain to another.

Lucius had his own form of magic, the gift of his ancestors. Perhaps he, too, could master the secret ways of the sea, and this is what had disturbed the monk. He had always envied Lucius's talent with magic, the one thing that belonged to Lucius rather than the invader.

Lucius took another sip of wine, letting it roll on his tongue. Yes, that was it. The monk could not bear the idea that Lucius was greater than he in this way, and thus fought to keep Lucius from learning more about this magic.

It is not magic. The monk's thoughts came slowly.

I can call fire to my hand, tell storms where to strike, and heal the most grievous wound. How can this not be magic?

You have magic, but the federation captains do not. They chart their courses by the mathematics.

But how can math tell them where to sail?

An image arose in his mind, a chart of the great basin, crosshatched by numbered lines, with mathematical formulas written in the margins. He saw a second image of a table with a compass and a metal instrument, hinged at the top, with a curved piece at the bottom.

The images made no sense to him, but the monk recalled them well enough to bring them to mind.

You know how to do this? Despite his earlier doubts, it did not occur to him that the monk would lie.

No. But I know where the knowledge may be found.

The monk's mental voice fell silent for a long moment.

In the library of the collegium, Lucius guessed.

Yes.

We must go there at once. Excitement rose within him. With this knowledge the Ikarian navy would be the equal of the federation. Perhaps even its superior, for the Ikarian Empire had far greater resources to draw upon.

The knowledge belongs to the Learned Brethren. I swore an oath to guard their secrets.

An emperor's duty is to his people, he thought, taking grim satisfaction in turning the monk's own words against him. Josan was not the only one whose life had been twisted beyond all recognition.

If he could no longer be the heedless prince, then it was fitting that Josan could no longer pretend that he would one day resume the life of a scholarly monk. They were yoked together, and both must share the burden of their twinned existence.

If we do this, we make an enemy of Brother Nikos. We may not survive if he turns the council against us.

Nikos is already our enemy, Lucius thought, trying to give the impression that he had already considered this. *He will not allow us to slip out of his control. At least this way we will be ready, rather than be taken unawares.*

I hope we live to regret this, the monk thought, displaying a rare flash of humor.

As do I.

Chapter 14

Captain Elpheme drove the *Dolphin* and her crew hard, ignoring the grumbles of sailors grown soft after two months in port. After the first day, the grumbles ceased as the crew settled to their routines. Even the *Dolphin* seemed glad to be back at sea, for she bore the contrary winds with ease, cutting cleanly through the water with a speed that few ships her age could hope to match.

Restless, Ysobel volunteered to take the night watch, grateful for a few hours when she thought no further ahead than a change in the weather or the coming of dawn. But even this was a temporary respite—at the end of each watch she carefully noted their progress on the charts, watching as each day's sailing brought them closer to Melene.

Melene. The pull of home was tempered by the growing fear that she was sailing toward a maelstrom. A prudent captain would chart a new course, one that took her ship far away from such danger. To Olizon, perhaps, or even as far as Vidrun. She had instructed her other ships to sail east. Why should she not join them?

But if she did that, she would be labeled a traitor and

stripped of her holdings. With four ships she could make a life for herself in exile. But she could never return home.

Nor could her crew. And it was this, more than anything, that stayed her hand. Though she wondered how many other captains faced similar dilemmas and what courses they had charted. How far did Quesnel's reach extend? She had made herself a target, but had he begun ordering other merchants into service? If he waited much longer, the great houses would send their best vessels and valued crews out on long trading voyages, where they would, alas, be too distant to be summoned.

She spared a thought for the house of Flordelis and hoped fervently that her father had paid heed to her warning and ensured that his prized ships were beyond Quesnel's reach.

Lieutenant Burrell had no duties aboard ship to occupy him, beyond keeping a close eye on the small contingent of marines that had chosen to accompany him.

She sympathized with his boredom, though he remained outwardly cheerful. Her initial attraction to him had strengthened, and she knew enough of his character that she no longer feared that he would betray her. He was everything that she looked for in a partner—handsome, well built, and smelling of the clean scents of the sea. And best of all, he was not in her employ. Of all the men upon this ship, only Burrell and his marines were available to her.

She had no doubt that they would find pleasure in each other. But a night's pleasure was all she could offer, and she sensed that Burrell wanted more from her. And this she could not give.

She could not sail into danger with a lover at her side. She would have to be satisfied with his friendship, instead.

Burrell had taken to bringing her a cup of hot tea at the end of her shift, and then lingering after she turned the watch over to Captain Elpheme. The three would speculate on what awaited them at Melene and spend endless hours poring over the charts of the Kazagan coastline. They agreed that the port cities might be attacked, and some of them even held for a short while. But without sufficient troops to occupy the countryside, it was inevitable that the invaders would be driven off by armies from the shore.

Surely King Bayard and his councilors could see the truths that were so obvious to the three of them. Perhaps Captain Justin's words had been meant to mislead them, to provoke Ysobel into rash action. Another trap, since she had eluded the others.

A fortnight after setting sail from Gallifrey they arrived off the coast of Melene, the jagged coast lit by the waning moon. Neither Ysobel nor Elpheme had ever had cause to visit the small naval harbor on the northern end of the island, so they anchored offshore, opposite the harbor beacons.

Dawn came, revealing a harbor crowded with ships of every size and purpose. Some bore the red-striped sails of naval vessels, but most were merchant ships, deepening her unease. A pilot boat came out to meet them, directing Elpheme to anchorage, while Ysobel took a gig to shore.

The naval headquarters was easy to find, but Commodore Grenville proved more elusive. Ysobel was left to cool her heels in an antechamber as others scurried to and fro. No one paused to speak with her, but she overheard scraps of conversation—some complaining over being impressed into service, others grumbling about lack of supplies or crew. Those she saw seemed harried, but purposeful, like a merchant who had three ships arrive to be unloaded on a day when he had expected only one.

She saw no signs of the panic she would have expected if war had been declared, and she took heart from this.

It was nearly noon by the time a young woman stood at the entrance of the antechamber and called out, "Lady Ysobel?"

"Yes," she said, rising to her feet. She followed as the woman led her through the main hall, where so many others had come and gone, toward a small door in the corner. The woman knocked once, then opened the door.

"Lady Ysobel," she announced, gesturing for Ysobel to enter.

Commodore Grenville was her father's age, with broad features that hinted at ancestors from the Northern Wastes. He sat at a large table so covered in scrolls that she could see only hints of the mosaic map underneath. His fingers were ink-stained and his complexion oddly pale for a sailor. She wondered when he had last spent a day at sea and whether this boded ill for his competence.

"Come," Grenville said. "Forgive me for not rising to congratulate you on your victory at Gallifrey. I spent too long on my leg, and the healers have bade me stay off it, lest I develop rot."

With his right hand he gestured toward the wall, where a wooden leg stood in a place of honor.

"I hope it is not a recent loss," she said.

Grenville shrugged. "I've had a decade to get used to it, and it doesn't slow me down on ship. On land, however, it's a damned nuisance."

There was no polite way to ask how he had lost his leg, though she doubted the tale was as colorful as the ones Brice told. It spoke well of his character that he had remained in service rather than accepting the king's pension.

At his gesture she took a seat on a stool at the opposite side of the table, so she was no longer staring down at him.

"Your clerk has my report, and a letter from Captain Justin," she began.

Grenville nodded. "I've read them. Captain Justin ascribes your victory to luck..." He let his voice trail off, waiting to see how she would react.

"We were lucky," Ysobel said. "And the Ikarians were careless, grown complacent from too many years without a challenge."

"They will not fall for such a ruse again," he observed.

Ysobel shrugged. Let other captains plot their own tactics—she was only responsible for herself and her own ships.

"What is it you wish me to do?"

Grenville brushed aside the scrolls that covered the portion of the mosaic showing the coast of Kazagan. It was a brilliant work of craftsmanship, made up of individual tiles each no larger than a pea. The sea was shaded from deep purple to lightest blue, indicating the depths of the ocean, while differing hues of browns, yellows, and greens indicated the details of the coastline. Such a table would have cost the whole of the profits from an entire trading voyage. Its presence spoke of Grenville's wealth, or his status within the navy, or possibly both.

Looking closely at the map she could see where wax pens had been used to indicate the positions of ships along the coastline. There were a dozen triangles, and a few scattered dots, bearing incomprehensible markings.

"As you see, we have a blockade along the coast of Kazagan. The eastern portion is controlled by ships from Sendat"—here his finger traced the symbols marked in red, then moved west to the symbols marked in black—"while my command covers the rest, all the way to the border with Ikaria."

"A blockade," she echoed. "As prelude to invasion?"

"A blockade for their own safety, as protection against pirates."

"And does anyone believe this?" she asked, not bothering to hide her scorn.

Now it was Grenville's turn to shrug. "If you had been home, you would have heard the proclamation from King Bayard and the minister of war. Too long have pirates harassed our vessels and those of other peaceful nations. The federation, as the preeminent force upon the sea, had taken it upon itself to stop these predations and ensure peaceful commerce."

"To ensure that only our ships have free passage. Tell me, how many Ikarian vessels have been seized as pirates? How many of their cargoes left to rot in harbor because we would not grant them the freedom to pass through the blockade?"

"Enough," he said. "Though my ships have been told to abide by their written orders, not all commanders are so strict."

She rose to her feet, unable to sit still. "Ikaria will not tolerate this interference. They will see this as an act of war. Lord Quesnel is a fool if he thinks they will not see through this pretense. Pirates, indeed."

Grenville grew in her estimation. He did not leap to defend the war minister, nor his policies. An invasion of Kazagan would have been sheer folly, but this was nearly as bad. Quesnel had not openly declared war on the empire, but he had set them on a course that would inevitably provoke the Ikarians into declaring war. And for what possible gain? Having the Ikarians seen as the aggressors might garner the federation sympathy, but it would bring neither allies nor ships to their cause. If the federation was truly set on war, better that they had risked all with a swift, sudden attack rather than waiting for the Ikarians to organize and arm themselves.

"I take it that I am to join this blockade?"

"Yes. Your station will be at the mouth of the Naryn

River," he said. "There are four other ships there, but their captains will be junior to you."

It would be highly unusual to place a merchant captain in command over a navy vessel, so she assumed that the four ships were other merchant vessels that had been drafted into service. It was unlikely that any would be commanded by a master trader—most were far too valuable to their houses to be caught in such a trap.

"I will need some time to equip my ship and bring on provisions—"

"You can have two days. And if you give any of your crew leave, you are responsible for finding your own replacements, or sailing shorthanded."

There would be no replacements to be found, not in a navy harbor where all the other captains would be competing to ensure they had a full complement.

Even the landsmen who worked the port would have grown wary, knowing enough not to walk alone after dark nor to accept a drink from a stranger lest they awaken to find themselves at sea.

"With your leave, I will retain Lieutenant Burrell and his marines," she said.

"Of course. And when you arrive on station, you will find another familiar face. One of your captains is already there."

That was not possible. She had given strict orders that should have kept her ships safe.

"Who?" she demanded.

Grenville glanced at the cryptic symbols on the map, then hunted through his scrolls till he found the one he wanted. He unrolled it, tracing the index with one finger until he found the entry he sought.

"The *Swift Gull*," he said. "She's been there this past month, under Captain Zorion. He was one of our first volunteers."

The fear in her belly turned to anger. Volunteered. This was no mischance—Zorion had deliberately chosen to put his ship in harm's way.

"If you will excuse me, there is much to be done," she said. She needed to leave before she gave vent to her anger.

"I will send your orders to your ship, along with new orders for the captains who will be part of your company," he said.

She left, striding so swiftly that those in the crowded outer chamber scattered before her.

Grenville had given her two days, but she would need only one. They would sail tomorrow if she had to set the sails herself. She had an old friend to see.

Four days later, the *Dolphin* arrived on station, helped by favorable winds. Three navy ships with their red-striped sails were at the mouth of the river, while two sets of plain sails were visible off to the west, where Zorion and the *Gull* were presumably to be found. Curiously, there was no traffic on the river, not even a single fishing boat to be seen.

She ordered Captain Elpheme to hoist the recall banner, with the signal flags below requesting a meeting aboard the *Dolphin* at sunset. A large cauldron was brought up on deck, and pitch fire set within it, producing a column of black smoke that could be seen for miles. If the *Gull* and her companion were not under attack, they would see the smoke and the sails of a newly arrived ship and hopefully return to station.

From such a distance it was difficult to tell whether a ship was advancing or retreating, though she checked their position periodically with the glass. Finally, after an hour, the lookout confirmed what her own eyes had told her a quarter hour before—that the sails were growing larger, and the ships were sailing east.

Precisely as the last rays of the sun fell, the three navy captains arrived. Captain Elpheme met them as they came aboard, and brought the captains to what was normally the quartermaster's office, where eight stools had been set up around the chart table. It was a cramped space, but it was the largest room she had unless they wished to meet in one of the holds.

Ysobel poured heavily watered wine for her guests and offered them sliced fruits and bread that had been baked only a few days before. They introduced themselves and spoke of trifles as she waited for the others.

Zorion was the last to arrive.

"My ship and my crew, they are well?" she asked.

"The *Gull* is as sound as the day she left the dockyards, and the crew are a credit to your house," he replied.

"Good."

He took the last empty stool, crowding his large frame in between Lieutenant Burrell and Captain Chiara, who had been the senior officer here until Ysobel's arrival.

"Elpheme has orders for each of you," Ysobel began, nodding to Elpheme, who began handing out the sealed missives to each captain. "I am taking command, effective immediately. Captain Chiara, your presence is requested in Melene, where further orders will be given you."

"May I ask why a naval captain was not sent?" Chiara, who was leaving and thus had nothing to lose, asked the question that was no doubt on everyone's mind.

"Are you questioning me? Or Commodore Grenville's orders?"

"Your pardon, I did not mean to slight you," Chiara said. "Of course the commodore would not send anyone he did not have confidence in."

"The navy is stretched thin, as you must know as well as

I," Ysobel said. "I did not ask for this command, but I am prepared to do my duty."

She'd been shocked to read Grenville's orders naming her to a command that included naval ships. In times of war, merchant ships were impressed to serve alongside the navy, not to take charge of them. Then, again, by placing her in command, she alone would bear the responsibility for any mistakes—which was no doubt what Lord Quesnel had intended.

Captains Sydney and Orville were too polite to express their doubts, but from their stiff postures she knew that they bristled at being placed under her thumb. Captain Durand, who commanded the other merchant ship, appeared more at ease, or perhaps it was simply that he was too young to properly appreciate the perils of their position.

He would bear careful watching. He might have achieved his position on his own merits, or his youth could be a sign that his house had sent their experienced captains off to safety, leaving the less valuable ones to be commandeered by the navy.

"As the woman who took Gallifrey harbor, I doubt that there are any challenges here that can match what she has already faced," Burrell said.

It would have been rude to laugh at their openmouthed astonishment, though Zorion beamed broadly.

"Enough," she said. Burrell's defense warmed her, but she would not stoop to the level of trading accomplishments with these captains as if they were sailors boasting of their exploits in a dockside tavern. "Captain Chiara, if you would be so kind as to explain to me how you are enforcing the blockade? I have general orders from the commodore, but you have firsthand experience."

Chiara, who had been leaning against the table, drew herself erect. "When we first arrived, I kept all ships here at the river's mouth, so we could inspect any ship that tried to enter or leave. Traffic has diminished, so from time to time I send one or two ships to sweep up and down the coastline, to see if smugglers are trying to land along the coves rather than coming into the harbor."

"And what do your inspections encompass?" Ysobel had done her own share of ship searches at the harbor in Gallifrey, and a tedious task that had been.

"We look for forged papers concealing their ownership, weapons, or hidden cargoes," Chiara said.

"Or a ship with too many sailors, or too few," Zorion added.

"Too many crew? Or too few?"

"Too many is a sign that they are smuggling soldiers," Chiara explained. "And too few is a clear sign that pirates have taken over the vessel, killing off the lawful crew."

Ysobel closed her mouth with an audible click. "Indeed," she said.

Chiara did not hear the sarcasm in Ysobel's voice, or else she ignored it.

"And what happens to the ships that do not pass your inspection?"

"We seize the ship and set the crew ashore. Depending on the vessel, we may send it with a prize crew back to Melene, or if it cannot be turned to our service, our orders are to burn the vessel at sea," Chiara said.

"Any suspected pirates are turned over to the local authorities to be hung," Captain Orville said. "Though I suspect most are simply turned free once we return to our ships."

Burning vessels and hanging their crews as pirates. No wonder there was no traffic along the river.

"And if a ship chooses to sail past and not be searched?" she asked, though she suspected she already knew the answer.

"Then we will know them for pirates, and take appropriate measures," Chiara said.

"I trust this has not happened often."

"We've seized over a dozen vessels and sent them to Melene," Chiara said.

"To our west, Captain Ancelin has hanged four pirate crews," Captain Durand chimed in.

"Ancelin is a tad . . . strict in his observation of the rules of engagement," Chiara said. "I have found it necessary to employ a certain amount of discretion, to allow the captains time to grow accustomed to our presence."

It was madness. Sheer madness. Whatever they did here, it would not be long before the Ikarian fleet returned the favor. There would be no safety for anyone.

Any captain with the sense of a child would steer clear of these waters. Which did not speak well for Zorion, whose own orders should have taken him far to the east.

But now was not the time for expressing her own doubts. She had already chosen her course, and that was to obey the orders she had been given, however nonsensical they seemed. She listened as Chiara explained the routine of the station and the duties of each of the captains under her. The other captains chimed in from time to time, though Zorion remained silent.

At last Chiara fell silent, and Ysobel could think of no more questions to ask.

"Captain Chiara, I thank you for your counsel, and wish you a swift and safe passage back to Melene," Ysobel said.

"I wish you well in your new command," Chiara responded. "Before I leave I will send over my charts and a copy of my logbook. Any personal letters may be sent over as well."

"I will have correspondence for you as well," Ysobel said. "Grenville has asked that we make plans to winter over in these waters, so each of you should prepare a list of the supplies that you need and send it along with Captain Chiara."

"Winter here? In the harbor, perhaps . . ." Captain Orville began.

"We are not welcome in their harbors," Zorion pointed out. These were the first words he had spoken in over an hour.

"It is not firm, but you should make your lists," Ysobel said. "Send a copy to me as well, so I will know what you have requested. Do not be extravagant, but do not be parsimonious either. Better to ask and be refused than to regret it later."

Her guests rose to their feet, the tallest ducking their heads to avoid the low beams.

"Zorion, if you will stay for a moment?" she said.

"Of course."

Lieutenant Burrell and Captain Elpheme escorted the captains topside. As the door closed behind them, Zorion rose, advancing as if to embrace her, but Ysobel moved away, keeping the table between them.

"It is good to see you," he said, bracing one hand against the table as the *Dolphin* rolled in the gentle swell.

"I cannot say the same. Tell me, did you not receive my letter?"

"The one ordering your ships on extended trading voyages to the east?"

His words crushed the slender hope that she nursed— hoping against all reason that her orders had gone astray, that his presence here was an unfortunate accident. Her heart had wanted to believe in him, even as reason told her otherwise. Grenville had said that Zorion had volunteered for this duty.

"Then perhaps you were impressed as you attempted to carry out my orders," she said.

"I saw the others off, set to winter in the east and return in the spring, then took the *Gull* to Melene. I'd hoped to join up with you there, but Commodore Grenville sent me here instead, saying that you would join me in time."

"You betrayed me," she said. "You betrayed your duty to my house."

Zorion's eyes darkened. "Without you, there is no house. I came because I knew this was where you would be, and I could not bear to see you sail into danger alone."

"Bad enough that Elpheme and the *Dolphin* are already lost to this madness. Now you would have me lose the pride of my house? The *Gull* is worth more than the rest of my ships together."

Zorion slowly circled the table. "The *Gull* is a fine ship, but she is only that. A ship. You are worth more than her, more than all your ships put together."

Her anger drained away, replaced by the bitter realization that there was no way to undo what had been done. This was why her aunt had not taken Zorion as a lover until he had left her service. Nothing must be allowed to come before duty to the house. She had known that Zorion regarded her as more than a mere trader, and yet she had allowed his affection, indeed she had used it for her advantage. Now they would both pay the price.

"When the navy is done with you, I will release you from my service," she said. "You will never sail for my house again."

She wanted to hurt Zorion, the way he had hurt her. But to her surprise he nodded calmly, as if he had been expecting her condemnation.

"As long as you are still alive to give that order, I will be content."

Chapter 15

The silk curtains of his litter were plain, unmarked by any imperial emblem. But any hope for anonymity was dashed by his escort of a dozen imperial guards, led by two tattooed functionaries, making a rare appearance outside the palace walls. As the small procession wound its way through the streets of Karystos, the usual city noises were overlaid with chants of his name as the populace vied for a glimpse of their reclusive emperor.

Empress Nerissa had often been seen in the city, her public appearances carefully crafted for maximum impact. But Josan had not left the imperial quarter since his coronation. Indeed, if he had been permitted to walk the streets dressed in a simple cloak, it was doubtful that any would have recognized him.

But he was not afforded that privilege. Instead he was under close guard—as much prisoner as protected.

The rocking motion of the litter abruptly stopped, and he swayed forward before regaining his balance. The curtains on the left side of the litter were drawn back, and the functionary he had named One extended his arm to help Josan alight. Despite the assistance, his exit from the litter was less than graceful as his long tunic tangled around his knees. He grimaced sourly, wondering if this was yet another skill that an emperor was expected to master in childhood.

A high wall surrounded the grounds of the collegium. On the north side a plain door marked the public entrance. Even during the day, this door was customarily locked. The brethren did not believe in granting free access to their domain.

His escort stared at the door, apparently bewildered by the lack of response.

"You will have to announce us," Josan said.

One bobbed his head, though his tattoos masked any signs of possible embarrassment. Striding forward, he pulled the bell cord and called out, "Open for his Most Serene Emperor Lucius."

Josan felt anything but serene at the moment, but he hoped his nervousness was not visible to all.

There was a long pause before the door slowly swung open, revealing the novice on duty—a beardless boy who was a stranger to him. It was disquieting to think that all of the novices would be strangers—orphaned babes left in the brethren's care, grown into youths while he was in exile.

"The emperor?" The novice's voice squeaked with disbelief. "But—"

"I am here to view the great library," Josan said. Protocol dictated that the emperor not speak directly with such a lowly one, but it seemed ridiculous for him to address the functionary, then have the functionary repeat his words. They did not have time to waste on such ceremonies.

The novice bent over in half, his bow so awkward it was nearly a parody. "Brother Nikos is not here," the novice said, addressing the cobblestones or perhaps his own sandals.

"I have come to see the library, not the worthy Nikos," Josan said.

Indeed, he had timed this excursion carefully for when Nikos would be occupied with Zuberi's weekly meeting. Once news reached Nikos, he would come scurrying back with all speed, but by then Josan would have what he wanted.

That is, if he wasn't forced to stand outside in the street like a common beggar.

The guards around him shifted closer, and he heard raised voices from the crowd calling his name.

The empress had been known to scatter coins to her people, usually on public holidays. It was not a custom Josan could follow. His own purse was flat—he could not even buy himself a cup of sour wine. His escorts had more coins than he did.

He panicked, as he realized that he was behaving as if he were a menial, waiting to be admitted by his betters. If he could not convince a mere novice . . .

"Lead the way or fetch someone who can," Josan said.

The novice blushed and hastily bowed low. "Of course! It will be my honor, your worthiness."

"You and Seven will accompany me, but our escort may wait here," Josan said.

One raised his eyebrows, his way of expressing polite disagreement. "I have strict instructions for your safety—"

"Do you doubt the loyalty of Brother Nikos and his monks? I am as safe in the collegium as I am in my palace," Josan said.

Perhaps safer. Count Hector's killer had never been found, after all.

As the novice bowed once more, Josan passed through the door onto the grounds of the collegium, trailed by the two functionaries. The novice scurried ahead. "This way," he said, though Josan had already turned right, taking the path that led directly to the library rather than the wide hall that led to the temple and the public rooms where visitors to the collegium were received.

Within the walls, the collegium was a collection of buildings connected by courtyards and colonnades. Most visitors ventured only as far as the first building, which housed receiving rooms along with private quarters for the senior members of the order, but there were also dormitories, classrooms, kitchen, a large gathering hall, and a small temple devoted to the twin gods. Dwarfing them all in importance was the great library, which lay at the heart of their order.

The dirty, chaotic city seemed impossibly distant as they strode through the colonnade that led to the library. The sound of young voices repeating their lessons drifted over the courtyard, reminding Josan of his youth. A brother crossing the courtyard stopped to gape at the procession, then turned on his heels and ran, presumably to alert whoever was senior in Brother Nikos's absence.

The library was located at the rear of the central courtyard, a mere two stories in height, though it stretched the full width of the courtyard. Over the years, several levels had been excavated underneath the building to hold the brethren's ever-growing stores of knowledge. Unlike the other collegium buildings, which mixed wood with marble and stone, the library was made entirely of stone, with bronze doors and a tile roof, meant to safeguard the contents from fire. A short flight of steps led up to a pair of large doors, which were propped open to take advantage of the cool autumn air.

The novice, who had never given them his name, dashed ahead into the library, calling out, "Brother Alexander! Brother Alexander! The emperor is here."

Josan could hear a low voice admonishing the boy for

disturbing the sanctity of the library with his fancies. The reprimands abruptly fell silent as Josan came into view.

"Emperor Lucius, how may the brethren serve you?" Brother Alexander asked, bowing deeply.

Josan knew Alexander, with whom he had shared classes as a novice. He recalled that Alexander's talent had been for organization, not scholarship. When it came time for their first postings, Josan had been sent on a voyage of exploration while Alexander had been named as Brother Nikos's aide.

Such a close connection with Nikos was not in his favor.

"Where is Brother Hermes?" Josan asked.

Alexander blinked. "Brother Hermes died five years ago, though he would be flattered that you remember his name. I had the honor of taking his place as librarian."

"How did he die?" Josan asked. He knew that he was being careless. Prince Lucius would not have known the name of any of the monks besides his tutor, Nikos. Nor would he have been likely to care about their lives or deaths. Lucius would not have cared, but Josan had to know.

"It was his time," Alexander said.

Impossible. Brother Hermes had been librarian since Josan had been old enough to read, legendary as much for his ill temper as for his near-perfect recall of the contents and location of every volume within these walls. He was supposed to be here, part of the fabric of the collegium, a place that had remained unchanged in Josan's memories during the long years of his exile.

Josan himself had been warped beyond all recognition, but he had clung to the idea of the collegium as a place of refuge, a constant in a world that he no longer knew. Despite Nikos's corruption, he still believed that most of the brethren were men of learning. He had once had friends within these walls though it seemed their numbers were diminished.

Remembering those friends made what he was to do next all the harder.

"I wish to see the journals of Brother Josan, collected during his last voyage," he said.

Alexander paled, his eyes darting around as if looking for Nikos, or some other brother on whom he could lay this burden. "Of course. It may take some time to find his journals, but I would be happy to read them and prepare a summary for you—"

"As the learned brother is absent from the collegium, the journals will be found on the lowest level, in a box marked with his name, on the shelves from the fifteenth year of the beloved Nerissa's reign," Josan said.

"But Emperor Lucius, it is not our custom to share our private teachings with anyone—"

"I am not anyone. I am your emperor and the patron of your order. By my grace, this collegium stands in Karystos. But should I revoke that grace..." Josan let his voice trail off softly.

"Of course." Alexander beckoned the novice forward, and after a few whispered words in his ear the boy scampered off in the direction of the stairs.

He could feel Alexander's eyes upon him, wondering how it was that Emperor Lucius knew of the writings of an obscure monk. Hermes would have known immediately why someone would want those journals, but he doubted Alexander shared his predecessor's diligence.

Alexander's curiosity would be equaled by that of the functionaries who stood at his back. They must be wondering why he had not simply sent a messenger to Brother Nikos, asking for what he wanted.

He breathed the familiar scents of the library—the must of aging scrolls mixed with the rich scent of leather, and under it all the tang from the precious whale-oil lamps that supplemented the narrow glass-covered windows. His eyes wandered over the broad stone shelves, with their precious burdens of manuscripts and scrolls carefully gathered over the ages. Those in this first semipublic space would be common manuscripts, copies of which could be found in private collections and scholarly libraries. The floor above was divided into smaller rooms, each focused on a particular area of study.

The levels beneath were the repository of the private scholarship of the brethren—knowledge carefully hoarded over generations, grudgingly doled out only when it would benefit the order. Even the least scrap of paper was jealously hoarded. They would not relinquish their treasures lightly.

He was conscious of time passing. Surely a runner had been sent to fetch Brother Nikos as soon as the emperor had arrived, and he wondered how long it would take for the message to reach Brother Nikos and for Nikos to make his way back to the collegium.

"If the boy does not return swiftly, or if he returns with less than the full sum of what I have requested, I will have you both arrested for treason," he said, not bothering to look Alexander in the face.

His words had the desired effect. "Perhaps he cannot find the box. I will go myself, to assist."

"Perhaps you should."

Three of the brethren were at tables in the rear of the library, but though their eyes were fixed on the imperial visitors, none dared approach. Josan wandered over to the nearest shelves, his fingers itching to pick up the books and examine them for himself. But he could not afford to indulge his own longings.

He heard the slap of sandals against tiles and turned as two monks entered behind him.

One was Brother Mensah, who had assisted Nikos during his coronation. Clutching Mensah's arm was Brother Thanatos, who presumably had been fetched as the senior brother present.

Josan smiled and took two steps forward ready to greet his favorite teacher. But he halted as he realized that Thanatos's own face bore no look of welcome. The brother saw Lucius, not Josan, and so it must be.

"Emperor Lucius?" It was not clear if Thanatos was questioning his identity or simply his presence here. Though surely the functionaries, with their distinctive tattoos, were proof enough of his status.

"Brother," Lucius said.

"What is your purpose here?" Thanatos asked. It was far from polite, but the elderly monk had been known for his study of mathematics, not diplomacy.

"Brother Alexander is fetching some scrolls for me," Josan said.

Just then Alexander and the novice made their appearance, each carrying a wooden box.

Josan moved to the nearest table. "Bring them here," he said, with an imperiousness that would have done credit to Lucius himself.

He waited impatiently as the boxes were set down. "Your knife," Josan said, holding out his hand to Brother Alexander.

Alexander hesitated, then withdrew a slender knife from the writing case at his belt. Josan took the knife, then carefully sliced through the wax seals that held the lid closed. Prying up the lid, he peered inside and saw a half dozen journals, each labeled with his own precise script. He opened each one in turn, paging through it to ensure that these were indeed his writings and not some other monk's works hastily relabeled in hopes of fooling him.

Satisfied, he replaced the lid, then turned his attention

to the second box. Inside he found a book of charts that he had brought back from Xandropol, along with four more journals from earlier that year.

Everything was as he remembered. His plan had worked—the mere presence of the emperor within their domain had startled the brethren into submission. They would have ignored a written order, or cobbled together a set of nonsense journals that would be useless to him. But by arriving in person, he had given them no opportunity to deceive.

Brother Thanatos came up beside him, peering over his shoulder at the boxes. "That is Brother Josan's writing," he said, wonderingly. "I thought Nikos had burned everything of his, for fear of contagion."

At the word *contagion,* Josan's escort drew back a pace.

But Thanatos, undaunted, reached for the journals with one trembling hand. Josan swiftly replaced the lid before Thanatos could touch the journals. It hurt to deny his former teacher, but if anyone were to be able to reason out the significance of these writings, it would be Thanatos.

"The empire has need of them," Josan said. Lucius would not have bothered to explain his actions but Josan felt he owed Thanatos that much.

"But you cannot take them," Thanatos said. "They belong to the order."

It seemed Thanatos had the courage that Alexander lacked. Or merely a poorer sense of self-preservation.

"The emperor has commanded them," One said, moving to place himself between the elderly monk and the emperor.

"But—" Thanatos objected.

"The knowledge in here must be studied rather than left to molder in the dark," Josan said. "It is what Josan would have wanted."

Even this was a lie. The scholarly monk Josan had believed that knowledge should be shared for the benefit of all. He would have been appalled at the idea that his work would be used for political gain.

Thanatos shook his head, seemingly unconvinced, but Alexander grabbed his arm, and Thanatos let himself be silenced.

At Josan's gesture Seven picked up both boxes, easily carrying them in one arm.

Josan paused for one last glance around the library. He was tempted to linger, for surely there were other books here with knowledge that he could use to his advantage. Books that would explain the source of Prince Lucius's magic, or perhaps even the spell that had combined their souls in a single body. But mentioning such topics would raise questions he could ill afford to answer.

As he turned and left the library, he knew that this chance would never come again. As soon as he left, the monks would begin moving their most prized manuscripts, burying them elsewhere or taking them out of the city to safety. Once he would have been in their number, eagerly protecting their precious knowledge from defilement. Instead he was the barbarian who had disturbed the sanctity of the collegium, bringing strife and politics within its walls.

But he was not the first to do so. Nikos had defiled this place long ago. Still, Josan's own hands were no cleaner.

He quickened his steps, as anxious to be gone from here as he had been to arrive. He was nearly at the gate when he saw Brother Nikos hurrying in.

"Emperor Lucius, I beg your pardon, I did not receive your message that you intended to call upon me. My most humble apologies for not being present to greet you when you arrived."

Nikos's words were gracious, but his face was flushed, as much from anger as from his hasty return. His eyes drifted from Josan to Seven and the boxes that he carried.

"What is the meaning of this?" he asked, his voice sharp. It was not the tone of a man speaking with his emperor.

"Seven, One, you will go outside and inform my escort to make ready," Josan said. "I would speak with Brother Nikos privately."

One glanced at Nikos, then back at Josan, before nodding. Brother Alexander and the young novice quickly discovered reason to be elsewhere, leaving only Josan and Nikos standing among the pillars.

"Is this a jest? Do you think to challenge me?" Brother Nikos asked. "You forget, with a word to Zuberi I can see you broken, sent back to Nizam where you belong. Zuberi already despises you—how long do you think you will live once he realizes that you are an abomination?"

Josan shrugged. "Punish me and you damn yourself," he said, pretending that he still believed this to be true. Once the threat would have worked, but Nikos had had months to destroy any evidence of his role in the cursed spell that had placed the soul of a dying monk in the body of the traitorous prince. It would be Nikos's word against Lucius's, and it was clear whom Zuberi would believe.

Josan needed proof of a different sort if he was to challenge Nikos. Proof that he had just obtained—but did Nikos realize this? Nikos had seen the boxes, but would he know what it was that Josan sought? Had he even realized what Josan had discovered before he condemned both man and his writings to obscurity?

If Nikos had been a true scholar, he would have known the value of Josan's journals and sought to disseminate that knowledge. But Nikos was a politician instead and assumed all other men thought as he did.

He must not suspect the true purpose of Josan's errand here today.

"I knew you would not help me free myself," Josan said. "If I am to break this curse, I must do so on my own."

Brother Nikos ventured a thin-lipped smile. "There are no scrolls that will help you. In his remorse, Brother Giles destroyed all records of what he had done."

Nikos turned as if to pass through the gate, and Josan knew he could not allow Nikos to examine the boxes. He must find something to distract Nikos's attention.

Summoning his anger, he demanded, "Where is my body?"

Nikos turned back to face him but did not answer.

Josan grasped Nikos's shoulders with both hands, and shook him. "What did you do with my body?"

It was a thought that had occupied him on countless sleepless nights, ever since he had learned that the body he wore was not his own.

He shook Nikos again, pleased to see Nikos's eyes widen as he finally realized his own danger. Nikos might have more political power, but physically he was no match for Lucius.

"Your disease-ravaged corpse was dumped in the harbor, along with the trash," Nikos said. "I imagine the scavengers made short work of it."

Josan's stomach roiled. He had known that his body was gone, but had hoped for a peaceful spot in the catacombs with the brothers who had gone before him if he was denied the honor of a funeral pyre. But to be dumped in the harbor like a criminal, his flesh torn apart by sea creatures even as his soul survived in another? It did not bear contemplation.

We will join you in the harbor if you do not leave before Brother Nikos suspects the true purpose of our errand, Prince Lucius murmured. *We will have our vengeance, but not today.*

The gods must be laughing if Lucius counseled patience.

Reluctantly, Josan released Nikos, then turned on his heel. He held his breath as he made his way toward the door, wondering if his gamble had succeeded. If Nikos tried to keep him here . . . He did not know whom the functionaries would obey.

But there was no raised voice, no footsteps behind him. Nikos thought Josan in search of a cure for the soul-madness, and assumed that the boxes he had taken were what remained of Brother Giles's studies. He should have inspected the boxes for himself.

Thanatos would never have made that mistake. Nor would Hermes or any of the other true members of the brethren. As Josan allowed himself to be helped into the litter, he vowed that Nikos's arrogance would be his undoing.

Josan had chafed at his confinement, yet he felt a sense of relief when he was finally within the palace walls once more. The crowds that had followed his litter had grown increasingly restive once they realized that he would not scatter coins, nor even show his face. The cheers had turned to jeers and loud-voiced speculation that the emperor hid because he was a disfigured eunuch. At this, he was grateful that Lucius slumbered—it could have been a coincidence, but it seemed all too likely that the slighted maidservant had indeed spread her tale far and wide.

If Josan had followed his first instinct and traveled without escort, he doubted they would have contented themselves with mere insults.

He was surprised to find he had been gone less than two hours. He needed to speak with Proconsul Zuberi, but if the past was any guide, Zuberi would still be meeting with his ministers and would not welcome any interruption. Instead he would use the time to discover as much as he could about the knowledge contained within his journals.

Josan startled Ferenc by commandeering his clerk's entire supply of blank parchment, then retreated back to his sitting room, where Seven had placed the two precious boxes. He emptied them on the table, arranging his notebooks in chronological order. Glancing through the book of charts, he made a list of which pages most urgently needed to be copied.

He opened the final journal of that year, paging through until he found the record of his calculations from the last day of his voyage back to Karystos.

He puzzled over the symbols, written in jagged script rather than his normal clear handwriting. His hand had trembled when he had written these formulas—perhaps from the motion of the ship, or perhaps this was the first symptom of the breakbone fever that had struck him down only days after his return.

A chill ran down his spine as he wondered if the contagion still lingered on these pages. The monks held that the fever came from the miasma that surrounded swamps, breeding in the stagnant water. But this was belief, not verified fact ...

Despite his fears, he did not move. It was not courage, but rather necessity, that kept his hand steady as he traced the symbols on the page. Their forms were familiar but their sequences were not. Still, this was proof that he had once understood the science of navigation, and what he had once discovered he could relearn.

These pages were the conclusions of his research, and he used the weighted stones on his writing table to hold the journal open to that page. Then he picked up the first journal of that year, from when he first began his studies in

Xandropol. He skimmed through his account of his arrival in Xandropol, then lingered over a sketch of a quadrant. He seemed to recall that the first quadrant he had studied had been flawed, without the engravings necessary to perform accurate calculations, and indeed it was featureless in his sketch.

He had once owned a quadrant made in the federation style, but it had not been stored with his writings. He would have to acquire another one, and he wondered if he could order Admiral Septimus to seize the navigation instruments from the first federation vessel he came across. Though such a tactic would give away the element of surprise. Instead, perhaps he could find a simple quadrant and transform it for celestial navigation. The details were surely buried somewhere within his notes—he would not have forgotten to record such vital details.

He continued reading, pausing from time to time to take careful notes. Lost in study, he was oblivious to his surroundings. He might have been in his cell at the collegium, or in the alcoves of the great university at Xandropol. Nothing mattered except unraveling the mysteries upon the page.

He heard a shout and lifted his head, wondering who had disturbed the sanctuary. He blinked in confusion, still lost in the memories of those long years ago.

"And what did you hope to accomplish with your little visit?" Proconsul Zuberi demanded. "A private consultation with Nikos, perhaps? Or do you wish me to believe that you went there to pray?"

Zuberi. The palace. The missing years came back to him in a rush, and his mind scrambled to make the transition from scholar to an emperor fighting for his life.

"You had no permission to leave the palace," Zuberi said, his voice tight with anger.

"I did not know that I needed your permission," Josan said.

"Anything you do requires my permission, or have you forgotten your place?"

Zuberi towered over him, but Josan remained seated. He would not allow Zuberi to provoke him.

"I did not go to see Nikos; I knew he was with you. I went for these," Josan said, indicating the journals on the table before him.

Zuberi barely glanced at the table. "The functionaries tell me that you went to the collegium and spoke only with the monks. Tell me, was this a test of how you were regarded in the city? Or a meeting with a conspirator who failed to show?"

Zuberi saw plots everywhere, except for the one that was right under his nose. It was time to enlighten him.

"Do you remember our discussions with Admiral Septimus?" Josan asked, leaning back in his seat. He knew his appearance of ease would infuriate Zuberi. "He reminded us that the federation ships outsail ours because they employ sorcerers."

"What of it?"

"Only this," Josan said. He picked up the journal he had been reading, turning back to the page that he had marked earlier. "I think you will find this interesting."

Zuberi stared at him for a long moment, then finally accepted the book. His eyes flickered back and forth as he read down the page.

Josan could see the moment when he reached the entry for *A study of the methods for calculating a ship's position using celestial reckoning.*

"What of it?" Zuberi asked.

"The federation captains do not practice sorcery. They use mathematical formulas taught from one generation to the next, preserved by oaths of secrecy."

"Impossible."

"Think on it. How many ships do they have? How many sorcerers would they need to craft magic tools for all of them? How could it be that all their captains possess the gift for practicing magic?"

Josan elaborated each point, but Zuberi was not swayed by mere logic.

"So you, the boy who could never be found for his studies, now fancies himself a scholar."

"I am not the man I was as a youth, but the same can be said for all men," Josan replied. "The secret to making our ships the equal of the Seddonians' is contained within these pages, waiting for me to decipher it."

"So you stole these books before Nikos could bring them to me? Seeking to prove your worth by claiming them for your own?"

"Nikos held these journals for years without speaking of them. He knew what they would mean to the empire, but he held his tongue rather than revealing the secrets of his order."

Zuberi was prejudiced, but he was not stupid. He turned the journal over in his hands as he considered what Josan had told him. Mere words would not be enough, but the evidence was in Josan's favor, from the boxes with their carefully labeled dates to the fact that the functionaries must have told Zuberi of the brethren's reluctance to part with the journals.

He still did not know if Nikos had understood Josan's discoveries and willfully concealed this knowledge, or if Nikos had simply overlooked the importance of the journals in his haste to hide all evidence of Josan's existence. It did not matter—even if Nikos was not guilty of deception in this matter, he was still guilty of far greater crimes.

"Why should I trust you?" Zuberi asked.

"I do not ask you to trust me. But I am telling you that

you cannot trust Nikos. He puts his own ambitions first, in all things."

"Nikos was the one who proposed you as emperor," Zuberi said.

"Nikos underestimated me," Josan said. "He remembered the man I once was and thought he could control me."

It was the truth, of a sort. He knew Zuberi would take his words as reference to the callow Prince Lucius, while in actuality Nikos had seen the young monk Josan, sworn to vows of obedience.

"You have five days to prove to me that there is worth to be found in these pages," Zuberi said, handing him back the journal. "I will deflect Nikos's anger for that long. But if you are proven a liar—"

"And when I have proven the truth of my claims, what will happen to Nikos?" Josan asked.

Zuberi smiled, his wasted flesh creating a ghastly resemblance to a grinning skull. "One of you is a traitor," he said. "And he will meet a traitor's fate."

Chapter 16

Ysobel peered at the charts spread across the table, the hanging lantern casting flickering shadows as the *Dolphin* rocked at anchor. She'd discovered a sheltered cove on her last patrol, and though it had been empty, the scarred beach showed that it had recently been used to transfer cargo. But it was at the edge of her area of responsibility— she'd only happened on it by chance. And if she shifted her patrol to extend this far, it meant leaving other equally accessible beaches unguarded.

Once again, she cursed those who had thought up this scheme. A blockade was a useful tactic for dealing with a port or river mouth, but impractical to apply to an entire country. Even if every ship of the federation was pressed into service, it would be impossible to keep watch along the entire coastline. All that Ysobel and the other captains could do was to watch the major ports and send periodic patrols out to catch those trying to sail around the blockade.

Before the blockade, Kazagan had dozens of thriving ports, serving local vessels as well as traders from Ikaria and Seddon. A few ships still sailed the traditional routes, submitting to the required inspections with poor grace. Others took to the open sea—perhaps because their cargoes could not stand inspection or because their captains did not trust the integrity of those enforcing these blockades. Some of these ships reached harbor safely, while others simply disappeared, their fates unknown.

Harbors that had once welcomed the rare goods brought by federation traders had turned hostile, and those who dared venture into Kazagan ports often found no one willing to buy their goods.

Established trading houses stood to lose fortunes if the disruption of trade continued, while the people of Kazagan would learn to adapt. What they could no longer gain from the sea, they could trade for overland from Ikaria or Thrasi. The longer the blockade wore on, the less important the sea trade would become.

The federation's strategy made no sense to Ysobel, and she wished she had been present for the deliberations of King Bayard and his councilors. Were they hoping that the Kazagans would recognize the federation's strength and be willing to join an alliance against Ikaria? Such a tactic might have worked if the Ikarian legions that occupied western Kazagan had been called north, but so far there was no sign of the hoped-for civil war. Instead of impressing the Kazagans with their strength, the federation had only succeeded in convincing them that they were not to be trusted.

No one with any sense believed that the federation was solely interested in pursuing pirates, though Ysobel did her best to ensure that the ships under her command followed their orders to the letter, offering no provocation to honest captains regardless of which country they claimed as their home port.

Originally, she'd stationed the two navy ships at the mouth of the Naryn River. Any ships entering or leaving the river knew that they would be searched, so it was unlikely they would find any contraband.

Captain Zorion and the *Swift Gull* had been dispatched to keep watch on the coastline to the west, investigating the numerous small coves and sandy beaches for signs of smugglers. She sent Captain Durand along with him. Should they encounter anything larger than a coastal dhow, they were instructed to observe and report back rather than engaging. But the slower speed of Durand's vessel made it an awkward match. Eventually, she detached him to duty at Naryn with Captain Sydney, and had Captain Orville join the *Swift Gull* on her patrols.

Zorion had not wanted to be parted from her, but logic dictated that Ysobel and the *Dolphin* should sweep the eastern routes. Of all the merchants, the *Dolphin*—with her armaments and contingent of marines—was best equipped to sail alone.

Her own patrols consisted of long periods of routine punctuated by a few brief hours of excitement. Thrice they had caught sight of sails fleeing their approach—one outsailed them, but the other two were caught and boarded.

There was little finesse required in these encounters—once they drew close enough, the ballistae fired linked chain shot to foul her opponent's rigging. Grapples joined the two ships together, then Lieutenant Burrell and his marines led the boarding party. The first ship fought back, its crew managing to kill two of the *Dolphin*'s sailors before being overpowered. The second ship was a dhow with a mere dozen aboard who surrendered at once when faced with the formidable *Dolphin*.

Neither of the captured vessels contained obvious contraband, but according to the rules of engagement, flight was seen as an admission of guilt. She seized the ships, placing their officers and most of their crews in chains for the journey back to Naryn. There she put the crews ashore, over the objections of Captain Sydney, who would have hung them as pirates.

Sending the vessels to Melene required prize crews she could not spare, but neither could she endure ordering good ships burned for no reason. In the end she cobbled together a small prize crew for each, with instructions to return on the next supply ship.

Every two to three weeks a ship came from Melene, bearing sealed dispatches and fresh provisions. Yesterday's ship had brought instructions from Commodore Grenville that they were to remain on blockade throughout the winter.

It was a risky gamble—merchant ships did not sail during the winter months, when frequent storms would catch ships on open water, driving them against reefs and coastlines. Storms arose with little warning—a fair day could turn into a tempest in mere hours. Sail too far out to sea, and a captain risked being caught by the worst of the storms, as she herself had been on one memorable occasion. Sail too close to shore and a ship would have no room to maneuver when caught by contrary winds. Only a sheltered anchorage provided safety, and the Kazagans controlled the best anchorages.

Only the foolhardy or those with no other choice sailed the winter seas. Which would make the task of enforcing the blockade simpler, since it could be assumed that any ship she saw was a smuggler or an enemy. Earlier dispatches had contained the news that the Ikarian navy was on the move, once again patrolling their coastline. Whether they would choose to challenge the federation's blockade during winter was anyone's guess.

Grenville had sent supplies, but provisions, canvas, cording, and spare timbers could only do so much. Ships needed time at dock to scrape the weeds off their hulls, replace aging spars or masts, and purchase any items that the crew could not fashion for themselves. Each of the ships in her command had scars to show for their encounters, and it was only a matter of time before one was damaged too severely to be repaired at sea.

She did not intend to be caught short, nor to have her ships fall victim to the storms. She knew she could not rely upon the navy to provide for her, so she sent Zorion, with his long experience of trading in these waters, to sound out the Kazagans. The river port would not have them, but to the west, the town of Samos had a decent harbor, and there were those there that still thought well of the house of Flordelis even as they despised the federation navy. Ysobel's personal guarantee of the debt brought agreement that their ships—including the two navy vessels—could anchor there in foul weather and obtain the services of a shipwright if needed.

She'd sent news of the agreement to Melene along with a request that the navy send the necessary funds. But she suspected that she would receive a letter praising her initiative while absolving the navy of any responsibility for her debts.

Making a final notation on the chart for her next patrol, she turned her attention to the list of supplies that Grenville had sent. As soon as Zorion and Orville returned from patrol, she would ask for a list of their stores on hand, so she could best determine how to allocate the supplies among her command. She had much to do, and little time before winter came.

Ysobel stared across the wardroom table at Captain Ancelin. "What would you have us do? We have a dozen ships between us, nearly half of them merchant vessels. The Ikarian navy has two dozen ships in the harbor—and the support of the natives."

"Our duty is to take Izmar and destroy the Ikarian vessels within," Captain Ancelin replied.

"We might as well challenge the Sea Witch," Ysobel said.

She was amused to note that Ancelin instinctively made the hand gesture to ward off evil as if he were a common sailor rather than a veteran naval captain.

Though what benefit his years of experience provided, she could not say. Responsible for patrolling the area west of her station, he'd reportedly seized numerous pirate vessels and hanged their crews, though in the privacy of her own thoughts she wondered just how many of his victims had deserved their fates.

The captured ships were property of the Ministry of War, but from the look of his personal quarters, it appeared that Ancelin had helped himself to a few things before dispatching his prizes. She'd never before been on a navy ship that boasted mahogany furniture, nor a table set with elaborate crystal and silver plate.

Ysobel was especially troubled by the silver—an impractical luxury aboard a ship where it would swiftly tarnish in the salt air. His crew must have spent hours polishing the silver in preparation for this dinner and would spend hours polishing it again after it had been used.

Captain Ancelin's orders gave him seniority over her, and his every action seemed designed to put her in her place. She wished that Elpheme were here, or Burrell, or even Captain Zorion, though their relationship was still chilly. But Ancelin had summoned only herself and the navy captains in his command to join him. The merchant captains were ignored, as were Captains Sydney and Orville, who were evidently tainted by being under her command.

The dinner consisted of seven courses, an unheard-of indulgence on shipboard, and Ancelin refused to allow any discussion of business while they ate. Instead he recounted stale gossip and tales of the exploits of his youth.

Only when the plates were removed did the conversation turn serious.

"Tell me, how is it that such a large detachment was able to reach Izmar undetected?" she asked.

Ancelin grimaced. "I was engaged elsewhere, as were most of my ships. I'd left one ship on station to watch Izmar, but they saw a strange sail on the horizon and sailed in pursuit, leaving the port unguarded. When they returned, they saw the masts of the Ikarians in the harbor and prudently retreated so they could report."

It was no explanation at all. Izmar was the most important port in his patrol area. It was a medium-sized town whose value was its proximity to the capital of Kazagan, which lay a week's ride inland. A broad road connected Izmar and the capital, and thus it was often used to supply the Ikarian troops garrisoned in the capital.

Anyone with the sense of a clam would have recognized that the road ran both ways. Izmar could be used to send supplies into the capital, or serve equally as well as a staging area for soldiers sent to help break the federation's blockade.

Ancelin should have stationed at least half of his ships to guard Izmar. A single ship was useless. Perhaps the captain had indeed sailed off to investigate another ship, or perhaps he had simply turned tail and fled when faced with such overwhelming odds.

Though in some ways one had to admire the Ikarians. They were merely adequate sailors, but nonetheless had undertaken an ambitious voyage in the midst of winter. Their presence signaled a change in imperial strategy. So far the ships had not challenged the federation patrols that still passed along the coast, but their mere presence at Izmar was a threat.

She knew Septimus from her time in Ikaria, and knew him well enough to know that his ambition would be tempered by caution. He would not have sent the ships here on an idle whim. Their presence was a reminder to the federation that Ikaria claimed all of Kazagan as its protectorate, from its beaches to the inland plains.

The Ikarians now had the advantage of numerical superiority. Should they seek out a sea battle, the sheer numbers of the Ikarian ships would overwhelm them. Fortunately, most of her ships held the advantage of speed and could simply sail away from danger.

But sailing away meant abandoning the blockade, and that they could not do.

Ancelin had dispatched one of his ships to Melene, requesting reinforcements and instructions. He'd dispatched a second ordering her to join him in keeping watch over Izmar. She and her ships had spent a week here on station, waiting for orders from Melene that never came. Either their message had never reached Melene, or Commodore Grenville had far weightier matters on his mind than the fate of two of his patrols.

Too impatient to wait any longer, Ancelin had summoned her to discuss plans for an attack. In vain, she tried to point out the folly of such a move, but he overrode her objections. His orders gave him seniority, and it was clear that he relished being able to put a master trader in her place.

"As long as they do not challenge us, there is no need for undue haste," she said. "The *Swift Gull* is the fastest of our ships. Let her carry your message to Melene, so that we may be certain that whatever we do next is in accordance with Commodore Grenville's will."

Heads nodded around the table, as no one wanted to take responsibility for provoking the Ikarians into open warfare. Though Ancelin's officers held their tongues, unlike a council of merchant captains that would have broken into lively debate. She had been told that such blind obedience was a sign of discipline, but to her it was far more frightening than the presence of the Ikarian fleet.

Ancelin stroked his chin thoughtfully, and for a moment she thought she had won. But then he spoke and dashed her hopes.

"No, I will not dally and be thought a coward," he said. "My orders were that no ships would be allowed to pass unchallenged. The Ikarian ships are a threat to those orders and must be destroyed."

She could not reason with him. He was the personification of the worst of the navy—overconfident in his prowess and slavish in his adherence to orders, even when circumstances had changed.

Had he been in a merchant's service, he would never have risen to an officer's rank—yet he now controlled Ysobel's fate and the fate of those who followed her.

It was almost enough to make one believe in the meddling of a malevolent god. Zorion would say that the Sea Witch was still angry with Ysobel for choosing politics over seamanship, though Ysobel had long ago repented that choice. Would that she could take comfort in believing herself a helpless pawn of the gods, but she knew that her own actions had helped to bring her here. Though there was blame enough to share, from King Bayard and his councilors, to Commodore Grenville, who had failed to keep Ancelin in check, down to the cowardice of those captains who sat at this table and yet refused to point out the risks inherent in Captain Ancelin's plan.

It was left to her to salvage what she could from this mess.

"Tell me of Izmar harbor," she said. "Have you been able

to spy out where the ships are anchored? How many other vessels are wintering over?"

Her abrupt change of subject caught Ancelin by surprise. He blinked once, then turned to his aide, Lieutenant Danel.

"Fetch the charts, and I will explain my plan," Ancelin said. "I think you will find that I have thought of everything."

Ysobel shivered as the damp winter wind cut through her cloak and tried not to think about how much colder the sea would be. From above her came the distinctive crack of canvas catching the wind, and she peered up into the darkness to see that the first course of sails had been set, the weathered canvas merely a lighter shade of gray in the dark night. In moments the second course was set and the sailors began to scramble down to the deck.

There were no shouted orders, and only the thin sliver of the waning moon to guide them as the sailors made their way to the port side and scrambled down the nets to the waiting rowboat. Ysobel waited by the tiller until she saw Captain Elpheme wave her right hand, indicating that the rowboat was safely away. A second rowboat was then launched, the six-man crew moving to take their position at the edge of the breakwater.

Crossing to the center of the deck, Elpheme uncovered the barrel of lamp oil that had been placed there, and tipped it over. A second barrel followed the first, and a thick pool of oil began to spread over the deck.

"Now," Ysobel said.

Lieutenant Burrell swung his axe and cut the anchor rope in two. The *Dolphin* lurched into motion, the fierce winds catching the sails. Ysobel held the tiller with both hands as the ship heeled to port, then righted herself and began heading for the mouth of Izmar harbor.

Behind her, spread out in a staggered semicircle, were the rest of Ancelin's ships, her own *Swift Gull* among them. They had spent the last four days refining their plans as they waited for the winds to turn in their favor. The winds were not as strong as she would have liked, but they were finally blowing onshore, and if they did not attack tonight, they would have to wait days before the moon would be bright enough to try again.

Ancelin lacked the patience for waiting, and Ysobel had not tried to dissuade him. It was victory enough that he had agreed to her plan. And if it must be done, it was better done swiftly.

As she passed the breakwater that guarded the harbor, she could see the dark bulk of the close-packed Ikarian ships, their masts like skeletons reaching toward the stars. There were faint pinpricks of light from each ship, showing that there were men on watch. She strained her eyes but could see no signs that an alarm had been raised.

They were complacent, confident in their superior numbers. The ships had anchored side by side, so close that sailors could jump from one ship to another at need. In case of an attack, defenders from the inner ships could quickly swarm to the defense of those on the edges of the anchorage.

The tight group of Ikarian vessels occupied the whole of the northern end of the narrow harbor, while native craft took up the rest. There was very little room to maneuver, which was precisely what Ysobel was counting on.

Captain Elpheme came to her side as they passed into the inner harbor.

"We'll hold to this course," Ysobel said.

As Ysobel held the tiller steady, Elpheme lashed it into place. Elpheme's face was studiously blank, showing none of the emotion she must feel. Ysobel wondered if her own visage was as bleak as she felt.

"We've been spotted," Burrell said, pointing off to starboard, where Ysobel could see someone standing in a small boat, waving a lantern in challenge. Ancelin had reported that there were no nightly patrols, but either his intelligence was faulty or this was something new since the Ikarians had arrived.

It did not matter. There was nothing the Ikarians could do to stop them.

Ysobel imagined she could hear the sound of bells as crews were hastily called to duty, shouted orders mixed with the sound of pounding feet.

For a moment she pitied those crews.

"It is time," Burrell prompted. He held out a torch.

Elpheme reached for it, but Ysobel stayed her hand. "No."

"This is my ship," Elpheme insisted.

"It is mine," Ysobel said. "My ship, my responsibility."

She took the torch, and Burrell uncovered the small brazier of coals that he had been guarding against the wind. The torch caught fire rapidly.

Ysobel walked toward the deckhouse, stopping as her feet reached the edge of the pool of lantern oil. "You were a good ship and served me well," she said. "I beg forgiveness for what I must do."

With a flick of her wrist she tossed the torch, which spun in an arc before landing on the deck.

The lantern oil caught fire immediately, and the flames began to spread, leaping up the oil-soaked rags that led from the deck to the rigging above.

Ysobel watched for a moment, until she was forced to step back as the flames approached her feet. Already the sails were beginning to catch fire—a sight sure to strike terror in any sailor's heart.

A fire-ship. The only defense was to run, but in the narrow harbor there would be little chance for escape.

Ysobel doffed her cloak, and the cold wind bit cruelly through the simple shirt and leggings that were all she wore underneath. Returning to the stern she saw that Burrell and Elpheme had stripped off their cloaks as well.

She could have done this without them, but they had refused to leave her. Untying her sandals, she placed her right hand on the taffrail.

"Once in the water, swim for yourselves," she said. "Don't wait, don't look back. Landers will be waiting with the small boat just beyond the breakwater."

"Yes, ma'am," they said.

"Go," she said. "I will be the last."

Burrell balanced on the rail for a moment before dropping into the water below. She held her breath until he surfaced, and began to swim. Elpheme jumped next, briefly disappearing under the waves before bobbing back up.

Ysobel hesitated. It felt wrong to leave a good ship to perish without a single member of her crew. If Elpheme had been here on her own, she might have chosen to stay with her ship to the bitter end.

But Ysobel had greater responsibilities. She vaulted over the taffrail and plunged into the water below.

The icy water cut through her like a knife, even as she struggled to the surface. Her lungs were paralyzed, fighting to draw breath. She turned away from the blazing *Dolphin* until she could see the white foam where the sea broke over the rocks, marking the entrance of the harbor. It seemed impossibly far away, and she cursed herself for delaying so long, even as she began to swim.

She saw a dark shape moving ahead of her, but lacked the breath to call out. The winter seas would sap even the strongest of swimmers. A man could endure a quarter hour at need. A half hour was possible, but any longer and they would become paralyzed and drown.

She swam as her arms burned, and her legs grew so numb that she no longer knew if she was kicking or merely dragging them behind her. She listened for the sound of shouts or muffled oars, waiting for the patrol boat to catch up to her, but there was no sound of pursuit.

At last she passed the breakwater and saw the crew of the rowboat frantically waving their lantern. The voices that called for her spoke her own tongue, and she redoubled her efforts.

As her fingers brushed the side of the rowboat, she stared up at it stupidly, wondering what to do next.

"Your hand," Landers said. "Give me your hand."

Ysobel reached up with both arms, which were swiftly caught. She was heaved on board, her belly scraping against the side of the boat until she was over the side, then she collapsed in a heap on the floor of the boat.

Strong arms helped her sit up, and someone threw a blanket over her shoulders.

She was too cold to shiver and knew this for a bad sign.

The sailing master held a metal cup to her mouth, and she gulped a mixture of lukewarm tea and brandy, which burned a trail down her gullet.

"Elpheme? Burrell?" she asked, as her teeth began to chatter.

"Burrell is behind you," someone said, and she turned her head to observe him huddled under his own blanket. "There's no sign of Captain Elpheme."

"She jumped before me," Ysobel said. "We will wait for her."

Elpheme had sworn herself a strong swimmer. Ysobel would never have agreed to her presence otherwise, no matter that Elpheme was the last captain the *Dolphin* would ever have.

Bracing herself, she rose from the floor of the boat, and the rowers moved apart so she could sit between them. She looked back into the harbor. The *Dolphin,* ablaze from the waterline to the top of her masts, had reached the anchored ships. She watched as wind-fanned sparks jumped from the *Dolphin* to the first ship, then to another, their furled canvas and pitch-coated lines providing ready fuel for the hungry flames.

The ships were too closely anchored together to avoid their fates. On a calm night, they might have had a chance, but the wind would spread the fires too swiftly for even the bravest crews.

Burrell moved to sit beside her, offering silent support. She resisted the urge to lean against him.

They watched in silence, save for one man who whispered a litany of prayers. The burning ships lit the harbor, and she could see signs of activity as desperate captains cut their anchor chains and tried to break for freedom. In such chaos they hindered each other, but at last one ship broke free and began heading for the harbor mouth.

"It's time to go," Burrell said.

There had been no sign of Elpheme. Whether by deliberate choice or the cruelty of the cold seas, Captain Elpheme had perished with her ship.

Ysobel was numb, as much from the events of this night as from the cold that had soaked through into her bones. She was responsible for what she saw. She alone had come up with this plan, and when Ancelin had refused to offer one of his vessels, she had chosen to sacrifice one of her own ships to carry it out.

It would be hailed as a brilliant success. Any stragglers that managed to escape the inferno of the harbor would be easily captured by Ancelin and his ships. By the time the sun rose, the Ikarian naval presence here would be destroyed.

Ancelin's plan for a daylight invasion could have cost them all their lives. She should take comfort in having won the victory at so little cost, but instead she felt the first stirrings of grief. She had a ship and a friend to mourn, and a weight on her soul that would never ease.

"Take us to the *Gull*," she said, and as the rowers bent their backs to the oars she turned one last time to look at the harbor before turning away.

Chapter 17

After Zuberi left, Josan continued his studies, waving off the pleas of his servants that he stop to eat and rest. As their requests grew firmer, so, too, did his refusals. Finally, only Eleven, the oldest of the functionaries, was left, along with a young boy to tend the lamps. The boy, at least, had the good sense to fall asleep. When Eleven went to shake the boy awake, Josan demurred. "I will call him when I need him."

Eleven merely grunted, settling back down on his cushion. The only sounds were the soft hiss of the burning lamps, punctuated by the boy's snores and the sound of Josan's pen scratching across parchment.

The journals were harder to read than he had expected. The handwriting was clear, but the words were not. They were filled with abbreviations and references to works that he no longer possessed. It was the language of scholars, one that he had not spoken for eight years.

He dimly remembered his journey to Xandropol, and his months of study that had culminated in the observations recorded in these journals. But he could not remember what it felt like to be that man—to unlock the secrets that the federation traders had so jealously guarded. The man who had written these journals seemed a stranger to him—distanced not just by the passage of years but by the sum of his experiences.

The monk who had gone to Xandropol had been a brilliant young scholar, already hailed as one of the finest minds of his generation. But for all his knowledge, the monk had been innocent—heedless of the wider world around him. He had maintained that innocence during the long sea voyage back to Ikaria, eager to share his knowledge with his brethren. But instead of the respect of his peers, he had returned to find Ikaria in the midst of rebellion and been betrayed by the very men he had trusted.

Josan shook his head to clear it of such bitter thoughts. It would not do to dwell on the past. Zuberi had given him only five days to relearn what it had taken him months to master. He could not afford to waste any time on self-pity.

Use Aeneades rev Great Map, div 12 sec, exc W o Tarsus, he read. Well that seemed clear enough. There were a number of versions of the map of the great basin which showed the sea and the countries that surrounded it. Aeneades's version was not the most popular, but this must be the version that the Ikarians used, or the closest one that could be found to it. He sifted through the pile of parchments in front of him until he found the list of references and added Aeneades's map to it. As soon as daylight arrived he would send the servants to scour the imperial libraries for the books he required.

The collegium would have what he needed, of course, but he could not go back there. It would take a full complement of Petrelis's guards to force their way into the collegium, and even then there was no guarantee that the books that he sought would still be there. If Nikos realized what Josan was researching, he would have removed any references that could help the emperor. He might have even ordered them burned.

The wanton destruction of knowledge was considered the ultimate sin that one of the brethren could commit, next to the sin of knowingly spreading false knowledge, and both were punishable by expulsion from the order. But Nikos had shown himself a man without honor. He would not hesitate to destroy the collegium itself if it preserved his power.

Which made it all the more vital that Josan succeed. Only once Nikos was defeated would the collegium be safe.

"The weather, what is it like?" Josan asked.

Eleven jerked his head up. "Highness?"

"The weather," Josan repeated. "Is it fair? Cloudy? Can the stars be seen?"

"Boy," Eleven called. "Boy!" he shouted again.

The boy sat up, rubbing sleep from his eyes. He picked up the jug of lamp oil and advanced toward Josan's desk.

"Run to the terrace and tell us what the weather is like," Eleven ordered.

The boy, still carrying his jug, ran out of the emperor's sitting room and down the hall. Only after he left did it occur to Josan that he could simply have arisen and crossed to the window to see the weather for himself.

In a few moments the boy returned.

"It's raining," he said, panting slightly. "And it's a cold night."

"Thank you," Josan said absently. It did not matter; he could not make true observations until he had a sextant and glass.

The boy's wide-eyed stare reminded him that an emperor did not acknowledge the presence of such a lowly one, and most certainly did not speak to him. In trying to remember the man he had been, he had forgotten the role he must play.

He could not afford to make that mistake again. If Zuberi or Demetrios had witnessed his lapse, they might well wonder about their emperor's unusual behavior, and he could not afford to rouse their suspicions.

"Check the lamps, then send for hot tea and sweet rolls for the emperor," Eleven ordered, having apparently decided that the emperor required sustenance to clear his wits.

Josan turned the page, reaching the end of the first journal. He had not understood the whole of it, but enough for a start. He stretched his arms out before him, then off to his sides, feeling the distant aches of a body held too long in the same position. Then he picked up the second journal and began to read.

Lucius was bored. Ever since their visit to the collegium, it had been Josan in control of their body. Lucius had been present for the confrontation with Zuberi. Then, having no interest in scholarship, he had let himself slumber as Josan began his studies.

When Lucius had surfaced the next morning, Josan was still in the same position as he had left him. The only difference was the size of the piles of books and parchment before him, and the bright sunlight that had replaced the lamplight of the earlier evening.

Lucius could feel his body protesting the lack of sleep and the aches from hours spent seated in a chair without moving. It was an itch under his skin, one that he could not scratch. He could not take control of their shared body, could not take the risk of displacing Josan's consciousness. The monk was the only one who could master the knowledge that would save them both.

Lucius understood the necessity, but chafed at its restrictions. He tried to return to unconsciousness, but he could not lose himself in the false sleep of unknowingness. Perhaps because he had not truly taken control of his body, neither could he truly release it.

Instead he was forced to wait, a silent observer, as Josan spent the day at his desk, alternating between frantic studying and barking orders at his servants. Here, at least, Josan behaved as an emperor should, brusquely ordering Ferenc to ignore his other duties in favor of making clean copies of mathematical tables, and sending the functionaries scouring through the palace and ministries for the books he needed. The imperial jeweler was summoned, his dignity affronted when Josan ordered him to engrave a series of markings on a curved device fetched from the storerooms of the Imperial Navy.

Lucius understood what it was that Josan was trying to do—determine how to calculate precisely the position of a ship at sea, so ships could reliably find the fastest currents and safest passages. All captains knew how to calculate a ship's position relative to the equator that divided the great basin between north and south, but accurately determining position east or west of a certain point required visible landmarks or the use of sorcery.

Not sorcery, math. And the knowledge of the precise position of the stars. Which formulas I would be able to determine, if you would stop distracting me.

It might as well be sorcery for all the sense Lucius could make of the monk's scribbled notes, but Lucius kept this thought to himself.

Josan's thoughts grew impenetrable, a maze of symbols that he could not follow, and Lucius lost himself in a wordless reverie. He drifted, only partially aware until he felt his body jerk to attention.

"Emperor Lucius, or should I call you Lucius the Scholar?"

Zuberi's voice came from behind him. Lucius could feel Josan's shock mingling with his own.

It had only been a day since he had returned from the collegium. Josan had not expected to see Zuberi this soon.

"They tell me that you have been at your studies all night and day," Zuberi said, walking around the desk until he was visible before them.

Careful, do not provoke him, Lucius warned, though he knew that Josan was already aware of the danger.

Ferenc rose, and after directing a stiff bow precisely calculated to include both of his masters, he gathered up his writing case and left. The servants also disappeared, as they did whenever Zuberi came to see Lucius. Though they were not truly alone. At least one functionary would be within earshot, and it was safe to say that there were other spies he could not see. Perhaps even the same spies who had reported his actions to Zuberi.

"Brother Nikos had an interesting tale to tell," Zuberi said.

Nikos must have realized the importance of the boxes Josan had taken. He had expected to have a few days' grace, reasoning that Nikos would enlist allies before acting against him. But it seemed he had misjudged Nikos's anger, or perhaps how much he feared losing control of his puppet emperor.

"Nikos would say anything to serve his purposes," Josan said. He lifted his eyes to meet the proconsul's gaze, then deliberately dropped his gaze back down to his desk.

"Nikos tells me that you have a madness within you, and the evidence before me seems to confirm his fears. What other reason could there be for Lucius, the idle wastrel, to have turned devoted scholar?"

Josan shrugged, seeming ready to provoke Zuberi, even

as Lucius wordlessly implored him to caution. "I was in exile for seven years, as you may recall. A man has to find some way to occupy his time."

"So you became a monk?"

Josan flinched.

Zuberi gave a cold laugh. "A monk," he repeated. "Is that what you claim?"

Demetrios already knows, Lucius reminded Josan. *We have nothing to lose.*

"Let us say that the secrets contained in these journals are not the only ones that Nikos kept from Empress Nerissa," Josan said. "For seven years he knew where to find me but said nothing."

Zuberi slammed his fist down on the desk, and scrolls tumbled off like leaves scattering in the wind. "You lie," Zuberi said. "One lie after another."

"We speak the truth. It is Nikos who has lied to you and lies to you still," Josan said.

"*We?* You style yourself in the manner of an emperor, but you are a mere pawn, of less use to me than the least of my slaves."

"You promised me five days," Josan reminded him. "Is that too high a price to pay for the truth? For knowing whom you can trust?"

Zuberi stared at him, trying to intimidate him by sheer force of will. Lucius tasted their shared fear, but Josan refused to be cowed. He did not even blink as he returned Zuberi's gaze, measure for measure, until Zuberi finally looked away.

"You have four days left," Zuberi said. "And then we will see."

"I will need one of the navy's captains to assist me, and Admiral Septimus must be recalled once I have proven my tale," Josan said.

Zuberi shook his head. "Save your breath. Your bold

lies will not convince me. In four days we shall see your true measure. And then I will give you cause to regret this insolence." He strode away, pausing as he reached the threshold. "Nizam has missed his favorite subject," he called over his shoulder.

Josan's eyes unfocused, lost in memories that were his own. Lucius felt the nausea welling up and the acrid taste of bile. Josan was paralyzed by remembered fear, so it was Lucius who commanded their body to stand, as he walked away from the desk, over to the table where his long-ignored lunch had been laid out. With trembling hands he poured himself a goblet of stale water and drank it down in swift gulps.

We have nothing to fear, he reminded Josan. *Once your calculations are proven, even Zuberi will have to see the truth.*

Will he? Or will he use this opportunity to destroy us and Nikos both, eliminating two rivals with a single blow?

To this Lucius had no answer.

The imperial gardens were a peaceful place, the sculpted paths lined with colorful flowers that were changed each season so that there were always fresh blossoms to delight the senses. But tonight there were no colors to be seen, nor perfume in the air, as the blossoms were closed tight against the chilly autumn night.

The watching servants shivered in their cloaks, grumbling under their breath about the madness of an emperor who would not allow a single brazier to be lit, lest it interfere with his view of the heavens. Josan ignored their grumblings, just as he ignored the demands of his own body. He, too, was cold and tired, having slept only a few hours over the past four days. But the sky was clear, and that was all that mattered.

Josan reached over to steady the quadrant as Lieutenant Chenzira sighted along it. "There, you see how the guide star is aligned with the axis?" he asked.

Chenzira nodded, disturbing the carefully positioned quadrant.

"Don't move your head. Just say yes or no."

"Yes," Chenzira replied. "Let me find it again."

Josan waited as Chenzira once again found the guide star.

"Now, keeping the quadrant steady, move the first marker arm until it is aligned with the Eye of the Gazelle," Josan said.

He watched as Chenzira complied. He had done this himself last night, but it was not enough that Josan be able to do this. The emperor was known as a magic wielder. To prove that this was mathematics, not sorcery, he had to show that an ordinary man could do the same.

At least Chenzira was willing to try. The first two captains he had been sent had been close-minded, unable to follow even the simplest of explanations. Given time, he might have been able to teach them, but time was a commodity that he lacked.

Ferenc had found Lieutenant Chenzira for him. Like the others, Chenzira was adequate at math, able to calculate distances and his ship's accounts. But unlike the others he was willing to listen to his emperor's explanations and follow his instructions, even as it was clear that he did not understand what it was that he was doing.

They had spent the afternoon practicing theoretical calculations, looking up star sightings and performing the calculations required to determine their position. Chenzira had been tongue-tied when summoned to the presence of his emperor, but by the time darkness fell he'd lost his reserve, not even blanching when Josan ordered an evening meal to be shared between them. It might have helped that

Josan did not look the part of an emperor. Unshaven and bleary-eyed with lack of sleep, his hands covered with ink stains, he might have been mistaken for Ferenc's assistant.

Josan talked Chenzira through the process of sighting the next two stars and recording their angles of distance from the guide star. According to his theory, only a single star was needed, but the slightest error in measuring the angle would result in a calculation that could be off by dozens of miles. Given the difficulty of taking readings while on the pitching deck of a ship, two stars were better and three were optimal.

Chenzira finished recording the final sight. "Do you want to check for yourself?" he asked.

"No."

He had to trust that he had taught his pupil well.

They returned indoors, much to the relief of their escort. The servants brought warmed wine, which Josan waved off. "Later," he said.

The sat side by side at the large table that had been moved into his sitting room, a copy of Aeneades's map spread before them.

Chenzira looked at the paper where he had recorded his measurements, then at the blank parchment before him. His hesitation was obvious.

"Start by looking up the Eye of the Gazelle in the chart," Josan prompted. "Write down the reading in the book next to the reading you have taken, and then do the same for each of the other two stars."

Chenzira had done this exercise at least a half dozen times already today, but Josan talked him through each step as if it were the first time, reminding himself to be patient. It was not that Chenzira was ignorant, but rather that he was unused to performing these types of calculations. No matter that Josan could have done the whole in his head in the time it took Chenzira to look up and write down his figures. What was important was that each time Chenzira did the exercise, he was faster than he had been before.

At last Chenzira was finished. The results of the final two measurements matched, while the first measurement differed in the final digit.

"What would you do now?" Josan prompted.

"If I were at sea? I'd ignore the first, assuming it was the result of a shaking hand," Chenzira said.

"And if all three measurements disagreed?"

"I would take their average. Unless, of course, they were wildly different, in which case I would start again with new readings."

Fair enough.

"So what have you concluded?"

Josan could read Chenzira's notes, but he wanted the lieutenant to state his conclusions aloud.

"The imperial garden is one degree north, and twenty-seven and a half degrees west of the center point of Sendat."

The star tables that the Seddonians had devised used the center of the island of Sendat as their base reference, which meant one more conversion was needed.

"Now trace that out on the map."

The map of Aeneades was divided into sections using the center of the great basin as the central point, rather than Sendat. But the distances were standard, so following the guidelines Ferenc had copied onto the map days before, Chenzira used his protractor to count off the necessary intervals. When he was done, the point of the protractor rested directly on Karystos.

Josan beamed with satisfaction, clapping Chenzira on the back. "There, you have done it."

"Done what?"

"Proven where Karystos is," Josan said, wondering at Chenzira's lack of enthusiasm. Didn't he realize what he had accomplished? Chenzira was only the second Ikarian to have performed these calculations. Ever. It was worthy of celebration. "Fetch wine for us both," he called over his shoulder.

"We already know where Karystos is. This proves nothing."

Josan stared at him in disbelief. "But—the star sightings. The formulas. You did the calculations yourself."

Chenzira gave him a pitying look. "This will not be enough to convince your doubters. A single measurement is not proof. You could have rigged these calculations to say anything you wished them to say."

"But that would be lying."

Chenzira laughed. "I can see why you have driven my uncle mad," he said. "What man would not lie in order to save his life?"

"Your uncle?"

Chenzira waited as a servingwoman placed two crystal goblets before them, and poured out a measure of dark wine into each. The wine jug was placed on the table, along with a pitcher of clear water.

Disdaining the water, Chenzira picked up the goblet. "To scholarship," he said.

Josan picked up his own goblet and sipped cautiously. He could not afford to be drunk.

"I am a bastard, but my father is the brother of Lady Eugenia, wife of the proconsul. He has privately acknowledged me as his nephew," Chenzira explained.

With his connections, if Chenzira had been legitimate, he would have already been a captain in the navy, or more likely appointed to a post in one of the ministries, where he could serve his uncle's interests while lining his own pockets. Even as a mere bastard, his uncle had done well by him. And he would be expected to be loyal to Zuberi in turn.

Did Chenzira understood what was at stake, or had he merely been sent to distract Josan, to ensure that there was time to train no other in his place?

"So what will you tell your uncle? That the emperor has succumbed to mad fancies?"

He wondered whom Zuberi had chosen to replace him as emperor. Did Demetrios's elder brother yet live? Was that the reason that he had not heard from his erstwhile ally in the past week? Or had another candidate emerged, the result of secret negotiations while Josan was huddled over his calculations?

He thought frantically but could see no way out of the pit he had dug for himself. He had run out of time.

"Your uncle's hatred of me blinds him to the truth," Josan warned. "We need this knowledge to fight back against the federation."

Chenzira nodded. "I know. I believe you."

Josan sagged with relief.

"Come dawn, I will convince my uncle to give this method a true trial," he said. "His affection for me is a slender reed, so we must think of something that can be accomplished in a day, no more."

Josan had always planned to demonstrate his method at sea, but had assumed that he would be the one to make the voyage. Still, he had no other choice. If Chenzira was to trust him by taking his part, then, in turn, Josan would have to place his trust in what he had taught his student.

"Have yourself taken aboard ship and blindfolded," Josan said. "Let the captain spend the day sailing, dropping anchor off a familiar shore at sunset. When it is night and no landmarks are visible, you will take your sightings and tell him where the ship is. If you are right, then we will both win."

"And if I am wrong?"

"Then you were duped by me and will return to tell your uncle as much."

And Josan would be sent to the dungeons below the palace, where Nizam could once again indulge his twisted desires.

That is, if Josan allowed himself to be taken alive. His summer strolls in the garden had not been entirely idle—he had slowly gathered a collection of foxglove seeds, which had been secreted in his chambers. It had been months since he had carried those seeds on his person, but he would find them tonight and tuck them in the lining of his belt. Given a large enough dose, not even Lucius's magic could save them.

Or so he hoped. Because the alternative was too grim to bear.

Josan spent the hours till dawn copying the tables that Chenzira would need. Fortunately, he already knew the date, and there was a limited distance that the ship could travel in a single day, so he only needed to copy two of the pages from the almanac. He put the tables in a document pouch along with a scale copy of Aeneades's map, and, after a moment's thought, tucked in the calculations that Chenzira had performed that evening as a guide.

Early the next morning, Chenzira came by with the news that his uncle had agreed to a sea trial. He did not say how he had managed this feat, but he must have awoken his uncle at sunrise. A brave man, or perhaps merely anxious to see this to the end.

Josan handed him the document case and quadrant and wished him good luck.

When his clerk Ferenc arrived at the usual hour, Josan bade him make a clean copy of the notes he had assembled detailing each step of the calculations. If Chenzira succeeded, he would need to teach others.

And if Chenzira failed, then Josan's last act would be to send his notes to Admiral Septimus for safekeeping. Given proper incentive, Septimus might be able to reason out what Josan had uncovered.

Then, with nothing else to occupy his time, Josan retired to his quarters and slept.

He awoke in the afternoon, feeling vaguely sick as he always did whenever he fell asleep during the day. The few hours of sleep that he had managed had done little to make up for the days without. Rather than refreshing him, his mind felt slow and stale, as if his wits were befuddled by wine.

For the first time in days he groomed himself properly, bathing in his chamber and scraping off the scraggly beard. He dressed with care, rejecting one tunic after another, until his attendant suggested a long overrobe of cotton tied with a wide silk sash. After the attendant had left, Josan went to his desk, opening a drawer to reveal a box of ground pigments ready to be mixed into ink. A twist of cotton held what looked like a coarse brown pigment, but were actually foxglove seeds, which he then tucked into the folds of his sash. It was unlikely that anything would happen today, but he would be prepared, just in case.

He visited his study and inspected the copy of his notes that Ferenc had prepared. "Have these sent to Admiral Septimus for his consideration," Josan said.

"Yes, your highness," Ferenc said. Though whether he would do so without first checking with Proconsul Zuberi was another matter.

The studies that had consumed his past days held no further appeal, and Josan gave in to Lucius's urging that they spend the afternoon strolling the grounds of the palace rather than seated at a chair. The exercise warmed his body, and slowly he felt his wits returning.

Lucius stirred within him, or perhaps it was merely an echo of his own worries that he felt. It was tempting to relinquish control of the body to Lucius, but he could not take that risk. If Zuberi were to ask for an explanation of his theory, or, more likely, if Nikos were to challenge his discovery . . . Lucius would be unable to answer and condemned as a fraud.

At sunset he ate a light dinner in his quarters, then retired to bed, after first tucking the foxglove seeds under his pillow.

He was brusquely shaken awake the next morning.

"Zuberi will see you now," One said. "Quickly!"

One threw open the shutters revealing a gray, cloud-covered sky, and the sight woke him more swiftly than One's frantic summons.

Josan had forgotten about the weather. What if it had been stormy at sea last night? If the skies were cloudy, no sightings could be made—but it was doubtful that Zuberi would accept any excuse for failure.

He dressed, blinking sleep from his eyes, remembering only at the last moment to retrieve the poisonous seeds. There was no place for them in the tunic that One handed him, but rather than waste time arguing Josan simply tucked them in his sandal, under the arch of his foot. They prickled a bit as he walked, but he was not limping.

The two guards on duty outside his chambers joined One in escorting him to the council room, then took up their posts outside.

As he entered the council room he saw Proconsul Zuberi, with Brother Nikos seated to his right. Demetrios sat on the other side, opposite Zuberi and Nikos.

There was no sign of Lieutenant Chenzira, nor the captain who had been assigned to supervise Chenzira's demonstration. Instead, Admiral Septimus sat next to Demetrios. He must have returned to Karystos sometime yesterday.

It was just past dawn, but the four men looked as if they had been awake for hours.

"I take full responsibility for the disaster at Izmar," Septimus was saying. "But even if I had been there myself, I doubt there was anything I could have done to change the outcome."

Disaster? What disaster?

Septimus broke off as he caught sight of his emperor.

"We will speak of this later," Zuberi said.

Meaning that he did not want to expose their disagreements in front of Lucius—or that Zuberi had decided that Lucius was irrelevant.

This did not bode well for Lieutenant Chenzira's errand.

"Proconsul, have you news from Lieutenant Chenzira?" Josan asked, as he took his seat at the foot of the council table. Perhaps Chenzira was merely delayed.

Zuberi scowled. "The lieutenant has returned and made his report."

"And?"

It was Septimus who answered. "Captain Matticus sailed a circuitous route and anchored off the southern tip of Eluktiri. According to his report, after an hour of fiddling with his instruments and reckoning his sums, the lieutenant correctly identified his location."

Josan sighed with relief, and he felt his muscles unclench. In his mind he heard Lucius's shout of victory, and he longed to echo it.

"It was a trick, of course," Zuberi said.

Brother Nikos nodded in agreement. "A good scheme, but you erred when you discarded the first two candidates as unsuitable. You must have been disappointed that the old blood ran so thin in their veins. Tell me, what would you have done if Chenzira had not carried the sorcerer's taint in his veins?"

Nikos was a poor scholar, but he had his own form of cleverness. With a few words he had neatly planted the seeds of doubt.

"It was no trick. It was mathematics. I could teach any of you to do the same," Josan insisted. He turned to Admiral Septimus. "Admiral, give me any man in the navy who is willing to learn, and I will teach him to do as Chenzira has done. Think of what that would mean for your navy."

"It would be a skill worth having," Septimus said, each word coming as slowly as if it were being torn out of him. Then, with a glance at Zuberi's red-faced visage, he added, "Though since I have not seen it for myself, I cannot rightly judge whether or not it is mere trickery."

"It is sorcery," Nikos insisted. "A scheme devised to discredit me, so as to divide this worthy council."

Anger welled up inside him—whether his own or Lucius's, it did not matter. He welcomed its heat.

"You are the one who lies," Josan said. "You would do anything to keep your place."

"Enough of this slander," Zuberi said. "I know one way to prove the truth of your words."

"How?" He had already done everything he could think of. If Zuberi did not believe his own nephew . . .

Zuberi smiled. "Let Nizam question you. He will get to the truth of the matter."

"You cannot mean that." Josan looked around the table, but neither Septimus nor Demetrios would meet his eyes, while Nikos openly smirked in triumph.

"You have nothing to fear," Zuberi said. "Unlike the rest of us, your sorcery will keep you alive when a better man would perish."

"Unless, of course, you are guilty of conspiracy, in which case you will be executed," Nikos added.

Josan began to shake. He could not do this. He could not endure another round of torture, and Nikos knew this. Nikos knew that Josan would not last long enough for Nizam to prove the truth of Josan's words. Whether by his own hand or another, Josan would die in those dungeons.

Hatred glittered in Zuberi's eyes, and Josan finally realized that this was not about the truth of his discovery. It was not even about whether Nikos had betrayed the council and Empress Nerissa before them. Zuberi hated Lucius not for what he had done, but for who he was.

Not simply because he was emperor.

He hates us, Lucius commented.

He envies us.

"It is not me you despise, but my magic," Josan said, rising to his feet. The recklessness that filled him was Lucius's, but the reason behind his actions was all his own. Holding his right hand out, palm upwards, he called fire to his hand.

Brother Nikos startled, then said, "Your petty tricks do not impress us."

Josan moved toward Zuberi. Anger gave rare color to Zuberi's face, but the rest of his skin was gray, his flesh sunken except where his belly bulged outward as if he were a pregnant woman. "You accuse me of treason, but it is you who are letting your envy blind you to the truth. I am trying to save the empire, while you can think no further than your own misery."

Brother Nikos reached for him, but as he touched Josan he drew his hand back as swiftly as if it had been burned.

"Guard," Nikos called out. "Guards!"

But it was too late. Josan had reached Zuberi. From the corner of his eye he saw Septimus leaping to his feet, but even he could not get there in time.

Josan could not stop. If he paused even to think about what he was doing, he would be lost. He let instinct be his guide, instinct and the rage within him that fueled his magic.

Zuberi scrambled backwards in his chair. "Touch me and die," he said.

"You will kill me anyway," Josan replied. Pushing aside Zuberi's robe, he reached with both hands. The silk tunic underneath tore as it if was mere paper.

Zuberi's distended belly was rigid, skin stretched tight over the tumor that was killing him. Josan put both hands on it, even as Zuberi squirmed under his touch.

"I can do nothing about the foulness in your mind," Josan said. "But as for your belly . . ."

He reached. There was no other word for it. He closed his eyes and reached. It was as if he put his hands in warm porridge, or the guts of a freshly slaughtered goat. The tumor was easy to recognize, an oily malignancy that slipped out of his grasp.

He reached again, catching it between both hands and pulled. It broke free with a sucking sound.

Josan opened his eyes. The tumor was the size of a summer melon—a putrid, stinking, lump of flesh that oozed pus from between his fingers.

He felt cold steel against his neck and carefully did not move.

Zuberi's chest heaved. His hand traced his belly, which was blistered as if from the sun, but showed no signs of wound nor blood.

"Proconsul?" he heard Balasi ask.

"Seize him," Nikos ordered.

"No," Zuberi whispered. He touched his belly with his right hand, drew one deep breath, then another. "What have you done?"

Josan straightened upright, though the sword followed his movements. "What needed to be done," he said. With a flick of his wrist, he tossed the tumor onto the table, then carefully wiped his hands off on his tunic. "Now you are like other men. You may live another forty years or be killed within the hour."

Demetrios leaned over his shoulder for a closer look at Zuberi's stomach.

Zuberi abruptly drew his robe closed.

"Guards, leave us," he said.

"See? He uses magic to gain his ends," Brother Nikos insisted. "It was as I have said all along."

But all eyes were on the emperor, not Nikos.

Zuberi caught Josan's gaze with his own. "I will not thank you," he said.

"I do not expect thanks, nor favors. I expect you to rule with your head and not be blinded by your fears," Josan said.

"You swear that you can teach Septimus's captains how to navigate the seas?" Zuberi asked.

"Any man who can reckon his sums can be taught," Josan said. "This I swear by the crown of my ancestors."

Nikos protested. "I will not stay here and endorse this folly," he said. "Lucius is a madman, who has dazzled you with his paltry tricks. If you listen to him, he will lead you to your dooms."

"The emperor's words have been sound," Demetrios said. "He convinced Commander Kiril to take on the traitor Markos, and it was Lucius who suggested Septimus could bring order to the navy when it was in disarray. I think all here will agree that both choices have served us well."

Septimus returned to his side of the table, then he and Demetrios both waited until Josan had taken his seat before resuming their own, a show of courtesy that they had seldom before offered to their emperor.

Nikos rose to his feet. "Zuberi, when you come to your senses you can send for me," he said.

Josan waited until the door closed behind Nikos. "He will make trouble," he warned.

"Leave him to me," Zuberi said. "Now tell me, what other secrets is he hiding? And how can we make best use of this knowledge to eliminate the Seddonian threat?"

Chapter 18

Ysobel threw open the shutters and stepped out onto the small balcony overlooking the central harbor of Sendat. Every possible anchorage was filled with ships of all sizes and descriptions, their pennants waving in the dawn breeze. She could see smaller craft moving about the harbor and knew these were lighters bringing supplies, and gigs transporting crew between their ships and the shore. Even at this hour, the wharves would already be bustling, the harbormaster's office crowded as captains petitioned for permission to sail or shift anchorage.

It was only the second week of spring, but the harbor was as busy as if it were full summer. Once she would have counted the ships and reckoned the wealth that they represented, but times had changed. At least half of the ships in the harbor were merchant vessels seconded to the service of the navy. Those trading ships that still ventured into Sendat harbor did so because they were too old or too slow to be impressed into service—or because their houses had already relinquished at least half of their ships.

As had she. While Ysobel herself had been ordered back to Sendat, given leave to resume the life of a master trader, the *Swift Gull*'s speed and large cargo holds were still being put to use carrying supplies from Melene to the ships that were maintaining the blockade off Kazagan.

She missed Zorion's support, and the loss of Elpheme still grieved her. She even missed Lieutenant Burrell more than she had expected to, and hoped for his sake that his new commander would prove worthy of his services.

Though she had longed to be set free to live as a trader once again, the price of her freedom had been even greater than she had feared.

She was not the only master trader who had lost a ship, but to her knowledge she was the only one who had destroyed one of her own ships in pursuit of victory. So far, at least, the *Dolphin*'s sacrifice protected her remaining two ships, which were sailing the eastern routes, bringing precious silks and rare teas back from the Olizons, generating a tidy profit. Her ships were based out of Alcina, where she had leased space in the Flordelis warehouses. She knew better than to instruct her captains to venture into Sendat or, even worse, Melene. If the war continued to go badly, any likely ship would be seized, regardless of how much that house had already given to the war.

Unless, of course, the owner was a member of the council. Each of King Bayard's councilors had made a show of designating one of their ships for naval service, but such a gesture meant little to houses that owned dozens of trading vessels. It was the smaller houses who were bearing the burden of Quesnel's war—traders without friends at the Ministry of War, who had no recourse when their finest ships and crews were seized for the war.

In public, at least, Lord Quesnel still proclaimed this a campaign to eliminate pirates. Ysobel was not privy to their discussions, but she would wager that he spun a far different tale for the councilors when they spoke privately.

She had not seen Quesnel since her recall to Sendat,

though she suspected that he was behind the orders that had released her from naval service. Some might see it as a reward for her achievements, but she suspected that her dual successes at Gallifrey and Izmar had irritated Quesnel. Rather than destroying her, his plots had only added luster to her reputation for boldness.

She hoped he was proving better at plotting against the Ikarians than he was against her.

Shivering in the chill air, she returned to her small bedroom, where she tied her sandals, then tossed a cloak over her shoulders. Leaving her apartment, she made her way through the narrow streets to the traders' guildhall. The wooden status boards inside the main door told the true story of the war—paper scripts fitted into the slats listed the names of over a hundred ships in harbor this morning, but only a quarter of them were marked as accepting cargoes. One of the new arrivals was a neutral vessel bearing a cargo of olive oil from Ikaria—though she wagered the news that the ship had brought would be at least as valuable as its cargo.

On the opposite wall a board held the names of the trading houses, along with ivory tokens for each of their ships. Plain tokens indicated ships on the business of their house. Tokens marked with red wax were those ships in service to the navy, while black indicated a ship that had been lost so that claims for compensation could be made by any who had dealings with that ship.

More and more ships were marked in blue, which meant their status was unknown. They could be merely delayed, or they could be lost at sea or even captured. At the end of a year without news, a blue token would be changed to black.

The boards were constantly updated by apprentices as ships arrived in the harbor bearing news, most of it ill. Ysobel scanned the board, having long ago memorized the position of each house so she did not need to pause to read the labels. Flordelis still had two tokens marked in blue—one was the *Palmatier,* captained by her cousin Nicola. But there were no tokens marked in black, and she took comfort from this.

Her eyes lingered for a moment on the black token next to her name that represented the lost *Dolphin.* The token would remain on the board until she had settled with the navy on the amount of compensation owed to her house. Their initial offer had been insulting—the worth of a fishing boat, not a merchant vessel that had carried over a hundred crew with cargoes to match.

Her presence in Sendat meant she could badger the clerks in person, and slowly she was grinding them down. Their most recent offer was merely distasteful rather than insulting. Instinct told her that the next offer they made would be one that she could accept.

As for Captain Elpheme's family, Ysobel had not waited for the navy, instead paying compensation from her own purse. Custom called for a captain to be paid the value of their last contract—Ysobel had trebled that payment. It was enough that Elpheme's parents could buy shares in a trading vessel if they so chose. If they managed those shares with skill, they could earn enough to ensure a prosperous future for their remaining children. Though whether they would send those children to sea...

"Greetings of the day to you," Gabirel Erromon said, breaking into her melancholy thoughts. A corpulent man whose girth almost exceeded his height, he spent his nights at lavish parties and his days in the guildhall, gathering intelligence that he could trade for favors. Those favors were needed now more than ever, as his house had relied heavily upon trade with Ikaria.

"Greetings, master trader," she replied. She did not like him, but he could be useful.

He fell into step beside her, wheezing slightly as he maneuvered his bulk around the crowded tables that filled the central hall, where representatives from each of the trading houses held sway as they recorded contracts, negotiated agreements, or simply paused to exchange the latest gossip. The low hum of dozens of conversations filled the hall.

A few paused in their conversations to call out greetings. A year ago these very same traders had shunned her, but these days her opinions were much sought after. Banned from trading with Ikaria because of her involvement in the doomed uprising, Ysobel had been forced to shift her ships to other routes, developing new trading partners. When the blockade cut off access to Ikarian ports, many traders had been left with broken contracts and warehouses filled with rotting goods, while Ysobel was unaffected.

To an outsider, her shift in trading alliances spoke of intimate knowledge of the council's plans, or uncanny ability to predict the future. Either made her an asset worth cultivating.

"Have you heard the news of Demetra?" Gabirel asked. "One of their ships arrived last evening—the first of the season from Vidrun."

"They must have left before the spring moon," Ysobel observed.

"They sailed with its rising, or so they claim, bringing a cargo of glass from Anamur," he said.

"An interesting choice." Generations ago, Ikaria had welcomed refugees fleeing Anamur, the so-called newcomers who had swiftly risen to power, displacing the old blood. Their craftsmen created ornamental glassware that was much in demand, but with the Ikarian markets closed, the house of Demetra had apparently chosen to return to Anamur, where the glassmakers' craft had originated.

Though it would be difficult to turn a profit on such a long voyage.

Gabirel murmured something that might have been agreement, but she refused to be drawn out further.

"I count Demetra of Demetra as a friend and know he would welcome the opportunity to hear your views on the new trading season," Gabirel said, finally arriving at the point of this encounter.

Nothing he did was without purpose. In return for arranging this meeting, Gabirel would expect a favor from Demetra in turn. She wondered idly how he calculated her worth.

A refusal sprang to her lips, but as she opened her mouth she reconsidered. The compensation from the navy would be enough to lease a ship, and she had yet to find a likely candidate. It would do no harm to sound out Demetra to see if he would be willing to engage in such a venture.

"Demetra is known to me as well," she said. "Though I thank you for your reminder that I have been remiss in paying the respects due to an old acquaintance. I will let the trader know that I would be happy to meet with him, at his convenience."

"I am pleased to have been of service," Gabirel said. With a shallow bow he took his leave, no doubt to rush to a member of the house of Demetra so he could claim credit for bringing Demetra to Ysobel's attention.

She found her clerk Balere at a small table in the rear of the hall. From the looks of it, Balere was studying a record of yesterday's trades—useful information to know even if she could not act upon it until her mistress leased a ship and began accepting cargo.

Ysobel pulled up the empty chair opposite Balere.

"Any news?" she asked.

"No news of our ships, as expected," Balere replied.

"The factor for Charlot is buying flax at ruinous prices, hoping to avoid paying forfeit. The house of Roquin holds the contracts, though, so most are reluctant to sell regardless of the price."

If Charlot could not deliver the promised flax, he would be forced to pay double its worth—a heavy burden on a house that had been strained even before the blockade. If Demetra had no likely ships to lease, she would approach Charlot. If they were sufficiently desperate, they might be willing to take a lower lease payment in return for receiving the entire amount at the start of the lease rather than spread into quarters as was customary.

"I want a list of the ships that Charlot has within the islands and their likely values," Ysobel said.

"I'll have it for you this afternoon," Balere said. "I've already started drawing it up but need to confirm the value of their current trading contracts and list of sailing routes."

"Prepare a similar list for Demetra, Searcy, and another house of your choice," Ysobel said. It would not do to show too much interest in any one house—letting them see that there were competitors for her favors would strengthen her bargaining position.

"Was there anything else?"

Balere rummaged through the parchment on her desks, then handed Ysobel a scroll marked with the seal of the Ministry of Trade. "Only this," she said.

Ysobel broke the seal with her thumbnail, unrolling the scroll to reveal a dinner invitation from Lady Solange, the minister of trade. The invitation was for this very evening, which showed Solange was confident that Ysobel was in no position to refuse.

"Do you know anything of the neutral ship *Ahwaga* that arrived last night, or the news she brought?" Ysobel asked.

Balere shook her head. "I have heard nothing, but I can make inquiries."

"Do so. I will return this afternoon to see what you have learned," Ysobel said.

In the meantime she would make her own investigations. Lady Solange had not summoned her lightly—and it was best to be prepared.

Servants circulated between the dining couches, some offering platters of delicacies while one did nothing but constantly fill up their wine cups. Ysobel sipped hers sparingly and noticed that Lady Solange did the same.

It was an intimate dinner party—Lady Solange shared a couch with her husband Millard, who spoke only to comment on each dish as it was presented. Ysobel's own dining partner was Telfor, who held no official post but was widely known as King Bayard's most trusted advisor. On any other occasion he would not have paused to greet her, but on this evening they shared plates as if they were equals or old friends.

She suspected that this was meant to be flattering—to lure her into confidences by presenting the illusion that she belonged in such rarefied company. But Ysobel knew that this was not a sign of true regard—if Lady Solange had wished to demonstrate her esteem, she would have held a large gathering where all might witness the favors that she bestowed upon Ysobel. This gathering was not a sign of any affection for Ysobel but rather a sign that Lady Solange wished no witnesses to what it was they were to discuss.

Ysobel's belly clenched with nervousness though she knew her features reflected none of her unease. She nibbled delicately at each dish, consuming just enough for politeness' sake. Finally, they were left with sweet wine and dishes of nuts roasted in honey. Ysobel repressed a smile as the reserved Telfor scooped an entire handful of nuts and began dropping them into his mouth one by one, much as a boy presented with a favorite treat.

"Lady Solange, what news have you from Ikaria?" Ysobel asked, after the last of the servants had withdrawn.

"You waste no time," Telfor said, punctuating his remark by cracking a nut between his teeth.

"There are others you could have invited for pleasant discourse, and I doubt that Lady Solange needs my opinion on the skills of her chef. That leaves Ikaria as the only reason for my presence—and the ship that arrived last night."

"Indeed," Lady Solange said. "The news from Ikaria was . . . unexpected."

Balere had been unsuccessful in her inquiries, and Ysobel's investigations had been similarly fruitless. Rumors from Ikaria should have been swirling, but surprisingly there were none. She'd spent a frustrating afternoon at the docks, lightening her purse, until she realized that it was the very absence of rumors that told the tale.

"The captain had nothing to tell you," Ysobel said. "No news worth mentioning because there is no civil war. Emperor Lucius remains on his throne, and by all accounts holds the loyalty of his people."

"It is perplexing," Lady Solange said.

"You may recall that I warned the council against underestimating him," Ysobel said. "We misjudged him once and must take care not to do so again."

It still rankled that she had been taken in by his pretense—judged him a coward, completely under the thumb of those who sought to use him. He had manipulated her, just as he continued to manipulate those around him.

"The Ikarian navy will not allow the blockade to pass unchallenged," Ysobel added. "Commodore Grenville cannot hold them off forever."

"An interesting position," Lady Solange said. "Considering that you are one of the few houses that has not had to pay a forfeit for lost contracts."

"I have already lost one ship. I do not wish to lose another," Ysobel said. "And if it comes to war, it will profit no one."

It was as blunt as she dared be, for all knew that Lady Solange's house was profiting from the blockade by virtue of her contracts to supply the navy. Her former rival Lord Quesnel also had much to gain, as he used his position as minister of war to buy captured ships at prices far below their true worth.

But true war was a different matter. The last full-scale conflict between Ikaria and Seddon had cost the federation dearly, as she had lost control of most of her foreign colonies. Entire trading houses had been obliterated, their surviving members forced to beg for refuge in other houses, forsaking both name and family.

If war came, there would be those who profited. Even the greatest of calamities could be turned to someone's advantage. But the survivors would need someone to blame—and it was unlikely that those present could remain in power, after bringing destruction down on their countrymen.

"Quesnel assures the council that it is only a matter of time before the emperor is toppled. Lucius is too busy securing his own power to move against us," Telfor said. His face was unreadable, giving no hint of his true thoughts.

"Quesnel is a fool," Ysobel said. "We have given Lucius what he needs—a common enemy that will unite his people. They will set aside their own concerns to move against us."

There were no murmurs of disagreement.

"They may have already done so," Solange said. "The captain held one bit of news confidential—the Imperial

Navy left its winter harbor two weeks before the first day of spring. They were weighed down with men and provisions."

"Where did they go?"

"They steered a course for open sea," Solange said.

This, too, was unexpected. The Ikarian navigators always kept land within sight. If they headed for open sea, it could only mean one thing—they meant to make sure that any watchers did not know their ultimate destination.

"Where are they going?" Ysobel mused aloud.

"I was hoping you could tell me," Solange replied.

Chapter 19

Josan hated sailing. He hated ships. He hated the whole of the great basin, and every wave upon it.

If there had been room for any other emotion within him, it would have been hatred for Septimus as well. Josan had elevated Septimus to the rank of admiral, and in return Septimus was doing his very best to unman his emperor.

"Any change?" Septimus whispered.

"The emperor is still indisposed," Seven replied. Younger than the other functionaries, he had volunteered to accompany the emperor on this journey, a decision he was no doubt regretting.

"The emperor wishes to die in peace," Josan said. He opened his eyes to glare at Septimus, whose windblown hair and reddened cheeks spoke of time spent up on deck. Septimus, who had always looked vaguely ill at ease in court silks, appeared in his element on the sea.

Josan could not say the same.

"You will feel better if you come take the air," Septimus said. He had repeated the same speech at least twice a day since they had left Karystos.

"Perhaps later. After the storm passes," Josan said, closing his eyes as Seven laid a cool cloth across his forehead. He clutched the rail on the side of the bed as the ship rocked beneath him. No matter what he did, he could not ease into the rhythm of its movements.

He had considered himself an experienced traveler, who had traveled the length of the great basin from Ikaria to Xandropol, in accommodations far less luxurious that those available on an admiral's flagship. But this was not his stomach in rebellion, it was Lucius's, and the prince was proving a poor traveler indeed.

"Storm?" Septimus's voice rose in puzzlement. "It is as fine a sailing day as we could wish for, with a steady wind from the west quarter. We've had nothing but fair weather since we left Karystos. My sailors say the emperor's luck sails with us."

"And will they say the same when they see me vomiting over the side?"

Septimus wisely said nothing.

Josan opened his eyes again. "How far away are we?"

"Five days, perhaps four if the weather continues to favor us," Septimus said.

Josan pushed himself into a seated position, half-leaning against the wall of the cabin. He bit his tongue as a wave of nausea swept through him.

Lucius had not made his presence felt since the first signs of illness had shown itself. It was his custom to flee misery, and Josan could not blame him. Though perhaps something of Lucius's presence still lingered—though it was difficult to believe that one man could command the weather.

It was far more likely that the fair weather was a natural phenomenon.

And if he felt this ill on a fair day . . .

Josan swung his legs over the side of the bed, and Seven

tied on sandals with soles of roughened leather that would not slip on the deck. As Josan moved to stand, Seven held his left arm and Septimus his right.

He stood, slowly, feeling his legs tremble as if from long illness. Bile rose in his throat, and he hastily swallowed. After a long moment, it subsided.

"Walk with me," Josan told Septimus. "I will take the air and you can tell me again of your plans for the Seddonian fleet."

Septimus had been right; the steady breeze made Josan feel better, even as it chilled him through the heavy woolen cloak he wore. The sailors on deck scattered as he approached, uneasy at the presence of the emperor in their domain.

This was not the imperial sailing ship, whose crew was well used to ferrying the imperial family between Karystos and their summer retreat on Eluktiri. This was a warship, with all that entailed. An emperor was as out of place as a dancing bear.

Emperors ruled from the palace at Karystos. Occasionally one ventured into the field to lead their armies—safely from the rear, of course. The first Constantin had been such a war leader, as had Aitor I. But no emperor sailed to battle—the risks were considered too great.

Josan had expected Zuberi to forbid him to accompany Septimus on this expedition. And, indeed, Zuberi had at first refused to consider the idea but had gradually allowed himself to be won over.

Despite months of training, Josan was still the best navigator they had, able to perform the calculations in a fraction of the time that it took the naval officers. And only Josan understood the theory behind their new weapons, though naturally Septimus's men had learned to operate them. Still, these reasons, compelling though they were, should not have been enough to sway Zuberi.

Unless, of course, Zuberi had his own reasons for wishing the emperor gone from the capital. The truce between them had held all winter, but they were merely temporary allies. There was no friendship, and little trust between them. Zuberi might have allowed Josan to go because he knew that the emperor's presence might mean the difference between success or failure.

Or he might have given Septimus a second set of orders—meant to ensure that the emperor did not return. Whether a martyred hero, or lost in a tragic defeat, it would be easy for Septimus to dispose of him. Zuberi would lead the public mourning, and, with his newly restored health, assume the throne that many thought should have been his all along.

A death at sea would be far more merciful than a slow extinction at the hands of the chief torturer. Josan grinned as he realized that, in his current misery, he would offer no resistance if Septimus were simply to push him over the rail. Though surely Septimus was enough of a tactician that he would not waste any advantage until after they had confronted the Seddonians.

"You find humor in the federation's standard line of battle?" Septimus asked.

Josan shook his head. "A passing thought, no more," he said. "Continue, I am listening."

Betrayal was easier the second time, Josan mused. Of all the lessons he had learned since agreeing to become emperor, it was this that most surprised him.

He had agonized for days over his decision to reveal the secrets of the Learned Brethren—torn between his duty to the empire and the oaths that he had sworn. Even the knowledge that these were his very own discoveries, secrets he himself had brought to the brethren, was not enough to assuage the guilt that had haunted him.

The second betrayal had been easier.

Josan stood at Septimus's side, watching as the nervous sailors poured heated pitch into the cauldron.

"Careful," he warned, as some of the pitch slopped over the sides. There was no room for mistakes—the final concoction would pose as grave a danger to their own ship as it did to their enemies.

He tasted the dampness of the air on his tongue as the sailors carefully measured the volatile powder. "Another quarter measure," he said.

The sailor looked at Septimus, who repeated the order.

For centuries, the secret of the Burning Terror had been lost—to all save the Learned Brethren. It had taken time for him to realize that the navigational secrets he had shared would not be enough to ensure their triumph over the federation's fleets. But once he realized the problem, he had barely hesitated before plundering the collegium's treasures for a second time.

He wondered if this was how Brother Nikos had begun his descent into treachery—choosing expediency over virtue once, then again, until he became so accustomed to it that he could see no other way.

It would be an interesting question to pose to Nikos, but Nikos had left Ikaria over the winter, taking the overland route to Kazagan from where he could catch a ship to Xandropol in the spring. Ostensibly Nikos journeyed on the business of his order, but all knew that Zuberi had given his erstwhile ally a choice between voluntary exile or imprisonment.

Brother Thanatos was the new head of the collegium, chosen by his peers and confirmed by the emperor. It was unclear how much the brethren knew about Nikos's dabbling in treason, but the selection of Thanatos as their head signified a wish to return to the old days, when scholarship, not politics, had been the focus of the order.

Josan had respected their decision, then had promptly dragged the order back into the realm of the political when he had scoured the libraries looking for weapons they could use against the federation. The brethren had claimed no such knowledge, but an afternoon's diligent searching had yielded the tome he sought.

He knew the brethren wondered about his intimate knowledge of their treasures—for while Brother Nikos had been Prince Lucius's tutor, it was also well-known that Lucius had been an indifferent scholar at best. The detailed knowledge the emperor possessed could only have come from one of the monks. They would be casting suspicious eyes upon one another, wondering which of their number had betrayed them.

Their suspicions would be correct, but they would never find the traitor. No one would think to cast suspicion on a man whom they believed dead for the past eight years.

A sailor, wearing leather gloves to protect his hands, picked up a wooden paddle and slowly began to stir the mixture. Josan leaned forward, inspecting its color and texture. It appeared a trifle thicker than in his experiments and he fretted, wondering how much the damp sea air had changed the elements.

He leaned too close and coughed as he breathed in noxious fumes. He took a hasty step back, Septimus's hand grasping his shoulder to steady him. Lucius's body had ceased its endless vomiting, but he still staggered around the deck with less grace than a newborn goat. If it were not for Septimus, he would have fallen a half dozen times already.

"It is ready for your blessing," the sailor said.

Josan sighed. Try as he might, he could not convince the sailors that the deadly concoction had nothing to do with magic. Even Septimus—who had readily accepted his teachings in the art of navigation—viewed these preparations askance, whispering a prayer to the old gods when he thought himself unobserved.

Or perhaps it was not the taint of sorcery that Septimus feared, but rather the power that Josan was about to unleash.

"See? The enemy has formed into two rows, as I predicted," Septimus said, pointing toward the waiting federation ships.

"Are our ships ready?" Josan asked.

Septimus conferred with his lieutenant, who was observing the signalers on the deck of each ship. "They are ready."

The Ikarian fleet consisted of two dozen ships—selected from the largest in their navy. Half of them held engineers whom Josan had taught to make the Burning Terror. These would form the front line of battle. The remaining ships were crammed with armed sailors who would form boarding parties as needed.

Naval tactics were simple in theory. When two enemy ships met, the weaker of the two would attempt to flee. If it could not flee, the two ships would maneuver for advantage. A heavy ship might attempt to ram its opponent and sink it. Or, if a prize was sought, once the ships were in close range, grappling lines could be used to bring the two ships together, and boarding parties would stream across. Such battles were usually won by the ship with the larger crew.

The theory was simple, but execution was not. A captain had to take into consideration the wind, weather, seas, and hazards such as shoals. The difficulties were multiplied when more than two ships were involved. In large-scale actions, your own ships could prove as much a hindrance as the enemy's.

A ship could give itself an advantage by installing ballistae, which were used to hurl lead balls, or linked chains to foul an opponent's rigging. Such tactics were useful only at close range, in preparation for boarding.

But Josan had found a new use for them.

As they approached the federation ships at the mouth of the Naryn River, Josan knew that the Seddonians must be feeling confident. They held the advantage in numbers, and their ships were more maneuverable, able to tack in the slightest breeze. The sudden appearance of the Ikarian fleet would have surprised them, but they had aligned themselves in good order, showing no signs of panic.

When Septimus had outlined his plans, he had expected to find only a small detachment here—perhaps a half dozen ships at most. Instead they had encountered a large force. Too big for guarding the river, it was either the vanguard for an invasion of Kazagan, or perhaps they were en route to challenge Ikarians in their home waters. What would have been a disaster under other circumstances was a stroke of luck. The more ships they faced, the more witnesses there would be to carry the tale.

The formula for the Burning Terror included a rare earth that was far more precious than gold. Every speck they'd been able to seize was being carried aboard this fleet. They had only enough for two engagements—perhaps three if they were frugal. They needed decisive victories that would cow the Seddonians into surrender before anyone realized that their supplies were limited.

Josan's hands clenched on the railing and he drew a deep breath as their ship sailed ever closer to the enemy. What had been a vague mass of ships separated into individual vessels. He could see their sails and the signs of purposeful activity on their decks.

The wind favored the Ikarians, blowing from the north, while the Seddonians were arrayed to the south of them,

with the Naryn River and the coastline of Kazagan in the
distance behind them.

"If the wind changes," Septimus murmured, so low that
only Josan could hear.

"It will not change," he said, then wondered why he felt
so confident. Perhaps there *was* magic at work. Or more
likely it was simply it his own desire speaking—if the wind
changed, they would surely fail.

Josan's heart pounded as they drew ever closer to the
enemy ships. Finally, Septimus was satisfied.

"By your leave," he said.

Josan nodded, his mouth so dry that he could not speak.

Septimus turned to address his crew. "In the name of
Emperor Lucius, who honors us with his presence, we will
destroy the treacherous rogues who foul the shores of our
trusted Kazagan allies," he bellowed, in a voice that could
be heard from one end of the ship to the other. "Today we
will achieve a victory that will be celebrated for generations
to come."

The sailors cheered, by rote rather than with any real
enthusiasm. Only the engineers and the sailors chosen to
assist them had ever seen the new weapons demonstrated.
The rest were trusting in the skill of their officers and the
courage of an emperor who was so confident in victory
that he had come in person to bear witness.

He knew their eyes were upon him. Josan did not know
how to wear the semblance of courage, so he assumed a
mask of boredom instead, as if any outcome other than
victory was unthinkable.

At Septimus's signal, the lead ships reefed all but a single sail, slowing their movement.

The ballistae were cocked, and a sailor dipped the first
of the rag bundles into the concoction, then carefully
loaded it in the bowl of the ballista.

"Aim for the center ship, with the commodore's pen nant," Septimus said.

Josan held his breath as the weapon was fired. It tum bled through the air, an unremarkable ball of white. He strained his eyes, but could not see where it landed.

"A miss," the lieutenant advised Septimus. The gear under the ballista were hastily adjusted, and then it wa loaded again. The second shot seemed to miss as well, and Josan felt the first stirrings of panic. The most powerfu weapon in the world would be useless if it could not reach its target . . .

Then he saw it. A small orange glow on the deck of the enemy ship. A fire so small that it could seemingly be smothered with a blanket. In a moment the ball doubled in size and then doubled again, racing hungrily across the deck as a second missile struck.

Septimus stood by his lieutenant, who bellowed order that Josan heard but did not comprehend. He had eyes only for the sight in front of him, as one after another, the federation ships began to burn.

The Burning Terror clung to whatever it touched. I could not be quenched by water or extinguished by beat ing it with rags. It would consume everything it touched until there was nothing left to feed upon. What happened when it fell upon a man's flesh was something he did no want to imagine.

He heard Septimus's sailors cheering, chants o "Septimus" and "Hail Emperor Lucius" nearly drowning out the distant cries of terror from the federation ships The Seddonians' disciplined ranks dissolved into chaos a those ships that had been spared in the initial volleys fled abandoning their hapless comrades. Sailors leapt from the burning decks of their ships, but no comrades would pause to rescue them.

Septimus approached, forgetting himself in the excitement of the moment as he clapped his emperor upon the back. Josan rocked forward with the impact, catching himself against the rail.

"By the grace of the triune gods, it's working," Septimus said.

Josan forced himself to smile, though he could not share in the excitement.

"By your leave, I will order our ships to seize those enemy vessels that are still in range," Septimus said. "Some may escape, but I doubt the rest will offer any resistance once we close with them."

"What of the men in the water?"

Septimus shrugged.

"We cannot leave them there," Josan insisted.

"If it is a choice between drowning or being hanged as pirates . . ."

The empire was not yet ready to declare war, so they had borrowed the federation strategy of declaring the enemy to be pirates, and pirates had no protection. Indeed, the law commanded that they be executed as a warning to others. Josan had known this from the start. But faced with the sight of men struggling in the water, he reconsidered his decision.

"Save the sailors," Josan said. "Set them ashore, so they may carry word of what we have done here today. You may hang their officers as you will."

"As you command, my emperor." With a hasty bow, Septimus began calling out orders, and his lieutenant started signaling the other ships.

Josan wanted to return to his cabin, but he forced himself to stand where he was, to bear witness to what was being done in his name. Hours later, as the sun set, the last of the surviving federation sailors was taken aboard an imperial ship. Septimus had refused to allow any prisoners on his flagship, out of concern for the emperor's safety, but had assured him that the ordinary sailors would be spared, told that their lives were a gift of mercy from Emperor Lucius himself.

Later that night, Septimus brought him the tally. Seventeen federation ships burned to their waterlines and sunk—more than half of their force. Nine ships captured, and two more pursued until they wrecked upon the shoals. Only five ships escaped—mainly smaller vessels that had been allowed to flee in favor of richer prizes.

By contrast, only a handful of Ikarian sailors had been killed when they boarded the enemy ships—most of the federation ships had simply surrendered. They had come close to losing one of their ships when a missile ignited while still in the ballista, but a quick-thinking sailor had chopped the arm of the ballista free and thrown it overboard before the fire could spread.

It was more than a victory. It was a rout—the complete and utter destruction of their enemy.

Josan dismissed Septimus and retired to his cabin, though he knew he would not sleep. It was exactly what he had hoped for, yet success had a bitter taste. What he had done could not be undone.

The emperor had brought victory to his people, while the monk had dishonored himself. Josan had once called himself a peaceful scholar and prided himself on his pursuit of knowledge. The man he had been would never have betrayed his order by teaching their secrets to another.

He thought back to the day when he had killed the assassin sent to murder the man who wore the body of Prince Lucius. That day marked the last when he could honestly claim to be a scholar. Every choice since then had taken him further and further away from the values he had once held dear.

Josan no longer recognized the man he had become. What difference was there between himself and Brother

Nikos? Both had perverted the knowledge of the brethren to their own ends. Both had sought power—and could he honestly say that his goals were any nobler that Nikos's?

At the time, each choice had seemed inevitable, but it was only now that he realized how far he had strayed.

He wondered what he would do, the next time he faced a challenge. Could he trust his own judgment? Or would the day come when he could no longer recognize the difference between good and evil?

Chapter 20

Lady Ysobel held her breath as the imperial functionary scrutinized her documents of office. Greeter, as he was known, had once been in her employ—blackmailed into providing intelligence on the empress's court. It had been his warning that had enabled her to flee Karystos before the empress's men could take her into custody—a gesture meant as much to conceal his own actions as it was for her safety. Today there was no trace of recognition in his face—he had not acknowledged her with so much as a glance. It was as if she were merely a vessel for the documents she bore.

The two guards who flanked him, however, glared at her with undisguised loathing. It was clear that her part in the unsuccessful attempt to unseat Empress Nerissa had not been forgotten . . . nor forgiven.

It was curious that Lucius had retained all of the late empress's retainers—from the ministers who ran the imperial bureaucracies down to the men who guarded his life and the functionaries who oversaw the imperial household. One would have expected that the new emperor would have replaced them with men personally loyal to him, but he had not. His main appointments had been to elevate Kiril to the rank of general, in return for his support against the upstart Markos, then to name Septimus the Younger to lead the Imperial Navy. If the emperor had interests besides the defense of his realm, they had not yet been revealed.

With a snap of his wrist, Greeter rolled the scroll closed.

"You will take her—" he began, then he paused.

Ysobel's heart raced. Was she to be brought to see the emperor? Or taken to the dungeons as a prisoner? Either was possible—King Bayard had selected her as his envoy to Ikaria in hopes that Lucius would remember Ysobel's past efforts on his behalf and be disposed to listen to her. But Lucius seldom did what was expected of him.

Greeter's gaze met hers. Despite the tattoos that disguised his features, she knew he was enjoying having power over her for a change. "Take her to the emperor, he is expecting her," he finally said, holding out the scroll of credentials so she could take it.

He stood aside as she entered the palace. Though *palace* was a misnomer—the imperial complex was a series of buildings connected by courtyards and colonnades. Her previous visits had been confined to the public spaces where the empress held her audiences and entertained her guests. Ysobel had expected to be brought to the central chamber where Nerissa had received petitioners, but instead she was led around the main buildings, through a courtyard dominated by a statue of Aitor I, and finally into a private garden surrounded by a low wall. A curved stone path, bordered by creeping lavender, led into the center of the garden, where Emperor Lucius sat on a stone bench next to a small fountain.

She paused as she saw that the emperor was alone. When she had been summoned to the palace, she had expected a formal audience—or imprisonment. Lucius, it seemed, had other plans.

She stopped the proscribed twelve paces away, and bowed low, waiting to be acknowledged. Her escort stopped immediately behind her.

"Lady Ysobel," he said.

"Most Gracious Emperor Lucius, I am honored to be received into your presence." As she straightened, she was conscious of the contrast in their appearance. She wore the formal uniform of the Ikarian court—a knee-length robe of embroidered silk over a tunic of unbleached linen, while Lucius was dressed in a simple linen tunic, banded in purple. His informal attire and the choice of location for their meeting was not meant to put her at her ease—rather it underlined her insignificance. He did not need the trappings of power to impress her.

She started as something ran across her foot, and looked down to see a bright green lizard disappearing beneath a bush.

"The gardeners encourage them," Lucius observed.

Of course. Lizards were the symbols of his house.

He rose to his feet. "Walk with me," he said.

She fell into step beside him, stealing a sideways glance at his expression. It would have been easier to read his features if they had conversed face-to-face. Instead they strolled together as if they were friends. He had learned to use intimacy as a weapon, thus robbing her of even the slightest advantage.

"I know why the federation selected you as their emissary, but I don't know why you accepted," he began. "You had no assurance that you would be welcome."

"King Bayard and his councilors felt that I was in a unique position to understand the needs of both our countries," she said, choosing each word carefully. "I am honored by their trust in me."

If the circumstances had been different, she would have taken pleasure in refusing the council's request. After all, she had repeatedly advised them against underestimating Lucius. But the new Ikarian weapons had changed everything. Faced with the potential destruction of the fleets upon which all depended, past rivalries must be put aside for the good of all. It did not matter who had led the federation to the brink of disaster—what mattered was who would find a way out of this mess.

It was the opportunity of a lifetime, and Ysobel had seized it with both hands.

"What could you possibly have to say to me? What can the federation offer?" he asked.

"Peace."

She let the word linger in the air between them. Lucius paused by a flowering rose tree, idly fingering one of the fragrant blooms.

"Tell me more," he said.

She pressed home her advantage. "Peaceful coexistence is the only true road to prosperity for both our countries."

Lucius turned to face her, his eyebrows raised in disbelief. "And this is why you encouraged Nerissa's subjects to rebel against her? Was it this desire for coexistence that drove you to seize our colony at Gallifrey and harass our ships at sea?"

"Mistakes were made," Ysobel said. "In our efforts to secure safe harbors for our ships, there were . . . unfortunate actions taken."

"Unfortunate," Lucius repeated.

It was difficult to negotiate for peace when there had been no war declared. Instead there had been a series of increasingly bloody encounters done in the name of ridding the sea of pirates, or defending oneself against unprovoked attacks.

"We regret—"

"You regret being caught," he broke in. "In your greed, you thought to take what spoils you could while my attention was occupied elsewhere. Now that our fleet has shown itself a match for your own, you come running here to cry peace."

She decided to return his bluntness with some of her own. "Both of our countries have suffered grievous losses. We could spend the rest of the afternoon reciting the wrongs that each of us has done to the other. But that is not why you summoned me."

He wanted something from her. She could feel it.

Perhaps his control of Ikaria was only an illusion, and unrest did indeed bubble under the surface. Or perhaps he feared that the federation would master the secret of the fire missiles, and Ikaria would soon lose the advantage they had gained.

Troubling enough that Ikarian ships had been sighted far out in the great basin, traversing routes that were once used only by federation captains. It seemed clear that some captain had been persuaded against his will to relinquish the secret knowledge. The wonder was not that the secret had been revealed, but rather that they had been able to keep it for so long, until no one even suspected there was a secret to be found.

Fire missiles had been the stuff of children's tales—ancient legends from kingdoms that had long since crumbled into dust. When the first reports had reached Sendat, they had been dismissed as exaggerations. The arrival of the first survivors had proven that the missiles were all too real—and a threat unlike any the federation had faced before.

It was said that Lucius himself had invented the weapons, and been so confident in their power that he had sailed on the flagship that had launched the first of a series of attacks upon the Seddonian fleet. Many had discounted these rumors as mere rhetoric, meant to inspire his subjects, but she believed otherwise. This, after all, was the man who had possessed the self-confidence to hand himself over to Empress Nerissa, gambling that she would not put him to death.

Lucius knew how to risk everything on a single chance—a quality that she prized in herself.

Once before he had chosen to make peace with his enemy rather than plunge his country into war. She was gambling that his goals were unchanged.

"We propose a truce between our two countries. Our fleets will return to their home ports to prevent any further unfortunate encounters. In token of our respect, we will give up our claims on Gallifrey and the other colonies that we occupied."

This was the condition that the council had most bitterly contested when they had discussed what terms they could offer. They would be arguing still, if news had not arrived of a second defeat, one that dwarfed the scale of the Battle at the Naryn River.

"That is a start. But I want compensation for each Ikarian merchant ship that was lost."

"And what of the ships that my people lost? And their crews?" she asked.

A look of sorrow passed over his face, but then his features grew cold.

"The price of your folly," he said. Gone was his earlier casual posture. He drew himself up to his full height so he could stare down upon her.

The council would not be happy with his terms—but they were more generous than she had expected. He could have chosen to press home his advantage, asking the federation to concede territories or demanding tribute instead of mere compensation.

"On behalf of the federation, I accept the general terms

of your offer, though naturally our representatives will need to negotiate on the specific details of the arrangements," she said.

"Of course. And as a sign of good faith, you will remain here in Karystos until the final terms are agreed upon. And if we should fail to reach agreement . . . there is still a writ of arrest with your name upon it." He smiled, the practiced grimace of a courtier that did not touch his eyes.

The threat was clear. Cooperate with him, or suffer the consequences.

"It would be my pleasure to do whatever I can to forge an alliance between us," she said, with a practiced smile of her own.

But there would be no lasting alliance. Lucius chose to make peace with the federation because it suited his purposes, not because he wished to spare both their peoples. Free to turn his attention to internal matters, he would use the interval to consolidate his power. He would attack again—driven by the prospect of conquest, or the need for a common enemy to unite his people.

She had bought the federation time to prepare. Even as she spoke, sorcerers and engineers from across the islands were busy trying to re-create the Ikarian fire missiles. If they could be duplicated—or a way found to protect ships against them, then the empire would lose its advantage.

The federation had underestimated Lucius once, to their great cost. She would not do so again.

About the Author

Patricia Bray grew up in a family where the ability to tell a good story was prized above all others. She soon realized that books were magical creations that let the author share stories with people he'd never met, and vowed that someday, she, too, would have this magic power.

A corporate I/T project manager by day, she wishes to note that any resemblance between her villains and former co-workers is entirely coincidental. When not at her home in upstate New York, she can be found on the SF convention circuit, or taking bike trips in exotic locations. Readers can find out more about Patricia and her latest projects by visiting her website at www.patriciabray.com.

Be sure not to miss
the stunning conclusion
to Josan and Lucius's tale in

THE FINAL
SACRIFICE

BY
Patricia Bray

Coming soon from Bantam Spectra

Here's a special preview…

Lady Ysobel slowly waved her fan, but there was no relief from the stifling heat of the crowded theater. Around her, the other patrons fluttered their own fans, filling the theater with a low rustling, as if a flock of birds had taken up residence. Certainly they were as colorful as any bird, though birds, at least, did not have to worry about sweating through costly silks.

Ysobel had chosen to wear a split robe of embroidered dark green linen over a high-necked cotton tunic—a fashion popular in her homeland, and far more conservative than the revealing, tightly fitted silks favored by the women of the Ikarian court. Her escort, Captain Burrell, wore his dress uniform—an unsubtle reminder that he was as much bodyguard as companion. The two stood out among the other patrons, as she had intended.

"Proconsul Zuberi's not here," Burrell

murmured, gesturing as if to draw her attention to the action on the stage.

She smiled as if he had said something particularly witty. "Unwell? Or secure enough in the emperor's favor that he need not dance attendance upon him?"

"Or perhaps he is the only sensible one among them, and has retired to the cooler breezes of the countryside."

It was possible, but not likely. Not as long as the emperor remained in the capital.

She glanced over at the imperial box where Emperor Lucius sat in splendid isolation, flanked only by his servants and bodyguards. There had been much gossip in the court over who Lucius would choose to share his box on this evening— but no one had expected him to attend alone.

Then, again, the emperor had repeatedly shown himself to be unpredictable. Which made him all the more dangerous.

It was Ysobel's job to understand him. To anticipate his next move, and be ready to counter it. The truce she had negotiated with Lucius on behalf of her country was merely that—a temporary cessation of hostilities while both countries retired to lick their wounds.

But if she could not guess who Lucius would take to the theater, then how could she predict when he would cast off the chains of peace and once more attack the Seddonian Federation?

Years ago, under the reign of Empress Nerissa, she'd woven a network of spies that spanned the imperial city, from the dockyards to within the very walls of the imperial palace. But most of her contacts had been killed after the aborted rebellion, and those that remained were unwilling to risk their lives—no matter what threats or inducements she offered.

She attended each session of court and a bevy of social occasions, gathering what gossip she could. But it was not enough.

Lucius was impossible to predict. One day he was a virtuous emperor, listening to the endless petitions from his subjects. On another he would hide himself within his chambers, canceling all his official appointments. Sometimes rumor placed him in the great library at the collegium of the Learned Brethren, while others said that he traveled incognito to the hippodrome outside the city walls, where he participated in mock races observed only by the grooms.

A year ago, he had ascended to the imperial throne under an extraordinary set of circumstances. The first of the old blood to sit on the throne in over one hundred years, many had expected that he would swiftly move to restore his followers to power. But instead he had followed Nerissa's policies as slavishly as if he were her own son.

The worship of the twin gods remained the official religion of the empire, rather than the triune gods favored by his ancestors. Nerissa's former ministers remained in power—all except her advisor, Brother Nikos, who had either left on a scholarly pilgrimage or fled ahead of the imperial guards, depending on whom you believed.

The newcomers retained all of their former power, while the old nobility grumbled—quietly—about Lucius's failure to favor his own people.

The only sign that one of Constantin's line sat on the throne was the lizard crown that he wore on state occasions—and the lizards themselves, which after years of being exterminated now flourished throughout the capital.

Ysobel shifted in her seat, envying Burrell's ability to remain motionless. He detested the theater as much as she did, but they were not there for pleasure. The unwritten rules of the Ikarian court demanded that she show an interest in whatever amusements captured the attention of the emperor. Indeed, she'd had to pay hefty bribes to secure a private balcony on the most desirable tier so that her presence could be duly noted.

She winced as the singers hit a particularly unfortunate note. Tonight's performance appeared to be about a shepherd courting the daughter of a wealthy merchant. Ysobel had caught only one phrase in ten, but she was certain that before the final act it would be revealed that the shepherd was actually the son of a nobleman.

The names had changed, as had the setting, but the plot was nearly identical to every other recent offering from this theater. There were frequent interludes where the central characters paused to allow barely clad dancers to take the stage. These interludes had grown longer as it was observed that the dancers were the only parts of a play guaranteed to bring the emperor's full attention to the stage.

As the young swain proclaimed his love, Emperor Lucius turned to survey the crowded theater. He nodded to her as he caught her gaze, a rare show of respect. She saw several others try to attract his attention, but his gaze swept over them.

The young lady ran from the stage, followed by her suitor. The music rose, loud enough to drown out the rustling fans, as the dancers took the stage.

All eyes turned toward the dancers—all eyes except hers. And the emperor's. Instead he gestured sharply at a servant who fetched him a cup of wine. He took a sip, and then turned to face the stage. It appeared that he was frowning, perhaps displeased by the wine, or perhaps even he had finally had his fill of insipid drama.

Then Lucius twitched, and his wine cup flew out of his hand, hitting one of his servants in the chest.

She blinked. "Did you see that?"

Captain Burrell shook his head.

The servants in the imperial box stood frozen, unwilling to attract the emperor's wrath. Could it be as simple as a fit of temper? Or had the wine been poisoned?

Lucius started to rise, then fell back into his chair. His servants hastened forward, but he waved them away. Grasping the arms of his chair, he pushed himself to his feet.

Immediately he was surrounded by his guards, hidden from view. The music slowly halted, the dancers forgotten, as the emperor and his escort swept out of the imperial box.

It had happened so suddenly that it was only as the emperor left his box that the other patrons realized something was wrong. All around the theater, heads turned toward the imperial box, and raised voices drowned out the sounds from the stage.

"Quickly, go after them, and discover what you can," Ysobel said.

Burrell hesitated, unwilling to leave her alone. "Go," she said. "I would do it myself if I could."

Burrell's uniform would make him stand out, but not as much as she would. Ikarian society had very rigid views on the roles of women. If she tried to force her way through the crowd, she would be looked at in suspicion, but Burrell could move freely.

Instead she remained in her seat, watching as the patrons put their heads together, trying to determine what had happened. Was it an assassination attempt? Was the emperor merely indisposed?

She had been looking directly at the emperor, and even she did not know precisely what had happened.

Lucius shook, as if in the grip of a fever, but he kept moving. He could not collapse. Not here, where he would be seen by all. Ahead of him, a functionary rushed to open the door to the private staircase that led from his box directly to the plaza below, where his carriage would be waiting. As he reached the stairs, which would shield him from curious eyes, he gave a sigh of relief.

But it was too soon, for his left leg gave way beneath him. He would have tumbled down the stairs, were it not for the guard behind him who hastily grabbed his arm, wrenching it in his haste.

Then another was on his right side, and between them, they hauled Lucius upright.

There was no room for humiliation as he struggled to regain his balance; there was only the bitter taste of fear.

"Gently," the functionary known as One admonished. "The emperor is unwell."

Lucius could not feel the left side of his body. His arm hung limp in the guard's grasp, while his leg trembled with spasms that he could not feel.

"I will fetch a litter," One said.

"No," Lucius insisted. "I will walk."

He looked at the guard who held his left arm, his eyes carefully downcast, as if this somehow made it acceptable to have laid hands upon the emperor.

"I will walk," he repeated. With his right leg, he took a step down. His helpers, after a frantic glance back toward the chief functionary, supported him between them, as he continued down the stairs.

It was not walking, precisely. If it were not for

the guards bearing most of his weight, Lucius would surely have fallen. But it was less humiliating than being carried, as if he were a fainting woman.

In his mind, he called out to the monk. *Wake. I need you.*

But there was no response. The monk's consciousness must be slumbering, something that had not happened for several months.

Finally he reached the safety of his carriage and was helped inside.

"I have sent a runner, and the healers will be waiting in your chambers," One said as he climbed into the carriage and took the seat opposite Lucius.

As the chief functionary and most trusted of the emperor's personal servants, One held a position of responsibility over all the other servants in the emperor's employ. At times, it seemed he would command the emperor himself—for his own good, of course.

"There is no need for a healer," Lucius said.

He could heal others. He had even healed himself, recovering from injuries that would have killed a lesser man. But whatever was happening now was no mere illness. Neither Lucius's own powers nor the skills of the imperial healer would be of any aid.

He could not confess the source of his affliction. No one must know that the emperor was the victim of sorcery, the victim of a spell meant to transform Prince Lucius into a willing puppet under the control of the Learned Brethren.

The spell had both succeeded and failed. The soul of a dying monk had been transplanted into the body of a prince, but the prince's own soul remained. Rather than a willing puppet, Brother Nikos had created an implacable enemy, as the souls of both men found common ground in their hatred of what had been done to them.

And now it seemed the spell had other, unintended consequences, as his gradually failing health would attest.

At least the trembling had subsided once he was in the carriage, though he still had no sensation on his left side. He could only hope it returned before he had to be carried through his own palace as if he were an elderly cripple.

Josan, he called in his mind. There was still no response. He shivered again, struck by a new fear, then turned his head so he would not have to meet One's gaze.

He had long chafed against the spell that had bound two souls in one body, wishing to be freed from the monk's persistent presence. Yet now that he was alone, he was afraid. What was happening to him? This was not the first time his body had betrayed him, but each attack was more severe than the last.

Josan was the only one who understood, the only one with whom he could share his fears. Yet, at the moment he most needed the monk's wisdom, the monk was gone.

He knew the rumors that swirled around the capital. The kindest said that the emperor was fatigued from the events of the past year, when he had simultaneously quelled a rebellion against him and personally led his fleet to victory over the ships of the Federation of Seddon.

Others were less kind, hinting at a fatal illness, or that he had been poisoned.

But more and more he heard the words *God-touched,* whispered when they thought he could not hear them. His attacks were seen as the consequences of the gods' favor—the price of the magic that he had inherited from his ancestors.

His left arm began to tingle, as if he had lain upon it. Slowly he flexed the fingers of his hand, welcoming the prickling pain.

Lucius, the monk's mind voice called. *Prince!*

Where have you been? Lucius demanded.

I was here, but you disappeared, the monk responded. *It was as if you had retired, but I could feel only part of our body. And I could not take control.*

He could feel the echoes of his own panic in the monk's thoughts. Normally, when Lucius could no longer maintain his grasp on consciousness—or when he was overwhelmed by tedium—he retreated into a kind of slumber, while the monk took control of their shared body. They had become accustomed to switching in this fashion, until it could be done within a heartbeat, while those around him remained completely unaware.

Yet this time something had gone wrong.

I could not feel my left side, Lucius said. *Nor could I hear you.*

And I could feel only the left.

There was silence between them. Then, finally, Lucius voiced what they must both be thinking. *The spell is failing, isn't it?*

I cannot say for certain, the monk replied.

Of course not. The monk never committed himself, instead choosing to study one musty scroll after another. Gathering knowledge, he would say. Collecting facts with which to build a hypothesis, as if their shared fate was a merely scholarly pre-occupation.

"Do you require assistance?" One asked.

Lucius was startled to realize that they had already reached the palace. He'd been so lost in his internal struggles that he hadn't paid any attention to his surroundings.

He wondered what he looked like when he and Josan were conversing. Did he appear as a man deep in thought? Or as a madman, his expressions changing in response to a voice only he could hear?

"I am recovered," Lucius said. The carriage door swung open, and One descended, then turned to offer his arm.

Lucius accepted the courtesy, as was his habit, but as soon as both feet touched the marble stones of his courtyard, he shook free of One's grasp. He headed toward his private chambers at a brisk pace, his servants scurrying behind him.

His body was under his command. But his relief was tempered by the knowledge that this was a momentary respite. At any moment, he could be struck down again.

He could not live like this. He could not rule an empire in this condition—a weak emperor was too inviting a target.

There was no more time for the monk's leisurely scholarship. Lucius had to find a cure, before they were both destroyed.